THE ORB OF BINDING

THE STARSEA CYCLE BOOK TWO

KYLE WEST

Copyright © 2021 by Kyle West

All rights reserved.

No part of this book may be reproduced in any form or by any electronic or mechanical means, including information storage and retrieval systems, without written permission from the author, except for the use of brief quotations in a book review.

1

"NO," Khairu admonished. "Wrong *again*."

Lucian heaved a sigh of frustration. "I did *exactly* as you told me."

Khairu's brown eyes narrowed. Three months since his acceptance into the Volsung Academy, the insufferable Talent still hated him. "Put the spear away, Lucian."

He hesitated only a moment before retracting the practice shockspear and latching it to his belt. Emma watched from the periphery of the training yard, though she was trying not to make eye contact. Maybe she was afraid of catching secondhand embarrassment.

"Let's take a step back," Khairu said. "What do you *think* went wrong?"

That was easy. She was not letting him do things his own way, as usual. He couldn't say that, though. Not unless he wanted extra chores.

When Lucian answered, his voice was properly meek. "I don't know, Talent Khairu."

But he was sure she was about to tell him.

Khairu's expression was stony, and she was all but throwing

up her hands in exasperation. She took a moment to collect her thoughts.

"*Always* remember your Focus," she said. "The Focus is the key to streaming all magic, always, all the time. Nothing more. Nothing less." To emphasize her point, she extended her own shockspear. Not a moment later, electricity sizzled along its length. Lucian stared, trying to fathom the inexplicable detail he was missing. It was as if she believed Lucian could learn to stream simply by watching *her* do it. But of course, that wouldn't help. Magic was something that had to be experienced, and unlocking its power was an internal journey.

When the electricity dissipated, Khairu's eyes opened and her features relaxed. "Now, *you* try."

"You're only showing me," Lucian said. "How do you expect me to learn just from watching?"

He had to keep his frustrations under control. Without calm, a mage was too distracted to hold his or her Focus. And without a firm grip on the Focus, streaming was impossible. At least, according to the teachings of the Transcends. Never mind the fact the only time Lucian had done it was during his fight with Dirk, and nothing like a Focus had even come into play.

How long ago that seemed. In three months, he thought he would have learned something more by now. Three months in the Volsung Academy and all he had were some useless meditations to show for it.

"You *can* learn," Khairu said. "You're just stubborn as a mule. Do you not remember *anything* I taught you about your Focus?"

Lucian *did* remember, but those instructions hadn't done him any good. Diligently, he had practiced maintaining his Focus every day. Every hour, even. It was usually a mental image such as a stone or tree, something simple a mage could recall with immaculate detail. That Focus became the gateway through which magic flowed, while magic itself stemmed from an incorporeal substance called "ether," which collected in the Focus and could be streamed outward. Ether was what powered magic and was drawn to mages through the "ethereal background," which was said to permeate the entire universe. While ether naturally built up over time, a mage could also extract more in a process called "overdrawing." When done in excess, overdrawing led to fraying.

For this reason, the mages of the Volsung Academy forbade overdrawing – only the ether which accumulated naturally in the Focus could be used for streaming. It was deemed safe enough, though of course, many mages said even that wasn't totally safe.

These were all foreign concepts to Lucian. Vera had never taught him as much, but then again, Vera hadn't taught him much at all.

The Focus Lucian had chosen was a stone he'd found on his first day of training. It was drab, gray, and could easily fit in the palm of his hand. He jokingly called it his "slate" because during his copious hours of meditation, he would stare at it. Three months at the Volsung Academy, he could close his eyes and imagine the stone for hours. He'd memorized every nook, cranny, and pockmark – all for the sake of learning to stream.

He hadn't known what to expect out of the Volsung Academy, but he most certainly had not expected to memorize a stone.

It was only once he'd gotten that down that the Talents allowed him to attempt streaming. That was hard to do when his mind rebelled against the Talents' methods at every turn. If he didn't learn to stream, and soon, he might suffer the same fate as Emma – Manifoldic poisoning. The buildup of ether would lead to sickness, seizures, and eventually, death.

Khairu was still staring at him. How long ago had she asked him about his Focus?

"That's what I don't understand," Lucian said. "The one

time I did stream, I didn't even *use* a Focus. I've tried your way, Khairu, but—"

"*My* way?" she challenged. "This is the Transcends' way! The Transcends, who have agreed to train you against all reason and logic. There's no place at this academy for those who spurn their teachings. You will learn nothing, Novice Lucian, until you place your faith in those wiser than yourself. *Control* your emotions. Streaming under duress is possible, yes. But it is dangerous. You are likely to overdraw, and overdrawing leads to fraying."

Khairu seemed on the verge of losing the self-control she preached. How could he take her seriously when she was about to fly off the handle herself?

Emma stepped forward, her features placating. "We should take a break. We've gone over time, anyway."

Khairu stared hard at Lucian a moment longer, and he responded in kind. The Talent was the first to relent, collapsing her spear and pocketing it. "Fine by me. We'll try again tomorrow. And Novice Lucian. Try to figure out what went wrong. Your progress is too slow. It behooves you to listen, even if listening goes against your nature."

She just *had* to get her shot in. It took great effort to bite back the sharp-worded response that wanted to fly off his tongue. This week with Talent Khairu couldn't be over fast enough.

He collapsed his own spear and stared darkly as Khairu retreated toward the academy.

Emma approached him, and he tried not to focus on the way the wind played with her hair, or her face filled with concern and pity. It was more than he deserved. Emma stood a safe distance away, so no impropriety could be noted. Even so, he found himself calmed by her presence. She was literally the only good thing about this place. Volsung's yellow sun cast her eyes an almost amber hue. He noticed there were fewer freckles on her cheeks now. Her face had gone paler under this northern, alien sun. He tore his gaze away, before he could feel too much and remember old feelings they had agreed to bury. That hadn't been easy, but it had been necessary.

"How are you feeling?" she asked.

He sighed. "I don't know what I'm doing wrong. She keeps telling me to use my Focus, as if that alone is supposed to infuse my spear with electricity. It doesn't work like that. *I* don't work like that."

Emma seemed to consider before responding. "Well, *I* haven't been successful, either. Progress doesn't come overnight, Lucian. Your Focus is a dormant muscle. You need to train it before you can use it."

Was that not what he'd been doing for the past three months? Several new Novices had arrived since he and Emma had joined the Academy. Novices who were already streaming, albeit in paltry amounts. Lucian would have taken anything at this point that signaled forward progress.

"It's been three months," he said. "If anything, coming here has *slowed* my progress. I streamed on board the liner. Here, I've streamed nothing at all."

"The point isn't *just* streaming, Lucian," Emma said. "It's to build a lasting base for long-term success. If you don't learn to sense your Focus, and through it your ether, you could overdraw. And if you do that..."

She didn't need to finish. The core of the Academy's lessons was to never stream beyond your ether, to draw from the Manifold itself. In that way lay rotting illness, along with the pain it unleashed and the slip from sanity that followed.

The path of the mage was one of balance. Don't stream too much, or too little, and you would be okay. Probably.

Talent Khairu had taught him to be aware of signs of overdrawing. Euphoria. The absence of pain. The unwillingness to let go of the stream, even as it burned you alive.

This was why the Talents instructed that magic must be streamed in an emotionless state. It *couldn't* feel good, because if it did, it would lead to drawing more and more, until one day, fraying resulted.

Plenty of mages had chosen that path. Xara Mallis, for one, and the Free Mages who had followed her. The result had been billions of dead, worlds ruined, and fleets obliterated during the Mage War.

Lucian hadn't just learned about Focuses and magic during his time here, but also history, much of which had been omitted from lessons on Earth. He learned things Vera had only mentioned in passing, if at all. He sometimes wished she were here, so that he could ask her opinion on things.

Of course, that was impossible. He had chosen to come here. Vera, Transcend White's twin sister, who was the most powerful mage in the Worlds...

He still couldn't believe she had offered to train him.

The Transcends had sworn him and Emma to secrecy concerning her. There was so much more to it, but Lucian didn't dare ask. It wasn't his place. In fact, a Transcend hadn't so much as *spoken* with him since his arrival here, outside of the weekly lessons one of them gave to Novices. As Vera had warned, it was the Talents who did most of the teaching, while the Transcends' own instruction was reserved for Talents.

He often wondered, if he had known then what he knew now, whether it would have changed his decision. Even he couldn't answer that.

How long had he and Emma been standing shoulder to shoulder along the cliff? She must have been lost in her own thoughts, too.

"We should go," Lucian said. "I'd like to get some lunch before the next lesson."

It was a moment before Emma responded. "You go on. I think I'll keep practicing."

Lucian stared at her in disbelief. "You're pushing yourself too hard, Emma."

"I need this, Lucian. If I can't figure this out..."

She didn't need to finish. She already suffered from wreakings, the first sign that ether had built up to dangerous levels. She, more than anyone, needed to learn to stream.

"I'm sorry," Lucian said. "I'm being an ass."

"Well, they say self-awareness is half the battle."

"All right. *You're* the ass now."

She giggled. "I can live with that. I mean, I feel the same way you do. I just manage to whine less."

"Easy for you to say. All the Talents *love* you."

"Maybe it's because I listen. You should try it sometime."

"Can't you be on my side for once?"

"Being on your side doesn't automatically mean agreeing with you. Sometimes, a good friend is the one willing to slap you in the face when you're not acting too clever."

"It's that bad, then?"

Emma nodded sagely. "Yeah. That last bout was pretty painful to watch."

Lucian sighed. It wasn't just the training. It was this cold, blasted world. It was this Academy. It was the Talents ordering them about on endless, pointless chores. And to top it all off, they often lacked food, proper sleep, and ample solitude to practice on their own. It was as if the instruction was designed to make them fail. There was little room for friendship here. Even this small conversation between himself and Emma was the first they'd had in weeks.

"If you need some time to train on your own, I understand," he said. "I'll leave you to it."

He turned to go but hadn't made it a couple of steps before she called after him.

"Lucian? Get back here!"

He turned to face her. Written in her expression was amusement, but also firmness.

"I mean this in the nicest possible way. Please, *please*, be more open to things. I know you don't like Khairu, but you're not going to get far unless you can keep your mouth shut. Lay down your pride and *learn*. If there's anything holding you back, it's that."

She was staring at him hard, her joking manner gone and replaced with a no-nonsense expression.

"So, you're really buying into all this stuff?"

Her eyes narrowed. "Yes. If I try to do this my own way, my life is at stake. As Novices, we're expected to submit to the will of the Transcends. And that means following the teachings of the Talents. That means doing chores. That means following the rules." She watched him closely. "I know you like to do things your own way, but here, you can't do that. The stakes are too high. You get what I'm saying?"

Emma and her rules. Why did she always have to lap up everything the Talents said without question? They were fallible, too. Rules didn't give salvation. One's own will and agency did.

Or was that Vera speaking? Why were her ideas so firmly rooted in his mind, months later?

"Whatever Khairu's trying to teach, it isn't working," Lucian said. "I streamed without even trying back on the ship. But down here on the surface, everything's different."

"It's not," Emma said. "It's only different in your mind."

Lucian knew she had him there.

She kept pushing. "Streaming without a Focus is the exact *opposite* of what they're trying to teach us. *That's* how you fray. What you did on the *Burung* was done in ignorance, and it could have killed someone. It might have even killed *you*. You're using one incident as the standard to measure everything up against. But that was a mistake that should have never happened. You need to learn to stream *properly*. And you can never do that if you stay stubborn about it."

Lucian knew she was right. That didn't mean he had to admit it, though. "All this about magic and ether confuses me, too. I'm not even sure of the difference."

"You *really* don't listen in lessons, do you? It's like magma and lava. Magma doesn't become lava until it surfaces. Similarly, ether doesn't become magic until it's streamed."

"Who told you that? Because now, it makes perfect sense."

"Transcend Yellow said it in the lesson last week," she said.

Lucian had probably been half-asleep.

"All this to say," she said, "you're not the only one who's struggling. And there are people with bigger problems than you here."

Lucian heaved a sigh. "You're right."

"Of course I'm right. You know what I think the problem is? You keep thinking of what would have been had you gone with Vera."

Lucian was struck silent. How had she known *that*?

"You need to let go of the past, Lucian. It's holding you back. The what ifs. The conflicting information. It's *all* holding you back. You've got to get Vera out of your head. Her way would have ended up killing you, anyway." She took his hand, a move that surprised him, since they were in view of the Academy entrance. Her expression softened. "You're *here* now. Nothing is going to change that. If you don't give up, you can make steady progress toward the goal day by day. You have to trust the process, even if it looks like you're going sideways."

Why did she always have to make so much sense? "I've always been skeptical of things, I guess. Seems that skepticism is holding me back right now."

"You can't let anything stand in the way of your training. You must leave everything at the door, including preconceived notions. You chose the Academy, right? So why are you wondering how things might have been?"

Lucian made himself nod, even if the movement didn't seem natural. "I don't know. Everything here isn't what I expected. You're right. It feels like I'm going sideways. It's cold here. I hate the long nights. And this tiny island makes me feel like a rat in a cage."

Emma rolled her eyes. "I get it. You're just venting, right?"

"I guess."

"Okay, I'll make you a deal." She held up her index finger. "You get one vent session per week, no more than ten minutes. And then we get back to learning to stream without killing ourselves. Deal?"

He couldn't help but laugh. "Sounds fair."

They lapsed into silence. The cool breeze whipped their brown novice robes, along with the heavier brown cloaks worn over those. Both drew up their hoods to keep warm. Everything they had brought, the Transcends had taken away. Lucian knew what the Transcends were trying to do; remove every aspect of their old lives and replace it with the new.

They stood at the precipice of the southern cliff, near the only tree on this plateau. The flame tree and its red, stringy foliage looked out of place up here. Indeed, flame trees were not supposed to grow this far north. And yet, here it stood, its white trunk thick, its roots deep, and its boughs spread wide. Maybe in time, Lucian could learn to be as rooted as that tree, able to weather any storm thrown his way. But that day seemed far away indeed.

The vast Ocean of Storms extended into the distance. That horizon seemed too near, still. Lucian wasn't sure his Earther eyes would ever get used to that.

Emma closed her own eyes, the wind gently tugging at her hair. Her composure seemed the opposite of his, one of acceptance and openness. It was hard not to be a bit resentful of that.

For whatever reason, he remembered something Vera had told him. The Transcends didn't want an individual. They wanted a vessel to mold. Isolated out here, that would be an easy thing to do. Already, he had changed. How long had it been since he'd thought of his mother? Little news reached the island, the only source being the occasional supply boat out of Karendas. For all he knew, the Swarmer fleet was glassing Earth and he had no way of knowing.

How long had it been since he'd held a slate in his hand? He had escaped Earth, but now he found himself in another kind of prison.

Then again, the whole universe could be a prison if he thought of it that way.

He wanted his slate back. He wanted to talk to his mother. He wanted to eat something other than the plain, if nutritious, food the Novices were responsible for preparing. He had grown weary of the regular fasting, sometimes for as long as a full Volsung day. He was sick of the mandatory meditations, the incessant training. He had never wanted this, and he was still having trouble accepting that this was his new reality. He had never dreamed he would be here, and it was hard to accept that this was his life now.

Emma was right that complaining didn't help. For some reason, he didn't want to let go of his past self. Maybe she was right in that he needed to do that. Maybe he needed to be molded into an obedient little mage, following the rules to a tee. It seemed to work for Emma, so why not for him?

Even knowing that, Lucian couldn't help but wonder what Vera's teaching would have been like. Different from this, surely. Conversations with her had been back and forth. Debates, even. When he disagreed with her, she fought for her position, as he did for his. He respected that. He usually lost those debates, but he learned more that way.

Here, there were no debates. You did as the Talents ordered, and if you didn't, well, then you were simply wrong. There was little in the way of reason or justifications.

He could see why the Transcends had been hesitant to take him on. Even he was self-aware enough to know his opinions were holding him back.

He was here for one reason, and one reason only: Transcend White's mysterious rivalry with her twin sister.

It was a moment before Lucian became aware of Emma's gaze. Lucian wondered how much of his inner thoughts had been written on his face.

"You're not alone," she said.

As he looked at her, he couldn't help but wonder. It was hard, but he had to give voice to his thoughts. If he couldn't tell her, then who?

"How much of us will be left by the time they're through?"

Emma was quiet for a long time. Lucian watched her, until at last, she responded.

"I don't know. This is reality now, and we must embrace it. Willing or not."

"Are *you* willing?"

She seemed annoyed by the question, from the way her eyebrows lowered. "I *have* to be. Sometimes, actions come first, and the heart second."

He didn't like that answer. "I'll try, Emma. I'll . . . do what they say. What's the harm, other than my pride? It's not like I have a choice."

"We always have a choice."

"We're stuck here," Lucian said. "Where's the choice in that?"

"The choice is in how we choose to view our circumstances. Wouldn't Vera have told you the same thing?"

Again, she was right. But it would take time for him to process.

"You are right about one thing, though," she said.

"What's that?"

She smiled. "It's far past time we ate lunch."

They went back inside the Academy, swallowed by its massive entrance. The sunlight hid itself behind a layer of gray clouds as the cold breeze blew harder from the north.

2

WHEN LUCIAN and Emma reached the small dining hall, a pot of stew was waiting for them on the serving table. The colorless, tasteless concoction had all the nutrition the human body needed, but the thought of eating it again made Lucian want to dry heave. Spices other than salt were a rarity. Food at the Volsung Academy was fuel for the body and nothing more. Even taste might serve as a distraction on a young Novice's path to Talent. Or so Lucian thought they would have him believe.

Whatever the food was, he hadn't died eating it. In fact, quite the opposite. He was the healthiest he had ever been, with more lean muscle mass than ever. He wasn't sure how that had happened, but his arms and chest had thickened. His thighs and legs had also grown, probably from the physical training and constant hikes up and down from the beach. He watched the same transition happen to other Novices who arrived at the Academy. They went from pudgy to lean, their features sharpening with strict diet and exercise. He was never truly hungry, except on fasting days, but he never really got to be full, either. He had noticed the same transition happening to Emma. It made concentrating during training sessions difficult.

Lucian and Emma filled their bowls and sat at one of the two long trestle tables placed in the hall. The other table was used by the Talents. It was later than Lucian realized – they were alone, meaning the other Novices had already eaten.

They ate quickly and without speaking. Lucian wasn't sure they'd have time to clean up before their next lesson, one of the weekly Transcend lessons that would be led by Transcend Green. Lucian downed the tasteless slop as quickly as he could. Once done, they cleaned their bowls in the wash basin, swept the floor, and scrubbed the empty serving pot. After that, they half-ran to the entry hall, where the lesson was to take place.

So far, Lucian had seen six of the eight Transcends. The only two he hadn't met were the reclusive Transcend Violet and Transcend Red. Transcend Violet spent almost every waking hour in meditation, while Transcend Red was said to be off world, hunting rogue mages.

As he and Emma hurried down the dark corridors, the Academy felt so empty. The place could have held a great many more mages than it now did. At its height before the Mage War, it was said a thousand mages had been based at the Volsung Academy. Such a thing was difficult to imagine today. Now, only a quarter of that number remained. Really, an eighth, since at any given time, half the Talents or Transcends were out, sanctioned by the League to run some errand or other that only a qualified mage could do. There were about a hundred Novices in total, who could never leave Transcend Mount except under supervision of a superior.

Still, the massive Academy was a sight to behold. Early colonists had built the original structure as a sort of way post for northern sea routes. Once those routes became outdated, it fell into disrepair until the mages repurposed it, expanding it to many times its original size. They added halls, entire wings, and towers with the aid of magic. Mages had carved the gray granite right out of the eastern cliffs. Those cliffs looked like giants' stairs all the way down to the frothing sea below.

Since then, the elements had weathered the Academy incredibly. For the worst cyclones, an energy shield was used to dampen the effects of the brutal weather.

They reached the entry hall, where about a dozen other Novices had gathered for the lesson. They stood in a single line, all in their brown robes, ranging in age from late teens to mid-thirties. As Lucian and Emma hurried into line, a wave of relief overcame Lucian. Transcend Green hadn't arrived and wouldn't know they were late.

Lucian was grateful for the warmth of the central brazier. The first nip of autumn was in the air, even though it was only late summer. Here on Volsung, winter came early, especially at this latitude. The cold was even more apparent since the doors to the yard always seemed to be open. Already, the temperature was colder than anything Lucian had ever experienced. Not cold enough to snow, but certainly cold enough to make him shiver if he were outside any longer than an hour. South Florida had never felt farther away.

It was late morning by now, but on Volsung, that would correspond to early evening by the standard clock. It was hard to decide whether the climate, or the fifty-four and a half hour days, were the bigger adjustment. Even after three months, Lucian wasn't completely used to it. Dayside, the mages woke a little before sunrise, and went to bed in early afternoon. They woke again just before sunset and slept just after midnight. Of course, this varied with the changing of seasons. Like Earth, Volsung had an axial tilt that made the winter days shorter and the summer days longer, though that tilt was not as pronounced. Days were filled with instruction at the feet of various Talents, individual training, and of course, chores. Nights were for meditation, self-reflection, and study.

Lucian tapped his foot and tried to stifle a yawn. Apparently, only Transcends had the privilege of being late.

As soon as he had that thought, Transcend Green strode into the light of the brazier. His verdant green robes shimmered the color of emeralds. Greenish shadows danced along the worn stone floor. It was said the Transcends' robes had been created with magic itself by the first Eight Transcends and had been passed down accordingly. Lucian watched Transcend Green, an elderly man who looked the part of the wizard with his long gray beard, astute dark eyes, and wrinkled face.

The line of Novices seemed to hold their breath as Transcend Green regarded them, one by one. When the Transcend's eyes met Lucian's, they seemed to hover a hair longer.

But the Transcend relented and turned to the opposite end of the line. "Novice Rhea." Though his voice was soft, it carried well. "Would you care to lead the lesson today?"

The blonde-haired, blue-eyed Rhea blinked in surprise. She was pretty, if a bit stuck up and a teacher's pet. Well, a *Transcend's* pet. She did have the most seniority of this group, having been at the Academy for two years and Tested. That meant she had participated in the grueling Trials before, held on the autumn equinox, though she had not passed them to become a Talent. That wasn't alarming – normally, it took at least five years or more before a Novice was proficient enough at streaming to become a Talent. Beyond those facts, Lucian knew little about her, other than the fact that she was extreme in her dedication.

She stepped into the light of the brazier. The light reflected off her pale, freckled complexion. Transcend Green stepped aside to give her space. She looked nervous under the weight of the Novices' attention.

"What shall I teach, Transcend Green?"

The Transcend gestured toward the Novices. Lucian wondered whether he wanted to give Rhea a chance to prove herself, or whether he simply didn't want to teach today. It was like in school when the teacher put on a holo that had little, if anything, to do with the subject.

"Today," Transcend Green said sonorously, "I'd like you, as the most experienced Novice here, to teach the things that have helped you to stream for the first time. Relate your struggles, and how you overcame them. Most here have not yet Emerged, and could do with a lesson in that regard."

A swarthy young man in his mid-twenties, well-muscled with coppery skin, spoke up. "I can help her, if you wish, your Eminence."

"No, Novice Damian," Transcend Green said. "I'd like Rhea to teach. There is no better way of learning a subject than having to teach it yourself."

At this observation, Rhea shifted her feet. "I'm not sure I'm qualified..."

"Believe in your abilities, Novice," Transcend Green instructed. "Two years you've been here. That is over a year longer than most here."

Rhea nodded, though from her face, she didn't look convinced. "All right, then. I'd like all of you to form your Focus..."

"What if we can't do that, yet?" one of the girls, about Emma's age, asked. She was small of frame, with short brown hair. Her plump cheeks told Lucian she hadn't acclimated to the diet of stew they subsisted on.

Rhea's face colored. "Err... sorry. I didn't consider that there might be some who haven't progressed that far yet..."

"Let them try, anyway," Transcend Green said. "Carry on with the lesson."

She gave a nod. "Okay. First, recall your Focus..."

Lucian did as Rhea instructed, imagining the stone. He imagined its scars, its pockmarks, the cracks, the various flecks of black mixed within. He recalled it, bringing the details in sharp relief, until the Focus dominated his mind.

"Now, starting with Novice Emma at the end of the line," Rhea said. "Try to move the flames of the brazier. Use the Psionic Aspect to do so."

He opened his eyes, keeping the imprint of his Focus fresh in his mind. Emma's eyes remained closed for a moment. Then, she opened them to stare into the flames with intense focus. After half a minute of concentration, those flames did not so much as flicker. At least, not because of a Psionic Magic. In the end, Emma shook her head and took a step back.

"Novice Lucian," Rhea said. "Your turn."

Lucian pushed down his nervousness, closing his eyes and firming his Focus. Once sure the image of the stone wouldn't flee his mind, he opened his eyes. For what seemed the thousandth time since he'd arrived at the Academy, he extended his hand to stream.

He reached *through* his Focus, seeking the ether to stream. But he felt nothing. He strained his concentration, watching those flames in the hope they did *something*. He not only had to stream, but isolate one the Psionic Aspect do so. So even if he did access his ether, he would have to contend with that.

At last, he could not hold his concentration any longer. His Focus shattered as he let out a breath.

"That will suffice, Novice Lucian," Rhea said, primly. "Novice Damian. Your turn."

"Give me another minute," Lucian protested. "I almost had it."

"You've had your chance, Novice Lucian," Rhea said. "Now, it's Novice Damian's turn."

"No, I *have* it."

Emma's voice was filled with trepidation. "Lucian?"

He ignored her. If he could move those flames, prove to everyone that he belonged here...

"What is this?" came a female voice, from behind.

Whatever resolve Lucian had evaporated that very moment. Lucian turned to see Khairu looking at him, seeming amused. What was *she* doing here?

He forced himself to look back at the fire, even as he felt her eyes on his back. Now though, the flames were moving, as if an invisible gust of wind were blowing over them.

Damian stood beside him, arm extended, his face a mask of concentration. Both of his hands were extended, palms facing outward, each glowing with dull, violet light.

"Very good, Novice Damian," Rhea said. "Now, for Novice Rolik..."

Lucian tried to hide his disappointment. That was difficult to do, especially when Damian had the gall to look over and smirk. The guy had been here over a year now. What was there to gloat about? Lucian kept his expression carefully neutral, not wanting to give him the satisfaction.

In the end, Damian was the only one who could stream Psionic Magic. The rest of the Novices had failed to do anything. It only made Lucian feel marginally better. A pale Novice named Lance, who was last, attempted the feat for about half a minute before giving up. Last of all, Rhea took a few steps from the flame. She extended her own hands toward it and assumed an expression of concentration. It only took a few seconds for the flames to extend sideways.

"Good," Transcend Green intoned. "Very good."

Rhea released her stream, allowing the flames to burn straight again.

"Remember," Transcend Green continued. "It is neither posture, nor hands, that allow for the streaming of magic. It is the muscle of the mind, your Focus, well-honed and practiced. Though progress may seem slow, every time you meditate, every time you recall your Focus, you are building a foundation. One day, with enough practice and patience, you will be able to do everything I can do." He looked at each of the Novices in turn, while Novice Rhea went to join the line. "Thank you for the lesson, Novice Rhea. Now, I ask that you pair off and face one another."

Emma and Lucian broke off from the rest of the group and stood a few steps away from each other.

"Continuing with the theme of Psionics," Transcend Green continued, "I want you to reach out to the other's mind and forge a Psionic link. Take turns. The person who *isn't* reaching, assume your Focus and be the recipient of your partner's link."

Lucian understood little of what Transcend Green was talking about, though he knew that "reaching" was the way a mage homed in on where his or her stream would go.

"You can go first," Emma said.

He hardly felt recovered from his failed effort to push the flames, but he didn't want to argue. Lucian assumed his Focus. Instead of struggling like last time, he allowed himself to relax. He waited until the image of the stone was firm, and he felt a calm permeating his entire being. Only then did he reach, seeking a connection to Emma's mind.

For a moment, it felt as if something were building up. Could this be it, the moment magic manifested? But almost as soon as he was aware of the feeling, it dissipated. He fought to regain control, but already, frustration was forming a block. He reached again, but there was no connection, no magic. Only him, fumbling in the dark of his mind.

"Lucian?"

He opened his eyes to Emma watching. "Nothing."

"It's okay. Let me try."

Lucian nodded. Clearly, it wasn't going to happen today. He recalled his Focus and prepared himself to accept her link.

And he heard her almost instantly. *Lucian? Can you hear me?*

He blinked. Had she really done it? It was Emma's voice, no

doubt of that. Lucian opened his eyes, thinking she might be speaking to him, but both her eyes and mouth were closed.

That meant only one thing. All he had to do was speak to her in his mind.

I heard you.

Emma's face became exultant. She squealed and smiled wider than he'd seen in weeks. "I did it!"

It was amazing how quickly the atmosphere in the room changed. All the Novices looked at her in surprise.

"Yes, I sensed a deviation in the ethereal background," Transcend Green said. "Novice Emma, congratulations."

Her eyes shone with tears. Lucian knew exactly why. She *needed* this. It would all but cure her from the wreakings that had plagued her for the past year. Wreakings that would have one day killed her.

He couldn't help but smile himself, especially as her gaze lingered on him a moment longer before turning to the others.

"Congratulations," Damian said, holding out his hand. "You nearly beat *my* time to Emerge."

"Good job," Rhea said, with a nervous smile. "Well done."

As happy as Lucian was, he couldn't help but feel a stab of jealousy. How had she managed it? He knew the feeling was inappropriate, given the situation. He didn't understand how he could be capable of such pettiness in the first place. Then again, being aware of it didn't make the feeling go away.

She was watching him now, expecting him to say something. "Well done, Emma. I'm proud of you."

"It's going to be okay," she said, the tears running down her face. "It's all going to be okay."

She didn't seem to notice him, surrounded as she was by the adulation of the other Novices. Lucian tried to let go and let her be. She had Emerged now, and he would be the one playing catch-up.

"This is cause for celebration," Transcend Green said. "I can order Talent Roland to have a cake for the Novices' table tonight."

This probably caused more excitement than the breaking of Emma's block.

They continued training, but Emma couldn't reproduce her results. Until she had trained further, her Focus would have difficulty latching onto her ether supply. That didn't take away from her elation, however. Breaking the block was the most difficult part. It became easier after that, at least according to the Talents.

The Novices returned to their training. Lucian set his mind to work but didn't feel closer to the goal. He should have streamed *something* by now.

He knew he had to tread carefully. If he focused on others instead of himself, it would be to his detriment. The Talents taught that each mage's journey was personal, to not measure one's progress against another's. But that was hard. And it rankled even more because he *had* streamed before. Could it be that if he had streamed the wrong way, he might never learn to do it the *right* way?

He was missing something. But what?

When Transcend Green called off the lesson, Khairu was waiting in the wings, having returned after watching Lucian's earlier failure. What did she want now? She approached Emma and didn't so much as look at Lucian.

"Novice Emma," Khairu said. "And Novice Lucian." She added his name as if he were an afterthought. "Follow me to the back courtyard. There are a few more things I'd like to show you."

Lucian almost started to protest. It was close to dinner, and he was exhausted. It wouldn't be a good idea, though, considering his performance.

He needed more training.

He faced Khairu, forcing a smile. "Can't wait."

3

THEY FOLLOWED Khairu to the courtyard, a promontory jutting into the Northern Ocean. Lucian didn't like it out here. It was windy, bleak, and small compared to the more sheltered southern yard, where the practice fields were. High cliffs fell several hundred meters to sharp rocks below, frothing with surf. Dozens of icebergs floated across the northern expanse. The island of Transcend Mount was only a couple thousand klicks from the ice cap, and it showed. One day soon, Lucian imagined, he'd see nothing out there but an endless sheet of ice.

"Stand here," Khairu instructed Lucian. "Emma, face him."

They did as they were told. Lucian was already exhausted, but a mere Novice didn't argue with a Talent. Being pushed beyond one's limits was par for the course in this place. Matters were only made worse by the bite of the cold wind, straight out of the north. If this were summer, Lucian didn't want to think about what winter would be like.

Even now, it had to be a few degrees above freezing, despite the blue sky and long daylight hours. A few purple flowers clung to life in the scrubby turf, the only thing of color in this place. If there was beauty here, it was of the bleak sort. It did little to lift Lucian's spirits.

"Draw spears," Khairu said.

Lucian withdrew it, extending it with only a thought that could be "read" by the spear through electric impulses beneath his skin. His was a practice spear with a dulled point – and that point would remain dull unless he ascended to Talent. He spun it neatly a few times, an action that was easy due to its lightness. He had deft hands; it was a shame he couldn't use the spear to its full effect.

"Stream," Khairu intoned, watching him.

Lucian recalled his Focus, that damnable stone he had imagined for the greater part of the day. He found meditative silence easy enough. If only streaming were as easy.

Emma seemed to be doing the same thing, standing only a few meters away.

"Feel the ether building within you," Khairu said. "Potential waiting to be unleashed. Let it go. Let it flow through the Aspect of Dynamism along the length of the spear."

As usual, Khairu did little in the way of explaining things. She didn't have the patience for it. It was one of the things that annoyed Lucian most about her. She expected her students to understand lessons immediately. For most of his questions, she just told Lucian to look it up in the library. That was how he had learned that Dynamism was one of the Seven Aspects of Magic.

But the mere world "Aspects" only reminded him of that strange dream he'd had on his first night in the Academy. The voice in that dream had told him to find the Aspects. What could that mean? An Aspect was nothing more than a manifestation of magic itself.

Emma gasped, breaking Lucian from his thoughts. Her spear was now glowing, shining with a brilliance that had nothing to do with the weak sunlight.

She'd done it again, with seemingly little effort. Electricity streamed from her hand and up the spear's length. That stream was weak, but there was no doubt. It was Dynamistic Magic.

"That's it, Emma!" Khairu said. "Imagine your Focus, imagine it expanding, fill it with the Aspect. *See* the spear in your mind's eye. *Feel* your ether flowing into it."

That was when Emma's hand ignited in a wreath of electricity. It flowed outward, dancing along the length of the weapon, crackling and sizzling. Her eyes went wide as she watched the display of power.

"Hold the stream," Khairu said, her face taking on intensity. "Now, the sequence I taught you!"

Emma spun, the spear snapping with unleashed energy. Lucian took a few steps back. The electricity collected at the spearpoint, the flows joining in a single ball of energy. The weapon gave off an eerie whir as Emma went through the forms, dancing with that spear as adroitly as Khairu. It was strangely beautiful, and Lucian found himself mesmerized.

"Let it flow!" Khairu said. "Good!"

Emma's eyes focused as she moved. Step forward, *crack*. Spin, cut, *static*. Emma's features were stoic with concentration, as if she were walking a tightrope over a pit of spikes. Lightning flowed along the flashing graphene weapon, and more and more energy collected at the tip. Emma's hair began to rise, as if it too were infused with energy.

"Yes!" Khairu exclaimed. "You've got it! Keep the stream flowing. It's open fully now. Keep it going until your ether is depleted. Hold on, and do *not* draw for more!"

Emma nodded, never breaking stride. Lucian watched as Emma went through the same sequence two more times. With each movement, less magic emanated from her hand, while the orb of light at the spearpoint pulsed. The final streams raced toward the point. With a final crackle, Emma whipped the shockspear, pointing it north toward the ocean.

A fork of lightning shot outward. It was hard to say, but it was at least a good ten meters long, its flash blinding in its brilliance. It was over almost as soon as it had begun.

There was no doubt now. Emma had broken her block, and had begun her first major step on the path to Talent.

When the energy dissipated, Emma's shoulders sagged, her chest heaving with exertion. Her eyes were dumfounded and disbelieving.

"Excellent," Khairu said. "I wanted to see it for myself. There is so much more to learn, but now your true journey as a mage can begin."

Emma seemed deaf to the praise. She only looked at her spear, incredulous. "I feel . . . empty. I can reach for my Focus, but there's nothing there. No power."

"That's the point," Khairu said. "Judging from the length of that lightning, you had quite the ether buildup. How are you feeling?"

She shook her head. "Empty. But . . . in a good way. I feel much lighter."

Emma collapsed her spear and pocketed it inside her robes.

There was a moment's pause as Khairu's attention shifted to Lucian. Her eyes no longer held praise. To Lucian, they seemed to hold only judgment.

"Lucian? Your turn."

Lucian looked at his spear doubtfully. "I don't know if I can do it."

"You must believe you can. You also have ethereal buildup. Let it go!"

He all but suppressed a sigh. He made himself nod and gripped the spear tightly. He recalled his Focus once again, for what seemed the thousandth time that day. He tried to feed his nervousness and doubt into it, to clear the way for the magic to flow.

"You can do it, Lucian," Emma said.

Lucian pushed everything from his mind, until only his Focus remained. Thoughts ran by in a stream, but Lucian did not attach himself to them. Why was it when he was trying to concentrate, all the thoughts came rushing in? He held that meditative stance until there was a curious tickling in the fiber of his muscles. Goosebumps covered his arms. Was that magic, the Manifold shifting the Shadow World, or was it only the cold breeze?

But the feeling subsided. The goosebumps faded, and that hint of potential dissipated. It slipped like sand through the cracks of his consciousness.

Lucian opened his eyes to see Khairu watching him. He tried not to think of that intense stare as accusatory. Emma's expression was a disappointed mask. She didn't even bother to hide it. It was as if she believed it would happen for him today, too.

Of course, nothing was ever that simple.

He let the spear fall to his side. "Not today."

Khairu nodded, as if she'd expected that. "Lucian, you can dedicate tomorrow's meditation on your block. You can report to me what you've learned the next day." She looked at Emma. "You did very well. I can see the results of your hard work." Khairu returned her attention to Lucian. "Until you dismantle your block, Lucian, you will continue to fail."

Lucian wanted to thank her for the "encouragement." But that would not be wise. He instead forced himself to nod at the harsh lesson. Remembering his talk with Emma, he couldn't let pride get in the way. "I will do my best."

"Not only that. You must listen to instruction. Your skepticism of our methods has not gone unnoticed." Was it Lucian's imagination, or was that a slight smirk tugging at her lips? "Pray that it escapes the notice of the Transcends." She glared at him a moment longer, before relenting. "Both of you, clean up. Dinner is in less than an hour."

As he and Emma parted ways, Lucian breathed a stream of curses. It seemed the only stream he was capable of right now.

He would show her. He would train until he got it right, until *he* was the one leaving everyone behind.

Because he couldn't go on like this.

4

LUCIAN CLEANED up in the bathhouse connected to the north wing. He didn't have time to warm the water, nor could he stream to do it, so he settled for scrubbing himself with soap and cold water and drying and warming himself by the hearth. He rushed through the back courtyard in a fresh brown robe, cutting across it toward the dining hall in the eastern wing.

Finally, it seemed, this long day was winding down.

The dining hall buzzed with conversation, mostly from the Novices, while the Talents had a more subdued conversation at the other table. In all, there were perhaps fifty people gathered. Though there were about a hundred Novices, not all ate at the same hours. Even with fifty here, it would be easy enough for Lucian to slip in unnoticed.

Lucian always wondered where the Transcends ate. Perhaps they subsisted on nothing more than ether itself. The thought was ridiculous, but it seemed to be the image they wanted to project. He knew their quarters and towers were on the third level and was barred to Novices and even Talents. One had to have a good reason for being there. Novices couldn't even go to the second level, where the Talents stayed, without permission.

Even though there were two tables, all the Novices crowded at the one farthest from the fire, where a large pot of stew simmered. There didn't look to be a single spot for Lucian to sit.

Lucian filled his bowl with stew, chocked with a smattering of ingredients haphazardly thrown in. The longest Lucian had seen the same stew simmer was about two weeks. It should have been flavorful, but a stew could only be as flavorful as the ingredients thrown in.

He noted the empty plate on the nearby serving table, where only a few crumbs of Emma's cake were left. He pushed down his ire at Khairu. If not for her, he would have been here in time to get some.

Lucian approached the Novices' table, at the end next to Emma. She made room, telling the others to scoot. They grumbled, but a small amount of space was cleared. Lucian was glad he had an advocate here, especially one as well-liked as Emma. She had no trouble making friends, something Lucian couldn't really boast for himself.

He took up his spot and ate. He hoped the conversation would focus on anything *but* him.

It didn't seem as if he would get his wish.

"How did training with Khairu go?" Damian asked him.

Thankfully, Emma was the one who answered. "Good. I don't think I could stream another drop."

"That's great!" Rhea said. "Looks like that block is gone for good, then?"

"I hope so," Emma said. "I've only had the wreakings twice since being here, so let's hope that's the last time."

"She looked like a Talent there for a minute," Lucian said. "She was streaming like she's done it all her life."

Emma's cheeks colored. "Really, it was nothing."

"Dynamism might be your primary," Rhea said.

"Primary?" Emma asked. "What does that mean?"

Rhea pursed her lips. It was against the rules for Novices to teach, unless asked by a superior of course. And that included casual conversation. That prohibition made it hard to acquire information. Even Talents didn't reveal much, only wanting to focus on the basics.

"Your primary is the Aspect you're best at," Rhea explained, slightly lowering her voice. "I won't say more. The Transcends like to reserve that type of teaching for themselves."

"What exactly *are* Aspects?" Lucian asked, somewhat cautiously. It was one of those things that everyone seemed to know. Everyone except him. He'd tried to look it up in the library once, but a passing Talent set him to work tidying the stacks. He learned enough to know that Dynamism and Psionics were two of them, but that still left five others.

Rhea seemed hesitant to say more, but Damian filled in the gap. "I don't see the harm of telling them the basics." Before Rhea could protest, he was already explaining. "Mages divide magic into Seven Aspects. They're the ways magic manifests itself in our world. Dynamism is one of those seven, for example. Rhea was saying Emma might be a Dynamist if that's her primary."

"What are the others?" Emma asked.

"You'll get to that, in time," Rhea said, casting a nervous glance toward the Talents. "For now, it's best if we don't overcomplicate things."

That only set fire to Lucian's curiosity, but apparently, more than a passing understanding was something frowned. It was clear things were done a certain way here.

Damian raised his clay cup. "To Emma! For those of you living under a rock, she broke her block today." Even some of the Talents were looking over now. "May it be her first step on the path to Talent!"

There were cries of "hear-hear," and the slamming of clay cups on the wooden table. Every Novice drank to Emma's progress, and most of the Talents, too. Lucian raised his cup with the rest. It felt wrong to do it with water. Lucian had been taught that was bad luck, but everyone else was doing it so he didn't want to stick out.

While the Novices chattered, Lucian added to the conversation only enough to not be noted. Despite the exertion of the day, he found he had little appetite.

"I have some cake left, Lucian," Emma said. "Would you like to try it?"

Everyone was looking at him. The stubborn part of him wanted to refuse, but he forced a smile. "Just a bite or two. You've earned it."

She cut off more than a bite or two, then watched him as he ate. The flavor hit was like a punch in the face. The cake was so creamy, with vanilla, buttercream, and raspberry jam, so light as to melt in his mouth. After months of porridge and stew, he had never tasted anything better. Despite his mood, he was powerless to resist the smile tugging at his lips.

Everyone was looking at him, watching for a reaction.

"We need to find the pantry," he said. "Where are they keeping all the sugar?"

The others had a laugh at that.

"Break your block, and you'll get your own cake," Damian said.

It was almost enough motivation to do it.

Once the Novices finished cleaning up, Lucian headed back to this room. Emma caught up to him in the corridor.

"Hey," she said. "Sorry about that back there."

"Sorry about what?"

There was an awkward silence. Did she suspect how jealous he was? If she could tell, so could everyone else.

"Never mind. I'm going to be dreaming about that cake for a while."

"Yeah, me too. Listen, Emma..."

He stopped in the corridor, and she with him. Her eyes

looked at him with concern. He didn't have the heart to meet her gaze. It would only make things worse.

"This is hard to say, but sorry if I'm acting weird. I'm happy for you. I really am. It's hard not to be a bit jealous, and that's not right." He felt his cheeks burn. "You've earned it."

"Oh." She touched his arm, and a thrill spread at her touch. "I understand how you feel. It'll happen for you soon. You'll see."

The words felt little more than a platitude. "I'm sure it will."

"It's hard to believe it's happened."

"You've worked so hard. It's inspiring, in a way."

She shrugged. "I had no choice. It's do or die for me."

Yes, that was true. "Anyway. Congratulations. Maybe you'll be good enough to stand the Trials this year."

"I'm not holding my breath. I'll see you in the morning. That is, two standard days from now."

Right. Because of night meditations. It was hard for Lucian to wrap his head around the schedule, even after three months. "See you then."

They watched each other a moment longer. Today, he'd talked to Emma more than he had in weeks. He didn't want the conversation to end, but there were appearances to keep up. If the Talents even suspected what he felt for her, it could ruin everything.

So, Lucian returned to his room. The walk back was cold and lonely. The outside air made the interior halls chilly, and Lucian only felt relief once he was in his room. Once he lit the candles, he closed the door to find himself in blessed silence.

Lucian settled into his bed, propping himself against the stone wall. He picked up a worn book from the Academy's library on his nightstand. He meant to finally get started on *Manifoldic Theory*, and almost didn't open the book due to his exhaustion.

But when he opened the cover, he found the title page was quite different.

"Prophecy of the Seven?"

Lucian heaved a sigh. Apparently, he was so exhausted that he had checked out the wrong book. It was still by Arian, so maybe there was something of value in it. The pages were faded. Arian had taught at the Academy during its early years, so the tome could be as much as a century old.

Lucian started at the beginning, but the prose was incomprehensible. Almost as if it were another language. The foreword, but some long dead Transcend or other, revealed that Arian had abandoned his conscious mind to enter the Manifold, giving his body to the fraying to delve its secrets. And this book was apparently supposed to be those hidden secrets, though most mages contended that the book was evidence that Arian had finally lost it, at the end.

Well, if anything, this would be a good resource to fall asleep on restless nights.

As Lucian read on, he doubted even the most hallucinatory drug trip could reproduce this text. The book was a symbol of everything else this place had to offer. Impenetrable, incomprehensible, and maddening.

He was about to blow out the candle when there was a knock at the door. With a frown, he stood to answer it.

5

LUCIAN WAS SURPRISED to see Damian standing there, beaming a friendly smile. There was something in his demeanor, though, that said this wasn't just a friendly visit.

"Mind if I step inside?"

"I'm pretty tired. Can it wait till tomorrow?"

Damian's smile widened. "This won't take long, I promise. I think you'll be interested in what I have to say."

Lucian suppressed a sigh and nodded toward his room. The swarthy Damian stepped inside, turning his wide upper body just to fit through the half-open door. Damian had the build of a sports star, an effect dampened somewhat by his humble brown Novice robes, which were a bit too tight. Maybe the Academy didn't have a set large enough for him. Damian was the first person from Luddus Lucian had met. That explained his muscles, something that happened to people living in a high-g environment.

Damian sat in the room's only chair, made of simple wood and without any sort of ornamentation. Lucian took a seat on the bed.

"What's up?" Lucian asked.

Damian watched Lucian for a moment, as if he saw him as competition. What a strange thought. Lucian was so far from reaching Damian's level of skill as to be laughable. Then again, Damian seemed to see *everyone* as competition. Even today during the lesson, he hadn't missed an opportunity to compare himself with others. Either he was confident or making up for something lacking.

"I hoped to offer you a bit of advice if you'll have it. As a new Novice."

"I've been here three months. There are some newer than me."

"As long as you haven't streamed yet, you're new." Damian leaned back in the chair. "I've been here over a year. I was a slow learner, too. At times, it felt like I would be left behind."

Were Lucian's shortcomings so obvious? If Damian could tell, most everyone could. "Why are you telling me this?"

Damian chuckled. "Don't take it the wrong way. I have a thick skull, and it can take a while for lessons to sink in." He gave a conspiratorial smile. "Takes one to know one, right?"

"Yeah. Maybe."

"Certain things were holding me back. The first six months were the roughest. I *hated* this place. Cold, miserable. Sea ice as far as the eye can see in the dead of winter. At least, as far as the eye could see when a snowstorm wasn't blowing through. Spring and summer were little better, but at least there was sun." He shook his head. "Luddus is warm and dry. My family has a nice estate by the Gartavian Sea. They grow wine, olives, that sort of thing. Fishing's good out there. Sea as calm as glass." His eyes became distant. "My dad always wanted me to take things over when the time came." He shrugged. "Well, my time did come. Just not in the way he imagined."

"You took your metaphysical."

Damian nodded. "That's right. Went in for my metaphysical one day, and within the week, I was being shipped here. Oh, how I hated that. Still do, sometimes, truth be told." He shook his head, as if the pain of the past were too much to talk about. "I missed home. Hell, I still do. It got in the way of training. Eventually, I learned to let it go. At least, enough to proceed. That was the source of my block."

"How'd you get past it?"

"I won't say it was any sort of eureka moment. I took it day by day. The past recedes if you let it." He chuckled, though Lucian thought the laughter held a bitter note. "Haven't heard a thing from back home. Of course, I figured out soon enough they don't allow that. Only if something drastic happens, like a death. Oh, they'll let you know then. Then you're *forced* to let go. They'll have you not only in body, but mind, too."

"You sound resentful."

"Do I?" He shook his head. "Well, I didn't come in here to talk about myself. And I see I've done nothing to encourage you. For all the teaching they give us about letting go of ego, there's still a lot of ego going on around here. A lot of Novices don't want to help the newbies. They see them as competition when the Trials come up. Yeah, I'm competitive, but I like competition as motivation to move forward. It's good for both people. Besides, I don't think I have much to worry about. My results speak for themselves." He flashed a smile. "There are Novices here who'll be nice to your face but trip you up the moment they get the opportunity. Some of them even go on to be Talents. Even Transcends, I suppose."

"Not shocking." Why was Damian sharing all this? Lucian couldn't help but wonder.

"What about you?" Damian asked. "What do you think's holding you back?"

"I don't know," Lucian said. "Of course, I miss Earth. I miss home." He paused. "I miss my mom, too, and my old life. I *still* don't want to be here. Not really." The following silence was uncomfortable. "I don't think that'll change any time soon."

"That's tough." Damian drew a deep breath. "Well, we both chose this place because it was the only real option. We have a new life. No choice but to accept it. The more experienced Talents can leave, but only for a specified purpose. And of course, the damn League must approve it. Visiting family doesn't fall under that." Damian's eyes became distant. "I wonder when *I'll* get to leave this place. Even if I went back home, what would it be like? My mom and dad older, maybe even dead. My little sister all grown up, married. It might be a decade or more before it even becomes possible to go back. And that's only if my mission takes me to my backwater planet." He shook his head. "Making peace with that is hard. The hardest thing about being here is the past. It's an anchor weighing you down. If you don't cut it loose, you're going to sink."

"I don't have much of a past," Lucian said. "I've been on my own most of my life."

"What about your mom?"

Lucian didn't want to talk about that. "It's complicated."

"All right, I get it. Well, remember what I said. Because of what we are, our lives can never be anything close to normal. Maybe one day the Transcends will have everything figured out and fraying will be a thing of the past. Until that day, we must atone for the wrongs of the past. We have a gift. A dangerous gift, but a gift all the same. We have the potential to help a lot of people out there in the galaxy. There's something redeeming in that."

Lucian nodded to show that there was, but he wasn't sure how he truly felt. The galaxy was a messed-up place, so what could one person do to right the wrongs of the past? It seemed a senseless errand. Better to love and protect those close to you than to try and be a hero.

That thought just made his mind turn to Emma. That was

something he had to let go of, too. Could that be what was holding him back, his wish that things would be different?

All he knew now was that he was tired, and he wished Damian would just go.

But Damian seemed inured to Lucian's wishes. "My main advice is to forget the past, Lucian. I took long walks around the island. Did a lot of meditation. I had to let go of who I thought I was. Sometimes, who we think we are doesn't line up with who we need to be. It's funny. We can decide who we get to be, any time, any day. And yet we don't want to let go and change. But that's the path to peace. No, it's never easy. It can be downright painful. I'll leave you with something Talent Relisa has always told me. She's my main mentor here. *Ego is the enemy.*"

"Talent Relisa. She's the Psion of Transcend Red, right?"

He nodded. "Yeah. I'm lucky she's patient with me. Without that, I wouldn't be sitting here now."

A stab of jealousy pierced his chest. Khairu was *anything* but patient, and she was far from being a mentor. And no other Talent seemed to take to him, either. He only had himself to blame for that, walking around as if his life were over.

"Where would you be without her?" Lucian asked.

Damian whistled. "Man, you're going to make me go there, aren't you?"

"What do you mean?"

Damian's eyes widened. "What? You don't know?"

At Lucian's look of confusion, Damian's expression sobered. "Well, I guess it's not talked about much. I knew coming in what would happen if I didn't prove myself. That's part of the reason I felt so pressured to succeed."

Lucian wanted Damian to just spit it out. And he also didn't want him to. A tendril of fear was snaking in his stomach.

In the end, Lucian had to prod Damian to continue. "If there's something everyone here knows that I don't, then it's only fair that I know, too. Especially if your whole reason for coming here was to help me."

From Damian's guilty expression, Lucian knew he had him.

"You're right," Damian said. "Well, here it goes. The timing of it varies, but after a certain point, if you haven't made enough progress . . ." Damian snapped his fingers. "You get on a boat, and you don't come back."

Lucian went quiet as he considered his words. They didn't make sense at first.

"You get on a boat? To go where?"

"Wherever mages go if they can't be in an Academy."

The realization struck Lucian like a thunderbolt. "No. That can't be right. Can it?"

Then, it hit him. Vera herself touched on the subject herself. What had she said? The Transcends had set up Psyche themselves after the war. At the time, he'd assumed it was just for the mages who'd fought with Xara Mallis, along with the rogues who wouldn't accept training.

But he saw now that wasn't the case. *All* mages outside an Academy's purview were bound for the Mad Moon. And that included those who couldn't make the cut here.

"I'm sorry," Damian said. "I thought you knew."

Of course, it made complete sense. If a mage were untrainable, of course there was nowhere else they could go but there.

"Have you . . ." Lucian trailed off. "Has *anyone* left since you've been here?"

Damian was quiet for a while, his face solemn. "Several times. The biggest cuts come a few weeks after the Trials. They cut slack the first few years, of course, but if you fail repeatedly?" He snapped his fingers. "Gone. We don't say their names anymore. We try to forget them as soon as possible. The most recent was this man named Biru. Traveled all the way from Hephaestus. Nervous guy who didn't talk much. He and Talent

Khairu set off on the boat a few months back. A couple days later, she came back . . . with you and Emma."

That gave Lucian a chill. Khairu, of course, hadn't said a word. He wondered if Emma knew.

"I don't know more than that," Damian said. "Of course, it's not something you talk about." Damian's face fell. "Biru went without a word or struggle. I'm sure it's not a decision made lightly. We're told the Transcends try not to admit Novices who can't make the cut. Sometimes, though, even they make mistakes."

All Lucian could think about was how they almost hadn't admitted *him*. At this very moment, his position here was hanging on the edge of a knife. One wrong move, one misplaced word, might be all it took. If they hadn't accepted him, he might even *be* on Psyche now. The moon was three Gates away, in the Cupid system.

Damian was already standing to leave, but Lucian remained seated, paralyzed. Damian looked down at him with a somber expression.

"Do what they say," Damian said. "Everything. Without question. There's no room for error, no room to do things your own way. I almost made that mistake. Without Relisa, I could've been on that prison barge, too." He gave a nod, as if to confirm that immutable fact. "I hate to leave you with this . . ." He smiled bitterly. "I came here to lift your spirits, not drain them."

"No, it's fine," Lucian said, half-dazed. "I appreciate knowing the truth. It . . . puts things in perspective, doesn't it?"

Damian nodded. "I wish you well, Lucian. I truly do."

"I appreciate it."

At last, Damian closed the door behind him.

Lucian sat there, a numb shock permeating his entire being. He sat there for a good ten minutes without moving a single muscle. And when he finally *did* move, it was only to pace the tiny room back and forth. This cell reminded him of his time in the brig. Coldly, he wondered how this was any different from that.

Of course, someone who couldn't be trained couldn't stay here, just as someone who showed signs of fraying couldn't. Lucian had barely been admitted into the Academy. And the only reason was because of Transcend White's competition with her sister. At least, that was Lucian's reckoning.

He had been a fool to give up that opportunity. Then again, the penalty for failing Vera might have been even steeper. Whatever the case, Lucian couldn't say Vera hadn't warned him. If he had known this beforehand, would it have changed his decision? It was impossible to say.

Lucian knew he couldn't change the past. He was here, locked in, and had no choice but to try his best.

The other option would be to suffer a fate worse than death. A mage prison planet, doomed to fray without the proper training, was the last place he wanted to spend his life.

A life which would, no doubt, be short-lived.

6

A KNOCK on Lucian's door jolted him awake, and Lucian groaned. *Again?* There was no way it was time to wake up yet.

He opened his eyes to see only darkness. The candles had burned out, and the tiny cell only had a small, high window to the outside. Which of course was dark and useless since it was almost always cloudy.

Lucian got up, throwing on a fresh set of brown robes and slipping on his leather boots. He stumbled toward the door, taking a while to find the latch. Whoever he saw on the other side of that door would be sorry for it.

When the door creaked open, it was the last person Lucian expected.

Psion Gaius, the apprentice of Transcend White herself, stood in the hallway. Lucian's eyebrows shot up – what in the Worlds was he doing here? He had to have the wrong door. Despite that, Lucian stood straighter.

The Psion's cold blue eyes stared at him, set in an angular face shrouded by heavy black brows. The brows were a stark contrast to his balding head, where a thinning ring of graying hair clung like a laurel. The respect due to someone of Psion Gaius's stature was almost equal to that of a Transcend.

Lucian lowered his head. "Psion Gaius." What was he supposed to say?

While he was debating that question, Psion Gaius's thick brows lowered. "Transcend White has summoned you."

Lucian's blood went cold. They couldn't be kicking him out so soon.

There was no choice but to obey. "Of course, Psion Gaius."

"I'm aware of the Quiet Hours," Gaius said. "This takes priority, per her words." He nodded toward his room. "Wash your face, straighten your hair, and do your best to compose yourself."

"Of course."

He debated whether he should shut the door. He settled for cracking it. He splashed cold water on his face, the shock doing a good job of waking him up. What did Transcend White want? Transcends simply didn't summon Novices, and the hour was clearly long before the usual waking time.

It couldn't be anything good.

Upon his return to the hallway, Lucian followed Psion Gaius down the corridor to a set of stairs. For the first time, he would be seeing the Academy's upper reaches.

They made it to the second-floor landing. The corridor extending outward looked much the same as the first floor. Lucian followed Gaius up the final set of stairs, until they were on the third and final level of the Academy. Gaius strode forward, sure of his destination. Other than the heavy silence, nothing about the Transcends' level was starkly different. At least, not until Lucian felt the coldness of a breeze caressing him from around the corner.

He immediately saw why. Around the corner was a long arcade open to the elements, supported by stone pillars on the left side. Open archways on the right led deeper into the Academy, but all of them were dark. Between the pillars stretched the wide, dark expanse of the Northern Ocean. The sky above teemed with foreign constellations. Anytime he saw the stars here, it only reminded him of how far he was from home.

They walked to the other side of the Academy, until they reached a wooden door which led into the Academy's north tower, the largest. This must be Transcend White's office and quarters.

Psion Gaius gave three firm knocks.

A reedy voice emanated from within. "Enter."

Gaius opened the door and bowed. Lucian followed suit, making sure to bow even lower than the Psion. He couldn't humble himself too far, especially considering what Damian had told him.

"Thank you, Psion Gaius," Transcend White said. "You may go."

The Psion bowed again before departing, casting Lucian a bemused expression that seemed to wonder what he was doing here.

Well, that was two of them.

The door closed, and the following silence was heavy. Transcend White seemed to ignore him, focusing on some papers before her. Lucian shifted his feet and tried to keep himself from wringing his hands. He focused on his surroundings. There was little in the room that might give Lucian a clue about who she was. There were no trappings – only bare walls, floor, and ceiling. A large fire burned in a small hearth near the Transcend's oaken desk, lending ample warmth. That desk was well-made, and had a few open books upon it, along with some old-fashioned pens that used ink. Today, her hair wasn't braided, and flowed as freely as her twin's. He suppressed a shudder. He might as well have been staring right at Vera. What was their story, and the nature of their disagreements?

Lucian valued his life, so he didn't mean to ask.

When the silence had gone on for a torturous length of time, Lucian wondered if he should be the first to speak. He held out until he could no longer stand it, even if it were a breach of decorum.

"What did you wish of me, your High Eminence?"

"Say not a word," she said, cutting him off. She scanned those papers, her eyes roving back and forth as if madly searching for some clue. Another minute passed before she leaned back in her chair and raised her eyes to meet his. That gaze was identical to the one she'd unleashed on him the day they met, three months ago.

Lucian had the feeling, as her eyes bored into his, that she was doing *more* than looking. A strange chill covered his skin, as if static were pulling at the hair on his arms. What *was* that feeling? In the end, he must have imagined it, because as soon as he noticed it, it was gone. Transcend White steepled her fingers.

"Sit, Novice Lucian."

Lucian sat.

"I've heard reports that you are struggling with the training."

He wasn't sure if he could speak yet, so he remained silent. She seemed to be waiting for an answer, so he decided to risk it.

"My progress has been slow, but I'm working as hard as I can."

"Are you?" Her expression seemed to question that. "I hope so." She studied him a moment longer. "It gives me no pleasure to say this, but it would seem my sister was mistaken about you."

He blinked. Was it happening already? "What do you mean?"

"I'm almost her equal in magic," Transcend White said. "And yet, I cannot *fathom* what it is she saw in you. Your progress *has* been slow. Completely unremarkable. My sister would not have offered to take you as her Psion unless she had seen something in you. And yet, your block remains resolute. You struggle every day to overcome it. For one reason or another, the Manifold remains closed to you. Enough to the point where I'm beginning to doubt your story." She shook her head. "But no, I can't deny it. You *did* meet my sister. She *did* see something in you. Only, why could that be?"

It was almost as if she were speaking to herself, each question spoken in a rhetorical tone.

"I told Vera myself there was nothing special about me."

Transcend White's eyebrows shot up. "And her reaction?"

"What I said before, your High Eminence. She didn't seem to think so. She mentioned something about prophecy."

"Prophecy means nothing. She must be gravely mistaken in that."

Lucian shrugged. It was not his place to offer an opinion.

"Well, you may be a slow learner. Why do you think that is, Lucian?"

"I don't know," he said. "My mother often said the same thing."

Her eyes widened slightly. Why would saying that surprise her?

"Yes, about that." She looked at him a bit longer. "This will not be easy, so I'm going to come out and say it. I didn't summon you here to talk about your progress. Though I am interested in that."

Lucian straightened in his chair and tried not to betray his nervousness.

"I hate to say this, especially when you are already struggling so much..."

Why was she hedging? He became more alert, his heart beginning to race.

"If it's about my progress, I promise to try even harder," Lucian said. "Yesterday, I felt like I was close..."

"It's not that, Novice," she said. "It was strange you mentioned your mother, because this is about her."

At those words, Lucian's heart nearly stopped. Before he could say anything, Transcend White continued.

"There was a battle outside Starbase Centauri. Though the League Fleet prevailed, Swarmer bombers destroyed the carrier your mother was stationed on."

Everything went cold, like a shock of cold water. But then, he felt resistance. It *couldn't* be true.

"Impossible," he whispered. "Chiron is a First World. If the Swarmers are in Alpha Centauri . . ." His *mother*. "No. You must be mistaken."

He leaned back in his chair, vertigo making him dizzy. That was when Transcend White pushed a piece of paper across her desk toward him.

"This is the dispatch."

Lucian picked it up with trembling hands. He scanned it, reading it once. Twice. Then three times. Numbness crept into his hands, down his arms, and into his heart. His eyes watered with tears, making the words difficult to read.

I regret to inform you, on behalf of the U.N.E. navy's Chief of Staff, Zira Giroux, of the untimely death of your mother, Captain Mira Abrantes. She died on 5 August 2364, defending humanity against a surprise Swarmer fleet. Her ship was shot down by a torpedo that slipped past the U.N.S. Refuge's point defense systems. The destruction was total. A service will be held on 10 August aboard the U.N.S. Encouragement. Given the impossibility of you or any next of kin's attendance, a subsidy of 2.5 Worlds Credits will be deposited in your name and can be collected at any League Fleet Office in the Hundred Worlds to make funeral arrangements. Again, on behalf of the Chief of Staff, please accept the Consolidated League Fleet's deepest condolences.

"No," Lucian whispered. "This is wrong."

Images of his mother flashed through his mind. The one brutal fact he was aware of was how little they had seen each other over the years. How precious and few their memories. The sense of loss wasn't only for what was, but what might have been. He had always thought there would be more time.

He'd been wrong.

He was blind and deaf to everything. He was barely even aware of Transcend White watching him from behind her desk, with not a trace of emotion on her face.

"You have my condolences, Lucian. It seems your mother was a brave woman. And it would seem the Worlds are in for dark days again."

Why was she saying "was?" The tears were flowing freely now. He wiped them away furiously. What would she think of him, not being able to control his emotions?

Through his blurred vision, he could see Transcend White holding out a clean kerchief. Lucian watched it for a moment, then took it to dry his face. He drew a deep breath to steady his nerves. He sat there, dazed.

"Take the night to process the news," Transcend White said. "Here on Transcend Mount, many come from . . . troubled pasts, and many have suffered a similar loss while training. As difficult as this situation is, know that you are not alone."

The words sounded trite and pointless. He wanted to be anywhere but here. "May I go now?"

"Of course. But one more thing, before you go."

Lucian stopped, his hand shaking on the door handle.

"Not a word about the Swarmers. If word gets out, we will know it was you. We Transcends will address the Academy in our own time. We don't want to cause undue panic or distract the Novices from their studies."

There was no choice but to nod his agreement.

He left her office, stumbling down the pillared arcade for the staircase. He clung to the dispatch in his hand. It was dated August fifth, and Lucian had no real way of knowing what that corresponded to here. He'd lost track of the standard calendar long ago. The months were the same on Volsung, but they had longer lengths, since Volsung's year was four hundred and four standard days.

If the dispatch was true, then it meant his mother had been dead a month. Possibly a little longer. The news must have just been freshly delivered.

The funeral had happened. For a whole month, his mother had had a *funeral*. He'd been training, struggling, fighting, and all the while – she had been cold and lifeless. Never to move, laugh, or breathe again. Had she been buried? What of her ashes? Or was she in a cold coffin floating in space, one among thousands of dead, silent and forgotten?

And why had Transcend White delivered the news herself? It didn't seem like something she would take upon herself.

Lucian couldn't think of that now. Whenever it happened, one fact was immutable. Lucian would never see his mother again.

Going down the stairs, all the old, sequestered fears from childhood became freshly open wounds. Back then, he would lie awake at night, wondering when he would get the news. He had mostly put those fears behind him. But now, they were manifested.

And he was here, lightyears away. Helpless.

She was dead. He would never hear her cheesy jokes. Never get her support. Never get another word of advice.

And the Swarmers were back. But out here, on Transcend Mount, that fact seemed so distant. He'd heard not a word about it, so how many knew? The Transcends, surely, and perhaps some of the Talents.

Lucian wandered the dark halls and corridors. He favored areas far from people. To his relief, he didn't pass anyone. He wandered down hallways that likely hadn't seen a footstep for weeks. Most of the Novices and Talents would be in their rooms or meditation chambers. Lucian walked in a half-dead haze. He felt as if he were in a dream, as if his spirit were floating a few meters behind his body.

Could she really be only a memory? Every time she deployed, she came back. Sure, she came back with more lines and wrinkles, but her eyes were the same.

And now, she would never come back.

It had to be true. Transcend White had no reason to lie about it, to forge an official dispatch. He thought of his conversation with Damian. How uncanny that he had mentioned they only told you about family in the case of a death.

He could only hope other parts of the conversation with Damian didn't prove so prophetic.

Somehow, without even realizing it, Lucian ended up in the courtyard. It seemed he was alone in the darkness. He strode toward the cliff, to the very edge of the promontory overlooking the dark ocean. There, he gazed at the bleak scene. How easy it would be to jump. Was there any point to staying alive? He would never be a proper mage, not with this distracting him and his progress so slow.

He *had* no control. All his hopes that things would turn out fine were illusion. His life now had two possible roads. He could follow the training, follow orders until he himself rose high enough to give them. Or he could fail. He would have nothing waiting for him but Psyche.

Of course, there was a third option. Take but a few more steps north, and all this would be over. Lucian doubted he would be the first to do such a thing. That rocky shore below had to be littered with at least some bones.

"I won't have it."

His voice sounded small, weak. Why had he come here instead of following Vera? Why had he let his mother go off to fight again? He should have convinced her to go to Halia to live with his Uncle Ravis. Would that have been so hard to encourage? As an executive for Caralis Intergalactic, he could have given her a job that paid as well, or better.

If only he had the power to change the past. But no one, not even a mage, was as powerful as that.

No matter what he tried, it would never be good enough.

"I won't have it!"

The wind carried his words away, rendering them useless and unheard. He curled his hands into fists. A hot, familiar fire burned at his core, spreading to every limb. That fire spread, suffusing his muscles and bones with a boundless, burning energy. The air warped before him, the stars elongating in long, bleeding streams curling against the black void above. This power demanded an outlet. The burn had become unbearable. It demanded release, but how?

Such pain. Lucian screamed, pushing the fire out of him in a concentrated wave of energy. That power found an outlet; a distant iceberg, floating about a kilometer out. Resistance pushed back against him. *Great* resistance. The iceberg was far, and Lucian knew his magic might not find a connection.

He needed more power. More ether. He was beyond caring at this point. His body burned hotter, and his consciousness extended to the iceberg itself. He tried to form his Focus, to control the rush, but the image of his stone collapsed in the torrent of magic. He pushed against the berg, feeling it buckle beneath the magical wave. His accompanying roar was eaten by the wind.

Then, the iceberg *moved*, crumbling into the dark water as a fissure tore through its center. A thunderous crack echoed off the northern walls of the Academy. Lucian's bones vibrated with its very force. The fire was extinguished, having been ripped from him completely. He felt... empty. Hollow.

His shoulders sagged, his lungs burning for oxygen. Lucian gasped for cold air. Sweat coated his skin. He watched, in fascination and disbelief, as the iceberg continued to crumble. Large, bluish chunks of ice splashed into the dark surface of the ocean.

He stumbled back from the precipice, his brown robes swirling in the wind. The iceberg was obliterated by now, broken into hundreds or even thousands of pieces. Flotsam of ice was being borne by the currents of the ocean.

He had finally streamed. It had only taken the death of his mother for it to happen.

He ran back to the Academy, fearful that someone might have seen. He had to get inside, before the noise drew people out here. He could only hope everyone was busy with their meditations. Otherwise, if anyone were looking out here at this moment...

He was almost inside the Academy when he thought he saw a face from the second-floor arcade. It was gone almost as soon as he spied it. The shadows were so deep that he couldn't be sure he'd seen anything at all.

He would have written it off, but for some reason he couldn't explain, he could think of no one other than Talent Khairu.

7

LUCIAN ENTERED the Academy and turned down a dark corridor. He clung to the shadows, waiting to make sure no one was coming. It was wishful thinking. Voices echoed from around the corner – voices that seemed to be coming his way. He shrunk into an open doorway, empty of articles except a dilapidated desk. Feet passed the door, making straight for the courtyard. He waited there at least five minutes as ten or so people passed, most speaking in hushed whispers. Lucian could join the flow and pretend as if he were investigating it himself. It was the natural thing to do. In fact, it might be more suspicious if he were the only one absent.

Lucian listened to make sure the hallway was clear. Then, he walked back out into the cold courtyard. Twenty or so people, Novices mostly but also some Talents, had gathered by the cliff. All were looking out at the shattered iceberg, talking in low voices.

Once Lucian was close enough, his heart racing, he could hear what they were saying.

"*Someone* hammered that thing," one of the male Talents said, whose name Lucian didn't know.

The person he was speaking to, Lucian *did* know. Gaius regarded the remnants of the berg in silence. Everyone seemed to watch Gaius for a reaction, but his expression was still as stone.

"The ether required to destroy that..." The Psion shook his head. "Someone overdrew."

Several gasped at that.

"Who?" a newer Novice asked.

Gaius clenched his jaw. "That's what I mean to find out."

"Hey."

Lucian jumped as Emma approached him from behind. "Oh. Hey."

"Just got here. What was that noise?" Her eyes went up to the destroyed iceberg, which was still in the process of breaking apart. They went wide at the sight. "Who did *that*?"

"No one knows," Lucian said. "Someone powerful with magic, that's for sure."

Maybe that would throw them off the trail. Some of the Talents shifted their feet. Lucian had been speaking more loudly than he thought.

Psion Gaius turned to face them. And with that action, he and Emma became the focus of everyone's attention. It wasn't a position Lucian wanted to be in. But the Psion's eyes went above them, seeming to address everyone gathered. "If anyone knows what happened, speak now."

No one suspected him. How could they? He hadn't streamed a drop of magic since getting here. No one would suspect him unless someone actually *saw* it. How long had he been out there? Two to three minutes? Most of the mages would have been at their meditations, though it was conceivable that one or two might have been looking out at the courtyard. The front yard was a more popular place to meditate, but it was too cold for many to do so outside.

Had that been Khairu on the second-floor arcade? No

doubt that if it were her, she would be reporting him at this very moment.

Transcends Blue and Green joined the throng. Their faces were stern masks, and all went quiet at their approach.

Transcend Green was the one who addressed the crowd, his long beard blowing in the wind. "What happened out here?"

"Someone destroyed the iceberg," a female Talent said, with a red sash that denoted her as a disciple of Transcend Red.

Transcend Green's attention immediately went back to the crowd. "Which of you did this?"

Dead silence was his only answer.

Lucian kept his eyes down. He couldn't risk looking at the Transcend. Vera and Transcend White at least seemed to have the ability to discern inner thoughts. Maybe Transcend Green did, too.

"If one of you did this," Transcend Blue said, scanning the small crowd, "a choice lies before you. To tell the truth, or pay the price for your silence. Either way, we Transcends will discover the truth of it, rest assured."

The two Transcends waited a moment longer, as if giving anyone a chance to confess. After that moment had passed, they turned back for the Academy.

In the absence of further instructions, Psion Gaius took charge. "All right. Get back to your meditations. There's nothing to see here."

At these words, the Novices and Talents dispersed with low murmurs. Lucian looked up at the pillared arcade where Khairu might have been earlier, but it was empty. He must have imagined it.

If it wasn't his imagination, his time at the Volsung Academy might soon come to an end.

LUCIAN RETURNED to his room to "meditate," but in reality he lay in bed, trying to process what had happened. Transcend Blue said they would find out, one way or another. The real question was whether Lucian should believe that.

The "right" thing to do was to confess, but that would only get him expelled. And that would be the end of his short tenure at the Volsung Academy.

There was only one person he could trust here. But Lucian didn't know where to find Emma. If she were in the women's Novice quarters, he couldn't go there. He would have to hope she was somewhere else on the grounds. Perhaps in the library, where she spent a great deal of her free time studying. It wasn't much, but it was all he had to go on.

The walk didn't take long. Lucian was always a bit awed by the library's scale. It was the only place in the Academy that opened to all three floors, extending to the height of the roof. Thousands upon thousands of books crowded the shelves. Since the use of electronics was forbidden, all the Volsung mages' knowledge was contained here. Metal spiral staircases circled to the upper levels. The entire space was lit dimly by oil lamps, while each mage at study had their own lamp by which to read.

Emma was sitting at one of the central tables along with a few other Novices, including Damian and Rhea. Each of them had their noses buried in a book, the only activity allowed on a meditation day. In complete obedience to the Transcends' mandate of silence, they didn't so much as look up at him as he approached.

Lucian stood by Emma. When she finally noticed him, Lucian nodded toward the open doorway and left. He was sure others had noticed that, but he needed to talk to her.

"What is it?" she asked, once they were out in the corridor.

There was no point in hedging. "It was me."

Her expression remained still, as if the news didn't register. And then her face blanched.

"No. It couldn't have been . . ." She looked at him, as if for confirmation. He nodded, and her face went even paler.

"Lucian. Oh, God."

"If they find out, I'll get kicked out of the Academy."

"What? No, you won't. This means you've broken through your block. That's what they want, right?"

"It's not that," he said. "Psion Gaius said whoever did it overdrew. So, if they figure out it was me . . ."

He sunk against the wall, putting his face in his hands. It was just now hitting him. The overdrawing, his mother dying, everything.

"Lucian?" Emma knelt across from him. "Can you tell me what's going on?"

He uncovered his face, his eyes meeting hers. "My mom died."

She blinked, her face not seeming to comprehend. "What do you mean? How do you know that?"

"Transcend White summoned me to her office," Lucian said. His voice was thick. "She handed me this."

He reached in his pocket and gave her the dispatch. She scanned it quickly.

"Lucian . . ." Her eyes filled with unshed tears. She reached for his hand. "I'm sorry. You must be hurting so much right now."

All Lucian felt was numbness. "It's . . . hard to believe. It doesn't feel real, yet."

"Lucian, it's okay to be sad. It's okay to grieve."

Grieve? How was it possible to grieve when it didn't even feel real?

"I don't know what to do," he said. "I can't leave. They already held the funeral weeks ago. I don't know what this means about the Swarmers . . ." He looked at her. "Don't tell anyone about that part."

"I won't." Her eyes were filled with sadness. "If you need anything, I'm here. Try to think of her, okay? Process it. Remember all that was good."

The last thing Lucian wanted was a lecture. He managed a nod.

"I should go. I . . . just needed to tell someone."

"Let me be with you. You shouldn't have to be alone right now."

"Maybe later. I just need some time to think."

She watched him a moment. "Okay. Don't bottle this up, okay? If you need anyone to talk to, I'm here."

"Thanks."

He left her standing there. It felt wrong to do that, but he just didn't want to talk about it right now. He didn't understand why he'd even sought her out to begin with.

Rather than return to his room, Lucian wandered the hallways again. He walked until he reached the front entrance of the Academy. The wide-open lawn outside was completely empty. He descended the outer steps until the short, lichen-like grass was beneath his boots. He didn't understand what he was doing, or why he was doing it.

He was heading to the flame tree, standing alone at the edge of the southern cliff. Its fiery foliage was thick above its white trunk. This very tree was imprinted on the stones of the Academy at various points. Though no one had ever told him so, Lucian figured it was something of a symbol for the Volsung Academy.

Lucian stood at the base of the tree, and after considering a moment, began climbing. He was probably not supposed to be doing this. But he had already broken one rule, in a big way, so what was another small infraction? Besides, he wasn't in the mood to care. Due to the thick foliage, there was little chance of anyone seeing him. He just wanted to be alone.

The foliage seemed to break the wind. Sheltered within the tree, he could sit here for hours and think. He'd have to mind that wind, though. The tree's limbs could whip violently if it were windy enough. Its limbs were far more elastic than any Earth tree, to better survive this world's storms.

There he sat and thought. And when he'd exhausted himself of that, he entered a silent torpor. It was as if he didn't exist at all, as if he didn't feel the cold. He realized he had unconsciously recalled his Focus, that he had been feeding his emotions into it, as into a flame. Oblivion was all he wished for. For a few hours, he might have it. The stars wheeled across the sky. Even Volsung Orbital passed along the southern horizon, about the size of Earth's moon. It was no more than a shadow blocking the stars above. He was content in that moment to exist, without thought or motive.

But the thoughts eventually returned, and they were cruel. If he had only mentioned her going to Halia to work for his uncle, she might be alive right now. She wasn't *supposed* to be a part of that battle.

His thoughts were broken by voices emanating from the direction of the Academy. Lucian didn't let go of his Focus, but allowed it to enhance his senses. He adjusted the limbs for a better view. What he saw broke through the numbness. Transcend White was strolling across the yard toward him, along with a red-robed figure that could be no one other than Transcend Red. She was back from the hunt, then. How long had she been here?

Lucian had heard Transcend Red was the youngest of the Transcends, being in her late thirties. As both Transcends drew closer, Lucian could see Transcend Red was a strikingly beautiful woman, with long blonde hair, full red lips, and a long, pale face illumined by the starlight. Her beauty was only slightly marred by a pinched, sour expression that gave her a mean look.

As they drew closer to the tree, Lucian remained still. If they knew he was in here, then there was little that could be done about it. It wasn't as if he could run without them noticing. To his relief, they stood at the cliff's edge about twenty meters away. They spoke in low voices, of which he could not hear a trace. The wind covered their words completely.

From the side profile of Transcend Red's face, Lucian could see her small but well-defined jawline, an aquiline nose, and creamy skin. The wind tugged at her light blonde hair as she watched Transcend White, whose back was to Lucian.

All Lucian could do was remain still. There were a couple of times where it *seemed* like Transcend Red saw him, but if she did, she pretended not to notice.

As she spoke, her demeanor was stern, and her gestures a bit harsh. What could they be arguing about, and why was she so angry?

All Lucian could do was hope they didn't look his way. The two Transcends spoke for at least half an hour. At last, they seemed to come to a consensus, at which point they began strolling back to the Academy.

Lucian waited another fifteen minutes before easing himself down from the tree. His muscles had gone stiff with inactivity, his hands numbed from the cold. The weather had grown even more frigid – cold enough for it to snow, perhaps. Shivering, he hurried back inside the Academy. He was grateful to find the entry hall empty, save for a young Talent in her twenties who was the night's Timekeeper, whose job was to light the fifty-five torches arranged in the entry hall, one per hour. Lucian warmed his hands at the central brazier before heading toward the dining hall.

He was almost there when a stern female voice apprehended him. "Novice Lucian."

He spun to face Khairu. Where had *she* come from? Though shorter than him by a good measure, she seemed to tower over Lucian from body posture alone.

"The Spectrum has summoned you."

All of them? That could only mean one thing. From Khairu's superior smirk, Lucian had a feeling that what he saw among the columns had not been his imagination.

Lucian almost asked her why she hated him so much, enough to rat him out to the Transcends, but pride stopped him. There was a faint chance this summoning could be about something else, small chance as it was.

"Make your way there now," she said.

Lucian nodded. This was a battle he could not win. Khairu walked away, her gray Talent robes swirling as she disappeared around the corner.

8

THERE WAS ONLY one reason the full Spectrum would summon him. They knew, and they knew because Khairu had told them.

He found it difficult to care, even if he knew he should.

Lucian collected himself outside the Spectrum Chamber. He assumed his Focus to steady his nerves. Then, he drew a deep breath and stepped inside.

Across the tiled floor, all eight stone seats were occupied. Each Transcend was regaled in their shimmering robes, each according to their color, and each of those seats was flanked by two small flames, burning with the Transcend's color. The inner chamber shone with multicolored brilliance, a rainbow of light dancing along the walls. Each of those faces wore a severe expression, expressions that Lucian couldn't meet for long.

From left to right, it began with Transcend Red. Illumined by red light, her sharp and beautiful features reminded him of a bird of prey. Then there was Transcend Orange, an overweight man of Indian descent with dark skin and white hair.

Next came Transcend Yellow, a willowy woman with skin of copper and long weaves with streaks of gray. Then came Transcend Green, with whom Lucian was already familiar. He stroked his long, gray beard, his face an inscrutable maze of wrinkles. Next to him, Transcend Blue stared at Lucian, his manner businesslike and brusque. Transcend Violet, like Transcend Red, was relatively young and beautiful for a Transcend – probably in her early to mid-forties. She had pale skin, wide blue eyes, and wavy brown hair. Those eyes seemed to pity him, if anything. Transcend Gray, the oldest save for Transcend White, stared at Lucian without expression. His sickly form was shriveled, and he seemed to be almost asleep, eyes half-lidded. Last of all, of course, was Transcend White herself, who stared at Lucian hardest of all.

The effect of their colorful array was like a rainbow, beautiful and terrible to behold. Each of those fires cast its own light on the figure sitting within each seat, deepening the colors of their robes, lending more power and majesty. The light even hurt Lucian's eyes, as if he were some lowly creature who couldn't bear to look at the radiance of gods. He had to lower his head as he approached. If humility was not chosen, then it would be forced.

Lucian knelt, and suffered the power of their collective gaze. He knelt for almost half a minute, a time that seemed to stretch into eternity. His own brown robes caught none of the colors of the chamber. It absorbed the light, rather than reflecting it.

"Your Eminences," he said, his voice hardly audible above the crackle of flames. "I've come in answer to your summons."

There was an uncomfortable pause as he awaited their answer. His heart thundered within, his throat clamped, and his stomach was doing leaps.

"Rise," Transcend White said, her voice reedy but powerful. "You need not hide your face from us, Novice Lucian."

Despite the pain, he could not refuse the command. To his surprise, the intensity of the glares had lessened.

"No doubt you know the reason for your summoning," Transcend White went on. "We sensed a large discharge of ethereal energy tonight. If not for Talent Khairu, we would have never figured out the source on our own."

So, it *had* been her. Small surprise there.

"Your Eminences..."

"*Silence*, Novice!" Transcend Red snapped. "You speak only when asked a direct question." She nodded toward Transcend White.

If any of the Transcends were fazed by this, they gave no sign. Transcend White least of all.

"As you may have guessed," Transcend White continued, "we do not take this lightly. What you did was terribly dangerous. A mage is *never* to use their powers so thoughtlessly, and in such a chaotic burst of emotion. *That* is the path to fraying." Transcend White's hard stare scanned her fellow Transcends. "We've gathered here today due to the seriousness of your case. We could not ignore it a moment longer. We are debating an important question about you, Novice." She paused, either for effect or because she didn't relish what she was about to say. "We were discussing whether it's time for us to dismiss you from the Volsung Academy forthright."

Lucian did his best not to quail under the verbal assault. She was right, of course. He had made a stupid, terrible mistake, and for what? Would they see grief as an acceptable reason? Somehow, he doubted it.

"Have you anything to say in your defense, Novice?" Transcend Gray asked. The man was alive after all.

Lucian shook his head. "What I did was wrong. I wanted to... vent, I guess."

Transcend Yellow addressed him serenely from her seat.

"And in venting, you did something that many of our own Talents cannot do. And at great range!"

Her tone held the unmistakable tone of awe. A Transcend, awed by what *he'd* done? Lucian did not dare look up; he could not let them think he was interpreting that as praise. But he could sense them watching him for some reaction, some sort of explanation. They were trying to figure something out. But what?

"Tell us where you've received training before," Transcend Blue finally said. "And why you didn't disclose such training upon your initiation."

Lucian looked at Transcend White. Something in her thunderous expression warned him to not breathe a word about her sister.

"I've received no training," he said. "Unless grief counts as training."

"What do you mean, Novice?" Transcend Yellow asked.

Again, he looked at Transcend White for permission to explain about his mother. At her slight nod, he cleared his throat.

"I learned today that my mother died in the battle in the Alpha Centauri system. I know it's no excuse for what I did, but it might offer some explanation for my ... lapse."

Lucian couldn't make himself continue. He knew he should be making his case, defending himself. But he didn't have the heart, even if the consequences of not doing so were perilous.

"We rarely give second chances," Transcend White said. "Especially when considering matters of this magnitude. The death of your mother, however, *is* a relevant detail. Of course, a mage should never stream under duress. But you are a child in this place. And children deserve more leniency than those who know better." She stared at him sharply. "There is no doubt among any of us that you are a mage of great potential. Only hours ago, I wondered whether we had made a mistake in admitting you. Again, I am wondering that, but for different reasons. Suffice it to say, we haven't seen a mage of your potential in this academy for many, many years."

"Not since . . ." Transcend Blue began to say.

Transcend White raised one of her gnarled hands, cutting him off. "No."

What had Transcend Blue been about to say? Lucian kept his face lowered, to hide his curiosity.

"Come, now," Transcend Red said. "Can we not share at least *something* of that episode? For instructional purposes?"

Transcend White stared her down. Transcend Red held that gaze for a moment, as if in challenge. But in the end, she broke away, her dark eyes smoldering.

Transcend White returned her attention to Lucian. "I'll say this much. Once, long ago, we made the mistake of training a powerful mage, despite clear warning signs. We were all humbled by that experience."

Some of the Transcends looked at her, surprised that she had said that much. But Transcend White's attention remained transfixed on Lucian.

"You must learn to *control* yourself, Novice. There will be none of this ever again. The Manifold is *not* something to bandy about. It does not exist to please our egos or quell our sorrows. We exist to serve *it*, to use it conscientiously and only at direst need. And we must *never* draw beyond our natural pool of ether. Overdrawing is the path to fraying. And your actions tonight are those of a frayed mage. The madness ether causes does not always seem obvious at first, especially to the one going mad."

Lucian kept his head lowered, not daring to speak.

"Rarely do we all gather on such short notice on the account of a Novice," Transcend White continued. She leaned back in her seat. "Consider this your first and only warning. Learn to stream the right way, with our training, or you can learn to do so in the pits of Psyche. Trust me; that school is much harder than ours."

Her face was as hard as stone, but Lucian thought there was something else. Disappointment, maybe?

"You may go," she said. "And consider yourself lucky. Meditate and do penance. Tomorrow, your training begins anew. It's clear that your powers have developed far beyond what any of us thought." She clenched her jaw. "We will keep you on for further training, though the rope you walk on is slender indeed."

Lucian lowered his head further. "Thank you, Transcend White."

"Fool," Transcend Red said, with vitriol. "Learn to be silent! If it were my decision, you would be banished."

Lucian bit his tongue.

"Do you dissent to my ruling, Transcend Red?" Transcend White asked, her tone dangerous.

Though there was no betrayal of emotion on Transcend Red's face, her hands seemed to clench on her seat. "No. But I must say that time will tell, will it not?" Her dark eyes narrowed on Lucian. "We will see if this proverbial slap on the wrist is enough to temper his wild proclivities."

"Mercy may be shown once," Transcend White said. "But only once."

At this, Transcend Red went quiet.

"If there is nothing more to discuss," Transcend White said, "you may leave, Lucian. Go with Transcend Red." Now, Transcend White gave a small smile, barely perceptible. "She will oversee your atonement."

Transcend Red's face became a mask of affront. But that expression only lasted half a second, and Lucian thought he was the only one to have caught it. One would think *she* was the one being punished.

Lucian stood, with Transcend Red also rising from her seat.

She regarded Lucian a moment with her intense, hawk-like gaze. If looks could kill, he would have been dead ten times over.

"Come with me, Lucian. We will begin immediately."

Lucian had no choice but to follow.

9

LUCIAN FOLLOWED TRANSCEND Red out of the Spectrum Chamber in silence. Not a word was spoken as she led him to the front yard. She walked quickly, as if to get this over with as soon as possible. The brown grass almost glowed under the light of the star-filled sky. Lucian's stomach rumbled – he hadn't eaten a bite since the evening meal yesterday. But he was not about to complain about it, especially now.

Once they reached the eastern cliff, they came to a stop.

"Stand here," Transcend Red instructed.

Lucian obeyed. Her red robes swirled at a gust of wind as she donned her hood. She looked like a pissed off version of Little Red Riding Hood. It took all his self-control not to laugh at that thought. When the wind blew her cloak aside enough to reveal a shockspear at her hip, his urge to laugh dissipated completely.

Transcend Red stood about five meters ahead of him. Her severe, pale face was stern. "Close your eyes, Novice."

Lucian didn't want to do that, but slacking in obedience would only make things worse. He closed his eyes. He tried to keep his mind off that spear. It was foolish to be afraid of that. After all, a mage's greatest weapon was magic, not a spear.

"You must learn to control your stream, Lucian," she said. "Those who cannot control themselves are dealt with severely."

His eyes half-opened of their own accord.

Her voice snapped like a whip. "Eyes closed!"

He shut his eyes.

"Imagine your Focus," she said. "Recall it well. Are you confused, Novice, that your punishment might only be further training?" She gave a throaty chuckle. "I find that punishment rarely has the intended effect. At best, it only makes the recipient fear you. Fear can be useful. But fear is not the goal here. Competency is."

Lucian nodded, to show he understood.

"Now, recall your Focus," Her voice was almost hypnotic. "Imagine it upon a black void. That part is important. There is naught but the Focus, the foreground against an endless black. . ."

Lucian followed her directions, imagining the black void first, and then his stone. The image held firmly, but at the same time, thoughts, fears, and memories intruded. The image swam in and out of consciousness.

"Now," she continued, "Feed everything into it. All your thoughts, all your fears, all your distractions. Feed them to the Focus. Each distraction only makes the Focus stronger and more dominant. As its roots deepen, so do yours." A pause. "*You* are the Focus. *You* are what grows in power. *You* are the conduit."

She was *training* him. How many Novices could say they received personal instruction from a Transcend? He wondered what her game was. With difficulty, he forced those thoughts into the Focus, until there was nothing but the stone in Lucian's mind. The world fell away, along with the cold wind and Transcend Red's droning voice. But the stone loomed larger than ever. A tendril of fear was growing, a sense of dread that went beyond the worries of the moment. At this nameless fear, his Focus collapsed, driven from his mind in a single moment.

He shook his head. "It's no good."

"Again," Transcend Red said. "I want you standing here until you learn to break your block the right way. Understood?"

Was the woman mad? "I'll freeze to death before that happens."

"Open your eyes."

Lucian opened his eyes, as Transcend Red's eyes narrowed.

"Then, you'll freeze to death."

With that, she stalked off, leaving him standing there on the cliff.

Was she *serious*? She couldn't be. But he didn't dare leave. One did not disobey a Transcend, no matter how seemingly insane the order.

So, he did what she said. He imagined that damned stone. He would learn to stream or die trying.

Lucian had plenty of frustrations to feed the stone. But for every frustration he fed, two more took its place.

Lucian didn't know how long he stayed out there. The coldness no longer bothered him. It seemed a distant thing beneath the deepness of his meditation. What must have been hours later, Lucian had no trouble holding the image of the stone in his mind, even as his hands and feet went numb and his muscles stiff.

It was progress, however small.

"Lucian?"

His Focus shattered as he opened his eyes to see Emma watching him with a worried expression.

"You must be freezing, standing out here!"

His mind had been floating in another reality, and it took a moment to rejoin this one. The stars had shifted positions. How late *was* it? Emma was still looking at him, awaiting an answer.

"Transcend Red told me to stand out here and practice my Focus, and to not stop until I'd learned to stream. So, that's what I've been doing."

"Transcend Red?" she asked. "*She* told you?"

Lucian nodded, and for the first time, realized how cold it had gotten. His teeth began to chatter. "It's my punishment. They found out it was me. Is it dinnertime yet?"

"It's over," Emma said. "Rhea mentioned she saw you out here."

"I see," he said. "Well, the Transcends decided to keep me on, at least for now. Khairu reported me. Apparently, she saw it all happen."

Emma shook her head. "Well, I can see her doing that. It's well below freezing out here, and they didn't even let you grab your cloak? You have nothing on but that robe."

"Builds discipline, haven't you heard?"

"Stop," she said. "Let's get inside. Some of the Talents were talking about a snowstorm and I don't want you to turn into a popsicle."

Indeed, a few flakes were already floating down, touching Lucian's face. A sheet of low, heavy clouds was approaching from the north, blocking out the stars. The hammer of a northern autumn was about to fall.

Once inside, Lucian and Emma warmed themselves by the central brazier. Then, they headed back to the dining hall, where there was still a pot of stew over the hearth. Hadn't she already eaten? He didn't understand why she was following him.

Then, he remembered. It was because of his mother. She wanted to be near him, to make sure he was okay. Just the thought of his mother made icy numbness spread outward from his chest. He wanted nothing more than for this day to be over, to sleep and know nothing more.

"I can't believe Transcend Red had you out there after

what's happened," she said, joining him as he sat down to eat. "I'd heard she was cold, but I guess we know personally now."

A couple of Talents, both women in their early thirties, entered the dining hall. They took up their bowls of stew and sat at the Talents' table. It was quiet for a minute, until Lucian overheard one of them talking.

"Who do you think did it?" Lucian thought her name was Pila. She had a pinched face and black hair set tightly in a bun.

Lucian continued eating, focusing on the conversation.

"They say Novice Lucian was out in the yard, doing penance," the other Talent said. Lucian couldn't remember her name, but he thought it was Lana. She was tall, with close-cropped hair and sharp blue eyes. From both Talents' purple sashes, they were disciples of Transcend Violet.

"Lucian?" Pila snorted. "I don't deny he was doing penance, but not for that!"

"Well then, who?" Lana asked.

"A Novice could never do something like that. Never."

The two lapsed into silence, and Lucian focused on eating. It was as if he weren't even there because they didn't bother to look over. Perhaps because he was facing away, they hadn't recognized him. He had half a mind to turn around and tell them off, but what was the point? He was a joke here, and his mother was dead. Why earn himself extra chores on top of that?

Emma was turning around, cheeks red, but Lucian touched her arm. "Don't."

"But..."

"Please," he said. "It's not worth it. They'll just give you extra sweeping duty or something." He let out a sigh. "I should go, anyway."

"You've barely eaten, though. And if you left now, it might look weird."

He was confused at first, until he saw her looking at the

other two Talents. Yes, it might look suspicious if he left so shortly after the Talents' conversation. Then, they would know he had heard, and perhaps had a guilty conscience.

They waited until the Talents had left, and then Emma and Lucian cleaned up. He had never felt so tired or defeated. The sooner this day was over, the better. He felt a sickness, in body and spirit, that was too heavy for words.

But he had to go on. He had to keep up a front.

Talent Eurice, who bore a green sash and had a pasty complexion, came in for his own meal. Lucian couldn't help but feel the older Talent's eyes on him while he cleaned. Finally, Eurice saw fit to break the silence.

"Is it true, what people are saying?"

Lucian didn't have the energy for this. "Is what true?"

"Did you do it?"

"Do what?"

"Stop playing coy, Novice. The iceberg."

"Are you kidding? I haven't even broken my block yet."

Talent Eurice studied him, his thick black brows knitting together on his pockmarked face. His giant ears made him look like a monkey. "You were summoned by the Spectrum, right?"

Lucian paused, considering his next response. "Where'd you hear that?"

"Half the Academy knows by now," he said. "I heard it from Talent Pila."

Emma watched the conversation with a worried expression, but didn't intervene.

"Whatever the Spectrum and I discussed isn't your concern. If you wish to know, maybe you can ask them about it."

If he didn't get the hint from that, Lucian didn't know what else to say.

Eurice didn't get the hint. "I've heard many things about you, Lucian. It's hard to guess the truth from lies."

"I'm sure you have heard many things. How could you not?"

Eurice looked confused for a moment, until Emma giggled from beside the fire, where she'd been cleaning up.

Eurice's cheeks, and then enormous ears, reddened. "This is unbecoming of you, Novice."

"Forgive me," Lucian said. "Talent *Ear*-rice."

Eurice's face reddened even further. "I'll see you on chamber pot duty for such insolence! Unless you have something else to add?"

"I do not. Goodnight, Talent Eurice. And for future reference, it's unbecoming of a Talent to take part in rumors that may or may not be true. That is, if we are both following the same rules prescribed by the Transcends."

When Lucian left, Eurice didn't push the issue further, nor did he give him any details about his "chamber pot duty."

Emma joined Lucian, and they headed back toward the dormitories. Once out of earshot of the dining hall, she turned to him.

"That was amazing! I've always wanted to tell a Talent off like that."

"I'm beyond caring at this point."

His tone seemed to pop her bubble. "Okay. Well, let me know if you need someone to talk to."

All Lucian could do was manage a nod. "Goodnight, Emma."

Lucian hurried back to his room. When he closed the door, he lit the candle on his nightstand. He sprawled on his tiny bed, a feeling of numbness washing over him.

It was all too much. Everything ran through his head in an interminable stream. It was as if he had three different channels on, each vying for control. There was his mother, the Spectrum, and his standing at the Academy. How could he *ever* survive here with his emotions spinning out of control? When he kept pushing Emma away, his only friend here?

He tossed and turned for the longest time, feeling possessed by a demon. Was *this* what fraying felt like? Was it happening? He felt a poison running through his mind, a nameless fear taking root. The poison of ether, or the stress of the worst day of his life?

It was hours before the oblivion of sleep took him.

10

WHEN LUCIAN WOKE UP, all he wanted was to close his eyes and go back to sleep. That wasn't an option, though. If he stayed in bed, his absence would be more than noted. It might even be enough to make the Transcends regret their decision of letting him stay.

The first thing he did was form his Focus; he found himself relying on that stillness to set aside all emotion. It wasn't natural yet, but one day, he wouldn't feel anything at all.

That day couldn't come soon enough.

The image of the stone collapsed, and all the pain from yesterday hit him like a dousing of cold water. His mother was dead. It was hardly any more real. And they expected him to go on as if nothing had happened.

His life had become a terrible nightmare, and all he wanted to do was wake up.

After he washed his face, he joined the flow of Novices heading to the lawn for morning meditation. Another cold, gray dawn on Volsung would not be long in coming.

Outside, half the Novices had already gathered, kneeling toward the western sky. In the distance, the gray tinge of dawn hinted at the coming daybreak. The wind cut like a knife; it was even colder this morning than last night. Frost crunched under his boots, clinging to the short, dead grass stiffened by its embrace. He made his way toward the cliff, picking a spot distant from the others, and knelt on the cold, bare earth. He hated this posture – the ground always dug into his knees. He had the suspicion that it was *meant* to be uncomfortable. Like everything else here.

He knelt toward the front, so if anyone looked his way, they couldn't tell whether he was doing the meditation. He opted to watch the gray ocean, wondering what lay across it while dreaming about another life. A life far from here, free from the curse of magic.

He closed his eyes and tried to picture his mother's face. To his surprise, the image was not as clear as he would have liked. He remembered her from five years ago, when she had come home from the first Swarmer War. Even then, she had seemed younger and lighter on her feet. They had spent a whole year together before she deployed again. From that point, they saw each other every six months or so . . . leading up to the last time. The time she had seemed the most tired of all.

Tears ran down his face, which he wiped away. When he opened his eyes, the barest glimmer of orange sun was peeking above the distant horizon. It cast its warm, gentle rays on his face – the only source of warmth on this forsaken island. The wind blew cold and bitter. That sun would rise later and later every day. The effect would be quite noticeable once the equinox had passed. He gazed over the cliff, toward the shoreline hundreds of meters below. There, the roiling surf crashed against the edificial cliffs.

Lucian started to think about what he wanted – from this place, and from himself. He was used to going it alone in life, but in the back of his mind, he always knew his mother would be there for him. He no longer had that safety. *This* was his only home now, and the thought was terrifying. This remote, northern island didn't seem much better than a prison. There were Talents who had been here for years, *decades* even, never having left. There were only eight Transcends, who had the power to leave at will, but there would never be more than eight. From the looks of things, it didn't look as if they got out much, either.

By necessity, the life of a mage was a life of limitation. No one trusted them. As well they shouldn't, after the Mage War.

Lucian wondered what the point of it all was. Everything seemed to go back to what Vera had told him on the *Burung*. The Worlds, as bickering as they were, agreed on one thing. Everyone with the spark of the Manifold, *every* mage, needed to be contained. If he ever got off this island, and anyone found out what he was, it would be his end.

But then there was an anomaly: Vera. Somehow, she had eluded not only capture, but fraying, the threat that seemed so present here. Lucian was reminded of it almost every day.

And now, Lucian would never discover her secret. He was the definition of a fool for coming here.

He formed his Focus, the stone materializing on a black void. He found it easier today, his concentration not breaking as much. He tried to feel his ether, where the power of the Manifold had gathered. But his block was resolute, as impassable as it had been two days before.

All he felt was hopelessness. How could he ever last here?

While eating breakfast, Lucian felt a tap on his shoulder. He turned to see Khairu.

"Walk with me."

The other Novices quieted as he followed her into the hallway.

She stopped a few meters away from the dining hall entrance.

"Transcend Blue would like you to attend the entry hall lesson today."

"What about my instruction with Talent Pila?"

"This takes precedence."

"Isn't this a lesson for the Novices who have already streamed?"

Lucian almost winced at those words. Of *course* he had streamed, just not in the right way.

"I don't make the rules," she said, eyes narrowing. "Just go, Novice."

After that, she stalked off in typical Khairu fashion.

Lucian went back to finish his meal, then headed to the entry hall.

Once there, Lucian took up a spot a few meters away from the central brazier at the end of the line of Novices. Most of them were Tested – those who had been through the Trials at least once. Lucian, Emma, and Damian were the only Novices there, out of twelve or so, who weren't. Rhea was among the group as well, along with others Lucian hadn't talked to yet – the Novices who had been here for years, in some cases. They acted as if they were Talents in their own right, sitting at their own end of the Novice table.

Transcend Blue stood in front of the central brazier, the fiery light dancing off his shimmering blue robes. Sunlight spilled through the open entrance. Lucian noted it still wasn't very bright outside, even though it was sunny. At this hour on Earth, it would be midmorning by now, but here on Volsung, that point was still several hours away. Transcend Blue's gaze hovered on Lucian just a moment too long.

"Today," Transcend Blue began, "we are going to touch on a subject most of you are already familiar with, with which you could do with a review." The Novices' chatter immediately stilled at these words. "Of late, we've had many promising new Novices who have yet to learn about the Aspects."

Lucian felt a chill at those words. The *Aspects*. He listened closely.

"The Aspects can be thought of as different manifestations of the Manifold into the Shadow World," Transcend Blue continued. "None are safe to use, per se. All lead to the fraying if overdrawn. But likewise, once a mage's powers have Emerged, the mage *must* learn to stream, as water must be released from behind a dam before it overflows."

Looking around, Lucian noticed a good half of the Novices looked bored. This was an old lesson for them.

"That said," Transcend Blue continued, "there are Seven Aspects, represented by seven colors, each worn by a Transcend. That Transcend, as you might have guessed by now, is the recognized master of that Aspect." He spread his arms. "I, for example, am Transcend Blue, the master of Binding. Binding is the ability to manipulate the very forces that bind matter together."

Transcend Blue retrieved a pen from the pocket of his cloak. He held it out in his hand, showing it to the line of Novices. Nothing happened at first. But after a moment, Lucian could see the pen giving off an ethereal, blue glow. Transcend Blue's hand also glowed blue. Not a moment later, the pen shot *upward*, hitting the ceiling far above at breakneck speed. There was a murmur of surprise as the pen remained rooted to the ceiling.

"It's Bound," Transcend Blue explained. "This is only one manifestation of Binding, of course. As two different things might be bound together, likewise they can be driven apart. The purpose of which I shall not show here, as it can be dangerous. Reverse Binding the natural bonds of matter can lead to drastic consequences. That said, it is exceedingly difficult to accomplish."

A young, fresh-faced Novice, named Elia, raised her hand demurely. He had missed her there since she was so short. She had arrived about a month after he and Emma, and like them, was Untested. The Talents must have seen her case as promising if she was being included here. Transcend Blue nodded to her.

"What are the other Aspects?"

"I was getting to that," Transcend Blue said. "The remaining six Aspects are Thermalism, represented by Red. There is Atomicism, represented by Orange. Then there's Dynamism, represented by Yellow. There's Radiance, the manipulation of light energy, represented by Green. Blue is Binding, which we've already discussed. Gray is Gravitonics. And Violet represents Psionics, the manipulation of kinetic and psychic energy."

So, this was what the Aspects were. He had mostly guessed it already, even if he didn't know the proper names.

"So, in summary," Transcend Blue continued, "there's Thermalism, Atomicism, Dynamism, Radiance, Binding, Psionics, and Gravitonics. They are sometimes labeled Red, Orange, Yellow, Green, Blue, Violet, and Gray Magic, due to the color of their streams when they manifest in the Shadow World. Of course, all mages have some skill in each of these Aspects. But their natural inclinations lean them toward one, or at most three, different Aspects. When a Talent apprentices him or herself to a Transcend, they must decide, one year after ascension, which Aspect and Transcend toward which to dedicate themselves. Usually, at the end of one year, one's primary Aspect becomes abundantly clear."

Emma raised her hand.

"Yes?" Transcend Blue asked.

"You said there are Seven Aspects, but there are eight Transcends. What about Transcend White?"

Transcend Blue smiled, as if pleased at her astuteness. "White contains all the colors, no? White is our leader, and being our leader, is the most powerful mage of our number. Transcend White is required to have a fair amount of skill at each Aspect. That said, Transcend White was formerly Transcend Violet before her ascension."

"There's something else I've been wondering," Elia asked, without bothering to raise her hand.

Lucian frowned. If *he* had spoken without being called on, he'd be chewed out.

Elia smiled primly. "I hope I'm not being disrespectful by asking, or proving my ignorance, but do the Transcends have personal names?"

Transcend Blue regarded her for a moment. "Our names are one of the many things we give up upon ascension. It is an outward symbol of our death to our old selves and our commitment to the cause of the Academy, and humankind at large."

That was something Lucian hadn't even thought about. Lucian wondered what Transcend White's had been.

Transcend Blue moved on with the lesson. "As Novices, your training will consist of being paired off with Talents of all the Transcends. In this way, you'll get a taste of all the Aspects, and learn which feels the most natural to you. Some of you may not even be able to stream certain Aspects at all, at least at first. But after several months of training, you'll find one that comes easier than others. That is how you identify your primary Aspect. Also, some are rarer than others. Psionics, for example, is the most common. It's able to be streamed by almost any mage, with notable rare exceptions. Atomicism, in contrast, is rarest. Transcend Orange only has two Talents under his tutelage. When practicing, they must travel afar to stream. Atomicism is particularly dangerous."

That was easy to imagine. Nuclear weapons were still the most devastating weapon of war, and fusion power was the engine of the interstellar economy. Splitting or fusing atoms through magic had to have consequences both incredible and terrible. Lucian could understand the reason the League wanted mages quarantined for that alone. Imagining what a maddened and frayed Atomicist was capable of was nothing short of horrifying.

Transcend Blue continued. "The onus is upon us to be wise stewards of our powers. That's why it's so important that you *never* stream beyond your inner pool. The temptation will be there, as it will every day for the rest of your life. But that path leads to fraying, and we must do whatever we can to prevent that. If we don't stream beyond our natural pool of ether, nor do we allow it to build up too much, we can walk the path of Balance. Balance is the inner state where all is in inner harmony. Knowing where the line is, and how to walk it, is the most important aspect of your training. Our emphasis on Balance is why our mages are the longest-lived in the League."

With Transcend Blue saying that, it was hard not to feel self-conscious about the previous night. Lucian only wondered what Aspect he'd used to destroy that iceberg. If it were kinetic force, then that would have been Psionic magic. If Lucian reversed the force binding molecules together, that would have been Binding. Or it could have even been Thermalism. Superheating a part of the iceberg might cause it to collapse on itself. And of course, it could have been a combination of all three, for all he knew.

That was when Lucian noticed Transcend Blue looking at him directly, along with everyone else. When some of the Novices giggled, he realized he had been asked a question.

"I'm sorry, Transcend Blue. I missed what you asked me."

"I asked, by way of example, what you believe to be the cause of the collapse of the iceberg last night?"

Had he read his thoughts? It was hard to keep a straight face, even if Transcend Blue's expression was a mask of innocent inquiry.

"I don't know," Lucian stammered. "I would think it was Psionics, but I can't be sure."

Transcend Blue looked at Lucian a moment longer, before turning to Damian.

"And what do you think, Novice Damian?"

Damian cleared his throat before answering. "Binding."

"And what makes you say that?"

He shrugged. "For an object that size and distance, it seems unbelievable it could be Psionics. But if it had collapsed from within, driven apart by a repelling force..."

"*Reverse* Binding," Transcend Blue said. "Even given the difficulty of a reverse binding, it's still easier than Psionics, especially at that distance."

Damian nodded. "My thoughts exactly."

Transcend Blue looked around at the gathering. "Novice Damian is correct, and his logic is sound. Binding, unlike some other forms of magic, is quite effective at distance. Psionic streaming, as Novice Lucian hypothesized, requires a shorter distance."

"So, who did it?" Damian asked. "That's the more important question to me."

Transcend Blue ignored Damian. "Now, since it is my day to teach, we will focus on Binding."

"Wait," Lucian said. "I have one more question."

He almost winced at that outburst, especially as Transcend Blue glowered at the interruption. "Yes, Novice?"

"These Aspects," Lucian said, feeling his heart race. "Are they anything physical?"

Some of the Novices had a laugh at that. But he needed to know the answer. There had been that dream, with that voice, telling him to *find* the Aspects. How could Lucian do that unless they *were* something physical?

Transcend Blue held up a hand, stifling the giggles. "That is a matter of debate. It's a strange story, a story that first gained popularity before the Mage War. But the physical manifestations of Aspects, most likely through hyper-concentrated ether, in our universe is only a hypothesis that has so far remained unproven. As far as we know, ether only gathers within the mage themselves, and it cannot be measured in any detectable way. Mages share particular dreams and thought-patterns that allow for their detection through metaphysical exams, but that is the extent of it."

Now, all the Novices were paying attention, even the ones who had been at the Academy the longest.

Of all people, it was Novice Rhea who spoke next. "What's the story?"

Transcend Blue cleared his throat, somewhat nervously. "It is nothing more than a story. It has no bearing on our lesson today."

"Now, I want to know it more," Damian said.

Transcend Blue sighed. "Well. I'm not one for tangents, but since you all seem interested... I don't see the harm."

Lucian listened, and Transcend Blue began.

"IN THE EARLY days of the Volsung Academy, the mages were many," Transcend Blue began. "They labored night and day to expand the ruins, and many came here to study. Magic then was much more of a mystery. It remains a mystery to this day, but back then, even more so. And it seemed the possibilities were endless..."

Lucian listened, rapt. Looking around, he saw he wasn't alone.

"They did not know the dangers of the Manifold, and the ether it Manifested. Not as we do today. In fact, such terms had not even been invented yet. The mages did not connect fraying to magic itself. That was still a few years off. As such, it was common for the first Transcends to delve the Manifold, seeking answers into the nature of its ultimate reality."

"Delve the Manifold?" Elia asked.

Transcend Blue nodded. "It means to form a Psionic link to the Manifold itself. Incredibly dangerous. It accelerates fraying greatly. But the mages of those days discovered a wealth of information. Some true, some false, some uncertain. That was how we learned of the Seven Aspects set in the Septagon. What they were, how they worked, how they interconnected – and most importantly, how a mage might stream them."

Transcend Blue paused, and from that hesitation, Lucian somehow knew he was about to get to the crux of the story.

"However," he continued, "there was something called the Prophecy of the Seven, written by one of the first Transcends, Arian." Lucian's ears perked up at that. That was the book he had on his nightstand. "The Seven were said to be beings living within the Manifold itself, each claiming control of one of the Aspects. Like gods, perhaps, or something else. He wrote of his journey into the Manifold, claiming to see past and future, among other things. He wrote them down. Our library contains a single copy of his work, entitled *The Prophecy of the Seven*. Transcend Arian planned to delve again to affirm his findings, and to make the text less obtuse to the casual reader. Only when he returned..."

Transcend Blue hardly needed to finish. It was clear enough what had happened.

"Frayed," Damian said.

If Arian had frayed, then that explained why the text was complete nonsense. Lucian could hardly believe that he had that book and checked out by mistake.

"Whether a mage frays or not upon delving is a coin flip," Transcend Blue said. "In the Manifold, there are horrors beyond our imagining. Horrors the human mind cannot comprehend." He shook his head. "Other Transcends have delved, of course, but the practice stopped long ago. It was simply too dangerous. No one has tried for decades."

"What about the Prophecy of the Seven?" Emma asked. "What about the Aspects?"

"We're getting far off base here. But never let it be said I left a tale untold." Transcend Blue cleared his throat. "The prophecy Arian wrote stated that magic goes through cycles of creation and destruction. The Prophecy says there are Seven Keys to this cycle. These keys are said to be orbs, ancient artifacts of great power, manifestations of pure ether in the corporeal world. With these orbs, a certain mage, called the *Chosen*, has the power to end the cycles."

The Novices stared at Transcend Blue, wide-eyed.

"Is any of that true?" Emma asked.

Transcend Blue laughed. "Of course not! Arian's delvings were the mad ramblings of a frayed man. It wouldn't be the first such false information uncovered during a delving. Nonetheless, it hasn't prevented certain mages from seeking these orbs, to no great success, I might add."

"And these orbs *are* something physical that can be touched?" Lucian asked.

Transcend Blue watched him shrewdly. "That's what Arian believed. And what his disciples, the Free Mages, sought to discover."

Some of the Novices gasped at that.

Transcend Blue continued. "It was much of their reason for breaking away from the Academies. It's safe to say that Arian's words cut the mages in two. And for that, he is certainly a divisive figure, even to this day." Looking around, he seemed to remember he had a lesson to teach. "I've spoken overmuch. Suffice it to say, Arian never intended for there to be a war, nor to be the basis of the belief that led to the defection of Mallis and her mages. One more thing. Each orb was said to be guarded by an Oracle, one of the Seven Beings. The Seven

Oracles, he said, were the givers of the Prophecy itself – hence the name of his tome. His belief was that the mages should seek and gather these orbs before the cycle of destruction returned. Unfortunately, certain mages took him quite seriously."

"And none have been found?" Damian asked.

Transcend Blue scoffed. "Of course not. It is a mad story. I won't say it's *impossible* for it to be true. But to me, it is the fantasy of a half-mad man. Had he never written his prophecy, there would have been no Mage War, and I don't use those words lightly. In fact, he may have ironically begun the cycle of destruction he prophesied merely by warning against it. Of course, some have supposed the fraying itself is the foretold cycle of destruction, and not the Mage War, or a *future* mage war." Transcend Blue shook his head. "Whatever the case, it is outside the object of our lesson here, and I will speak no more of the subject."

The Transcend continued the lesson, but Lucian found his mind drifting off. To others, it was only a story. But what about his dreams? What about the voice that told him to find the Aspects? How could his mind have thought of something so crazy with no prior information? Was it prophecy, or madness? There *had* to be something to it. Unless *he* were going mad as well, hearing things directly from the Manifold just as Arian had...

The mere prospect made him sick.

As soon as the lesson concluded, Lucian wanted nothing more than to return to his room. But he had an obligation, along with Emma, to attend a training session with Talent Khairu.

11

WHEN LUCIAN JOINED KHAIRU, the Talent gave no sign she had ratted Lucian out the night before. The lesson proceeded normally enough. *Normally* meaning Khairu criticized Lucian's every move.

"Center yourself," she said. "Embrace your Focus."

The teaching only made Lucian more anxious. Telling her as much wouldn't help matters, though.

Instead, Lucian tried to take her advice. He formed an image of his Focus, that damnable stone, once again. The picture took root as if it stood right before him. At least he had this part nailed down.

"Good," Khairu said, in a rare bit of praise. "I can feel the potential of your Focus, even now. The next step is to reach for your ether and stream electricity through your spear."

For a moment, Lucian felt a curious pressure forming in his mind. No matter how much he tried, though, the Dynamistic Aspect wouldn't manifest itself. Lucian clung on, letting his Focus remain resolute. This time, he was determined to not let it shatter.

"Calm," Khairu said. "You're doing well. *Focus.*"

Something in her tone made Lucian think she was surprised at his progress. It was if she were *trying* to get under his skin.

All at once, Lucian felt a surge of power, a fire prickling beneath his skin. It was *here*. His eyes opened in shock.

"*Control it,*" Khairu said, firmly. "Let it flow through the spear."

Lucian imagined the energy leaving him in a steady stream. He *saw* the spear alight with electrical energy. He could *feel* the graphene infused with his magic. The wind began to pick up, and the spear was glowing, the spear turning red-hot. Awesome amounts of heat began to radiate outward, heat which began to flow into his hand.

"Stop!" Khairu said, eyes wide with fear. "Stop right now! Cut your stream off!"

It was like trying to stop a rushing river. The only thing he could do was drop the spear. It fell to the frosty ground, hissing and smoking in the process. Khairu hopped back as if it were an adder while Emma watched with widened eyes from the side.

At last, the fire within Lucian subsided. He was breathing heavily, as if he had sprinted across the entire lawn. Khairu's expression was one of shock, her mouth slightly agape.

"*Why* did you do that? You were supposed to stream Dynamism, *not* Thermalism!"

Lucian blinked in surprise. So, *that* was why the metal had started heating up.

"I don't understand how to stream one Aspect over another," Lucian said. "How can I do that without practice? What's more important is that I broke my block, in the way you told me to."

Khairu folded her arms. "The way *I* told you to? No, far from that! You could have gotten yourself killed with a bit of misdirected energy. What would have happened if the heat had spread to the handle?"

"Well," Lucian said, "at least I managed something this time."

Her look was all-too knowing. "Let's not pretend. We *both* know what you're capable of. Next time, do as you're told and *nothing* different!"

Arguing was pointless. He nodded meekly, as much as it grated him. "Yes, Talent Khairu."

This mollified her, if only a little. "This bears repeating, since it seems my lesson from earlier didn't take hold. You must *imagine* the thing you wish to manifest once your Focus is formed, and only *then* stream. What were you thinking about to produce a Thermal stream like that?"

He thought he *had* been thinking of electricity. Until he remembered he had also been thinking about that fiery feeling beneath his skin. Perhaps that had been enough for the magic to come out that way, too.

Khairu reached for the discarded spear, which had cooled by now. She handed it back to Lucian, and then gestured toward Emma. "Your turn."

Of course, Emma had no trouble streaming electricity through her own practice spear. She held it aloft as the magic raced from handle to point, crackling at the spear's tip. After half a minute, she cried out suddenly.

"It's getting harder to hold!"

"Let go of your Focus," Khairu said. "Your ether is almost depleted."

Emma nodded and immediately stopped. The electrical magic dissipated, from the handle to the tip. She breathed heavily from exertion.

"Not bad," Khairu said. "You'd make a good Dynamist. That would depend on your spear work, though."

"I'm not much of a fighter," she said, between breaths.

"Dynamists do more than spear play," Khairu said. "There's shielding and warding, too."

Shielding sounded like fighting to Lucian, too, if only in a defensive way.

"Why are we being trained to fight?" he asked. "I thought the mages were forbidden to use their powers for war."

"The Volsung Academy is one of the few that remained loyal to the League. We fought against Xara Mallis. We serve the League at its discretion, though we maintain control over our own matters."

"That doesn't answer his original question," Emma said. "Why are we taught to fight at all?"

"Because," Khairu said, "we've proven ourselves invaluable. The League guarantees our right to exist, and one day we may be needed for the League's defense. We helped with the last Swarmer War, though I was still a Novice at the time. I don't know much else about it."

With the Swarmers back, that only begged the question. Would the mages be getting involved once again?

"The other academies train their mages for warfare as well," Khairu went on. "There are only two others officially sanctioned by the League: the Irion Academy, and the Mako Academy. However, the League has decreed the Volsung Academy ascendant. Transcend White not only leads us, but all the academies, if war ever returns."

Lucian almost informed her that war *had* returned, until remembering Transcend White's prohibition.

"What Transcend White says, goes then," Emma said.

"Correct," Khairu said. "Those academies are so distant that they are almost fully autonomous. If there ever is another war, that will change. Until then, our job is to vet every mage who can be trained."

"And if they can't be trained?" Lucian asked.

Khairu glowered. "You know what happens, Novice Lucian. It's not something anyone relishes, least of all the Transcends."

Emma looked at him in warning. But he had to know. "But there are mages who aren't part of any academy. Right? Rogues, I mean."

Khairu's eyes narrowed. "Yes. Rogue mages slip through the cracks. The Border Worlds especially lack the infrastructure for widespread testing. When a report reaches the Academy about a rogue mage, a team of Talents deals with it. Depending on the severity, a Transcend might go as well."

"It must be rare, because I haven't seen many Talents come and go," Emma observed.

"Oh, our Talents are out there. The more experienced ones. It takes a lot before the Transcends are willing to trust a Talent with such a task. They must be absolutely sure of their loyalty and abilities. Rogue mages are highly dangerous, and it's not unknown for Talents to be killed in the hunting of them." As an aside, she added, "Usually, one of the Talents sent is a Radiant. Radiants are good at Sensing." At Lucian's confused look, she added, "That is, detecting deviations in the ethereal field, which can pinpoint a mage's location. That can ease the search."

Emma's eyebrows arched at that. *She* had the ability to do that, at least when she was close to another mage. From her silence, she chose to not share this with Khairu.

"This is only a fraction of our number," Khairu said. "At any point, half or more of the mages are gone on errands. This can be anything from consulting local governments, seeking out new mages, conducting research . . ."

". . . or hunting rogues," Lucian finished.

"Yes, that too. Transcend Red recently returned from such a hunt." Khairu collapsed her spear and stashed it inside her robe, signaling the end of the lesson. "It's a rarity when the entire Spectrum is here. In fact, I can't ever remember such a thing happening, and I've been here almost seven years."

"And a Talent for how long?" Emma asked.

Lucian wondered why Khairu was volunteering so much information about herself, especially to Novices like them.

"Four of those years," Khairu said. "I advanced quickly, but that's because they saw my dedication."

If becoming a Talent in three years was considered quick, then Lucian had no hope of getting off this island. Not for a long, long time.

12

HOURS BLED INTO DAYS, and days into weeks. Lucian threw himself into his training and studies, using them to forget his old life. He dedicated himself in a way he never had before. Isolated on the island of Transcend Mount, there were no distractions. There was only the training, and those beside him on the same journey.

It was amazing how quickly the concerns of the outside world fell away. Even the fear of a new Swarmer War seemed distant. As he acquired new knowledge, former mysteries began to make sense. When he wasn't learning about the mages, their history, or the Seven Aspects, he was meditating on them, strengthening his Focus, learning to isolate each Aspect, and streaming each one under rigorous concentration.

Some were easier to grasp than others. Psionics came easiest to him, while Dynamism was the greatest struggle. Still, he trained, building his Focus until he could imagine the stone with perfect clarity and hold the image for hours.

And then his Focus underwent changes. One day, when he imagined the stone, he could see seven lights floating around it: red, orange, yellow, green, blue, violet, and gray. At first, he thought he was losing his concentration. But the more his meditation deepened, the more vivid the colors became.

When Lucian shared this with Damian, he nodded as if it were normal.

"You're transitioning."

"Transitioning?"

"The stone you chose is just a training tool. A mage's Focus – their *true* Focus – is them using their mind to connect to the Manifold. And the way that reality manifests is the Septagon, the shape on which all seven Aspects are placed."

"The Septagon?"

"There are some charts you can look up in the library, but it's basic Manifoldic theory. They don't teach the Novices early on because they don't want them getting distracted. As their Focus grows, it naturally becomes the new Focus."

"So, should I start imagining this Septagon?"

"No!" Damian said, with a laugh. "You aren't ready for that yet. Let it transition on its own, but now that you are aware of it, you won't be alarmed as it happens. In the meantime, try to sense it, isolate each of the Aspects, and stream through those lights. Now you know why we call each Aspect by its color. It's because those lights you're seeing are common to all mages once they become strong enough to detect them."

Strong enough. Was he finally getting the hang of things? It was a good, if unfamiliar, feeling. He might not get expelled after all.

As Lucian trained further, he tried to do as Damian said. He continued to use the stone as his Focus rather than the Septagon. In the meantime, he did his own reading on the subject, checking out a book from the library – the correct one this time.

The first time he saw the Septagon, with its labeled Aspects, his eyes nearly popped out of his head. It was rendered almost exactly as he had imagined it in his mind. It looked like some strange, occult symbol, something that would scare the living daylights out of a Believer if they ever saw it. It not only showed each of the Aspects at one of the Septagon's seven corners, but lines interconnecting the Aspects. Aspects were connected by the border of the Septagon, but additional lines connected Aspects two apart.

He learned what the lines meant: the closer the Aspect to one's primary, the more easily and efficiently it could be streamed. Dynamists, for example, found streaming Atomicism and Radiance easier than streaming Gravitonics. Lucian wondered if his primary was Psionics since it was the easiest for him to stream. It would explain why he found Dynamism so difficult and unnatural, which was three slots away from Psionics.

Then again, he learned there was another school of thought that said the Septagon shouldn't be taken too seriously. If a mage believed they would be bad at something, it was a self-fulfilling prophecy. Belief was an important component of streaming. It was generally agreed that a mage had one strength, one or two secondary Aspects they were middling in, and tertiary and quaternary Aspects that were far weaker. Lucian was still too early in his journey to know where he fell.

Five months into his training, the autumn equinox passed, and the days grew ever shorter. By now, Lucian could almost always stream, even if it were only a little. Without his emotions to fan the flames, it was difficult.

At least he was no longer the least accomplished. New Novices had arrived, and one day, without any sort of warning, another was exiled. She was a quiet young woman named Katya, who had jumped at every shadow. What was more, she was one of the Tested. The Novices talked about that in hushed tones the day they realized she was gone. And after that, she was never mentioned again.

The Novices worked much harder at their studies, with less

joking and laughter. No one wanted to be next. And the Trials were on everyone's minds, drawing closer and closer.

Lucian tried not to concern himself with the successes and failures of his peers. And he did his best not to let emotion enter the picture. At night, he only felt numbness. The only way he could weather his inner turmoil was by not acknowledging its existence. The change startled him, but in his mind, it was a necessary change.

If emotions ruled him, he would never make it here.

Even his feelings for Emma, which had seemed so powerful at first, had dampened. Or had they merely been displaced? Whatever the case, that prospect was receding into the past. Yes, his heart still ached at seeing her. Those feelings threatened to undo his accomplishments. But every day he denied them, the closer he came to walking the path of Balance.

He was changing. He didn't allow himself to think whether that change was for the better. This was reality, and any change was for the sake of not being the next exile.

As the weeks passed, he and Emma saw less and less of each other. Aside from mealtimes, he might not see her at all. She focused on her studies, and he on his. They were assigned to different Talents and different Aspects almost every week.

From Psion Gaius, Lucian learned Psionic theory, the manipulation of kinetic energy itself. He learned to recognize its pulsating flow with greater ease than the other Novices. Each Aspect had its own peculiarities. Psionics was all about releasing powerful waves of magic, with almost no control. And for some reason, Lucian showed much promise at it.

Dynamism remained challenging. It seemed to rip right out of him and had to be held tightly to remain in control. Thermalism was steadier than Dynamism, but once built up, became powerful. The classic test for the Novices was to either heat a pot of water to boiling or freeze it into a block of ice – using a classic forward stream, or a reverse stream, respectively.

He found it easier to control than Dynamism. Damian far surpassed him in Thermalism, a fact Lucian learned when both were paired with Talent Relisa for training. Damian could instantly cool a pail of water into ice and sublimate it within seconds. Relisa all but doted on him, even more so because she was from Luddus, too.

And so it went with each of the Aspects. Every week, the Transcends paired Novices with a new Talent. That Talent taught the Novices everything they could about their Aspect. A few times a month, they might receive advanced instruction from the Transcends. But as autumn took hold, this happened less often. The Transcends were busy with their own concerns.

By his sixth month, Lucian could stream basic Psionic, Thermal, and Binding magic with confidence. The other Aspects – Radiance, Gravitonics, and Dynamism, came with greater difficulty, mostly because he had received less training with them. But he could at least tell the difference between the Aspects now, and how they manifested. The one Aspect he did *not* learn was Atomicism, which was not streamed on Academy grounds due to its danger.

As always, the conversation shifted to the Trials. Novices who passed would rise to the mantle of Talent. If they failed, they had to wait until the next year's Trials. And of course, failing them too often or too spectacularly placed a Novice in danger of expulsion.

By the end of his sixth month of training, there was only one Aspect Lucian had yet to learn about: Atomicism. The subject was only taught twice a year, in the spring and in the autumn, in dedicated day trips to a distant island.

Talent Isaac, an Orange Talent, informed the Novices who had not yet received a demonstration that the trip would take place the next day.

For the first time in months, Lucian was leaving Transcend Mount.

The deck of *Lightsail* was a welcome escape. The day proved warmer than the past few weeks, though the breeze was bitingly cold. Before setting sail, the Academy's two Orange Talents, Isaac and Hamil, gathered the Novices near the bow. The Talents didn't speak until the Novices had settled down.

"Before we leave, we would do well to review Atomicism," Talent Isaac began, his sandy brown hair whipping in the wind. His heroic, square-jawed face seemed to be carved from stone. More than a few of the female Novices gazing at him with admiration. "First, it's the only Aspect that Novices are *not* allowed to stream. Besides being difficult to master, it is dangerous. We only give two lessons a year, and that lesson consists of listening to everything we say. And *not* attempting to stream." He looked around. "Is this understood?"

Lucian could not help but notice the disappointed faces around him. One of the Novices, named Erik and a native of Volsung, spoke up. "I understand Atomicism is dangerous, but how are we supposed to learn anything if we can't even stream it?"

Talent Isaac watched him sternly. "*No one* can stream the Atomic Aspect until he or she is accepted as a Talent by Transcend Orange. The Atomicists under Xara Mallis laid waste to entire systems with their magic. They also overloaded the fusion reactors of League warships. *They* were the greatest weapons of the war. A weapon the League's fleets could hardly defend against."

Isaac looked at each of them, to better let his point sink in. The Novices, having received that lesson, remained silent.

Talent Hamil stood at Isaac's side, his thick, hairy forearms folded beneath his barrel chest. That thick arm hair was a sharp contrast to his completely bald head. His defining feature was a long scar slashing from his left temple to the bottom of his nose.

When he spoke to the Novices, his voice came out in a low growl. "We're heading to a nearby island for the demonstration. Should take a few hours."

"Are you going to create a nuclear reaction this time?" Damian asked. "Last time, it was only a bit of transmutation."

Talent Hamil growled in response. "We are not here for your entertainment, Novice. If you disagree, maybe scrubbing the bathhouse floors for the next week will teach you." That made Damian go quiet, and the rest of the Novices stood to attention. "Creating a viable nuclear reaction uses a lot of ether. *A lot*. Enough to make us fray, even. And a frayed Atomicist is the last thing you want to deal with."

"So, how is Atomic Magic applied in real life?" Lucian asked.

"Finally, a good question," Hamil said.

Lucian blinked in surprise. Was that praise from one of the Talents, for once?

Hamil continued. "Say a starship is low on fuel or has the inability to refuel. Well, it would be possible to transmute some simple matter into the helium-3 needed for a starship's reactor. It would only need to behave as helium-3 for as long as it took the reactor to use it. Now, *true* Transmutation that sticks around takes a lot more work and is more dangerous. Flux transmutation – that which only lasts a moment – is safer, and more common. Assuming there was enough matter on board, Atomicists could keep the ship going without the need to refuel. The fleets commanded by Mallis, for example, moved more quickly than conventional fleets. They could maneuver in ways that were impossible without Atomicists."

"They were close to winning, weren't they?" Damian asked.

Talent Hamil surprised Lucian with his answer. "Yes. They changed warfare forever. Mallis was perhaps the most powerful mage there ever was. She was a brilliant strategist, albeit half-mad with the fraying." He shook his head. "Half the things we know about magic and the Manifold is because of her, for all the ill she's done."

"Why did she start the war?" Emma asked.

"We're getting off track," Hamil growled. "Time to set sail."

The questions were cut short as the Talents went to the bridge. The *Lightsail* embarked. Despite the cold wind and choppy water, Lucian couldn't help but smile. It was the closest thing to freedom he'd experienced since his arrival. Nothing made him happier than seeing the gray, dismal island of Transcend Mount receding into the west.

For the first time in months, the Novices could laugh, play, and joke around. At least, until the two Talents gathered them on the deck to make use of all the directionless energy. Within minutes, the Novices were back to practicing meditation and forming their Focuses. Forming his Focus was simple for Lucian now; it *should* have been after six months of doing little else. The stone floated in the void of his mind. His feelings were something to be considered, not embraced. Even the cold, whipping wind was something distant.

More than that, the stone seemed to thrum with potential power. Lucian knew he had only to allow that power to grow, and he would be streaming. Beyond his pool of ether was the Manifold itself. Against that, his ether was a speck of dust against a star, or maybe the entire universe. He couldn't help but wonder what it might be like to stream that kind of power.

A dangerous thought. The kind of thought that had surely started Xara Mallis on her path to madness. Lucian refocused on the stone, as he had been taught. *Any* kind of thought while streaming could be dangerous.

Time itself slipped away as Lucian held his Focus. When his eyes opened, the boat was slowing. The temperature was warmer, almost pleasant, and the sun shone brightly. Before the ship was an island. Nothing more than an outcrop, really, but it excited Lucian all the same.

The other Novices were emerging from their own meditations as well. Everyone went to the railing to watch the ship's approach. There was only a single landing point. They anchored in the surf about fifty meters out. They cast off in two rowboats, each holding a Talent and eight rowing Novices.

Once on shore, they ate their packed lunches on the rocky beach. Once done, they climbed the steep slope to the plateau above.

Lucian wondered what the Orange Talents had in store for them.

13

"LINE UP," Hamil called out.

Lucian stood with Emma on his right and Damian on his left. He risked a glance in her direction, and their eyes met for a moment. She offered a small smile, but before Lucian could return it, the Talents were coming back. He faced forward.

Lucian judged this small island to be more desolate than even Transcend Mount. For one, it was smaller, and didn't have a single building, or even a tree. There were likely tens of thousands of such islands scattered across the face of Volsung. It was cold, too. Whatever warmth the sun had cast earlier was now hidden behind a layer of clouds. The weather here was fickle. Lucian longed for the warmth of his home city he had long taken for granted.

It was only a little past midmorning, and the only sign of life on the island were the odd patches of pink lichen clinging to rocks. The sky was heavy with clouds and seemed ready to unleash a tempest of snow or ice at any moment.

As the Novices huddled closer, Isaac and Hamil found a fist-sized stone. Facing each other, they held the stone together, staring at it intensely. When the hairs of Lucian's arms stood on end, he knew it had nothing to do with the cold. The Talents were streaming.

The stone glowed with orange light. Subtly, at first, but then with increasing brilliance. A collective gasp escaped the Novices as they shielded their eyes. Lucian didn't see how the Talents could hold that stone without their hands burning. The rock should have been scalding by now.

When the brightness receded, Lucian tried to blink the spots in his vision away, noticing that the other Novices were doing the same. The world that returned was dim in comparison to the stone's former brilliance.

What was once a plain stone was now a small, yellow, and glinting nugget of what had to be pure gold.

Before Lucian could even marvel, Isaac chucked it as far as he could. The gold nugget sailed in a wide arc toward the water below. Even the cloudy sky couldn't keep it from glimmering before it was lost to sight.

"What'd you do that for?" Damian demanded.

Isaac shrugged. "We can always make more. This was for demonstration purposes."

"But..."

"Gold isn't even worth much, anyway," Talent Hamil said.

"It is on Luddus."

Lucian wasn't sure why Damian was trying to argue with the Talents. Pointless didn't even begin to describe it.

"This is but a taste of the power of Atomicism," Hamil said. "Now, pay attention. See that outcrop out there? Watch."

Hamil took a few steps until he stood at the southern precipice of the island. He focused on a rock rising about a hundred meters away. That craggy outcrop had been battered to hell and back. It was thinner toward the center, where entire chunks had been ripped out of it. This could be seen from the rocky flotsam piled at its base, through which the violent surf churned.

The Novices stood, watching. Not a moment later, everyone jumped as the outcrop became a fountain of earth and rock, shooting high into the air. Everyone ducked, even though the rain of rock had no chance of hitting them. Most of the debris shot straight upward, and many of the stony pieces were splashing into the gray ocean below. Once the dust settled, Lucian could see that the outcrop had a new hole blown in it. It teetered for a moment before steadying. After that treatment, even the slightest wind might be enough to crumble it for good.

"Thought I might actually kill it," Hamil said. He turned to face the Novices. "Any guesses on what I did there?"

Novice Elia raised her hand timidly. "An explosion?"

Some of the novices laughed at that. But Hamil surprised Lucian by nodding. "That's right. No need to make an answer more complicated than it needs to be. This demonstration was to show you that you don't need to use fission or fusion to create a lot of havoc with Atomicism." He licked his thin lips. "I focused on the middle of the rock, and transmuted some of the atoms into carbon, oxygen, and nitrogen. I bound these atoms to create a modest amount of trinitrotoluene. Which I heated with a thin flow of Thermalism to create an explosion."

"What's trinitro...whatever you called it?" Emma asked.

"TNT, as it's more commonly known," Talent Isaac said. "A somewhat primitive explosive that's still sometimes used in mining operations. As you can see, Atomicism is as much about chemistry as it is about magic. Of all the Aspects, it requires the most study. Get one atom in a molecule wrong, and things can get deadly amazingly fast."

"What about atomic reactions?" Rhea asked. "How are those done?"

"If you mean fission or fusion," Isaac said, "that is beyond either Talent Hamil's or my abilities. We understand the theory of it, though. A lot of complicated reactions occur within a short period of time. If you don't know what you're doing, you'll end up doing a lot of damage. As such, it's forbidden magic here at the Volsung Academy."

"What about simple Transmutation, then?" Emma asked. "Why can't we try that?"

Isaac chuckled. "Simple? No, nothing is ever simple. It took a couple of years of intense study for me to do something as simple as transmute hydrogen into helium."

"Wouldn't that be fusion?" Emma pressed.

"No," Hamil answered. "That would be *combining* two atoms of hydrogen, for example, to create helium. That's not what we mean by Transmutation. Through the Manifold, we can use magic to bend the rules of the Shadow World. *Our* reality. The closer two atoms are to each other on the periodic table, for example, the easier the process. It's easier to trick hydrogen into being a certain isotope of helium, for example, rather than tricking it into being tungsten. And there are two types of transmutation – flux transmutation, which lasts on the order of nanoseconds, and permanent. Permanent transmutation requires more magic, plus the setting of a ward, usually Dynamistic in nature."

"Now I'm even *more* confused," Emma said.

"That is beyond the lesson for today," Hamil said. "Suffice it to say, it took two of us combining our streams to create that gold earlier, and it drained most of our ether. Talent Isaac is better at supplying the ether, while I'm better at rearranging molecules, the actual chemistry of it. The point is, you have to *feel* what's there. Atomic Magic requires sharp senses, as well as being skilled at other Aspects. That's why there's so very few of us. Of course, it's better to use what's there rather than to Transmute your own raw material. Much less dangerous and ether-intensive."

Though Lucian had only been here six months, he was always surprised by what magic could do. Atomicism seemed like a powerful Aspect indeed.

Hamil and Isaac continued to lecture the Novices for the next hour. There were no more demonstrations.

When the sun had reached its zenith, the Novices were still huddling from the biting wind. The Talents ended the lesson, and everyone returned to the boats. After rowing out to sea, they lifted the vessels back on board. Once all was secured, everyone crowded into the bridge as the ship set sail. Isaac brewed some hot tea for everyone to share in the wardroom.

The water grew choppier, the wind blustering against the hull with powerful gusts. The storm that had threatened all morning was now falling upon them. The ship flew across the water as a dismal sleet pelted the deck, coating it with ice.

Volsung winter was coming. The cold filtered through the cracks of the door, and ice coated the windscreen in a layer of ice. Lucian was grateful the ship was completely automated, or they might have been in trouble. The wardroom was cozy, and the tea did a lot to refresh him.

"In a few months," Hamil began gruffly, to an audience of Novices hanging on his every word, "the entire Northern Ocean will freeze over. It gets cold out here. Damned cold. It'll freeze the blood in your veins if you're out too long in it. You'll know true cold a couple months after the Trials are over; that's when the worst of it happens. And you better believe they'll have you training out in the lawn, even when a blizzard's blowing."

He took a sip of his tea, hardly having time to swallow before Emma pelted him with yet another question.

"How long does the ice last? What happens if someone needs to leave?"

He looked at her with an amused expression. "You don't. You can expect half the year to be completely impassable. But once the ice is thick enough, this very ship modifies into a hovercraft. It'll do that once the ice is thick enough to hold it at rest."

Transcend Mount would become an island of life in an icy

desert. Then Lucian would be *truly* stuck here. For some reason, the iced over ocean seemed a greater barrier than boundless water.

The rest of the trip back was mostly quiet, save for the blustering wind.

Lucian was relieved when the ship pulled into the short dock. Once *Lightsail* was moored, the party made the long climb to the Academy. The weather was still foul, snow mixing with freezing rain. The cliff broke the worst of the gusts coming from the north. All was a monochrome gray; the visibility was too poor to even see the ocean from the trail. This cold was nothing Lucian had ever experienced – it even hurt his nostrils to breathe.

The dismal scene made Lucian realize how far from home he was.

Once they were back inside the cavernous entrance of the Academy, Lucian heaved a sigh. This place that had seemed so strange and forlorn at first had quickly become his refuge. It was hard to completely hate it, as he had just a few weeks ago.

There were positives he had never considered. There was structure he had been lacking before. And even if the training was difficult, his devotion made other worries fall by the wayside.

There were new worries, though. There was always the fear of not being good enough, and the consequences of that were very real.

No. He couldn't think about that now.

This place, his training, was all he had left to live for. What kind of life was that?

He realized, with growing coldness, that the question didn't matter. This *was* his life now, for better or for worse.

The sooner he accepted that, the better things would be.

14

GOOD AS TALENT HAMIL'S word, the weather grew colder. *Much* colder.

By the passing of the equinox, the entire front lawn and back courtyard lay buried beneath a thick layer of snow. The Novices had to shovel it without the aid of magic. If the drifts grew too high, they brought in the Talents to blast them with Thermal Magic. Which meant the Novices had to clean the muddy slurry that remained. It was backbreaking, repetitive labor. But at least the constant work kept Lucian warm under his thick winter robes. Most of the time.

The days, too, grew short, until what remained of "day" was about as long as a typical Earth day. That meant the mages of the Academy spent most of their hours in darkness. Lucian's spirits fell along with the sun, and he noticed a similar reticence in the other Novices. It was getting harder to remember what it was all for.

He knew he needed motivation that went beyond survival. But he didn't know what that was.

Vera had foretold that there would be no room for self-expression in this place. Not for the first time, Lucian noted how right she had been.

Here at the Volsung Academy, it was either the Transcends' way, or no way at all.

For all his inner rebellion, Lucian did exactly as he was told. Two more months ticked by, and the anticipation of the Trials grew closer. Lucian had lost count of the standard calendar. He was almost one hundred percent certain his birthday had come and gone, which would make him twenty-one. He didn't bother telling anyone. It seemed there was never any reason to celebrate here unless it was a tangible milestone. A Novice breaking their block might earn special food, but there was little to look forward to beyond that.

And as much as Lucian wanted to learn about the Trials, Tested Novices were forbidden to speak of it. And trying to pry information from the Tested was like pulling teeth. They set themselves apart from the Untested, and unless you were good friends with them, they just weren't going to share their secrets. The Trials pitted the Novices against each other. A small bit of advice might be enough to tip the scales. The Transcends only selected a few Talents every year, at most. Sometimes, they raised no Talents at all.

When the rolls opened for the Novices to enter, Lucian signed up for it on the first day. He knew he wasn't likely to pass. Generally, it took at least two years of dedicated training and study to even have a chance. But the knowledge of the Trials alone would be worth the price of participating, and anyone could join if they had been at the Academy for at least six months. And Lucian didn't want to wait another year.

Besides, the Novices who didn't try out would be stuck doing the chores of those who were. For that reason alone, Lucian thought it would be worth it.

Assuming the Transcends chose him – which he knew wouldn't happen – the next step was to take a year to decide which Aspect to dedicate himself to. He would become a Talent of one of seven Transcends. Transcend White herself did not teach, aside from her personal Psion, Gaius.

There was still so much to learn. And like most of the Novices participating, Lucian was nowhere near ready. Only the ones who had been here for years had a chance of wearing the gray robes and colored sash of a Talent.

Rhea, of course, was one of the top contenders. Though she had only been here a little less than two years, she had apparently had promising results in last year's Trials. Damian seemed confident that he'd learned enough as well, despite being at the Academy for only a year and a half.

As for Lucian himself, he didn't have much hope. Though his progress had seemed to pick up, he still lagged most of the others.

No new Novices had arrived since the equinox, nor had any been sent home. More experienced Novices whispered it was *after* the Trials that dismissals would come. Lucian tried to keep his mind off that, as difficult as it was.

As the Trials neared, as the late autumn snows fell, Lucian labored all the harder. He could identify and stream the basics of all six of the Aspects permitted to him, even his weakest Aspect, Dynamism. His streams would not be as practiced and efficient as someone like Rhea, but he was proud of how far he had come.

The question was, would it be enough?

AT LAST, the day came.

After a crowded breakfast, around fifty Novices and a third that number of Talents gathered in the Spectrum Chamber for Trial assignments. Lucian was surprised that there were *so many*.

It only meant more competition. Not that he had a chance, anyway.

It was at least an hour before the subdued murmuring subsided. The Transcends stole into the room, taking up their stone seats. Red, Orange, Yellow, Green, Blue, Violet, Gray, and finally, White. As each sat, the sides of their seats lit with colored flames, casting the chamber in rainbow brilliance. Lucian's eyes widened at the sight, and noticed several other Novices staring as well. The Transcends' colorful robes shone with radiance that was almost too bright to look at.

All attention was on Transcend White, seated in the far-right seat. Rarely did they get to see the entire Spectrum arrayed in their dazzling colors.

Soon, the Novices would know who would rise, who would stay another year, and who would be sent away.

Transcend White's steely gaze scanned the assembly. "Today marks the first day of the Volsung Academy Trials. You will be split into seven groups of equal number, and the Trials will last for the next seven days. For those of you unfamiliar, this is how it works. You will spend each day with one of the Transcends. They will test you on their respective Aspect. If you fail *any* of the Trials, then you will not be raised to the mantle of Talent. These Trials are a basic competency test that will form the basis of more advanced training." Transcend White allowed a pause to let the point sink in. "Do I make myself clear?"

"Yes, Transcend White," came the unified response.

"Good," she said. "Then let the Trials commence!"

The Novices were split into their Trial groups by the gathered Talents. The assignments must have been decided for a long time because it went fast. Lucian was placed in a group with Damian, Rhea, and a new Novice named Marcus. There were fourteen groups in all. Half of those groups would undergo the Trials in the morning, the other half in the afternoon. Lucian was in the morning group.

None of the Novices dared break the silence. The Trials may have already begun, and Lucian figured no one wanted to mess that up.

They waited while the Transcends conferred amongst themselves. At last, Transcend White nodded. Each of the Transcends went to a predetermined group of Novices. Transcend Blue was making his way over to Lucian's group. His dark, grandfatherly face, with its trim gray goatee, betrayed no emotion.

"Your first Trial will be with me," he said. "It will be in a training room on the second level."

Transcend Blue, without a word, led the way down the corridor outside the Spectrum Chamber. They went up the staircase to the second level.

The second level wasn't much different from the first. A long corridor stretched before them for well over a hundred meters. Blazing torches lined the walls, and many open doorways and arches led into interior rooms. Most of the cells they passed were dark and empty. The sun still hadn't risen, despite it being past midmorning.

About halfway down the corridor, Transcend Blue entered an archway on the left. It opened into a spacious room with training mats spread across the floor. A large chest stood in the middle of the room. The setting made Lucian wonder if they were going to be pitted against one another in duels. Mages could certainly use Binding in a fight.

Looking around at everyone else's nervous faces, Lucian could see he wasn't alone in wondering what came next.

"Stand in a line, about a couple of meters between each of you," Transcend Blue instructed.

They hurried to do as instructed. Transcend Blue was

already opening the chest. He retrieved a spherical stone, about thirty or forty centimeters in diameter.

"We are starting with Novice Damian," Transcend Blue said. "Take this sphere from my hand using a Binding tether."

Damian's eyes widened. He looked at the other Novices for a moment, as if shocked he'd have to perform in front of everyone else. That had to be purposeful. The Transcends wanted to see if the Novices could stream under pressure.

Damian extended his hand with his palm facing outward, closing his eyes. It was dead silent for a long moment. Damian had often bragged that Binding was one of his strongest Aspects, but Lucian knew that couldn't be the case, because he also claimed Thermalism was his strongest, and that was on the opposite side of the Septagon. Now, Damian had the chance to put his money where his mouth was. A small part of Lucian wanted him to fail. Humility was not Damian's strong suit.

Just as Lucian had this thought, the side of the sphere Transcend Blue held emitted a bluish aura. It shot toward Damian's open hand, also glowing blue, while a line bridged the two points. Upon contact, Damian's fingers clasped the sphere. The Novice opened his eyes and let out a breath.

Lucian had to keep from gaping. Damian had made it look *easy*.

Transcend Blue nodded. "All right. Now, Bind it to the chest to put it back in."

This part didn't take as long. After a short moment, the top of the open chest glowed blue, and the sphere shot out of Damian's hand. It bounced off the lid's inner casing to land snugly inside. He closed his eyes, breathing a sigh of relief.

There was no chance Lucian's test would go as well.

Next up was Novice Rhea. As soon as her Trial began, a good five minutes passed without anything happening. To Lucian's surprise, Transcend Blue didn't call anything off. He only watched her intently. Lucian couldn't help but feel bad for her.

But that feeling subsided when, in a sudden burst of energy, the sphere glowed and shot into Rhea's hand. It moved so fast that it *had* to have hurt as it made contact. However, Rhea betrayed no pain in her expression.

"Now, Bind it into the chest," Transcend Blue said.

Rhea did so in even less time than Damian. But the effect was ruined when the sphere bounced too hard, causing it to roll across the floor.

Transcend Blue retrieved it with his own Binding, placing the sphere inside smoothly. Rhea's pale complexion burned red with embarrassment.

"Novice Marcus."

The nervous youth had been at the Academy for almost as long as Lucian. Lucian had never seen him stream. They had to wait for at least half an hour. Sweat collected on the Novice's brow, dripping on the mat below, his face a mask of intense concentration.

After a few more minutes passed, Transcend Blue cleared his throat. "That will be enough, Novice Marcus."

He sputtered, his eyes widening. "Transcend Blue, if you could give me but a moment longer..."

"You have had your chance, Novice. Thank you."

That cut off any more arguments. Marcus nodded, his face coloring.

That was when Transcend Blue's attention turned to Lucian. "Novice Lucian. Tether the sphere, if you would."

Lucian drew a deep, centering breath, closing his eyes as he formed his Focus. His stone appeared in his mind's eye. Hours upon hours of practice had manifested into perfect calmness. He was no longer in this Trial. There was nothing but the Focus, his breath, and his pool of ether waiting beyond consciousness.

There was the stone of his Focus, and then the sphere Transcend Blue held. That sphere would become the bound object. Both floated, and melded, in his mind's eye. But even beyond his Focus was the desire to succeed, to outdo the rest of the Novices. To prove himself the best and most worthy.

At this thought, the hairs on his arms stood on end. He felt the coolness of the chamber in sharp relief.

Now, all he had to do was stream in the way the Blue Talents had taught him.

He reached through his Focus, feeling the smooth outer surface of the sphere in his mind. That surface became infused with blue, Binding Magic. The Binding now only awaited a focal point toward which to be drawn. That point would be his hand.

He might be the first to complete the Trials with less than a year of training. Who said it *wasn't* possible? If he was the first, then his position would be secure. No one could ever doubt him again. It was fuel to keep going. To keep pushing.

While maintaining the anchor point on the sphere, Lucian streamed the focal point on his outstretched hand, just as he had been taught. Lucian tested the tension between the anchor point and focal point; balance was important. Too much power in the focal point, and the stone would fly too fast, causing injury or even death. Too little, and it would move too slowly, unable to resist the pool of gravity. Something as seemingly simple as this had a lot of moving components, and Lucian's concentration couldn't slip for a moment. He was competing not only against this group here, but *all* the groups that would go through this same Trial. Was it worth the risk to add his own flourish to catch Transcend Blue's eye?

Lucian had delayed too long, already proving himself less proficient than Damian. If he wanted to stand out, he *had* to do something special.

Before he could doubt himself, he streamed more magic

into both the anchor point on the sphere, and the focal point on his hand. When Lucian opened his eyes, he saw a long line of brilliant blue extending from his open palm to the stone. What was *this*? There was no time to wonder at it. He increased the magic in the focal point, and watched as the stone floated slowly toward him, spinning like a top at the same time, the air filled with a curious thrumming.

Ether burned through Lucian in a torrent. Whatever he was doing, it was draining his pool too quickly. Cold sweat trickled off his brow. There was nothing left but to see this through. A fire was burning beneath his skin, with intoxicating hints of sweetness coupled with flashes of pain. That pain – the same he had felt during the fight with Dirk – was a sure sign he was overdrawing. It wasn't *supposed* to hurt like this.

But to complete the Trial, he'd have to stand the pain. And below that, the sweetness of the additional ether made it difficult to let go.

He had to finish this quickly, before anyone could guess he'd crossed the point of no return. Lucian sped the rate of the stone's passage a bit. When it touched his hand, he closed the stream off with great effort, cutting himself off from the Manifold. He let out a gasp, his arm shaking, and his skin bathed in a cold sweat. When reality returned, an acrid taste burned his tongue, and the fire beneath his skin was a molten afterglow. It felt as if he had a sunburn beneath this skin, while he was panting as if he had sprinted five minutes straight.

Now, for the hard part: moving the sphere to the chest. He had already used up all his ether, but to complete the Trial, he had to overdraw. He knew what he should do – refrain from doing the rest of the Trial. But even if he failed this one, he still couldn't get out of the rest of the Trials. The Transcends had made that clear. Once a Novice took part in the Trials, they had to be completed, unless the Novice were somehow incapacitated during them.

Now, for the shift. All Lucian had to do was the same thing, only flipping the anchor point and the focal point, so that the focal point was streamed onto the top of the chest. He drew more magic, which entered his pool like white-hot fire. The sphere shot from his hand, bouncing off the top of the casing and bouncing inside.

He let out a breath and let go of his stream, his arm trembling.

"Good, Novice Lucian." Transcend Blue's neutral mask betrayed no emotion.

Did he know he had overdrawn? Lucian couldn't begin to guess. Certainly, he had never created a stream so strong, except perhaps when had destroyed that iceberg.

In contrast to Transcend Blue's neutral expression, the other Novices stared at him. Marcus's eyes burned with envy and anger. Rhea's face was pale, even ashen. Damian seemed suspicious, with a single eyebrow arched.

"This concludes the Binding Trial," Transcend Blue said. "Tomorrow, you'll meet with Transcend Gray in the entry hall after breakfast. Don't be late." Transcend Blue looked at each of them in turn, and Lucian last of all. It seemed he looked at Lucian longer than the others. "You are dismissed. Use this time to rest and study for the Gravitonics Trial tomorrow."

The Novices left the training room, walking down the stone corridor to the stairs that would take them to the first level. Lucian hung back, hoping the others would go ahead of him. But Damian walked at his side, only speaking when the others were well ahead.

"What was *that*?" he whispered. "What did you do?"

"I'm not sure," Lucian said. Maybe he could play dumb. "I think I streamed too much by mistake."

"You think?" Damian asked, drily. "You overdrew, didn't you?"

"I don't know."

"You've been here over half a year and you *still* don't know your limits?" Damian shook his head. "It starts to hurt like a muscle cramp, but all over the body. Like your entire body is on fire. As soon as you feel *that*, you know you've gone past your limit."

Well, that answered that. "I don't know. I guess it felt a bit like that."

"Tch. Yeah, okay. You realize you can get kicked out for streaming too much? They will *end* you."

Lucian realized that he had already gotten a pass back when he had destroyed the iceberg. If Transcend Blue knew he had streamed too much, drawing beyond his pool . . .

"I know it's tempting," Damian continued, "but you've got to control yourself, man. It gives you an unfair advantage over the rest of us who are trying to pass fair and square."

"I wasn't trying to cheat," Lucian said. He couldn't help but feel defensive, even if he knew Damian was right.

"Sure," Damian said. "It's only a friendly word of advice. They aren't just testing us on our skill, Lucian. They're testing for other things, too."

"Other things like what?"

By now, they had made it to the first level. They stopped in front of the staircase.

"Do you *really* have to ask?" Damian asked. "I can't *prove* you overdrew, but no Novice can do what you did. If I was thinking it, others were, too."

"I've felt that fiery feeling before. Several times, in fact."

"Then you better watch it. I'm only trying to help you. Good luck tomorrow. You're going to need it. They say the Gravitonics Trial is always a killer."

When Damian walked away, Lucian couldn't help but be glad. This wasn't Damian's business, even if the older Novice had something of a point.

Even if overdrawing had been a bit painful, it had also felt . .

. rapturous, for lack of a better word. He wanted to stream again, if only to catch that feeling.

But sanity prevailed. The last thing he needed was more ether. He needed rest, especially if the Gravitonics Trial was going to be as difficult as Damian hinted. He hadn't had much training in Gravitonics. All he'd learned so far was to stream anti-gravity discs to levitate stones and the like. The effect was close to Binding, only the Aspect to get there was different.

Lucian had a feeling that the Gravitonics Trial wouldn't be like the Binding one. It wasn't likely that two Trials would be so similar, even if the Aspect of Magic were different.

Lucian made it to his room. The last thing he wanted was to be around people. Having time to rest was rare, so he wanted to take advantage of it.

Lucian could only relax when he closed the door behind him and had the candle lit. He sprawled on his bed. A wave of exhaustion coursed through him. It wasn't even lunchtime yet.

Before he knew it, he was dozing off. When he awoke, he was unsure how much time had passed, but he did know he had a throbbing headache. That acrid taste on his tongue was back, his entire mouth feeling as if it were coated in filth. An aftereffect of overdrawing, perhaps?

He got up, brushed his teeth, and vigorously cleaned his tongue. It helped. Until a sudden wave of nausea sent him into a dry heave.

He couldn't get sick. Not now.

He lay down a few minutes longer, until the world stopped spinning and the nausea subsided. He needed to eat to keep up his strength. For all he knew, it was evening now. But he had no appetite at all. Is this what happened when a mage went beyond their limits?

Damian was right. He'd streamed far too much. He was sure his pounding headache, foul breath, and nausea was a side effect of reaching too far. Ether was poisonous, a fact proven by the fraying.

What he had done was not only dangerous, but stupid. And to boot, he had most likely failed the Trial.

He would have to learn from this mistake and resolve not to give into the temptation again.

Lucian left his room for the dining hall.

———

WHEN LUCIAN RETURNED FROM DINNER, all he wanted was to sleep. He was about to do so, until he saw the book.

The Prophecy of the Seven by Arian was so unassuming on the nightstand, with its plain and worn leather cover. There it had sat for the past two months, so long that Lucian had nearly forgotten it.

But Transcend Blue's story returned to him. Despite his weariness, he lay back in the bed, propping his back against the wall. By the light of the lantern, he began reading.

He forced himself to read through paragraphs of nonsense. He didn't understand why. There something about the words that were – intoxicating, as if he were reading poetry in another language. That sentiment was reflected by the actual text. Words out of order, words made up, all running together in a nonstop stream of consciousness.

Because of that, he reeled when he reached a part that was decipherable:

I SAW SEVEN KEYS, floating Orbs in the Black Void. Red, Orange, Yellow, Green, Blue, Violet, and Gray. The Aspects of Magic. Ether unadulterated. They spun like jewels of a Septagon crown, whorls of color and heavenly light. I stared for eons into the timeslip of eternity. They ... whispered to me, secrets of Starsea and Creation ...

They told me to find them. They told me to bring them together. The Cycle must be completed. And the lights faded, and with each fading, it felt like death untold.

And then there was an eighth orb, shining like a black sun in the center of the Seven. And it spoke unto me...

Find them, it said. Bring them to me. I can cure the darkness. I can stop the Cycle...

Starsea shall rise again.

LUCIAN SHUT THE BOOK, unable to make himself go on. As he read the words of that voice, it was if he had heard it in his mind. Could it be the same voice that had visited him? No. Impossible. And he was no longer sure that had even happened.

Lucian forced himself to read once again, but it had become gibberish again . . . even the passage he had just read. A quick scan of the rest of the text revealed much the same. He searched pages, all the way to the beginning of the book. Had it changed, or had he nodded off and gone into a dream?

He was simply tired. He didn't know why he was bothering. He had much greater concerns, so this was the last thing he needed. If he allowed distractions, it could mean the difference between passing and failing the Trials.

Lucian lay down. Despite the troubled nature of his thoughts, he was quick to sleep.

15

THE NEXT DAY, Lucian woke with a pounding headache. He groaned at the mere thought of having to go through another Trial. It was day two, and he was already over it.

Worse, rumors had been flying around last night that the Trial was on the beach. The Novices who had already participated wouldn't say more. At least, not to him.

There was nothing for Lucian to do but get up, wash his face, and get dressed. He layered himself in his thick, fur-lined winter Novice robe. He expected this Trial to be hell, but after a hot breakfast and some tea, he *might* be feeling more up to it.

Almost everyone in his group was up by now, sitting at the end of the Novice table. Lucian grabbed a bowl of porridge and joined them. Rhea and Damian chattered about the Trial ahead, while Marcus and Lucian ate in silence. Emma's group sat next to them, and only she was able to draw him out of his sullen silence.

"Nervous?"

He cleared his throat. "A little."

"Same. Gravitonics is one of my weaker Aspects. Too much concentration."

"It isn't so bad," Rhea said, overhearing the conversation. "Just takes a bit of practice."

"Gravitonics is her primary," Damian explained. "Along with seemingly everything else."

"Hey," she said, playfully. "Don't be jealous."

Damian's eyebrows shot up. "How could I *not* be? You're a shoo-in for Talenthood."

At this, Rhea's cheeks flushed with pride.

"And what about me?" Emma asked.

Damian gave a winning smile. "I wouldn't be surprised. You broke your block quickly."

"I was only joking," Emma said, though Lucian could tell she liked the praise. That was Damian, though. His words were always honeyed, and it made him want to barf.

"We have a tough Trial ahead of us," Marcus said, coming out of his silence. He hadn't eaten much. Of all the Novices undergoing the Trial today, *he* had the least chance of success. Lucian didn't understand why he'd sought to undergo them. Then again, he was hardly one to judge.

"That we do," Damian said. "It will be a good experience, if nothing else. I really hope it doesn't last long."

"I suppose it'll be even colder when I go out after you guys," Emma said. "*Why* does it have to take place outside?"

"I guess we'll find out soon enough," Lucian said.

As more Talents filtered in, the Novices shifted the conversation away from the Trials. Lucian forced himself to eat his porridge, even if his stomach was unsettled. Damian, unflappable as ever, returned with seconds.

"If only they'd built an Academy on Luddus," he said. "It's warm year-round. And no seasons. Gentle rains once every few days fall like clockwork. You only have to get used to the gravity."

"Even *this* gravity is hard for me to get used to," Emma said. "It's getting better, though."

"It takes about a year for a spaceborne to get used to higher gravity," Rhea said. "I was the same way."

Lucian realized he had never heard Rhea's story. "Where are you from?"

"Mimir," she said. "Just one Gate away. Similar world. Just darker and drabber. A backwater if there ever was one. Still, some people like it for the Yggdrasil trees."

"I've heard they're beautiful," Emma said. "I wish I could see them!"

"I suppose I never noticed them," Rhea said.

The conversation was cut short when it was time to get moving. The morning groups bussed their bowls and headed for their meeting spots.

"Good luck," Emma said.

"Thanks," Lucian said. "You, too."

Lucian walked with Damian, Rhea, and Marcus toward the entry hall. When they arrived, they were the only ones. They warmed themselves by the central brazier, gathering as much warmth as they could before the inevitable.

A few minutes passed before Transcend Gray appeared. He was short and shriveled in his silvery robes, approaching without a word. He walked with the aid of a cane, seeming so frail that a stray gust of wind would blow him away. Outside the Spectrum Chamber, Lucian noted how sickly he seemed. His skin was mottled and pallid, and his face ashen beneath his scraggly white beard. He wheezed as he breathed, and the two Gray Talents flanking his either side seemed ready to catch him at a moment's notice. The first Talent was a tall woman in her thirties with hawkish features, and the other a short, brown-skinned man of similar age. The Novices stood straight as the Transcend approached, lowering their heads in supplication.

"These are my Talents, Gail and Zaren," he said, his voice scratchy. "They will be helping me administer the Trial today." His rheumy eyes seemed to take in each of them before he spoke again. "We will begin immediately. The Trial will be on the beach."

The dreaded moment had arrived. They followed Transcend Gray and his two Talents into the dark, frigid night.

WHEN THE FIRST breeze whipped at Lucian's robes, his thick winter robes seemed to be for nothing. The wind cut to the bone, and he put his hands inside his sleeves while throwing his hood overhead. The cold air stung his nostrils as he drew breath. The scrubby grass crunched beneath everyone's boots, the only sound to be heard besides the wind. He could only hope the shoreline was more sheltered.

There was nothing to do but plod on. They hiked down the steep trail leading to the beach. On the south side of the island, the wind wasn't as bad. But Transcend Gray set a slow pace that was quite maddening. The way was lit by a single light orb set by Talent Gail, which followed the group, Lucian supposed, with a simple Binding. Down on the beach, Lucian could see an orange light. There was a fire, at least. There was enough starlight to see that ice already encased large stretches of the rocky beach.

It took a half hour to reach the bonfire at Transcend Gray's glacial pace. Once there, everyone huddled around it for warmth for a few minutes, the Talents included. Transcend Gray seemed inured to the cold, as he took a few steps toward the ocean. The madman wasn't going *in*, was he? All the other Novices seemed to be wondering the same thing, as they watched Transcend Gray with widened eyes.

The Talents released the light orb, leaving only the fire by which to see. It was amazing how dark it was. The only thing Lucian could see beyond the fire's glow was the ice building up on the shoreline. Even after eight months on Volsung, Lucian wasn't used to the lack of moon. The waves were smaller here, created by wind alone. On a windy night like this, though, the surf was almost as high as it would be on Earth.

Rhea and Marcus's teeth chattered as a particularly cold breeze gusted. That wind sprayed them with bits of icy water. Transcend Gray conferred with his Talents for a moment, nodded, and then turned to face the Novices. The Talents walked with purpose toward the surf. Lucian stared in disbelief. They *were* going into the water.

"Gravitonics has many uses, and is complicated to stream," Transcend Gray began. "If you feel you lack the experience required to complete this Trial, speak now. I will make an exception given the danger of being unprepared. There is no shame in attempting it again next year."

It was true that Lucian had almost no training in Gravitonics. He had done nothing more than float stones. But to Lucian, there was no point in giving up, especially not when he'd have to wait another year to try again.

"As you wish." Transcend Gray turned back toward the surf, raising his hands as if in benediction. "Tonight, we walk on water."

It was at that moment that Lucian noticed that Gail and Zaren had stolen off. Shadows moved out on the surf, supported by nothing more than glowing gray discs painted upon the dark surface of the water.

"I can't do that," Marcus said, his thin voice almost eaten by the wind.

Lucian only stared in disbelief. He *couldn't*. His short lessons with Talent Zaren taught him nothing more than basic antigrav streams, good for nothing more than levitating stones. If Lucian attempted this Trial, he'd have to be insane. He tried not to think of sinking into that freezing, dark water.

"Those of you who choose to take part," Transcend Gray said, his voice sonorous, "approach the tide line now."

It was now or never. Lucian tried not to focus on the ice chunks floating on the waves. About fifty meters from the shore, the Gray Talents stood, silent and shadowy sentinels. The gray discs underneath their feet might have been just another piece of ice from this distance. He'd have to walk there and back to shore without sinking.

Damian was casting a glance his way. His expression was determined and competitive. It was almost as if he was telling Lucian to give up. That he couldn't do this.

That all but firmed Lucian's resolve as he looked back out at the ocean.

"Your Trial," Transcend Gray called, his voice resounding, "is to walk out to the Talents and back." He nodded toward Rhea. "Novice Rhea will begin."

She recoiled at the mere mention of her name. "I . . . might need some time to prepare my Focus, Transcend Gray."

"I encourage you to do so," Transcend Gray said. "And I suggest all of you do the same."

Lucian closed his eyes and latched to his Focus easily enough. The surrounding world faded. He still felt the coldness, the wind piercing his robes. But his Focus was a layer of mental armor that insulated him from the elements. He knew it wouldn't be enough to save him if the worst happened, if he sank into that cold, dark water . . .

But for now, all eyes were on Novice Rhea. The wind gusted through the Novices, Rhea's long blonde hair whipping like a banner. The Novices waited, not wanting to pressure her. Five minutes must have passed before Lucian heard the crunch of the gravel beneath her boots. He paid close attention; there might be some clue about how he could pull this off himself.

Rhea paused about a meter from the edge of the swirling surf, and drew a deep, steadying breath. Then, she stepped onto the water. The same gray disc Lucian had seen below the Talents appeared beneath *her* boot. He shifted his Focus, until it was upon the disc itself. There wasn't much time; he memorized every aspect he could before it could dissipate.

Rhea took her next step upon another disc, and the original dissolved like smoke on water. Lucian shifted his Focus to the next disc, but Rhea was moving faster now. He couldn't hold his Focus for more than a couple of seconds for each one.

As she became more distant, it became much harder for his Focus to follow. He was forced to let go; he was already streaming too much trying to learn to do this.

He felt Damian's eyes on him, but he didn't dare look. Lucian wasn't sure if what he had done was against the rules, but he didn't want to face those accusing eyes.

Lucian watched as Rhea made her way over the dark water, her form only visible from the light of the discs. She made it all the way to the two shadowy figures in the distance, and then turned back. Lucian suppressed a shiver as a particularly chilly gust blew. Transcend Gray watched, the cowl of his hood obscuring his pale skin as his long white beard blew in the breeze.

After a few minutes that seemed to take an eternity, Rhea returned. The bottom of her robes was soaked up to the knees, but she hadn't sunk any lower than that. She was shaking, and her face was paler than usual, making it seem as if a ghost were approaching from the waves.

As she stepped onto the shore, Transcend Gray lent her a hand.

"I got a little wet on my boots," she said, between shivers. "It was the surf. I hope that doesn't count against me."

"Go warm yourself by the fire, Novice Rhea. Well done."

Rhea did as instructed while Transcend Gray turned to Lucian. "Novice Lucian. Your turn."

What, already? Yesterday, he had gone last, and for some reason he had expected the same thing here. He was nowhere near ready. But he couldn't refuse. He had to take what he had learned and use it, little as it was.

Of course, he had the option to sit this one out and wait until next year, when he was better prepared. It would be the wise thing to do. The water here would be dreadfully cold. It would be terrible to fail, and perhaps even fatal. Just because there were two Gray Talents out there didn't guarantee they would reach him in time if things went awry.

But he had come this far. He would try his best.

"Yes, Transcend Gray," Lucian said, making his voice firm. "I'm ready."

Lucian reached for his Focus. The stone appeared upon the black void. At least this part was easy. Lucian made sure the image held before reaching for his ether. With luck, it would be enough to get him through the Trial.

He needed to stream antigravity discs beneath his feet, perfectly balanced against Volsung's gravity. That was no easy thing, but assuming he found that balance, it was just a matter of whether could ration his ether long enough to finish the Trial. And after burning through his ether so quickly yesterday . . .

No. There was no room for doubt. He deepened his Focus, trying to access the memory of the stream Rhea had used to create her discs. Before Lucian could second-guess himself, he reached for the Gravitonic Aspect. It was difficult to isolate it since he hadn't much practice. Everything was muddled in his mind's eye, his Focus intermixing with the Septagon. Until he streamed, he couldn't be sure he was using the right Aspect.

He streamed and could do nothing more than hope that what came from his hand was Gravitonic Magic. An unseen force pushed an incoming wave outward, in a way that would have been impossible with Gravitonics. His hands gave off a low, violet aura, a sure tell that he had isolated Psionics, not Gravitonics.

He reset, clearing his mind for a second attempt. He tried to ignore the other Novices' stares, to not think of their perception of him. He had to deepen his Focus until only magic remained.

When he streamed again, a sudden burst of light went off like a firework over the water, illuminating the dreary beach in a blinding flash of brilliance. Lucian hastily cut off the stream. The wrong Aspect, *again*. That must have been Radiance.

Lucian blinked away stars and found his Focus again, his heart pounding. He should just give up. It was obvious he didn't know what he was doing.

"There is no shame in deferring the Trial, Novice Lucian," Transcend Gray said.

A twinge of annoyance curdled Lucian's stomach. "Please give me one more chance, Transcend Gray."

Transcend Gray said nothing more, but now the pressure was unreal. If Lucian didn't stream the right Aspect now, he would end up looking even more incompetent. Stopping while he was behind was the wise action, especially after streaming the wrong Aspect twice.

But he couldn't give up. To give up meant failure. It meant waiting another year. And another year was just that much longer to wait before he even had the chance of leaving this island.

He reached for his Focus again, probing at an unfamiliar Aspect. It felt . . . *heavy*. Its unfamiliarity told him it was either Gravitonics or Atomicism, the two Aspects he had the least experience with. If he streamed the latter, they would kick him out of the Academy for good, if not outright doing some irreparable damage or perhaps even killing himself.

It was a coin flip. The stakes were just too high, and it was irresponsible to go on.

But Lucian couldn't bring himself to give up. He had come this far, and this was his chance.

He wasn't going to throw that away.

He took a deep breath and streamed, summoning as much confidence as he could. It wasn't Atomicism, that much he could feel. So, it had to be Gravitonics. He fought to remember Rhea's discs, allowing Gravitonic Magic to fill the grooves. He directed his Focus to the surface of the water, into which magic flowed, like hot metal filling a mold. Now, all he had to do was hold the stream steady. The nature of the stream was incomprehensible to him. He was only doing what he had seen Rhea do.

Lucian opened his eyes to see a gray disc bobbing on the surface of the water about a meter in front of him, with intricate lines and curves that swirled from its center. He drew a deep, steadying breath, then took a bold step outward. His foot held on the disc. It was perfectly balanced against gravity.

He could hardly believe it. He only had to hold the design of that disc in his memory. It was simply a matter of imprinting it a few more dozen times before returning to the shoreline. The only question was, did he have the ether to complete the Trial?

There was only one way to find out. Lucian created another disc another meter out. He took a long stride, and was pleased to find this one held, too. It was unreal to see the dark, cold water passing beneath his boots. He released the original disc to conserve his ether, as he had seen Rhea do. Holding multiple streams consumed far more, and he'd never have enough to finish the whole Trial if he didn't manage his ether well.

He moved forward, creating more discs and taking long strides to bridge them. They oscillated on the surf like lily pads. By the time he'd streamed his sixth, he couldn't help but look back at the shoreline. He didn't know whether he was looking for reactions, guidance, or encouragement. Everyone stared with neutral masks, the light of the fire casting them in orange radiance.

Lucian refocused on his task. One after another, the discs manifested before him. He tried not to think about the cold, deep water. Lucian gasped when a particularly high wave sloshed against him, chilling him to the bone. His Focus threatened to crumble, but with sheer stubbornness, he held onto it like a lifeline. Already, he couldn't feel anything beneath his shins. But if the discs held, Lucian would be fine. The warm fire back on shore would be his reward for a Trial completed.

Nervousness fell by the wayside as his Focus deepened. He let intuition do the steering, and the discs appeared, one after another. He was halfway to the waiting Talents, silhouettes in the distance. So long as he streamed at a steady and efficient rate, he would have enough ether to go the entire distance.

That was the thing, though. He was burning through his pool quickly – *too* quickly. But if he lessened his stream, the discs would not be as effective. He had two choices, as he saw it. He overdraw or find a way to stretch his limited reserves.

Or move faster. Much, much faster.

Damian's warning from yesterday resounded in his mind. The Transcends were testing them not only for competency, but wisdom. He may have gotten away with overdrawing yesterday, but that was no guarantee he would this time. The only solution was to stream more efficiently, or to move faster.

He slowed the rate of his stream, while also moving faster. But somehow, slowing the stream changed the nature of the discs. They were darker now, almost completely blending in with the water. In fact, they seemed to be failing, no longer strong enough to keep him above the surface.

Lucian heard some shouting in the distance, but he could hardly pay attention to that. His knees had already slipped underwater. The icy surface pierced his skin, stabbing like a knife.

Lucian scrambled to stream properly again, but the water was up to his waist. It was so cold that the breath went out of him. Whatever was left of his Focus completely shattered.

Worse, he was only getting *heavier*. Something was wrong with the stream. He shouldn't be sinking *this* quickly.

It was time for desperate measures. There was still a chance to save this.

Lucian had to overdraw.

He deepened his Focus, desperate for any drop of ether, even if it made him sick, even if it would someday kill him with fraying. Because if he didn't have it now, he would die. But even that was not to be. A wave crashed against him, knocking him off what remained of his disc. He streamed Gravitonic Magic below him, desperate to do anything to get out of this death spiral. Even as the fire burned beneath his skin, icy water pricked at it from above. And he only sank lower.

He tried to swim, but he was so heavy. It was impossible to fight the gravity pulling him down. He took one final breath before the icy water claimed him. He was a meter underwater now, and already the darkness was near absolute.

He gave up trying to stream Gravitonics, instead opting for Psionics. In an uncontrolled burst, he pushed the water surrounding him. It blasted away long enough for him to draw a deep gulp of air. But the water returned, heavier than before. Lucian clawed, trying to swim upward. But he was still too heavy, as if he wore leaden boots.

He was sinking, deeper and deeper toward the bottom of the Ocean of Storms.

16

LUCIAN SUNK INTO A COLD, silent world, the botched gravity stream doing its deadly work. He fumbled and attempted to reform his Focus as the water crushed him. How far had he already fallen? His lungs burned for air even as this watery, icy hell surrounded him. His heart pounded, but already, it was beginning to slow...

It was quiet down here. Peaceful, even. And he was so tired. But Lucian knew that if he closed his eyes, even for a moment, he would never wake up again.

A strange sense of déjà vu struck him, as if he had lived this before. It was like the first dream during his metaphysical all those months ago. The reminiscence was dashed when he struck the rocky bottom. Lucian made a feeble attempt to push himself up, but he was still so heavy.

This *couldn't* be happening. He felt terror, yes, but mostly he felt disbelief. He thought of Emma, how he would never see her again. Of his mother, whom he might see in some form of an afterlife. Assuming there was one waiting for him.

He opened his eyes to see a shimmering rope descending

from the surface, the only light in the darkness. By its reflected radiance, he could see swarms of fish and teeming eels.

A voice entered his mind.

Reach for it, Lucian.

It sounded like his mother, but that couldn't be. She was dead. The rope was too far. *How* could he reach it?

And yet, the rope was there, drawing nearer. What if he touched it? What if he tried to save himself? It wasn't too late.

Lucian reached, but his hand found nothing but cold water ... water so cold that it burned. The rope was just an illusion, then. With that realization, Lucian relaxed. There was nothing left to fight with, and nothing left to fight for.

The voice returned, unmistakable and snapping like an authoritative whip.

Stand!

Lucian stood on the rocky bottom. That wasn't his mother at all. That was ... Vera?

This isn't the end for you. Reach beyond your strength and take what is yours! Are you going to die here at the bottom of this forsaken sea? The Manifold means greater things for you if you have but the courage to reach. If not, then I was wrong about you ... so very wrong.

Vera? How are you even ...?

Reach. Reach now! Do it!

Something within him stirred. Lucian formed his Focus. It materialized in the void, firm and sure. Fire burned within him, and warmth – *real* warmth – spread throughout his limbs. He was streaming Thermal Magic into his very bones, reviving his body which had gone cold. How had he known do that? Before now, he would have never dreamed such a thing was possible.

But it wouldn't save him, only buy him time. His lungs burned for air. Might he Transmute the water into air within his very lungs? That was too complicated. He needed something simpler, something more direct ...

The solution came to him in a sudden burst of clarity.

Lucian formed a new gravity disc beneath him. This time, he formed the imprint that had sent him to the bottom, only he did so *backwards*. It was a long shot, but any shot at all was better than nothing.

He reached for his Focus but found it empty. So, he reached even farther, for the Manifold itself. The Manifold was there, waiting, roaring like an oncoming tsunami, one that promised life and freedom.

There was nothing to do but embrace that gargantuan force, and let it carry him wherever it may. Even if it carried him to fraying.

Ether passed through him in a torrent. He drew the disc on the rocks beneath him and streamed as much Gravitonic Magic as he could. As soon as the stream was complete, Lucian released.

The disc rose beneath him, carrying him with it. Cold water rushed past his face, and Lucian clung to the disc, holding on for everything he was worth. Faster and faster, he surged upward through the water, the pressure lessening. The disc was gone, lost somewhere on the way, but Lucian's momentum was too great. He was still rising and had somehow broken the Gravitonic hold that had dragged him down.

Just as he was about to draw a deep lungful of water, he broke the dark surface, hacking and coughing as he arced through the air. He drew a deep, sputtering breath before crashing back into the water. He clawed upward until he was swimming among floating chunks of ice. He treaded water, trying to find the direction of the shore, the rush of magic ebbing.

Half-delirious with cold, he swam.

His Focus was gone, and he could not recall it. He no longer had the strength. His only hope was to get to that bonfire or die in the attempt.

And yet the will to live overpowered all else, even if it was tempting to give up and let the sea take him. It took a minute of swimming before his feet could reach the bottom. At first, he wasn't sure he could touch it, because his feet were so numb. He shambled out of the water on frozen legs, the wind freezing the water to his skin. Frost framed his face and solidified on his cloak.

Forward. He had to keep moving forward.

How was he still alive? How was he still walking? He could see the fire in the distance. He opened his mouth to shout, but his voice escaped as a groan that was eaten by the wind.

All this effort to save himself was wasted. The fire was too far, and they would never know to look for him here. By the time daylight revealed his frozen body, it would be too late. He was so tired. So awfully tired...

He took a few more pointless steps. At some point, his body would stop working, no matter his determination. He was no longer even shaking. Every ounce of his energy went to his legs, moving toward the fiery light in the distance. There was a good fifty meters to go, and it was too dark for anyone to see him. He coughed and hacked, salty seawater spewing from his lungs. His leaden legs were so heavy that he could hardly lift them. How ironic it would be to die here, just a few steps away from warmth...

Lucian stumbled, his vision fading. He had one hope left. If there was no ether to complete it, then death would find him soon.

With his last bit of consciousness, he reached for the Manifold again, wresting enough ether to stream an illuminating burst of light.

He could only hope it was bright enough as he collapsed to the ground.

As Lucian faded in and out, he could see the ground moving beneath him. He heard voices, too, talking soft and low. He didn't even have the energy to let out a groan.

Then, he swam through dark dreams. Most of them were nightmares, one fading into another. In the first, he got on a boat, to go on a long journey from which he could never return. A cold, gray island, where he was waiting for . . . something. Something terrible. And then, a vast golden palace set in the foothills of some impossibly high mountain.

When Lucian opened his eyes, he burned with fever. He was warm, but at the same time, chilled. A fire crackled in the stone hearth about two meters away. When his eyes focused, he saw he was in a small room. It held several similar beds, all of which were empty. The masonry told him he was in the Academy, but he didn't know where. He became aware of a gray-robed Talent seated next to him on a stool, reading a book. Her wide, pale face and slate blue eyes, coupled with her gray sash, told him it was Talent Gail.

Lucian coughed, and the Talent set down her book while clicking her tongue, as if to chide him. "Some of us were wondering if you'd wake up."

Lucian was too tired to argue. For his own part, he couldn't believe he was still breathing.

He closed his eyes, not having the strength to even stay conscious.

When he woke later, there was a familiar voice. It filled him with calm, and he longed to open his eyes and see the face behind it. Despite the sheer difficulty, his eyelids fluttered open. Emma's face materialized, his eyes finding hers.

"Emma?"

Her brown eyes looked at him as she smiled. "How was your swim?"

She would joke now, after almost dying? "Cold."

"Well, that much is obvious."

She reached for a nearby clay cup and held it to his mouth. When the cool water touched Lucian's lips, he realized just how thirsty he was. He drank greedily. His throat felt like sandpaper.

When she took the cup away, Lucian motioned for more.

"Hold your horses," she said. She went away, and a moment later returned with a full cup.

Lucian drank again. Once finished, Emma set it aside and looked down at him.

"What were you *thinking*, Lucian? Or were you thinking at all? You're lucky to be alive."

Did she think he didn't know that? "Something went wrong with the stream. I don't know anything beyond that."

"They say you made a gravity amplification stream," Emma said. "It doubled your weight when you stood over the disc." She looked at him seriously. "All you had to do was jump off and it would have been fine, but they say you fought to reverse it instead."

Jump off? Had it really been as simple as that?

"I was in over my head," he said. "Where am I, exactly?"

"The infirmary."

"Well, I'm alive." Lucian didn't feel the sheer gratitude that should have accompanied those words. "I guess my light worked."

"What light?"

Lucian had trouble remembering. "when I got to the beach, I streamed some light. I guess it got people's attention."

"Oh," she said. "I suppose it did." She shifted in her seat. "It's morning now. I came by to check on you before going to my own Trial."

Morning. If he could only summon his strength . . .

But Emma placed a hand on his chest. Even with that feeble weight, it might as well have been a gravity amplification stream.

"You're not going anywhere, Lucian. Besides, they wanted

me to take your spot in the Trial. I guess in hopes you might be better for the afternoon."

He couldn't so much as move, not with her pressing down on him like that. Her hand went to his face.

"Geez, you're burning up.

"I've ruined everything, haven't I?"

"Truth is, neither of us had much of a chance. I bombed the Gravity Trial."

"What happened?"

She sighed. "I got the first few discs fine. It was the ones after that I couldn't hold." She smiled. "At least I only dealt with water up to my waist."

"Count yourself lucky."

Emma stood, smoothing her robes as she did. "I should get going. The Trial will be starting soon."

"Good luck," he said. "At least it's not over for you."

"We'll see about that. Don't push yourself too much, Lucian. If you haven't learned your lesson by now, then I don't know what to say. Just don't be stupid, okay? Is that too much to ask?"

It was harsh, but she said it kindly enough that it didn't matter. "I'll try."

She smiled. "See you later."

She walked out of the room, leaving nothing behind but her empty presence.

———

LUCIAN SLEPT A COUPLE MORE HOURS, but when he awoke again, all he could think about was how all the other Novices were busy at their Trials. And here he was, out of the running because of his own stupid mistake.

To his surprise, he felt much better, though his fever still ran hot. All was quiet in the sick room, save for the crackle of flames in the hearth. His condition, he supposed, was stable enough for no one to watch over him anymore.

He didn't know where the Radiance Trial was taking place, and even if he did, what good would it do? Was he in any state to stream? He realized this nausea could be from drawing too much ether as much as from his icy plunge. Every time he closed his eyes, his head spun.

"Feeling better?"

Lucian startled at voice. Psion Gaius stood in the doorway. What was *he* doing here?

Lucian did his best to recover. "Not really."

"Well, you're awake, so that's something. Do you have the strength for a walk?"

Lucian wasn't sure, but neither did he want to refuse Gaius. He planted his feet on the stone floor, finding his socks and boots waiting for him. He laced them and stood. His head swam for a moment, but it was only for a moment. His vision steadied, and he walked over to Talent Gaius, who watched him with neutral blue eyes.

Lucian knew he should still be in bed, but he was also curious about what Gaius wanted. Being asked to do something by a Psion was almost as serious as a Transcend asking.

Once out in the hallway, Lucian followed Gaius to a set of steps leading to the Talents' level. He worried the climb would be much too strenuous, but he held onto the railing and took deep breaths. Gaius waited for him at the top, even giving Lucian a moment to catch his breath.

Gaius led Lucian toward the arcade on the Academy's northern face. Lucian felt the cool wind, warmed only a little by weak daylight. Once they reached the first columns, the breeze stole whatever warmth the sun gave. The day was gray and bleak, and visibility poor. In short, it was another day on Volsung. The cutting wind only served to remind Lucian of his ordeal. But he didn't want to show weakness by requesting a warmer spot.

"About yesterday," Psion Gaius said. "I've heard everything. Novices killing themselves with their own stupidity is more common than you would think. It often saves the Spectrum the trouble of having to expel them."

Lucian resisted the urge to wince. "I guess everyone knows by now."

Gaius's cold blue eyes regarded him. "There's at least one death a year. Usually more. Magic is dangerous, and we Talents and the Transcends can't shield you from that danger. The best we can do is train *you* to make the wisest choice. That's why we leave it to the Novices to decide on whether they're ready for the Trials."

Lucian had never thought of it that way. All he'd done was compare himself to his competition. He should try to be more like Marcus, knowing his limits, rather than like Damian or Rhea, who'd been here a year longer.

Gaius continued his lecture. "Magic is any action that tampers with reality as it should operate. It is a gift, and a curse, far beyond our understanding. We can't be sure at all times of the *true* effect of our magic. Even those of us who have been doing this for years are caught off guard by how unpredictable magic can be. We've only scratched the surface of what is possible. Of course, safety is relative when speaking of the Manifold. Therefore, we warn novices that they can never be too careful. We watch for those whose competitive fire can lead them awry." Gaius smiled, and that smile was almost as cold as the wind blowing through the columns. "Your ambition has been noted, Lucian. Courage is never a bad thing – except when it gets you killed for no good reason."

Lucian tried to make his voice as respectful as possible. "Psion Gaius, why are you telling me this?"

He shrugged. "I don't even know myself. As you know, I'm

Psion to Transcend White. My master has taken a keen interest in you. That much is clear. For one reason or another, she expects great things from you."

As Gaius watched him, Lucian did his best to make his features a mask of humility. He didn't want Gaius to know just how nervous that made him.

"My only advice is don't do anything stupid."

Him, too? At this point, Lucian wouldn't be surprised if Transcend White herself came to tell him the same thing.

"Let yesterday be a lesson," Psion Gaius said. "Take your time. Don't burn yourself out. And for the Manifold's sake, commit yourself to your training. You have the potential to go far here. Even if none of us can see what Her High Eminence sees. Having her favor in this place is a rare thing indeed. But that favor can shift faster than the weather."

"I don't feel like I have her favor at all."

"It's her favor that got you in here to begin with," Gaius said. "Her favor is the only reason you aren't on your way to Psyche right now. You'd do well to remember that."

Those words made him go cold. And it didn't help that he felt like a fraud. And as soon as everyone else discovered that, too, they would certainly exile him.

"I've got it, Talent Gaius. I'll be careful."

"Watch your attitude, Novice," Gaius said, with an edge. "When your superior gives you advice, you'd do well to be humble and take it."

Lucian resisted the urge to grit his teeth. "Yes, Psion Gaius. Forgive me."

Even if it sounded forced, Gaius made no comment about it. "If you're feeling up to it, the afternoon Radiance Trial will begin in half an hour in the back courtyard. You can tell Transcend Green you have my permission to take part."

It was a testament to Psion Gaius's authority that his word was good enough to override Transcend Green's, at least in this situation. Lucian almost protested, throwing back the Psion's own words at him. Hadn't he said to take things slow? Then again, Lucian *did* want to take part in the Trial. And if Gaius was encouraging it, it was a tacit admission that Lucian wasn't out of the running yet.

"Are you sure?" Lucian asked.

"Go," Gaius said. "And remember. *Nothing* stupid."

Lucian left the Psion standing by the columns and rushed down to the courtyard.

17

LUCIAN APPROACHED the group of four Novices standing by the cliff at the edge of the courtyard. Their faces registered shock upon seeing him. Everyone likely saw him as the stupidest Novice at the Academy. And for all Lucian knew, he probably was.

So, Lucian stood away from the group, and tried to ignore their hushed whispers.

Out here in the cold, he was starting to feel a bit sick. But he didn't want to lose face by going back inside. Gaius had hinted things might not be over for him. There were five other Trials to face, and if anything, Lucian wanted the Transcends to note that he hadn't given up early.

He couldn't help but feel the Novices' eyes staring at him. He didn't know these people. Two of them, fresh-faced girls with light brown skin and dark hair, probably had less business doing the Trials than Marcus. Both were making a concerted effort not to shiver. Like Lucian, they probably had come from a warmer climate.

The other two were older, among the Tested, and Lucian had seen them around the Academy. Lucian couldn't remember their names, but both were in their mid-twenties. The closest of the two was kicking rocks off the cliff. The other watched, guffawing when the kicker tripped over his robes.

If this was the competition, Lucian might have a shot of passing after all, sickness or not.

"You're Lucian, aren't you?"

One of the girls had spoken to him. She was pretty, her eyes set in a heart-shaped face. The other girl was tall with long hair, and her eyes held a mocking quality.

"That's me," he said.

The male Novice who had been kicking rocks had lost interest in the activity. "I thought you were dead."

"Not yet."

"You *did* almost die though, right?" the tall girl asked,

"Unfortunately."

"You aren't supposed to be talking about the Trial," the other young man said, his face stern. "Where's Emma, anyway?"

"She did the Trials this morning, Petros," the girl said. She looked back at Lucian. "You're friends with her, right?"

"Yeah," Lucian said.

"I like Emma," the girl said. "She's really nice. My name is Hana. I'm from Sani, too, like Emma."

Lucian knew Emma was born on Sani, even if she'd lived most of her life in other places. "Nice to meet you. I'm Lucian."

"Yes, I know that," she said. She nodded toward the other girl. "This is Corinne. She's from Sani, too, but we didn't know each other from before."

Were all women from Sani so beautiful? Lucian almost mentioned that, before thinking better of it.

"Quiet," the rock-kicker said. "He's coming."

Everyone went still as Transcend Green walked into the courtyard from the back entrance of the Academy. He had no Talents with him. Perhaps this Trial would be simple.

If Transcend Green was surprised to see Lucian, he gave no sign. The Novices lined up and stood to attention. Transcend Green surveyed them for a moment before beginning.

"Today's Trial will be relatively straightforward and will consist of two parts. First, I need you to stream a basic light orb, to be held and maintained for one full minute. After that, you must receive and interpret a radio stream I send. You must stream the answer to me, again by radio. That is the essence of today's Trial."

The first one sounded simple enough, though Lucian had never held a light orb for as long as a minute. Ten seconds, at the most. Unless there was some trick to holding the orb longer, it should be rather simple. The second task, however, would be tougher. Lucian had not learned much about streaming radio. Mages usually opted for Psionic links since Psionic Magic was more common between mages and there was no risk of interference. But radio streams also had their place, being more efficient on ether reserves.

"Novice Lucian," Transcend Green said. "We'll begin with you. Stream a light orb and hold it for a full minute. You may start when ready."

That was it, then. No time to even prepare himself.

He reached for his Focus, grasping it with ease. However, the mere act of forming it sent waves of nausea coursing through him. He let go, bending over and drawing a deep breath.

This might not go as well as he'd hoped.

"Are you well, Novice?" Transcend Green asked.

Lucian made himself stand straight. "I'm fine. Please give me a moment, your Eminence."

He didn't feel fine, though. His eyes drifted upward, to the columns of the second floor. To Lucian's surprise, Psion Gaius was still there, watching.

He couldn't back down. The Psion would note his refusal to

take part. And that information would be inevitably passed on to Transcend White.

Lucian waited a moment longer to get his bearings. His ether had regenerated somewhat from last night. With luck, it would be enough to get through the Trial.

Lucian closed his eyes, and reached for his Focus, becoming one with it. He could feel the power of the Manifold waiting beyond, but he could not let himself draw directly from it. Not today. All he had to do here was stream a light orb and hold it. Simple enough. Radiance was one of his stronger Aspects.

The only question was whether he could do it while feeling so weak.

He could feel the Aspect ready to be streamed. The light orb grew in his mind's eye. All he had to do was release it and keep the stream steady.

Lucian allowed the magic to flow. To his satisfaction, an orb of light materialized about a meter ahead, halfway between himself and Transcend Green. So far, so good. It shone bright enough to make the other Novices shield their eyes.

"Not so bright, Novice," Transcend Green said.

Lucian nodded, and slowed the stream. To his relief, the light ebbed. He held it, only feeling the strain after the first thirty seconds had passed. It felt like holding his breath, only . . . different. He maintained his Focus, not allowing any other thought to intrude and disrupt the flow. Passing the Trial depended on that. For something so simple, it had to be executed unfailingly.

That minute seemed to take forever, and the longer it went, the harder it was to hold the stream. Ether burned through him at a steady clip. Just a few seconds longer . . .

Just when he felt in danger of losing control, Transcend Green nodded. "Good."

Lucian let out a breath and stemmed the stream. He had executed it almost perfectly.

"Novice Garrett," Transcend Green said. "You're next."

Rock-Kicker cleared his throat and shifted his feet. He was so gangly that his robes billowed outward with every stray breeze. His cheeks were rosy, as if someone had pinched them. Garret closed his eyes, and after a full minute of intense concentration, a light orb appeared before him, too. But his was dimmer than Lucian's, and its intensity warbled notably, especially toward the end. Garrett held the orb for a full minute, letting out a breath when Transcend Green called time.

"Novice Petros," Transcend Green said. "Your turn."

Petros started at the mention of his name. But when the time came, his orb was perfect, in both intensity and duration. It didn't deviate for a moment, while not being too bright to look at.

Next were the two girls from Sani. Hana could only hold her orb for half the time, and it was too bright. Corinne's sputtered in and out over the duration.

Once everyone had finished, it was clear that only three Novices had a shot at passing.

"Good," Transcend Green said, stroking his gray beard. "Now, for the second part of the Trial. Go stand over there, by the bathhouse wall, while I move to the opposite end of the courtyard. I'll stream a radio wave to each of you. Your job is to receive my message and relay the answer back to me. We'll go in the same order as last time." He looked around at the Novices, his face as wrinkled as a prune. "Understood?"

"Yes, your Eminence," they all said.

Lucian went to the appointed spot and reached for his Focus. He waited for Transcend Green to arrive at the opposite end of the courtyard, about a hundred meters away. Was he streaming already? Lucian couldn't feel anything yet, and he wasn't sure if he should have.

And his head was already swimming with the effort from

earlier. He hoped he had enough energy to not only complete the Trial, but to figure out how to do it in the process.

He knew from his reading that receiving and transmitting radio waves using magic was all about finding the right frequency. Given he could do that, he might have a shot of passing this.

Lucian began by releasing a thin stream of Radiance. Radio waves were long, requiring little ether. He expanded his Focus, becoming aware of the Radiant Aspect in the world before him. Details sharpened. It seemed he could see farther, a sign that his magic was allowing him to interpret the visible spectrum more efficiently. This too had its uses, though it wasn't the purpose of today's Trial. He needed to slow the stream, until he could perceive radio waves.

The world shifted entirely. He saw new colors – violet beyond violet, and he let out a gasp at its vibrancy.

No. This was the wrong way. He knew he was seeing into the ultraviolet spectrum, burning what remained of his ether at an alarming rate.

But there was time to correct it. The ultraviolet spectrum subsided, until all became as red as blood. Redder than red. Until the red stretched so far that the world itself disappeared into a black void. Here, he could "see" an unintelligible babel of voices. Yes, there it was. Radio waves.

The din was overwhelming. On-world, off-world, and even farther out than Volsung System. There were *thousands*. He had the strange thought that if there were a God, this was what it would be like to hear everyone praying all at once.

Of all those voices, he had to isolate Transcend Green.

That was easier said than done. Lucian was aware, even under the cacophony of noise, that there had to be an easier way. He tried to block everything out, limiting the reach of his Focus. Voices fell away, until there were only a few conversations within the garbled static. He limited the range even further, honing it down, sensing for the right frequency. He felt the rate of his ether burn increase. Seeing radio waves was easy. *Distinguishing* the right one among thousands was the hard part.

And there was only so much time before his ether ran dry.

After a couple of minutes of searching, just as he burned what remained of his ether, he found one he *knew* to be the right one, though he couldn't have said how.

Congratulations. You've passed the Trial. That is, if you can find a way to thank me.

Lucian opened his eyes to see Transcend Green watching him from the other side of the courtyard. Hearing the transmission was one thing. Lucian still had to respond to it.

He kept his Focus attuned to the frequency. Once sure, Lucian responded.

I heard you. Thank you, Transcend Green.

Transcend Green nodded, and Lucian felt their connection sever. He let go of his stream and let out a breath.

He'd done it.

"Next, Novice Garett," Transcend Green called.

Lucian stood aside, in disbelief and exultation. He'd done it. Against all odds, he'd finally managed to not screw something up.

He looked up at the second-floor arcade, but Psion Gaius was gone.

Lucian watched the other Novices go through their own tests. It was impossible to see if they had failed or succeeded, the only clue being their facial expressions. Garrett seemed confident and sure. The two Sani girls' pallid expressions revealed they were out of their depth. Petros's face was an unreadable mask, but Lucian's suspicion was that he had completed the Trial, given his performance during the first part.

Once all were done, Transcend Green called a halt for the day.

"This concludes the Radiance Trial," he said. "Lucian, you will be with your assigned group for tomorrow."

Lucian lowered his head. "Of course, Transcend Green."

After Transcend Green was out of earshot, the Novices gathered to discuss the Trial.

"Do you think you passed?" Garrett asked Petros.

"Of course I passed," he said. "Radiance is my primary."

"I did well enough, I think, for my secondary," Garrett said. "What about you, Lucian?"

Lucian shrugged. "I think I did well."

"Took you a while to find the frequency, didn't it?"

Lucian nodded. "Yeah. Look, I should go. I'm pretty beat."

"Suit yourself."

The girls were already inside the Academy, likely not wanting to discuss their Trial. Lucian made a beeline for the Academy as well, where it would be warm. Now that he was no longer streaming, he was starting to catch a chill. And his head felt as if it were floating, and it was all he could do to keep himself moving. He had been drained to his limit, to the point where he wasn't sure how he'd be ready for the Dynamism Trial tomorrow morning. Since he'd been moved to the afternoon group today, he'd have less time than the rest of his group to recover.

Normally, it would be too early for dinner, but during the Trials, food was always kept ready. Lucian headed for the dining hall, bumping into Emma in the line.

"Up already?" She took one look at him and seemed to guess where he had been. "Wait. Don't tell me you did the Trial?"

He nodded. "I'm feeling better. And they let me, so why not?"

"I thought I told you to take it easy!"

"I feel fine," he said. He filled his bowl with a generous portion of stew, even if he was feeling a little sick.

"Okay," she said, sounding unsure. "How'd it go, then?"

"I did well," Lucian said. "It wasn't easy, though."

She ladled stew into her own bowl. "Well, as long as you didn't kill yourself this time."

"*You're* the one killing me."

She smiled. "You know I'm joking. You do look a little pale, though."

"A warm fire and a bowl of stew is all I need."

She moved on from the line, Lucian joining her at the table. Emma took one bite, her nose wrinkling.

"I'm so *tired* of stew," Emma said. "What I wouldn't give for a big, juicy burger! With lots of cheese and onions."

"You like American food, huh?"

"I like *all* food," she said. "Just not stew. There was this American place on L5. Burgers, fries, milkshakes, all that sort of stuff." She stared at her stew wistfully. "I'll never get to have real food again, will I?"

"Become a Talent, and you could make that restaurant your first stop if you'd like."

"Stop."

"I thought we weren't complaining about things anymore."

She rolled her eyes. "I'm starting to regret those words. Complaining feels so good sometimes." She sighed. "I only have to sink ten more years in this place, then maybe they'll trust me enough to on expeditions." She poked the stew with her spoon glumly.

"Poor Emma," Lucian said. "Maybe one day, when I'm a Talent, I can bring you back some real food."

"Ha. What makes you think *you'll* make Talent first?"

He shrugged. "I *am* rather talented."

"Well, so am I! I think you're full of yourself, Lucian."

"You do?"

"Yes. Quite full of yourself for someone who took an unintentional swim in the Ocean of Storms."

"Well, it's not just everyone who can make it to the bottom and tell the story about it."

"Maybe so," she admitted.

"And you must have found it impressive, since you came to check on me today."

"What can I say? I have a soft spot for the charity cases." She turned and put a finger on his chest. "And you are most *definitely* a charity case."

"We'll see if you're still saying that when I come back with some real food. Someday. I might even warm it up for you with a little Thermal magic."

She smiled. "Wow. If you did that, I'd have to eat my words." Her mood became glum again. "With the way my Gravitonics Trial went, anyways, so there's no way I'll make Talent. Not that I had a chance, anyway."

"Well, I'm not making it, either. I did well enough on the Radiance Trial, but the rest is a shitshow."

She laughed. "Yes, that's quite . . . apt. And we must pass all of them to even have a shot. And all these Trials are supposed to be *basic* competency. Can you imagine what the advanced training will be like?"

Lucian couldn't. He'd never even seen the Talents train on the second floor. Surely, they were practicing things far more advanced than what the Novices were doing. The closest thing he'd seen was Khairu's practice on board the *Lightsail* on their way here.

If her work with a shockspear and Dynamism was any indication, then the Talents had earned their namesake.

"We'll be much better prepared for next year," Lucian said. "We've got Dynamism tomorrow. If our lessons with Khairu are any sign, I don't expect to do too well there."

"I should do well. Dynamism comes pretty naturally to me."

"Maybe you can give me some tips. Or some training."

"Training?" She laughed. "I need my energy for tomorrow." She got up. "Good luck, Lucian."

After they cleaned their dishes, they went their separate ways. He knew he should head to the library to study, but he was too sick and tired. All he wanted was to sleep.

But first, he went to the bathhouse, finding the male side empty. He filled the tub with cold water from the basin and placed it over the flames to warm. He could practice his Thermalism here by warming his water with magic, but he didn't want to drain himself further.

He waited a good fifteen minutes for the water to warm, and then stepped inside. There he soaked for half an hour, luxuriating in the feeling of warmth reentering his bones.

Once done, he headed back to his room to sleep. He could only hope to get enough rest to perform well at the Trial in the morning.

18

LUCIAN DREAMED OF DROWNING. The icy cold of the Ocean of Storms was as real in his nightmares as it had been yesterday. Lucian tossed and turned, finally waking up with his heart racing and a sense of impending doom. His body was burning one moment, and cold as ice in the next. He wanted nothing more than to scream as he closed his eyes, only to see images of his death playing out repeatedly...

A knock resounded from the door. He had no idea what time it was. After hours, conversation between Novices was forbidden. He hurried out of bed to answer.

When he opened the door, Talent Khairu glared at him, seeming to tower over him despite the fact he had a full head and a half on her. Her face was stern, and very Khairu-like.

"Transcend Yellow demands your presence."

Lucian blinked drearily. "What? *Now?*"

"Yes, *now*," she answered, brusquely. "Follow me."

Without waiting to see if he would follow, Khairu led the way. All Lucian could do was shake his head. He was due to have his Trial with her tomorrow. What could she possibly want?

"The Trial," she said, her tone taking on a bit of impatience. "I don't like repeating myself. Would you like help, or no?"

He almost asked if this was even allowed, but he didn't want to call her integrity into question. That was not something a Novice did.

There was only one right answer here. But if anyone got in trouble for it, it would be Lucian.

"This isn't a test, is it?"

She rolled her eyes. "Of course not. It's only fair, seeing as you had to participate in a later Trial today. Your ether won't be as regenerated as your peers."

Lucian didn't buy that, but refusing her outright was a good way to fail the Trial tomorrow. "If you're really offering help, I'd be a fool not to take it. May I ask why, though?"

"That's simple," Transcend Yellow said. "I sense great potential in you. I'm of a mind that that potential should be celebrated, not stymied. True, you haven't been here long, but I've been watching your progress with great interest. Even if what you have done isn't exactly . . . condoned . . . anyone would be a fool to not recognize your potential. That potential might be tempered into something useful under the right hand. Of course, there is what happened on the ship on your way here. Your power is directionless for now. But it need not be. I would not like a repeat of the Gravitonics Trial, and Dynamism is just as dangerous, if not more so." She leaned back, seeming to think for a moment. "Transcend Gray should have given you some help as well, but given his condition . . ."

"His condition?"

She shook her head. "Never mind about that. So, what do you say?"

"I . . . guess that makes sense."

She stood, and with that action, Lucian realized that they were starting right here, right now. "First, stream an energy shield for me, as Talent Khairu has taught you."

Lucian blinked in surprise. "In your office? What if I mess something up?"

Transcend Yellow, in response, pointed to the space before her desk in front of the door. "Take great care then, Lucian. Let my books and artwork serve as a reminder that the Manifold must be handled with care. That is something you should have remembered at the Gravitonics Trial!"

Lucian saw that he would have to do exactly as she said. More than that, he couldn't make any mistake. So it was, under the pressure of her watchful gaze, that he formed his Focus. He still felt drained from the previous Trial, but some ether had regenerated. He only hoped that whatever this training consisted of, that it wouldn't exhaust him too much.

He reached for the Dynamistic Aspect, and per her instruction, streamed a basic energy shield around himself. He'd come a long way in the months since his first training sessions with Khairu. Dynamism was one of his weaker Aspects, but even so, it was passable for a Novice of his short tenure. The thin layer of energy reflected the yellow light cast by the lamps. He held the stream, not daring to let go until Transcend Yellow gave another order. The effort was taxing, but what choice did he have? It occurred to him that she might be *trying* to exhaust him before tomorrow. Maybe she didn't *want* him to pass.

Whatever the case, he knew he was a puppet, and she the one pulling the strings.

Without warning, Transcend Yellow's hands became awash in electrical energy. Yellow sparks flew from her fingers as she slammed her palms into Lucian's shield. The shield fizzled out with a thunderous crack. Transcend Yellow gave a coy smile.

"When I say shields up, Novice," she said. "I mean it. Again!"

Without hesitation, Lucian raised his shield again, streaming his ether much more rapidly, thus producing a stronger barrier. It was so strong that Lucian was confident

Transcend Yellow couldn't make a dent. However, his reserves were draining, and fast. Transcend Yellow watched, a cat considering how she might gut the mouse she'd caught.

When Lucian could hardly hold on any longer, she smiled. "Stop."

Lucian released his stream, and the shield dissipated. "You didn't attack."

"Another lesson," she said. "When in a duel with another mage, the one who runs out of ether first, loses. If you strengthen your shield, but no one's attacking, you will lose. Defend yourself closely, yes. But awareness is the best defense."

Lucian could only wonder when he might *ever* need to duel another mage. He was aware that the Talents did sometimes as practice. It was possible, he supposed, for there to be another mage war, or a battle with a rogue or perhaps even a group of rogues. In that case, he would need to be ready. But it was hard to imagine that day ever coming.

"So, how do I know when the other mage is about to attack?"

In answer, Transcend Yellow's hands became wrapped in electricity. Lucian threw up his own shield to block it. It was a weak attack, sizzling against his barrier.

"Like that," she said. "Watch. Learn. Gain experience. Those things my Talents learn to do very well. Depending on your performance tomorrow, you have the aptitude to be a Yellow Talent."

"But Dynamism is my weakest Aspect."

Her face became a storm cloud of anger. "Don't *ever* say such a thing. *Never* limit your beliefs. You shouldn't be buying into this talk of primaries and secondaries. Some Aspects will be harder to learn, yes, but it's our beliefs that limit us the most, *not* our natural inclinations." She watched him for a moment, letting the point sink in. "Do you understand?"

Lucian nodded. He couldn't get over that she had hinted he

might soon become *her* Talent. That would give Talent Khairu apoplexy. It seemed imprudent to ask her to clarify that, so he did his best to make his face smooth and expressionless. The way Transcend Yellow looked at him, without the trace of a smile, suggested she was quite serious.

"Now," she said, "do you know how to stream lightning?"

Lucian shook his head. "That's too advanced for me."

"There you go again," Transcend Yellow said. "With the Manifold, *belief* makes reality. That is the most basic lesson. If *that* hasn't been drilled into your head yet, this academy has failed you. *Never* say something is *too advanced,* or impossible. Anyone who believes in impossibility *makes* impossibility their reality. Either the sky is the limit, or the limit is the sky." She gave a half-smile. "Which belief is more productive?"

"The first one."

Transcend Yellow nodded. "Now, I ask again. Do you know how to stream lightning?"

"No," Lucian said, "but I would like to learn."

She smiled, as if pleased with that answer. "It's simple. Take all that effort you made into making a shield. Instead, imagine your stream manifesting as a single line of hyper-concentrated magic. Imagine the anchor point in your hand, and the focal point as the object you wish to strike."

Fear twisted in stomach. She *couldn't* be asking him to stream lightning in her office. And he was already so tired, his ether so depleted...

"I've almost exhausted myself, Transcend Yellow," Lucian said. "If I stream any more..."

"*Do it,*" she said, her tone brooking no argument.

There was no arguing with a Transcend, whatever her motives. Transcend Yellow oversaw the Trial tomorrow, and Lucian was likely to fail if he didn't follow orders.

Once again, Lucian reached for his Focus. While he found

it, it felt slippery, a sure sign he was tiring. Would he have enough to stream an unfamiliar Aspect?

"Do I attack you with it, or something?" he asked.

Transcend Yellow nodded, her manner somewhat impatient. "You can't hurt me, Lucian. Do it now!"

With that order, Lucian streamed through his Focus, imagining the Dynamistic Aspect. First came the anchor point of his hand, as instructed. He felt potential building there. Next came the focal point – which he formed right at Transcend Yellow's center. Whatever ether he had left, he concentrated there. But for all that build-up, only a shower of sparks streamed from his outward-facing palm.

"Stop doubting yourself," she admonished. "Let it flow!"

This was too much. If he did as she asked, then he would overdraw, something he was strictly forbidden to do. He released his Focus and shook his head. "I can't. I'm not supposed to go beyond my pool, and if I did as you said, I would."

She looked at him for a long moment, and Lucian was sure she was about to tell him to do it, anyway. He didn't know what he'd do, then.

But in the end, she nodded, though her face seemed disappointed. "Very well. Perhaps I got carried away. I don't wish to overtax you. I just don't want you to limit your beliefs. It would be a shame if you did that." She heaved a sigh that was strangely sad. There was something more going on, but Lucian didn't know what. She returned to her desk and sat. "That will be all, Novice Lucian. Return to your room and get some rest."

It was all Lucian could do not to heave a sigh of relief. "Of course, Transcend Yellow."

Lucian left the office, gently shutting the heavy wooden door behind him. He walked down the corridor, hoping that no one saw him here on the Transcends' level at this hour. He didn't want anyone asking questions.

He only felt safe once he was back in his room. He sat on his bed, wondering if all that had really happened. Why was she going on about his potential? And if that was something she had noticed, had other Transcends noticed as well?

He didn't have the time or energy for such questions. He blew out the lamp and fell into an exhausted sleep.

19

"YOUR STREAM ISN'T STEADY, Novice Damian," Transcend Yellow said, interrupting him in the middle of his Trial. "Any mage with half a brain could cut it off with a Psionic block."

His face darkened as his brow scrunched further in concentration. After his energy shield steadied, Transcend Yellow gave a nod. Talent Khairu stood with shockspear in hand, electricity streaming along its length, flashing a predatory smile. It was the only time Lucian had ever seen her happy – if that terrifying expression could be considered happiness. Through the open archway of the entry hall, the nighttime chill gusted inside.

Khairu charged. Damian cried out as his energy shield ate the impact of the Yellow Talent's shockspear. When the shield collapsed with a sizzle, Transcend Yellow clapped her hands.

"Enough, Novice Damian."

Damian returned sulkily to the line of Novices, his head hung low.

Transcend Yellow nodded at Lucian. "Novice Lucian. You're up."

He stepped forward, feeling slightly guilty over the help

he'd gotten last night. It wasn't like he could have refused it, but it still made him a little sick. Khairu was already twirling her spear. Even if the tip was blunted, the electricity sizzling along its length was all too real. Lucian felt inadequate as he drew his own spear, extending it with a metallic whir. He didn't even bother streaming. Remembering Transcend Yellow's lesson, he needed to save every bit of ether he had just to survive.

For that was the point of this Trial – to last as long as possible against Khairu without "dying." Lucian had the feeling Khairu would go extra hard on him. Because why shouldn't she? Even more so because she had to have suspected the training Transcend Yellow had given him.

Khairu glared, seeming ready to pounce at a moment's notice.

"Spears up, Novice," Transcend Yellow said.

Lucian did so without hesitation, holding the spear out with both hands in a defensive posture. He remembered well how suddenly Transcend Yellow had attacked him the night before, so he began by streaming an energy shield, keeping it as weak as possible to conserve his ether. He could strengthen it at will, once Khairu attacked. It was more efficient on his ether than streaming something suddenly and swiftly.

In his peripheral vision, he could make out Damian's hard stare and Rhea's stony mask.

Khairu launched into her attack. Electricity shrouded her hands and danced along her spear as she swung with far more intensity than she had with Damian. But Lucian was ready, anticipating the blow and strengthening his shield to match. It ate the impact easily, strong enough to make the Yellow Talent grunt and take a step back. She scowled, glancing at Transcend Yellow for further instructions.

"Not bad," Transcend Yellow said. "Shields down."

Lucian released his stream with relief. But as soon as the stream cut off, Khairu attacked again, perhaps at an unseen signal from Transcend Yellow. Lucian tried to raise his shield in time, but he couldn't do so before eating a nasty shock streamed from her spear. It sent him sprawling to the floor. The other Novices gasped in surprise as Lucian rolled a few times, stopped only by a pillar. Anger and shock coursed through his veins. Khairu stood a few meters away, her face gloating. She was all but daring him to get up again.

But Transcend Yellow had not called the match for Khairu, meaning that Lucian wasn't "dead" yet. It was a minor shock, admittedly, something meant to toy with him rather than delivering a death blow. Well, that would be her mistake. With Khairu bearing down on him, Lucian scrambled up, shockspear at the "primus" position, pointed out at a forty-five-degree angle. It was a basic posture, but it was really all he knew.

"Never let your guard down, Novice," Transcend Yellow called. "Not until you're *sure* the threat has passed."

Khairu took a swing, which Lucian easily parried with a clang. He backed away a few steps, granting some space. Khairu smirked.

"It's not fair!" he called. "You *told* me to let my shield down."

"Do you expect things to be fair in a real fight? A harsh lesson, but a lesson you must learn."

Khairu seemed to be waiting for his move. Lucian deepened his Focus. It was time to go on the offense. But before he could attack, Khairu herself came forward, putting Lucian back in survival mode. Her shockspear spun in a wide and powerful arc meant to maim. Before the weapon could connect, Lucian unleashed a primal shout. From the anchor point of his palm, he set the focal point aimed directly at Khairu. Then, he streamed a wild burst of Dynamistic Magic.

A fork of lightning shot right out of his palm directly at Khairu. Her face registered the slightest hint of surprise, but she strengthened her own energy shield just in time. A shockwave rebounded off Khairu's shield, pummeling him and sending him staggering back a few meters. He managed to keep his feet – just barely. It was well that he did, because only a few more meters would have sent him into the central brazier.

His ether reserves were near empty, and he got the feeling Khairu had plenty left. He'd have to play this carefully. As Transcend Yellow had said, the mage who ran out of ether first, lost. Khairu's face was a severe mask as she approached. It was clear she hadn't expected this much trouble – not from a Novice she all but regarded as useless.

Lucian knew she not only wanted to save face. She wanted to put him in his place. And he didn't intend on letting her do that. From the sidelines, Lucian could see the Novices watching open-mouthed, while Transcend Yellow's dark eyes drunk in the sight greedily.

With a growl, Khairu approached, stabbing with her electrically charged spear. Lucian tried to throw his shield up, but it was too weak. He was forced to retreat until his back was hot with the flames of the brazier. He braced himself to make his last stand, setting his spear in a defensive posture. Khairu's dark eyes were superior and gloating as she paced back and forth a few meters ahead of him. She stabbed with a flurry of strikes, each aimed at a different part of his body. Lucian sidestepped the first, and parried the second, while his shield ate the third. She easily sidestepped his counterstrike, grabbing him by the wrist. Lucian tried to wrest free, but her grip was too strong. Next thing he knew, the point of her spear was at his neck while hot flames were at his back. Even if no one had said anything yet, he was undoubtedly dead, and he knew he was expected to yield.

There they stood for a long moment, eye to eye. His back was hot; one more step backward and his robes would be eaten by the flames. But he would not give her the satisfaction of yielding. She scowled, pulling him harshly from the brazier. She turned her back on him and walked away.

He had lasted about twice as long as Damian, so he had that going for him at least.

"Why did you stream lightning, Novice?" Transcend Yellow asked. "Had you not, you might have lasted thrice as long against her."

Her voice wasn't accusing, but at the same time, Lucian found it hard to answer. He could feel the stares of the other Novices, along with Khairu.

"I don't know," he said. "I wanted to win, not just survive."

Transcend Yellow smiled. "But the Trial *was* to survive as long as possible. A bit of advice. If you're going to take a risk like that, you better be damned sure you can win." She nodded toward the line of watching Novices. "Your Trial is over, Novice Lucian."

Lucian hardly paid attention as Rhea and Marcus went through their own Trials. Rhea did well, of course, and even Marcus made a respectable showing, though notably, neither lasted as long as Lucian had. The experience was foreign to him. He was used to being left behind, but outclassing Rhea and Damian was something else entirely.

Maybe Transcend Yellow was right about his "potential." Could it be he might make Talent, where no other Novice had? He couldn't let himself get distracted by such thoughts.

Once they were dismissed, Lucian and the other Novices made their way toward the dining hall. No one said a word until they had rounded the corner, out of earshot of Transcend Yellow and Talent Khairu. Both Damian and Rhea fell in beside him.

"Did you listen to *anything* I said after the Binding Trial?" Damian asked.

"What are you talking about?"

"Don't play coy. You *overdrew*. Don't say you didn't. No Novice can do what you just did."

"Well, it looks like *I* did."

"Yeah, right. I don't know how you did it, but just know that in this place, cheaters never prosper."

Lucian saw that there was no convincing him. "Whatever."

Rhea's voice was accusing. "I'll be honest. You'll be lucky to even stay here after that Trial."

Well, he hadn't asked her opinion, either. Maybe he *had* cheated, but not in the way they thought. Besides, it wasn't as if he had a choice to refuse Transcend Yellow's training. If he told them the truth right now, their heads would probably explode. Then they could lecture Transcend Yellow about fairness, not him.

When they reached the dining hall, the long wooden tables were already filled with Novices. He could only hope they didn't blab about what he'd done, but he didn't have much hope of that. The last thing he needed here was more infamy.

He sat away from his group. By the time he finished eating and cleaning up, he made his way back to the Novice wing. That would at least keep everyone off his back.

Lucian found a warm meditation chamber near his room. He sat on the stones, using a prong to stoke the hearth within. Once settled, he assumed his Focus, allowing time itself to slip away. He went to a place where he felt nothing, physical or mental. That was the only place he could feel peace, and to allow that peace to speed his ether regeneration.

After a long time had passed, he returned to the entry hall, muscles stiff with idleness. He didn't know how long he'd sat quietly, but he felt more refreshed. Outside, from the field of white snow, a storm had blown through during his meditation. The chill spilled in through the entrance. Even the central brazier and torches couldn't take the edge off. Outside, several Novices were sweeping snow off the steps. Lucian would have turned for his room at this point, but he saw Emma among them.

Lucian found a broom and shovel leaning against the wall

and joined the Novices. No longer holding his Focus, it felt as if there were a hole in his consciousness. Something missing. Strange, how something he had so reviled was now a part of him. He reached for it again, and the meditative trance the Focus gave him was something of a buffer against the harsh cold. While the other Novices shuddered and shivered, Lucian worked methodically. Even the despair of seeing how much snow needed to be swept before the night was over couldn't reach him here.

Emma sidled over and began sweeping beside him. "You're working like a droid," she said, her teeth chattering. "You okay?"

"Fine," Lucian said, letting his Focus go. The mental state was meant to strip oneself of all emotions. Useful for streaming and meditation, but not for conversation with a friend. "I'm trying to prepare for the Trial tomorrow."

"Same," she said. "Thermalism is one of my weaker Aspects."

"I'd advise against talking about it."

A few meters away, Rhea swept. If there was anyone who would rat them out to the Talents for breaking the rules, it was her.

"I will say this much," Emma said. "I don't know what will be harder – the Trial or surviving Transcend Red if I happen to make a mistake."

Lucian almost shuddered. His one interaction with Transcend Red hadn't been a pleasant one. There was a spitefulness to her he didn't much like. Unfortunately, he would have to deal with her tomorrow. He had streamed the wrong Aspect during the Gravitonics Trial, so he hoped he didn't commit the same error.

"Well, seems like we're going to have fun tomorrow."

"You have nothing to worry about," Emma said. "In fact, it seems you're making some people jealous."

Lucian had a feeling he knew who she was talking about. "Who?"

"Damian was saying things about you."

He resisted the urge to roll his eyes. "Things like what?"

"Nothing directly accusatory. He's implying you might be overdrawing to pass these Trials. He said no one of your experience level should have been able to last that long against Talent Khairu."

"Well, I did. He's just a sore loser. He can't stand being second to anybody." He looked around to make sure no one was listening. "I'll admit I did overdraw during the Binding Trial. And during the Gravitonics Trial, too, but only to keep myself from drowning."

She stopped sweeping for a moment, as if in shock, before starting up again. Lucian had the feeling she would have had a stronger reaction if there were no one around.

"What were you *thinking*? I understand the Gravitonics Trial, but what happened with Binding? Did Transcend Blue notice?"

He shook his head. "I don't think so. But of course, that'll be impossible to know until the results are in."

"And the Radiance Trial?"

"That was all me. For the Dynamism Trial, Damian's running his mouth. I didn't overdraw."

He felt a tinge of guilt at that. He didn't want to talk about Transcend Yellow's private lesson, but Emma was the only one here he trusted. He couldn't bring himself to lie to her.

"There's something I need to tell you. I'm not sure what to make of it..."

When he told her about the training, Emma's eyes went so wide that Lucian thought they would pop out of her head.

"She summoned *you*?"

"Yeah. That's weird, isn't it?"

She didn't react for a moment, as if processing the news.

Finally, she spoke. "Have any of the other Transcends done the same thing?"

"What, given me private lessons? No."

"Hmm." Her brow scrunched in thought. "She must see great potential in you. But to give you private instruction that would give you an edge on the eve of a Trial? I don't want to question a Transcend, but that's an unfair advantage. Do you think she was testing you in some way?"

"I asked her point blank and she said *no*," Lucian said. "I didn't want to question her. When a Transcend says *jump*, you ask *how high*."

"I understand," she said. She swept a large snowdrift down the steps. "Or when they say sweep out in the cold, you ask *how long*."

Lucian chuckled. "I suppose that's how this all got started?"

"I was minding my own business, walking back to my room to get some sleep. Then, the Talents go through the halls and handed us these." She held up the broom, shaking her head in disbelief. "You'd think we'd get a little leeway with the Trials, but nope."

"I was in meditation, so I guess that's why they didn't bother me."

"Wait. You're here by *choice*?"

"Yeah. I guess."

"You just wanted to hang out with me, didn't you?"

"So, about this Transcend Yellow business," Lucian said. "It seemed like you were going somewhere with that before we got sidetracked."

"It's this. You had a rough start, right? But now, something's changed and people are noticing. You're rocketing past everyone right now, me included. At this rate, you'll make Talent before any of us."

"It doesn't feel that way," he said. "There's still so much I don't understand."

"You might even make Talent this year."

He could hardly believe that. "Remember the Gravitonics Trial? I almost got myself killed."

"Even when you fail, you fail impressively," she said. "Hardly any training in Gravitonics and you make an impressive showing. Most everyone else would have probably died."

She went quiet after that. From her tense expression, it looked as if she had something else to say.

"If there's something on your mind, you can tell me," Lucian said.

"There is. Remember how they seemed hesitant to train you at first?"

Where was she going with all this? "How could I forget?"

"You're proving them wrong. In a big way."

"Am I, though?"

"Maybe you're skeptical, but you have great talent. But those with great gifts are burdened with even greater expectations. It's not only Transcend Yellow who will be courting you to be her Talent. Others will come out of the woodwork soon enough. Especially if you make history as the first one to pass the Trials on the first try."

Lucian couldn't believe what she was saying. "Seriously? I nearly killed myself, and somehow that qualifies me to be a Talent? Someone entrusted with not only learning more, but training the Novices?"

"Wait and see," Emma said. "That might be a bold prediction, but I wouldn't be surprised if it happened. My advice is to keep your head down. If you continue doing well, that might paint a target on your back."

Lucian thought of Damian. "I'll try."

"Just imagine the other Novices' perspective. You work hard, and then someone who's been here less than a year starts overtaking you. It can't be a good feeling."

"No, I guess not."

"If Transcend Yellow is vying for you already, how soon before others start making their moves? They might not even wait until the Trials are over. Why else would she want to help you?"

He knew she had him there. "I'm only a Novice, though."

"In name. You're forgetting Vera. But trust me, *they* haven't."

Vera, who Transcend White said was the most powerful mage in all the Worlds. Yes, there was that minor detail. Lucian had almost managed to put it fully from his mind.

"You have a point," he admitted.

"Of course I do. I'm only looking out for you. Things can get dangerous when you're caught in the crossfire of powerful people."

Lucian felt as if there was a story there, but he didn't get the opportunity to ask.

"We should turn in," she said. "The job's done and we're the only ones still sweeping."

Lucian looked around to see that she was right. The stairs were clean, and the still night had grown even colder.

They went to the central brazier to warm up. Emma watched him from across the flames. He saw worry in her eyes. And something else, maybe. His throat clenched, and he had to look away before old feelings resurfaced. Feelings he had mostly suppressed in favor of his training.

"You okay, Lucian?"

He softened at the concern in her voice. "I'm as fine as I can be."

"Are you sure? It seems we barely talk anymore."

That was what this place did. It was late, and if anyone caught them here together, it would raise eyebrows at best. They should disperse to their rooms, but Lucian didn't want to go.

The truth was, he did miss her. That night on the *Lightsail* on the Ocean of Storms seemed so long ago. Like it had happened to another person.

"Do you ever think about that night on our way here?"

She recoiled a bit at the question. "I do."

"I've been trying to put it from my mind ever since. Some days, I succeed. But other days, I just think about what we've lost."

She went quiet again, but she didn't leave. Finally, she looked up at him. "Such talk is dangerous."

Maybe he didn't care. Maybe he wanted to do things his own way for once. Did the Talents and Transcends really believe that the men and women here forwent all romantic attachment? Now that he thought of it, he noticed Damian and Rhea often looked at each other a hair too long. Maybe it meant something, maybe it didn't. But nothing could ever move beyond looks and the most subtle of flirting.

Not here.

"I hate it." It was all he could manage to say.

Emma came around the fire and touched his arm. That was daring a lot. More than he would have guessed from her, who'd always maintained distance.

She said nothing more, leaving him by the fire. Despite its warmth, all he could feel was coldness within.

20

THE THERMALISM TRIAL WAS ALMOST... *simple*, for lack of a better word. For the sake of show, Lucian feigned struggle as much as the other Novices. Even Transcend Red's nerve-wracking effect wasn't enough to break his Focus or make him slip. She hovered right behind him, practically breathing down his neck. It gave him the creeps.

Damian didn't cast any dirty glances his way, even if Lucian executed the Trial without flaw. Then again, Damian's performance had also been perfect. Rhea aced it, too, while Marcus, who had some training in Thermalism, did well enough. Despite Transcend Red's harshness, it was the most basic one so far. All they had to do was heat a pot of water to boiling, then freeze it, then sublimate it. That last bit was trickiest, but achievable with a high burst of Thermal Magic streamed evenly throughout the ice. Lucian wondered when this would *ever* be applicable to real life outside of heating bathwater, but he was wise enough not to question it.

The next night was the written examination of the Atomicism Trial. Lucian had been studying for it with every spare minute. The questions required detailed knowledge of atomic and chemical theory as it related to Atomicism. Of course, he wouldn't know the results of that test until the Spectrum deliberated. That could take anywhere from a few days to a few weeks, from what he had heard. They considered each Novice in turn, casting votes on who was ready to ascend. In the case of a tie, Transcend White's vote decided the ascension.

That left only the Psionic Trial. Transcend Violet was an enigmatic and reclusive figure that Lucian had only seen once, back when he had been summoned before the Spectrum. The only ones who had access to her were her Talents. That said, Lucian felt Psionics was his strength.

They met in the rock garden, located on the Academy's isolated western cliff face. It was little-used due to its small size, and it had an air of neglect and abandonment.

"The goal of this Trial is simple," Transcend Violet said, in a lilting Scottish accent. Her pale face was serene, with curly black hair falling to the shoulders of her purple-tinged robe. The wind of the courtyard wove through her hair. Age hardly touched her features, besides the shallow crinkles at the corners of her eyes. She was beautiful, in a dreamy way, an effect only pronounced by her sharp blue eyes.

Lucian could hardly believe it was almost over. All he had to do was finish this one out with a bang, and then it would be out of his hands.

She surveyed the Novice group. "I have four large stones here," she said, nodding toward the stones on the ground before them. "One for each of you. Do something with these stones that would impress me, using only Psionic Magic." She looked at each of the Novices. "Who would like to go first?"

"I will," Damian said, without hesitation. Maybe he thought by going first, he would "impress" her.

She stood aside, motioning for the rest of the Novices to take a few steps back as well.

There was a long moment as Damian gathered his Focus.

Then, with a sudden outcry, he thrust his hands forward, palms outward. His stone went rolling toward the cliff's edge, hurtling over the side in a wide arc. He opened his eyes and lowered his hands, his chest heaving with exertion.

Transcend Violet nodded. "Good. Who's next?"

Rhea stepped forward, doing much the same thing as Damian. Lucian's hunch was that she had meant to do it faster and harder, but her stone only rolled more slowly. Damian gave a smug smile, while Rhea shot him a withering glare.

Marcus stepped up next, to Lucian's surprise. He managed to get his stone almost to the cliff before exhausting himself. He shook his head, then went to stand in his former spot.

Now, all the attention was on Lucian. He took a couple of steps forward, until the heavy stone stood a few meters before him. Lucian found his Focus; the action was almost as natural as breathing. Lucian reached for the Psionic Aspect.

He had no doubt he could do this.

They're going to fight over you. Emma's words echoed in his mind. *Being caught in the crossfire of powerful people is a dangerous thing.*

A new thought occurred to Lucian. He could bungle this, and not have to worry about them raising him to Talent all year. That had to be a pointless concern. He wasn't going to make it, anyway. Lucian could feel Transcend Violet watching him closely. If he *did* throw it, would she know the difference? Lucian couldn't answer that. But those gifted in Psionics could often read into another's intentions.

No. He had to give this everything he had.

Holding his Focus, he reached for the stone, latching onto its physicality. Then, Lucian released a rushing stream of Psionic Magic, pushing the stone *up* from the ground.

It levitated in midair, rising higher and higher, faster and faster. Magic tore through him in a torrent. He kept pushing until the stone could hardly be seen in the gray sky above. Within seconds, he'd burned through his entire ether pool.

"Novice Lucian," Transcend Violet said, her voice tense. "That's enough."

But his ether was already exhausted. The stone was falling.

There were screams as the other Novices realized what was happening, jumping out of the way. But before it could land, the stone flew in the direction of the ocean, far out of sight.

Lucian hadn't done that. He opened his eyes to see Transcend Violet glaring at him, her arm extended in the direction of the water. Lucian guessed that this wasn't what she had in mind when she had said to impress her. Damian, Rhea, and Marcus all stared at Lucian in mute shock.

"This Trial is over," Transcend Violet said. "Novice Lucian. Walk with me."

The other Novices cast curious glances his way before heading back into the Academy. Feeling a leaden weight in his stomach, Lucian followed.

She stood close to the cliff's edge. One step or bit of clumsiness was all it would take to make her fall, but from her serene expression, this was far from her mind.

Lucian stood beside her, more than a meter away from the edge of the precipice. She broke the silence.

"What possessed you to do something so dangerous, Novice?"

Her voice was snappish and demanded an answer of him that wasn't a foolish justification. Lucian found himself at a loss for words.

A ghost of a smile spread across her lips. "If you were aiming to impress me, well, you've accomplished that much. If your performance on the other Trials was anything like this. . ."

All Lucian could think about was his failure at the Gravitonics Trial. It was best not to mention it. It seemed Transcend

Violet was separated enough from the day-to-day to not know of his failures.

Emma's warning echoed in his mind. He would need to answer her carefully.

"I was sure you were going to punish me."

"Well, I can hardly do that when I encouraged the behavior." She let out a sigh. "I must admit, I was getting concerned that you would raise the stone too high. Psionic Magic becomes less efficient at distance – at least, active Psionic magic that isn't warded. *That* was what grabbed my attention. Despite the distance, you retained control of the stone, even when it was a good fifty meters above us. I was ready to step in at a moment's notice, and that's why I told you to stop. I didn't want anyone to get hurt."

Lucian nodded. "That makes sense. If I overstepped anything, I apologize."

"You did," she said. "But I can't deny that your powers have developed far beyond what any of us were expecting." She frowned, as if she had more to share, but in the end thought better of it. "Tread carefully, Lucian."

He almost did a double take at the use of his name. It wasn't like a Transcend to be so familiar. But before he could react, she withdrew, heading for the northern path that snaked its way down the cliff.

Lucian stood for a while, feeling a sense of fading shock. Tread carefully. How could he do that when he had no idea what he was even doing?

One thing he was sure of, though. The Trials were over, and with luck, he might get some decent rest from his labors.

21

THE FIRST THING Lucian did after the Psionic Trial was head back to his room to take a well-deserved nap. From the empty corridors and common areas, it seemed most Novices were of a similar mind. He slept so long that he missed dinner.

When Lucian woke up, it was night. He went to the entry hall with a mind to go outside, despite the cold. Psion Gaius, of all people, was Timekeeper. He didn't seem to notice Lucian as he lit the Witching Torch, signifying the last thirty minutes of a Volsung day.

Lucian would have never guessed someone of Gaius's stature would be Timekeeper. Especially during such an important week in the Academy.

Once done lighting the torch with Thermal Magic, Gaius made his way over to Lucian. Lucian lowered his head in supplication, as was fitting for someone of Gaius's station.

"One day, Novice Lucian, you might have the honor of lighting the Time Torches. It could be one day very soon."

His tone was approving, a far cry from his usual dismissive attitude. It took a moment before Lucian could find the right response.

"I'm not worthy of that honor." Before Gaius could say more, Lucian continued. "Are all Talents responsible for the torches?"

"Yes. A privilege it is, though not easy. Each day . . . *Volsung* day, that is . . . a Talent must keep vigil and be Timekeeper for the rest. It's a task too important to entrust to a mere Novice."

Lucian wondered why it was so important. Surely a simple clock would not be too much technology, even for the Transcends. Sometimes, their luddism made no sense.

"So, you haven't slept in fifty-four hours?"

He nodded. "It isn't easy, but when you've done it before, and you've trained your mind, you can forgo the need for sleep. For a time." He stifled a yawn. "My vigil ends at the passing of the Witching Hour. At that point, Talent Khairu will extinguish the torches and begin the vigil anew."

"It doesn't sound like much of an honor," Lucian said, choosing not to filter his thoughts. Talent Gaius seemed in a conciliatory mood.

"It may seem that way on the surface," he said, "but keeping vigil is a rare opportunity to rest. You will one day learn how grueling the Talent training will be, if the Transcends see fit to let you ascend."

Staying up for over two standard days was a *break*? If that was so, then the training must be especially harsh.

"Is it true that no Talent has been raised after their first Trial?"

"That's true. I came close. Transcend White told me herself. It was her vote that decided I needed to train another year." He gave a throaty chuckle. "How angry I was. And how blind. She was right. Sometimes, it's not our abilities that are lacking, but our conception of them. And our maturity."

From the way Gaius was looking at Lucian, he seemed to question Lucian's own maturity. Lucian wondered whether he should share his own misgivings, but decided it was too great a risk.

"I've come a long way," Lucian said. "Not only in my handling of magic, but my attitude. For the first time, I think I'm at peace here. That I could even make a life here."

Gaius nodded approvingly. "That's good, Novice. That is the most important step. A heart that is ready and willing to serve."

A small part of Lucian quailed at that. But it was only a small part. Being one hundred percent sure of something was a rarity. If he could commit himself, he had the rest of his life to figure things out.

"I wish to become a mage of the Academy," Lucian said. "I wish to become a Talent."

Gaius watched him for a moment, seeming to weigh him with those inscrutable eyes. "It's well that you wish that, Novice. For you *are* a mage already. It must be more than survival, for survival is insufficient. It is only when you become a Talent that you will find your true purpose. And when that purpose is found, it does make it easier to endure the hardships."

Lucian's curiosity was stoked at that, but he knew it was prudent to remain quiet about that. "Then I will work hard every day to make it reality."

"I'm pleased," Psion Gaius said. "You should be resting. Opportunities to do so are rare indeed. Tomorrow will be a Day of Contemplation, not only for you Novices, but for the Talents and Transcends as well. There will be as many Days of Contemplation as the Transcends need to decide who ascends and who must wait another year."

"And who leaves."

Talent Gaius nodded. "Yes. And who leaves. Never pleasant, that, but the Academy cannot waste resources on lost causes. This is the way of things."

To Lucian, Talent Gaius didn't sound too sad about that, but it could be that he was inured to reality by now. After two decades here, he'd have to be.

"How long will it take them to decide?"

Gaius shrugged. "Who knows? Sometimes, a day. The longest I've seen is two weeks. Usually, it takes two or three days."

"We should know soon, then."

"That we will. I've heard you've performed beyond expectations. Don't let that go to your head. I thought I would be the first, too." He smiled. "It's not only magic and controlling our stream that the Transcends wish to teach us. There are ethical values, too, patience and humility being foremost. The Transcends err on the side of conservatism when the decision isn't obvious. They've . . . made mistakes before."

"What mistakes?"

Gaius shook his head. "I've said overmuch. Sleep, Novice. If it's food you're after, you must wait until tomorrow. You will learn the results soon, I assure you."

Lucian nodded, and turned to go. When given a direct order by a Psion, one was wise to obey.

Lucian lay on his bed, wondering at the mistakes Gaius had hinted at. It was hard to imagine a Transcend doing such a thing. The Psion might have shared so much because he was sleep deprived. Most saw the Transcends' decisions as inerrant. That *they* could make a mistake was not something much talked about.

Lucian's last thought was whether those mistakes might have had something to do with Vera.

LUCIAN WOKE to a rapping at his door. He couldn't have been asleep for more than a few hours, judging by his grogginess.

He was surprised to see Transcend Blue standing there, of all people. He stared at Lucian shrewdly.

Before Lucian could think to bow, the Transcend was speaking.

"I have need of you, Novice. Follow."

Lucian did his best not to betray any emotion, reaching for his Focus to better control himself. He had expected a well-earned rest, but that wasn't in the cards, at least for now. Lucian followed Transcend Blue down the stone corridor leading to the entry hall, wondering just what it was he wanted.

Lucian wished he'd brought a heavier cloak to wear. Lucian noted five torches lit, with Talent Khairu presiding over them in the corner. There were hours yet before dawn.

"Forgive me, Transcend," Lucian said, "but might I ask where we're going?"

Transcend Blue continued, as if he hadn't heard Lucian at all.

When they went outside, the wind was cutting. Lucian could only hope they weren't out here long. It wasn't until they stood below the boughs of the flame tree that Transcend Blue broke the silence. Whatever he had to say, it was clear he didn't want anyone to overhear it.

"I have an offer for you," he said. "I was quite impressed with your showing at the Binding Trial. In fact, you did quite well on most of your other Trials, too, from what I understand."

Lucian wasn't sure what to say. He remembered what Emma had said and could hardly believe her words were coming true. He had to be careful, here. "You are kind to say so, your Eminence."

Transcend Blue waved a hand, as if to dismiss the honorific. "I'm a very direct man, so I'll cut to the chase. I'm willing to raise you to the mantle of Talent."

There it was, plain as day. Emma had predicted it, but Lucian never expected it to happen.

"I'm nowhere near ready for that," Lucian protested. "Besides, wouldn't I need the votes of the other Transends?"

"Don't worry about that. It is your part to accept this generosity, which I've never given to any other Novice."

Did Lucian's opinion not matter? Clearly, Transcend Blue seemed to think so.

Transcend Blue continued. "This is an opportunity many Novices would kill for, and I assure you, I won't offer it again. *Many* factors impact a decision on who to ascend, and your stars have aligned." He watched Lucian, his wizened face severe. "You would be a fool to say anything but *yes*."

Lucian's shock hadn't dissipated. It was worse because Transcend Blue seemed to want a quick response. And being on a Transend's bad side was a recipe for disaster.

"That's a very generous offer," Lucian said. "I have to ask, though. Why me, and why now? Especially with the Gravitonics Trial..."

"It's clear that your failure there was due to a lack of training. Considering that, you did as well as could be expected. Even better. You have done well in most of the Aspects, in fact. That's a rarity. It's expected for a Talent to choose his Aspect at the end of his first year." He looked at Lucian appraisingly. "If you favor the Blue, my vote is yours . . . along with some personal training in the meantime I only offer to my Psion."

Transcend Blue watched Lucian for a reaction, but he was still too stunned to say much at all. He cleared his throat. "That's a huge honor. At the same time, I'm not sure I'm worthy of it."

"You weary me, Novice." Transcend Blue glanced back at the Academy, as if to see whether they were being watched. "Don't take too long to consider. A couple of days, at most. If I haven't heard from you, well, then I'm afraid my inclination is to vote a different way. You have such great potential in Binding; it would be a shame to lose you to another. It was Binding

Magic, after all, that saw the destruction of that iceberg several months ago."

With a conspiratorial wink, Transcend Blue departed, leaving Lucian open-mouthed and unsure of what to do. Once again, Emma had proved perceptive. Transcend Yellow had already given him personal training, something that would have been unthinkable to him before. Now, Transcend Blue was straight up saying his vote was for Lucian, if he agreed to become a Blue Talent.

But could he really commit to making Binding his chosen Aspect?

Besides, what happened if other Transcends made a similar offer, as Emma thought might happen? Lucian had a lot to think about in the coming days. From what he understood, once a Talent chose an Aspect, it was for life.

He couldn't make this decision without due research. But how could he know for sure in just a couple of days?

It was too much to think about. And yet, Lucian had no choice *but* to think about it.

His very future at the Academy depended upon it.

HE HEADED BACK to the Academy and warmed himself by the central brazier. By this point, some of the early risers were up for nightly meditations. Lucian knew he should be joining them, but he instead headed for the kitchen to help prepare breakfast. No Transcend would intrude on him there.

But breakfast was ready, and eaten, in too little time. He headed to an out-of-the-way meditation chamber, using lesser-used corridors far away from the entry hall and dorms. Once settled in, Lucian sought his Focus and the clarity it brought. It was becoming his refuge, his guide. It reminded him of what Vera had taught him – to seek his path in the heart of silence. He needed that guidance now, and he hoped to find it soon.

Even if he managed to push intruding thoughts aside, he couldn't ignore his unease. His Focus was like staring into a deep ocean, not being able to see anything. The answers were at the bottom, but he also knew countless monsters lurked in the darkness beneath. They were monsters he'd have to fight to discover the truth. His *own* truth. Who was he, and which Aspect was he best suited for? He knew the other Novices would kill to have this problem, but Lucian would have killed to have it go to another.

One thing he knew for sure. He was a mere Novice, and his plans for his own future paled in comparison to those of the Transcends. There was little agency in this place, especially for a Novice. He wondered how many of the Talents got a choice for their Aspect to begin with. He remembered most mages could only use one or two Aspects with any sort of skill. Despite Lucian's growing pains, he was progressing well in *all* the Aspects, more or less. That put him in a unique position compared to others.

Transcend Blue was right in saying many Novices would kill for the opportunity. With only a few words, he might even be the first to ascend.

A female voice spoke from behind. "Novice Lucian?"

He jumped. It was an unwritten rule to never disturb a mage at meditation. It was one of a few times even a Novice could find privacy. But clearly, that rule didn't apply here.

He turned to see Transcend Violet, her blue eyes looking at him as if she wanted something. Her, too?

"Yes, Transcend Violet," he said, standing and bowing.

"Forgive me for intruding. But I have something important to discuss with you. Walk with me."

Lucian followed her to the rock garden, where the gray northern sunlight did little to bring warmth. Transcend Violet seemed inured to the frigid air. Lucian had to suppress his need to shiver.

"Is it too cold for you out here?" Transcend Violet asked.

"A little," Lucian admitted.

"Everyone is inside today," she went on. "This is the best place to speak. Have any of the others... spoken with you?"

Lucian felt himself in a bind as Transcend Violet watched him closely. Those sharp blue eyes didn't seem to miss a detail. He couldn't lie. She was Transcend Violet, after all, master of Psionics. And those hypnotic eyes seemed to be doing more than looking at him. He found himself compelled to answer truthfully, to trust her, even if it was against his interests.

"Transcend Blue did this morning," he said. He meant to keep the next part to himself, but he found himself blurting it out all the same. "He said he'd vote for my ascension if I chose to dedicate myself to Binding."

She gave a bitter laugh. "Did he?" She shook her head, her dark curls swaying with the effort. "Your talents would be wasted as a Binder. Your gifting is with Psionics. Even Transcend Blue must see that."

All Lucian could do was nod politely. But it seemed Transcend Violet expected some sort of response from him. "Why do you say that, your Eminence?"

"I haven't seen *any* Novice control a Psionic stream the way you did yesterday," she said. "Many of my own Talents would be hard-pressed to do such a thing. Did you have training before coming here?"

Lucian realized that none of them knew of his affiliation with Vera – none but Transcend White. He would have to answer with caution. "No, Transcend Violet."

"Remarkable," she said. "I don't believe you. Have you considered his offer?"

"Not yet," Lucian said.

"We begin deliberation this afternoon," Transcend Violet

said. "If you're interested in exploring the full extent of Psionics, then I will vouch for you and come to some sort of agreement with Transcend Blue. Indecision, I'm afraid, will be your worst enemy."

Lucian was surprised at the severity of her expression. This was no game. He had never asked for this, and all he wanted to do was run, but running was hard to do when you were surrounded by thousands of kilometers of icy ocean. He should have bungled the Trial after all.

"What should I say to Transcend Blue, then?" Lucian asked. "Or for that matter, any others who might approach me? How am I supposed to choose *anyone* when I don't know which Aspect is the right one?"

"A fair point," Transcend Violet said. "Allow me to convince you. Transcend White was a Psionic herself. It's often said the Psionics are the most gifted of the mages. And with your potential, you would go farthest with us. Your progress would be swift. Within a few years, you might be good enough to go on expeditions outside the Academy."

Lucian tried to hide his surprise, but he knew doing so was impossible with Transcend Violet. "So soon?"

"Anything is possible," Transcend Violet said, smoothly. "The only limit is your own beliefs and your willingness to learn. I can also offer... *extra* instruction."

Lucian almost choked at that, his mind going to a place it shouldn't have gone. He had he imagined the seductive tone of her voice? The mere idea of it was madness. Before he could even respond, she continued speaking, as if nothing untoward had happened. "As I said, the greatest crime would be to see your potential wasted... *especially* as a Binder."

She seemed to be standing closer to him. He tried to create more space, but it was hard to think straight. He could smell her perfume, a heady aroma that made it difficult to hold onto any thought for long. What need did a Transcend have for perfume? But there was something beyond that. Was she . . . *doing* something to his mind, flaring urges he had learned to repress? The feeling intensified for a moment, until he it felt like was being reduced to a slavering dog. Just as he was about to give his answer, an answer that was beyond all thought and reason, the feeling instantly dissipated as if it had never been. Lucian blinked, bewildered by emotional whiplash.

"There are many things I can teach you," she said. "Magic frowned upon by my colleagues. And yet, always useful to have. After all, you never know when it might come in handy."

Long after she had gone, Lucian stayed behind in the cold, hoping that would clear his head. Whatever she had done to him, *that* was power. Psionics wasn't only the mastery of kinetic magic, but manipulation of the mind itself. It wasn't supposed to be done to other mages – that was against the rules. But clearly, she had violated those rules. Was she trying to send a message, that she could teach *him* to do the same thing? Plenty of male Novices had joked about Transcend Violet in that way, but it was just banter. But this was no game. It was his future.

Now that it was out in the open, the question was, would he accept the offer?

Nowhere was safe. Just when it seemed he was getting his bearings, learning to accept his lot, *this* had to happen. Wherever he went, the Transcends would fight over him.

He just didn't want to get ripped to pieces in the process.

22

OVER THE NEXT FEW DAYS, every Transcend except for White, Gray, and Red approached Lucian. Transcend Yellow gently reminded him of her generosity in giving him extra training. Transcend Green made a friendly offer while Lucian was sweeping the corridor. He said the Greens looked forward to him joining their ranks. He also mentioned several archaeology expeditions around Volsung. If Lucian wished, he could join he and his Talents as soon as the weather permitted. Transcend Orange observed that Lucian had done well enough on the Atomicism Trial and would give him personal lessons as soon as he was ascended. Provided he opted to join the Oranges, of course.

Transcend Gray's disinterest was understandable, given Lucian's performance at his Trial. Transcend Red also wasn't surprising, given her dislike of him. Transcend White, of course, had no Talents herself, only a Psion.

"I don't know what I should do," he said to Emma one day as they walked the back courtyard.

"I would go with the Aspect I'm most suited for, regardless of the politics behind it," Emma said.

"That's the thing," Lucian said. "I don't know *what* I'm most suited for. I used to think it was Psionics, but Transcend Violet seems . . . strange." Lucian hadn't mentioned his suspicions about what she'd done to him. It was so out there that he wasn't sure he would be believed. "Each Transcend thinks I'm best suited for their *own* Aspect. I mean, do *you* even know what you're best at after being here less than a year?"

"No," Emma admitted. "Radiance, maybe? You'll have to choose, though, and let your chosen Transcend know soon."

As the rest of the week passed, the deliberations continued, and Lucian did not get approached again. He knew the ball was in his court.

He took long walks around the island, to better avoid potential confrontations. The Transcends' overtures didn't go unnoticed by the Novices, either. Not every Transcend was as covert as Blue or Violet. Lucian noticed Damian and Rhea distancing themselves. Whispers seemed to take over any time he left a room. Talents were becoming friendlier toward him, even as he felt distance building between himself and the Novices.

Everyone seemed to think an unfair exception was being made for him. Even if it wasn't decided yet, Emma told him there were rumors that he had overdrawn for all his Trials. Which was true in the case of the Binding Trial, and the Gravity Trial if people were going to be nitpicky.

Lucian tried to ignore it. There was little else he could do. Emma was the only Novice who was still friendly to him.

After a standard week, the Transcends were *still* deliberating. And then another. At two weeks of deliberations, it was the longest the Transcends had ever dedicated in living memory. Lucian knew he was the reason. Lessons were put to a halt as every day and night became a time of quiet contemplation.

And then, on the fifteenth day, the Transcends emerged from the Spectrum Chamber. They began summoning the

Novices, one by one, taking about half an hour with each to go over their results.

Rhea was one of the first summoned. She happily announced she was being raised to the Talents. She chose to dedicate herself to the Grays, even if such a decision wasn't necessary for another year. No sooner had she made the announcement, she joined the Talents at their table. Tradition raised an invisible wall between her and the Novices. The change was sudden, and it was clear she had long been ready for her ascension.

The Transcends almost raised Damian, too, at least according to him. He'd only failed two Trials, Gravitonics and Dynamism.

As the days passed, Lucian only grew more nervous. They couldn't get through all the Novices in a single day. Most, of course, failed the Trials. By the time it was Emma's turn, only two other Talents had been raised. She received good marks for an Untested, but the Transcends said she needed more training.

Everyone seemed to be called before Lucian. Something was wrong. That feeling was only amplified as stares and whispers followed him wherever he went.

Eventually, they would summon him to stand before them. Then, he would find out the truth. Would they raise him or not? He hadn't chosen *any* of the Transcends ahead of time. Had Rhea received a similar offer she was being quiet about? Did this happen to *every* Talent?

But then, one full week after the reviews began, only Lucian was left. One day, a few hours after he had gone to bed, Psion Gaius himself knocked on his door, his manner somber.

"You have been summoned by the Spectrum," he said, his voice full of gravitas. "Follow."

The moment of truth had arrived.

THE ORB OF BINDING

The atmosphere in the Spectrum Chamber was tense – even tenser than the last time Lucian was here. The Transcends' expressions were grave, with exhaustion written on their faces. As Lucian walked forward to the central stone dais, he saw that it was not only the Transcends that were here. Each Psion was present, too, except for Psion Yellow, who Lucian knew to be away from the Academy. Khairu stood in her place. None of the Novices had mentioned to expect the Psions. Something was happening. Something different.

And Lucian didn't like it.

They had saved him for last for a reason, and he was about to find out why. The realization made the hairs on the back of his neck stand on end.

"Let this Trial Review begin," Transcend White intoned. The Transcends shifted in their seats, though none looked at him directly. "Novice Lucian, before we Transcends speak, we invite you to give an account of yourself, and why you feel you are ready to ascend to the rank of Talent."

The Transcends watched him like vultures as he cleared his throat. "It's just that, your High Eminence. After much meditation, I've decided that I'm not ready to ascend – should that be the inclination of the Transcends. I respectfully ask that all such consideration be put off until next year, when I'm better able to control my magic."

From the silence that followed, it was as if the air had gone out of the room. Lucian didn't know how much time had passed, but just looking at all those stony expressions made him feel as if he'd made a terrible mistake.

At last, Transcend White relented, and spoke. "Transcend Blue. The floor is yours."

Transcend Blue shifted in his seat, stroking his trim goatee. "Novice Lucian . . . I regret to inform you that you have failed my Trial. Despite an impressive performance, you overdrew. A mage's path is one of discretion and caution. As we iterate constantly, the path of Balance must be walked. Such reckless streaming on your part has been proven to speed up a mage's fraying. Raising you to the mantle of Talent a risk too grave to consider."

The words came as a blow. Even if Lucian had expected that opinion, he didn't expect it to be put in such harsh terms. Apparently, Transcend Blue took Lucian's refusal as a slight. There was no point in defending himself.

But there were six other Transcends who had yet to pass their judgment.

"Transcend Gray," Transcend White said.

"Novice Lucian," he began, his voice raspy, his pallor pale, "you have also failed my Trial. You streamed two different Aspects before identifying the correct one. Your Trial began promisingly enough. But a simple mistake made in ignorance almost saw you killed. It is true you wrested yourself from the situation, but fluctuations in the ethereal field clearly means you overdrew to do so."

"Overdrawing was better than dying," Lucian said, unable to help himself.

The mood in the chamber became icier, several of the Transcends shaking their heads, while Transcend Red smirked.

Transcend Gray frowned before continuing. "If that is your belief, then you should have remained on shore. But in your pride, you deemed yourself adept enough to pass the Trial with little to no training. As such, you have failed. Not only in your failure to complete the Trial, but in your error of judgment."

Lucian bit his tongue. There was a moment's pause as the Transcends regarded him severely.

"Transcend Green?"

Transcend Green stroked his long, white beard. Lucian

relaxed, knowing there was no way he could have failed his Trial.

"You made an impressive showing at your Radiance Trial. However, your stream was not as efficient as I would like for one of my own Talents. It took you too long to find the right frequency during the radio portion. And once you did, you streamed your ether inefficiently. That only proves your inadequacy with Radiance. You have failed my Trial, though I admit you are a mage of great promise."

Transcend Green's tone suggested that Lucian had wasted that promise. What had happened to two weeks ago, when he had all but *begged* Lucian to consider the Greens? Something strange was happening. Lucian had performed as well, or even better, than the other Novices at the Trial.

Something was amiss.

"Transcend Orange," Transcend White said.

"You failed your written examination on the Atomicism Exam abominably," he said. "Never have I seen a worse performance in my thirty years as a Transcend."

Now, how could *that* have been possible? Lucian had studied day and night when he wasn't practicing the other Aspects. But questioning Transcend Orange would only make things worse. He knew that was a complete fabrication, but how could he challenge him? If this was a conspiracy, was there any point?

Had the Transcends come to some sort of consensus, each agreeing to fail him one by one as punishment for rejecting them all? It seemed they had decided that if he hadn't chosen any of them, then *none* could have him.

"Transcend Yellow," Transcend White said.

She looked at Lucian for a long time with a mournful expression, though he couldn't help but feel as if she were toying with him. If she also denounced him, then it would all but confirm his suspicions.

"Despite great promise," Transcend Yellow said, sorrowfully, "I regret to say that you have failed my Trial as well."

She paused, as if giving Lucian an opportunity to respond. That slight smile she wore was simply too much to bear.

"I did well. Anyone there could have said that. I lasted longer than either Damian or Rhea, and Rhea is a Talent now."

"While that is true," Transcend Yellow said, "you would have not passed if not for one thing. There are . . . certain Talents . . . who have come to me, suggesting that you asked them for outside help with your Trial. While all my Talents deny helping you, it seems you knew exactly what to expect. Indeed, you performed *too* perfectly. My suspicions were stoked, and at my questioning, my own Talents admitted it."

"That's a damn lie!" Lucian said. "*You* were the one who helped me, Transcend Yellow!"

"Silence!" Transcend White called. Transcend Yellow recoiled, as if he were a viper, her face a perfect mask of affront.

Lucian's face burned with anger, but there was nothing more he could say. Why would they believe him over one of their own?

Lucian looked at Khairu, desperate enough to ask for her help, even if it was pointless. "You were there, Khairu. You led me to her office the night before the Trial. Speak in my defense!"

She looked at the stones below. "I remember nothing of that nature."

He knew Khairu hated him, but to *this* extent? He then realized that even if she wanted to, there was no possible way she could side with him. To do so would be to defy a Transcend, and that Transcend was also the leader of her Aspect.

"You will stay silent for the remainder of this examination," Transcend White finally said, coldly. "Do I make myself clear, Novice?"

It took everything he had to push down the comeback that

wanted to fly from his lips. "You do. Abundantly, your High Eminence."

He couldn't keep the anger out of his voice, but already, Transcend White was moving on. "Transcend Red."

She gave a knowing smile, so poisonous it marred her beautiful features. "Lucian did well at my Trial. Certainly not the best, but beyond acceptable. He passed."

Several of the other Transcends looked at her, as if she had stepped out of line. She settled back in her seat, smiling primly, her robes and lips the color of blood.

"Transcend Violet," Transcend White said, "you gave Lucian his last Trial. How did he fare in Psionics?"

Lucian only had to look at her sorrowful gaze to know that she, too, was going to fail him. "He began promisingly enough. Until his Psionic stream took things to dangerous levels. I had to step in and correct his lack of judgment." Her face was a mask of severity. "I fail him."

What was the point of protesting? He was a mere Novice. What was his word against theirs? If he outed them right now about their offers, they would flat out deny it. The truth didn't matter, here. But why were they going so far, even to the point of lying, to cast him in the worst possible light? Why not just tell him he wasn't ready to be a Talent, something he himself agreed with? They could have simply failed him. Only they hadn't.

They had gone far beyond that.

"As spoken by the Spectrum," Transcend White went on, "you have failed the Talent Trials. Normally, this is where the hearing would end. But we have further business with you." She clapped her hands twice. At the signal, the Psions exited the chamber, leaving Lucian alone with the Spectrum. Their manner, if anything, grew even colder.

"Novice Lucian," Transcend White said, "your negligence is a great affront to this academy. We have seen your great potential. But that potential has corrupted your mind. Once before, we were blind to these things. Once before, we chose poorly. Our academy was broken in two, and the Mage War began. Only I, Transcend Gray, and Transcend Green remember those dark days. Far be it from us to ever repeat that tragedy." She rose, and pointed a long, gnarled finger, her face a thunderstorm of anger. "You are no longer a Novice of this academy. Considering what has been said here, and considering malfeasance we've let slide until now, we strip you of robe, title, and spear. You are expelled forthwith from the Volsung Academy. We sentence you to exile on the Isle of Madness, where you will await transport to the prison moon of Psyche." She sat back down, her features losing none of their intensity. "All in favor, let your voice be heard."

"Aye," came the single, unified response.

That horrifying, discordant sound was like the utterance of a demonic beast, shattering Lucian to the core. His lips moved, but no words came. He didn't know where to begin. "Can I say nothing in my defense?"

"This is not a trial, but a sentencing," Transcend White said. "Your trial was every day you lived and breathed in the Academy. But now, you are to leave this place forevermore. And you are to leave immediately."

"Wait a minute..." he began. "All of you lied to me. This is a conspiracy against me!"

But it was already too late. At some unspoken signal, the Psions returned. Gaius, along with the swarthy Psion Gray, a man named Usban, grabbed hold of his arms. Others he recognized, like Psion Isaac and Talent Khairu, waited in the wings.

"Will you come peaceably?" Psion Gaius asked.

Lucian tried to tear himself away. "This isn't fair. All of you are traitors! Vera was right about you!"

He was already damned, so there was no reason he couldn't damn himself further. And if anything would influence them, it was that. Clearly, the Transcends recognized that name, because their expressions were as if he'd doused them with ice water. Even Transcend Red's face was one of shock.

But Transcend White's eyes smoldered. "Enough. Take him away, Psion Gaius."

A pressing force surrounded him, pushing into him. He reached for his Focus, and while he found it, something blocked his access to his ether. Somehow, they had cut him off. He thrashed about, but with seven Psions, plus Talent Khairu, there was nothing he could do but accept his fate.

"They're lying," Lucian said. "All of them! All of them tried to make a deal with me."

Gaius leaned forward and whispered in his ear. "Do you not remember? I *told* you to tread carefully. And it would seem you've fallen through the ice."

Lucian screamed, but that scream was cut off with a sharp pain in his head, followed by a loss of consciousness.

23

HE AWOKE in darkness to the creaking hull of a boat. His head felt as if it had been hit with a hammer. A groan escaped his throat. The floor below him rolled, making it hard to sit up.

No, not floor. *Deck.* Rough wood ran beneath his numbed fingers. What was he doing here? He bit back the scream that wanted to tear from his throat. He fumbled along the curved side of the ship. The wood under his hands was cold as ice. For good reason – centimeters on the other side was the wintry Ocean of Storms, almost certainly laden with copious icebergs as the sea was freezing over.

They were taking him out to sea *now*?

It was impossible to tell how much time had passed since the Trial review. All he knew was that it was dark, and it was cold. The only light came from a crack in what had to be a door. Shadow blocked part of the light. A person standing guard?

Whatever the case, he was here. And there were eight of them, and one of him, and his ether was blocked.

Not just long odds, but *impossible* odds. And even if he did try something and managed it, he would find himself in the middle of the icy ocean. But he had to try *something*, because if this was happening, there was only one outcome.

And Lucian did not want to go to Psyche.

Feeling his way around a bit, he realized he wasn't in one of the cabins. A cargo hold, maybe, or a sequestered space within the cargo hold. His area was small, though larger than the brig on board the *Burung*.

"You awake?" The voice was muffled through the door. Lucian couldn't tell who it was, but for some reason, he thought it might be Psion Gaius.

"I'm here," he said. "Who're you?"

The door opened, much to Lucian's surprise, revealing a white-robed figure holding an oil lamp. It was Gaius, then. While the light emitted was dim, it was blinding to Lucian's eyes. He threw up a hand to block the aura as the figure approached, scraping a crate from nearby to sit on. As Lucian's eyes adjusted, he could make out two more shadows in the corridor beyond the open door. No chance of escape, then.

Gaius set the lamp down and regarded Lucian in silence.

"Let me ask again," Lucian said. He straightened himself so he could address his captor on somewhat equal terms. "Why are you doing this?"

Gaius turned his head, nodding to the two figures in the corridor beyond. They withdrew.

"A bit risky, to be alone with a dangerous individual like me," Lucian said.

"You *are* dangerous," Gaius said, coolly. "Make no mistake. Trust me, it never gives us pleasure to do this."

Lucian had trouble believing this was reality. "Where are we going? I'm clearly on the *Lightsail*. What is this Isle of Madness?"

Gaius looked at him, his face incredulous. "You really didn't see this coming, did you? This wasn't the end I imagined for you. I can help you make sense of it. It's the least I could do."

Lucian bit back the pithy remark that had been forming on his lips. This might be his only shot of understanding what was happening, and why. He couldn't squander it. So, he nodded and remained silent.

"Usually when a mage is exiled, it's because they don't have enough talent," Gaius began. "In your case, it's the opposite. They *fear* you, Lucian. And if you give them signs that you can't be controlled, they mean to destroy you before you can ever become a threat."

"What do you mean, they *fear me*?" The idea was ridiculous. "So, my only crime was progressing *too* quickly?"

"In a way. They might have permitted that, had you played their game." He seemed to think a bit before continuing. "Transcend White lets me into her counsels. She told me as much before making the decision. She was hesitant of accepting you in the first place, as I'm sure you remember. You knew you were facing a mountain from the very beginning. All Novices do, of course, but yours was twice as high, and thrice as treacherous. Worse, this was not told to you outright, and could only be discerned from subtle clues." He shrugged. "The purported reason for your exile is your abuse of the Manifold in the Trials. But of course, that's not the real reason. You had a choice – seven choices, actually, if we're including Transcends Red and Gray, who might have accepted you had you shown initiative."

Lucian watched Gaius's stubbled face and square jaw, profiled by the dim lamplight. The Psion wore an amused smile.

"Seven choices, and you told them your answer loud and clear with your silence." He chuckled. "It's the Psions' duty to escort exiles to the Isle of Madness, where they await transport to Psyche. Usually, only one or two is all it takes. The Transcends saw fit to use all they could spare. Your one chance was committing yourself to an Aspect early. By doing so, you would have fallen under that Transcend's protection. And they would

THE ORB OF BINDING

have guarded you, quite jealously. But if you would have none of them, then none had a reason to protect you."

"The Transcends are supposed to be above such pettiness," Lucian said. "What did I do, wound their pride?"

"No," Gaius said. "As a practical matter, they don't see a place for you anymore. They are . . . cognizant of the dangers represented by a mage with as much potential as you. Long ago, they chose to cultivate someone of similar ability who refused to play their games." Gaius shook his head. "It didn't turn out well. For anyone."

"I know," Lucian said. "Vera. Transcend White's twin."

From Gaius's lack of surprise, it was clear he knew about her. He wasn't lying about being deep in his Transcend's counsels.

"No, Lucian. She was talking about Xara Mallis . . . Vera's *Psion*."

The words Gaius spoke seemed to be a different language. Xara Mallis had been Vera's *Psion*? What had happened sixty years ago at the Volsung Academy? Had Vera been a Transcend then, along with her sister? And did Vera leave with Xara to lead the Free Mages in the war six decades ago?

"I'm not like Xara Mallis," Lucian said, feeling lightheaded at such a revelation. "That *can't* be the reason. Can it?"

"You don't think so? Once upon a time, I would have agreed with you. But the days are dark for mages. Fifty years since the war, and we are no closer to curing the fraying than we were back then. The last thing the Transcends want is for another one like her to rise. The League couldn't survive it . . ." He shrugged. "So, they err on the side of caution. If there's even a ten percent chance you're the next Xara Mallis, they won't risk it. No matter your potential."

"But I wouldn't do *anything* like her. It's unfair."

"That's where you're wrong. You received training, however briefly, from Vera herself. And Transcend White *hates* her sister. If there's any wonder at all, it's that they didn't send you to Psyche right away. No one knows what instigated Vera and Xara to leave the Academy. But it's thought Vera's influence began Xara down that dark path. And Vera has been missing for so long, that until *you* showed up, Lucian, many believed her dead. Not Transcend White, though. Never her."

Could such a thing be true? If she was believed dead, then that meant Vera had recently come out of hiding. For what purpose? None of it made any sense. And none of it mattered, anyway. Lucian would be spending the rest of his days on the Mad Moon, assuming he could make it on this so-called Isle of Madness. The name didn't sound promising for his survival prospects.

Lucian should have picked somebody – *anybody*. Even Transcend Red would have been better than the hell he would soon face.

He had been such a fool.

"I suppose it's too late to change my mind."

Gaius nodded. "That it is, I'm afraid. Even if they accepted you back, you would always be the one they almost consigned to Psyche. And they would fear your retribution, however much you tried to smooth things over."

"Why are you telling me all this?" Lucian asked. "What's the point?"

Gaius shrugged. "Do my reasons matter? I admit, what has happened to you is unprecedented. I've never seen anything like it in my life. Usually, all the exiles are shipped off at the same time. But Transcend White made it a special point to send you off immediately." Gaius eyed him critically. "You don't seem dangerous, but looks can be deceiving. The Transcends see things far beyond the capabilities of one such as me."

"You overestimate them. They're fallible, Gaius. If you had eyes, you would see that." Gaius didn't respond to this point.

Lucian continued. "If the Transcends were never questioned, then what's there to keep *them* in check?"

"Well," Gaius said. "I suppose you can get away with speaking such things, since you have nothing to lose. Of course, the Transcends aren't infallible, but more often than not, they are right. They were raised for that very reason."

The two lapsed into silence for a long time. There was nothing but the creaking of the hull, swaying in the dark water, and the rush of water outside the hull.

"What is the Isle of Madness?" Lucian finally asked. "I figured those bound for Psyche would be sent directly to the spaceport."

"No," Gaius said. "Things are not done that way. The Isle might be the most desolate, remote, forsaken place on all Volsung besides the ice caps. Escape is impossible. There are several thousand kilometers of ocean between it and the Ostkontinent. Unless you intend to waterwalk that distance, then you will be stuck there until a prison shuttle arrives to convey you to a prison barge."

"And that barge will take me to Psyche?"

"One day, yes. The barges make a circuit around the League. When it comes to Volsung, a shuttle will descend to the Isle directly. It could be days, weeks, or even months from now. But one day, it will happen."

"Is there food, water, and shelter at least? You said this place is remote."

"The ocean currents keep the island somewhat warmer than most places this far north. There are edible plants, and even game and fish. That said, it will be quite cold. There are warm springs, and cabins built in the middle of the island. We'll be giving a supply of food to start you off with, along with a survival handbook in case the shuttle is late."

"How kind of you." At Gaius's smug expression, Lucian's face twisted with disgust. "You're *enjoying* this, aren't you?"

Gaius rose from his crate, and regarded Lucian in silence, his expression unreadable. All Lucian wanted was for the White Psion to leave him be. Lucian reached for his Focus; like yesterday, he could assume the tranquility with ease. But he couldn't find his ether. How had they cut him off? The thought crossed his mind that it was permanent, but that was too horrifying to imagine. But if that were the case, then they wouldn't have needed eight mages to escort him to the island. That meant he would gain access to his ether once they left him.

"How much longer until we get there?" Lucian asked.

"Soon," Gaius said, turning for the door. His expression became distant, and for a moment, his lips moved as if he had something more to say. In the end, however, he shut the door, leaving Lucian in cold silence.

24

LUCIAN JUDGED that several days had passed, though of course, it was impossible to tell in the dark hold. The hull creaked so much that Lucian was afraid it would rend. He half-expected the siding to give way and for dark ocean water to immerse him in an icy tomb. Then again, that might be a kinder fate than what awaited him on the Isle of Madness. Still, he sat as far as he could from the siding, huddling for warmth.

They fed him at regular intervals. The food was much the same as back at the Academy, so he suspected he was eating the same meals they were. It was hard to keep them down, though, with the rolling of the waves. Apparently, winter didn't mean calmer weather on Volsung. Even if the ship were being perfectly steered by some computer program, didn't it stand to reason that with enough icebergs, that might not even matter?

At least Lucian didn't have to watch the journey. But that left him with nothing to do. He asked for a light and something to read, but he was denied. He replayed his actions and the Transcends' judgment, over and over. He should have just gone with one of them, any of them. But back then, he would have never dreamed this would be his fate.

Anger burned within him. Anger, and regret. Mostly at himself for even coming to this place. There had been another option, after all.

Thinking about Vera was worse than useless. Besides, what did he expect? For her to rescue him after refusing her training, even if against all odds he managed to break the Psions' block and forge a Psionic link across lightyears of space?

No, he'd dug his own grave. Stupidly. And now, he would die for it.

He drew his legs close and buried his face in his knees. For what seemed the hundredth time, he formed his Focus, but there was no ether to reach for. Someone always seemed to be standing guard outside the door.

It went on like this for a while. The only time the door opened was for meals, or for a Psion to have the unlucky task of relieving his chamber pot.

By now, everyone at the Academy would know what had happened to him. He'd lost everything – his place in the Academy, his mother, and now, even his freedom. And he had lost Emma. Thinking of her was a painful thing. What stories were they telling back there? Would she believe them?

He should have cried, and in fact, he *wanted* to cry. But all he could feel was numb.

There didn't seem to be any reason to go on. His only hope, the Academy, was now gone.

Sometimes Gaius would talk to him, but never about anything serious. Lucian only wanted him to go away.

But one day, Gaius opened the door, setting down a worn canvas backpack that seemed quite heavy. Lucian looked at it cautiously.

"Inside, you'll find a book on edible flora and fauna that can be found on the island. There are survival tips, too. Of course, you'll have your magic back. You should be able to stream as soon as we've pulled away from the island. You may need to survive on your own for a while – at least until the shuttle comes."

Lucian remained quiet.

Gaius looked at him almost pityingly. How Lucian *hated* that. "I'm sorry for the way it happened."

"I don't want your condolences."

Gaius pursed his lips. "Very well. Well, the pack is there. You have provisions for a week, a pot and utensils, among other things you'll find useful. We try to make it out here every couple of months to drop off supplies if the shuttle hasn't come through."

"I don't know why you bother. Why not take me to the nearest cliff and push me off?"

Gaius' expression was grave. "Certainly, some choose that option. Were it me . . . well, I suppose there's no harm in saying it. Suicide is a legitimate choice. It's what I would do, and what many mages choose for themselves if they know the fraying is taking them." He chuckled darkly. "You realize Transcend Gray has it? No one speaks of it, but it's plain as day. The rot seems to have only affected his skin, but it's only a matter of time before it warps his mind."

Yes, he had always looked rather sickly. "And yet, you let him stay there where he can be a danger. Funny how justice falls more swiftly on the powerless."

"I don't deny that. Of course, you're young and may want to live still. In that case, you must wait for the shuttle. Who knows? Life might be worth living, even on Psyche. The will to survive is an amazing thing."

"I don't need your lectures."

Gaius stood there a moment longer, as if he had something more to say. In the end, he shut up and bolted the door behind him.

As much as Lucian was afraid of the future, it would be good to get out of this stinking hold. He would be outside, free to walk around as he wished. No doubt the Isle of Madness would be inhospitable, but at least he would be free to do as he pleased within its bounds.

At least until he died.

But Lucian didn't plan to die. He would find a way off that island, and if it came to it, a way off Psyche, too.

It wasn't likely, but he wasn't going down without a fight.

When the door opened again hours later, Lucian had hardly slept a wink. But the vessel had come to a stop. The Psions filed in, along with Khairu, who all stood next to Gaius with solemn expressions. What would they do, he wondered, if he sat here and didn't move a muscle? Something told him it wouldn't matter. They would chuck him out into the ocean if that was what it took.

"Think about it," Lucian said, finally. "All eight of you, the Transcends' chosen, taking days of your time to move me here." He chuckled. "A massive waste, isn't it?"

None of those stony masks responded, though he thought he could see Khairu glowering. The light was too low to be sure.

"You *are* dangerous," Gaius finally said. "And we trust the Transcends' judgment." He nodded toward the open doorway, leading into the corridor outside. "The weather is good today, but we expect a storm a few hours from now. We're putting you off in daylight, but that too will be gone in about ten hours. There's a trail leading inland from the beach. If you walk fast enough, you should make it to the cabins by nightfall."

"All right, then. I can see myself out."

He hoisted the pack onto his shoulders, and tried to put on a brave face, even if all he wanted to do was scream. He'd already gone through the bag's contents and was surprised to find a collapsed shockspear in there. He was sure having it now was against the rules. He looked at Gaius, who stared at him with a neutral mask. Had *he* put it in there? If so, why?

Of course, the opportunity existed for one last-ditch effort for revenge. But Lucian knew it was pointless. The Psions were only following orders and fighting back would do nothing but secure his immediate death. The fact that the spear was in his bag told him there were dangers on the island, and he might need to face those dangers with more than his bare hands and limited knowledge of magic.

He felt their collective gaze pressing on him as he walked into the corridor. The Psions parted to give him space. The gray daylight from the bridge, though dim, was bright to his eyes. Through the windscreen lay the endless expanse of the Ocean of Storms under a slate gray sky. To his left was the island – larger than expected – stretching far in both directions. Several rocky hills rose farther inland, and the sky in that direction was blue. Judging from the position of the sun, they were on the island's south side. There was no discernible vegetation. Even Transcend Mount had trees on its lower reaches. Perhaps they were even farther north than that.

When Lucian walked onto the deck, the icy wind only confirmed that suspicion.

"Lucian?"

Gaius handed him a thick parka and snow pants, both heavily furred. Lucian doubted that fur was real, but it certainly looked warmer than what he had on.

"Take it," the Psion said. "Just in case."

Lucian put down his pack and threw on the heavy layers. The Psions gave him some thicker winter boots, thermal underwear, and fur-lined gloves. Even if Lucian was being sent into brutal conditions, he saw the Psions did not intend for it to be a death march. For the first time, he realized they really did want him to survive long enough to see Psyche.

It was either mercy or torture. It was too early to tell.

Lucian took a ladder down to one of the rowboats, where four male Psions, including Gaius, rowed him to the rocky shore. As a test, Lucian probed for his ether, but it was as absent as it had been on board. It was clear the Psions were leaving nothing to chance. The rest of the Psions, along with Talent Khairu, watched from the deck. He met Khairu's gaze for a moment. He expected a smirk, but all he got was a stony stare.

When Lucian stepped out into the surf, not a trace of water entered his boots. Good quality, then. As soon as he was ashore, the Psions pushed off, without so much as a good luck or a goodbye.

He stayed on the shore a few minutes, watching them row back out. He reached for his Focus, not finding it any easier to stream. He supposed he could wait until he felt his ether again, and take a parting shot at the last minute. But the fact remained that there were eight of them, and one of him, and they likely knew how to defend against any such attack.

Besides, that wasn't who he was. He wasn't mad. Not yet.

He walked down the rocky shoreline, scanning for the trail. It didn't take long to find a set of steps carved into the hillside. He made his way toward it, climbing hand over hand. It took about ten minutes to crest the first rise. He scanned the surrounding landscape, finding it bare, gray, and almost lifeless. There was some pink lichen, coated like paint over some of the rocks. Those rocks varied in size from his fist to the size of a house. This broken land made it seem as if a giant's fist had slammed it from the sky. There was nothing resembling a tree, or even a shrub. Ice entombed most of the shoreline. The place they'd rowed him in was one of the few places that was ice-free, while the sea itself was filled with icebergs. If they had waited another week, *Lightsail* might have made the journey in hover mode.

Toward the north, the gray land stretched all the way to the horizon. The trail, at least, was clear of rocks and debris. It was then that Lucian noticed one of those odd-shaped rocks *moving*. A crablike creature with a long, stalky neck scuttled sideways and hid in a crevice. Maybe he could eat those, he wasn't sure. He hadn't been able to read the survival guide in the darkness of the cargo hold.

He looked back at the ocean. In the distance, he could see the ship's sails full, pulling away with surprising speed. When he reached for his Focus, he found it easily – as well as sensing his ether. Despite the situation, he heaved a sigh of relief.

Lucian continued his way inland, walking as fast as he could. The sooner he reached shelter, the better.

25

AFTER A COUPLE of hours of walking, daylight was already failing. The sun had hardly shown itself above the south-western hills. Now, it was dropping back down. The wind blew cold, carrying with it small bits of sleet, even though there was no snow on the ground. Strangely, the rocks were warm through his thick-soled boots. At first, he thought it was all the walking, but when he knelt to touch the ground, it confirmed his suspicions. It wasn't exactly *warm*, but it was warmer than it should have been. It had to be ten degrees below freezing out here, if not colder.

It was only after cresting the next hill that Lucian saw where all the sleet was coming from. A solid wall of white mountains expanded from east to west beyond the horizon. It was hard to judge the distance, but Lucian thought at least twenty kilometers.

After walking for several hours, Lucian paused by a still pool to fill his canteen. He wanted to drink it straight, but he knew that wasn't a good idea. The water was lukewarm – how was that possible? Given the temperature, it should have been completely iced over. If it was due to geothermal energy, that might mean there were harmful chemicals. But he hadn't had anything to drink all day, and his thirst won over good sense.

He retrieved the pot from his pack and filled it. He reached for his Focus, extending his hand to release a steady stream of Thermalism. For the first time in his life, he was streaming in the real world, and not as part of some training or test. Despite the situation, he found he liked the feeling.

His hands emitted a subtle red glow, and within a matter of seconds, steam curled from the top of the water. A few seconds later, it was boiling. He let the water go for a couple of minutes before drawing the heat out with a reverse stream. He went too far – it began to ice over, forcing him to reverse the stream again. It felt nice to not have a Talent watching over his shoulder, criticizing his every move.

When he was confident that the water was room temperature, he filled his canteen with it. It had a gritty, metallic taste. Hopefully, there was nothing in it that could poison him. He supposed he would find out soon enough. He had to get his water from *somewhere*, and all he had seen so far were these pools.

He continued walking, the land darkening. It wasn't dim enough yet to need a light orb, but it was getting there. The trail grew rougher the deeper inland he walked. Even if Gaius had told him he was alone on the island, he got the sense he was being watched. Lucian remembered that the Transcends had exiled one of the Tested just a few months back for not meeting benchmarks – a Novice by the name of Katya. Could *she* still be here? There were too many stray boulders, clefts, and cliffs that someone could easily hide behind. If there were someone – or something – out there, he'd have no way of knowing.

He remembered the shockspear then, retrieving it from his bag and extending it. It gave a metallic whir and he used the weapon as a walking stick. He continued at a faster pace than before. At this rate, he might not make it to the cabins before nightfall. Perhaps they no longer existed, or he had taken the wrong trail.

But it was at the top of the next hill that he found what he was looking for. Below was a valley with a ring of five stone cabins at the bottom. They were shabbily made, with flat, earthen roofs and no windows, slightly lowered into the ground. The trail led to the center and died away. There was nothing but those cabins, sitting low in the gathering gloom. Lucian almost didn't want to go down there. But where else would he sleep tonight? Certainly not out here, among the rocks where anything might be lying in wait.

He hurried on, trying to will away his nervousness. Within ten minutes, he was in the middle of the cabins, looking at them one after the other. All the doorways were wide maws of darkness that could be hiding anything.

"Hello?" he called out. "Anyone here?"

Lucian streamed a light orb. It was too bright, so he slowed the stream until it was the right luminosity. As he walked, he also streamed a simple binding tether to the orb, so it would follow him. As he approached the first cabin, he set a focal point for the orb inside the cabin. No way he was going in there without a light first. The orb floated over his shoulder, illuminating the interior.

There wasn't much. A cot with some furs, a bare earthen floor, a stone table. A smooth rock next to it served as a stool. Dust and gravel lined the floor. The wind and elements had made a real mess of the cabin, over a period of weeks or even months. The door hung open, weather-beaten and wide open. Ice encased the hinges, having frozen the door into place.

He withdrew from the cabin and made a survey of the rest, finding much the same thing. In one, he found the chitin shell of some many-legged animal, as if it had sheltered and molted there. In another, the cot had been overturned and the stone table split clean in two. The others were intact, but the last one was pungent with the smell of spoiled meat, even if there was no clear source for the rot.

Lucian chose the fourth cabin. He didn't see any water source, so he used his canteen to make a stew out of the food in his pack. He used magic to warm up the pot every few minutes, before realizing that wasn't a wise use of ether. It would be much better to find some fuel for a fire, and to keep it maintained. That was, if he could find anything here that burned.

He ate quickly, finding there was nothing to keep him busy after. Outside, the wind blustered against the stones. Some of the draft entered through the cracks, chilling him.

He went to the cabin's hearth, finding nothing but ashes. That told him that *something* on this island could be used for fuel. There were no trees, at least not that he had seen. Could the fuel be that lichen that seemed to cover everything?

He went outside, and after a few minutes, gathered an armful of it, the browner bits that were clearly dead. The stuff was surprisingly heavy, so he hoped it burned a long time – if it burned at all. He threw it in the fireplace, forming his Focus once again. He reached for the Thermal Aspect, hoping the stuff would catch.

After just a few seconds of concentrated heat, the lichen caught quite well, to his surprise. Unfortunately, it had a nose-scrunching sulfurous smell. He would have to choose between staying warm or the constant smell of flatulence. With the frigid weather, the answer was obvious.

The door was still stuck open from the icy hinges, so he had to stream again to warm them. Only then could he shut the door against the cold night. He hacked at the smell and could only hope it wasn't poisonous. He fed the flame and judged what he had on hand should see him through the night. He was already getting used to the smell and having the warmth of the fire felt good.

He peeled off his gloves and warmed his hands as the wind howled outside. Looked like that storm was blowing through. He wondered who had built these little hovels – the mages of the Academy, or the castaways they had sent here? Something told him it was the second option.

He busied himself with tidying the cabin, such as he could. Anything to keep thoughts at a distance. He straightened the cot and the furs on top. Unfortunately, there wasn't so much as a broom to sweep away the dust and pebbles strewn about. He ended up using his hands and collected quite the pile of debris over the next hour near the door. Once done, he opened it and pushed the pile out.

He washed his hands off with some water from the canteen, which left him only a few mouthfuls. He should probably use his water for drinking only. It was a half hour hike back to the nearest pond he'd passed, so there had to be something closer. It wouldn't make sense to build cabins here if there were no water source. Wherever it was, it would have to wait until morning. However long away *that* was.

The furs on the cot had a rank smell, but if his nose wasn't too close, it was manageable. He lay on top of them while remaining fully clothed. He wanted to be ready for anything. These furs didn't seem synthetic, so they had to have come from *something*. In his short time on the island, he hadn't seen any large mammals. Then again, previous exiles might have brought them here, too.

Lucian got up, to make sure the door was well and truly shut. Only then did he return to his cot, placing his shockspear, still extended, by his bed. When he closed his eyes, unwelcome thoughts returned. Loneliness was a knife tearing him from the inside out.

When he fell asleep, he was tormented by nightmares. The wind kept waking him, and the isolation was unbearable. It permeated his entire being, as if he were at the bottom of the ocean again. He reached for his Focus, to better not feel that sorrow, but it did little good.

No one was here. No one could hear him cry. His mother was dead, Emma was back at the Academy, and the new life he had been coming to accept had been snatched away. Within weeks, or even days, he would be on a prison barge to Psyche.

Assuming he didn't die here first.

The sobs were small at first, but they soon became gut-wrenching. They tore through him so hard that he was in physical pain. He had never known such darkness, such horror. It was like standing at the event horizon of a black hole, one foot in, one foot out, the gravity ripping him to his core.

When he couldn't mourn anymore, only numbness remained.

A cold thought struck him. Was the shockspear really for his protection, or to make a certain decision . . . easier? The shockspear was Gaius's solution. Placed to the head or neck and streaming at himself would ensure he'd never have to endure Psyche.

Lucian took the spear by the handle. Its carbon alloy point was incredibly sharp, forged by Thermal and Atomic Magic. He didn't even need to stream electricity. It would cut him sure and true, and within minutes, he wouldn't have to deal with this anymore.

He remembered then something his mother had told him:

You must always hope, Lucian. No matter how dark it gets, the human spirit can push through as long as it finds a silver lining and clings to it with everything. Never forget that.

He didn't know if he would find a silver lining, but one thing he did know was that he needed to try, if only for his mother's memory. It was the only thing he had left. She had never raised him to give up.

"I'll try."

It was all he could manage to say. He placed the spear next to the cot, rolled over, and went to sleep.

26

WHEN LUCIAN AWOKE, the fire had burnt out and the wind was howling even more fiercely. Lucian stoked the fire, throwing on more of the lichen while streaming Thermalism thinly to get the blaze going. He coughed at the sulfurous stench.

Lucian cracked the door, only to see snow blowing sideways in the darkness. Even if that weather was cold beyond cold, nature called. He only made it a few steps into the storm to relieve himself before rushing back inside to warm himself by the fire. He used the rest of his water to make another soup, setting the pot over the fire this time to conserve his ether. As it cooked, his stomach growled at the savory aroma.

He took the pot off the flame and set it on the stone table. In the cold air, it cooled rather fast. It was bland with no spices, but the warmth and sustenance were welcome. He hoped this blizzard didn't last long. If it went on for days, he might run out of food. He needed to be out there now, seeking resources. Instead, he was stuck in here until it blew over.

What he wanted most was a hot bath. Between the passage

here, the long walk inland, and the reek of the fire, he was the ripest he'd been in his entire life.

Not that there was anyone around to smell him.

On the second day, the blizzard still blew. He ventured outside during a lull in the storm, scraping as much lichen as he could with his spear, having to use Thermalism to melt thick snowdrifts. He made it back inside right before the storm returned with cold fury. Lucian passed the days by reaching for his Focus, practicing isolating his Aspects while studying his survival guide. Anything to keep his mind occupied.

If the Academy would no longer train him, then he would have to train himself.

Every day, he picked a new Aspect to concentrate on. It was only when he reached Gravitonics, on the sixth day, that the howling wind died enough for him to open the door.

A snowdrift as high as his head tumbled inside. Despite the height of the snow, the temperature was warmer than during the storm. The air smelt clean and odorless.

He wondered how he'd ever find *anything* buried under that snow. Unless the shuttle came soon, he would die in this valley. He needed snowshoes, but there was nothing with which to make them. And even if there were, the instructions in his survival guide were a bit confusing.

That was when he spied a column of smoke to the west, beyond the rim of the valley. Was that smoke natural, or was there someone else on this island?

Another person could mean food. Then again, it could also mean conflict. Lucian looked at his own chimney. A thick column of smoke curled upward into the bright blue sky.

Well, they would know about him, too. Either he could go investigate, or they would investigate him. If it turned out they were dangerous, he always had his magic. Then again, assuming they were exiled mages, they would have magic, too. Could it be Katya? Lucian couldn't imagine who else it might be. If she were still alive after all this time, without a shuttle coming to get her, then maybe his odds weren't so bad, either.

He returned to his hovel, shut the door, and warmed himself by the fire. After a couple of minutes, he made his decision. He put the collapsed shockspear in his parka pocket. These last seven days hadn't been easy. Not in the least. But with the breaking of the storm and the blue sky, Lucian found a small kernel of hope.

His spear was a weapon and a tool now, not an instrument of self-harm. The fact that there was another *person* here, or even *people*, changed everything. He wasn't sure how far that smoke was, but he knew the direction. Could he wait any longer? The weather might not hold up, and his food reserves were getting low.

Lucian didn't see how it was possible to cross the deep snow. It was taller than *he* was. But he had no choice. He couldn't stay in this valley forever. He had to explore the island and find enough resources to survive. And that included finding other survivors.

He filled his backpack with everything he'd unpacked. He made a fresh canteen of water from snowmelt and made sure every drop of soup was eaten. He fed the last of the lichen to the fire, relishing in the intense warmth.

Once warm enough, he put on his gloves. As warm as his clothing was, it wouldn't hold up for many hours in the cold, especially as darkness fell, which would be soon. How cold was it? Five below? Ten? At some point, it became impossible to tell. It was just damn cold.

He drew a deep breath and went back outside. A landscape of deep snow stood before him, so deep, that only the upper halves of the cabins were visible. Getting out of this valley wouldn't be easy, but it would be necessary.

And he would need magic to do it.

He extended his hands and streamed Thermalism. The

snow in front of him melted instantly, collapsing into a thick puddle of slurry. It sloshed in his direction up to his ankles. Any more of that, and his boots would be completely soaked, waterproofing or not. Besides, blasting the snow with heat would consume far too much ether. His pool was limited, and it needed to last long enough to get out of this valley and defend himself if it came to that.

It was a tall order, but an order he had to ensure. Outside the valley, the snow would probably be less deep. He might even be able to walk without using magic.

This was real life, not the controlled setting of a Trial. If he made the wrong choice, he would die.

He thought about how to proceed. He could stream antigrav discs and attempt to walk above the snow. But the distance was much farther than his Trial on the beach. He was almost sure to run out of ether before reached the top of the valley. Nor could he use Binding to pull himself across the valley. The amount of ether required by a Binding tether was a function of both distance and mass. Since the distance to the valley's crest was far, and his mass was far greater than anything he'd ever Bound, he would run out of ether in seconds. And blasting the snow with Thermalism was a no go, for the same reasons as Binding himself.

But then an idea came to him – an idea so ambitious that it scared him. But the more he thought about it, the more he realized it was his only choice. Perhaps Binding himself would be impossible, but what if he could bind something with little to *no* mass?

He'd read about a technique in the library called "dual-streaming." It was possible to combine the streams of two different Aspects, if they were complements – that was, if they either bordered each other on the theoretical Septagon, or were two spaces apart. It meant he could combine a gravitational disc with a binding tether. And a gravity disc itself had no mass other than the energy used to produce it, which was far less mass than he himself. All to say, Lucian *might* be able to connect a Binding line to an antigrav disc, setting the focal point for the ridge above. This would allow him to skim above the snow, assuming he could manage to stay on the disc, and the Binding output would only be costly in terms of distance, not mass.

Theoretically, it *should* work, but dualstreams were an advanced technique not taught to Novices. And assuming he could pull it off, it would burn through his ether like crazy. Dualstreams used *quadruple* the ether of a single stream, making them highly impractical in most situations. He'd even read about tristreams that used *nine* times the ether, but it was thought to be impossible for a mage to tristream without overdrawing, so the technique was forbidden at the Volsung Academy. At least, according to the book he'd read.

Theoretically, with Binding and Gravitonics being complements, Lucian could float across the valley quickly enough to make it to the rim before his ether ran dry. Assuming, of course, dualstreaming was less costly on his ether than Binding himself directly. Hopefully, it would be over with quickly, before his ether ran dry.

He saw no other way to go about it. Using the rough stones of the hovel's wall, Lucian climbed to the roof until he stood above the deep snow. The unbroken white covered the entire valley, about half a meter below where he stood.

It was now or never.

He began by streaming a antigrav disc right above the surface of the snow. He made no deviation, remembering well how slowing the speed of his stream during the Trial had *doubled* his gravity. To set the stream, he only had to maintain a thin flow of magic. The silvery disc floated above the snow, just a step away. He couldn't wait long; his ether was burning.

He stepped onto the disc and was pleased to find it held.

While maintaining the Gravitonic stream, he reached for the Binding Aspect. He was burning ether at an alarming rate, so much so that he shook with the effort. Brimming with potential magic, he directed the new stream by designating an anchor point on the antigrav disc. To his relief, it connected with a burst of bluish-gray light. The streams were now fused as ether roared through him anew.

There was no time to waste. He'd run out in seconds at this burn rate. He streamed Binding at the focal point on a distant boulder at the top of the western rise. Once both points were set, anchor and focal, he held it, the binding line between brimming with energy. The longer he held it, the more his magic infused into the line. And the more magic, the faster he would go.

Kneeling, he held the binding line as long as he could. Then, he let it go.

He almost fell off the disc as it glided smoothly above the surface of the snow, following the glowing blue binding line.

"Whoa!"

As the disc picked up speed, the wind roared past his face. He couldn't help but let out a whoop, even as his ether burned away. If he ran out before reaching the rise, he would crash through the snow. Both of his hands glowed with silvery blue radiance. As long as he maintained both streams at the incredible burn rate, he had a shot of making it.

He knelt, his heart racing, and almost lost the focal point several times. The longer he went, the more slippery the streams were to hold. He deepened his Focus, streamed more ether, and fed each stream the necessary magic to be maintained. The disc flew along, as if reeled by a fishing rod.

His ether pool was depleting. As the disc flickered below him, he felt himself sinking. He re-streamed the disc, solidifying it, but the speed of the binding line slowed as the focal point started to fade.

Focus. He had to maintain Focus.

He was over halfway now, and almost completely out of ether. The dualstream was beginning to sputter. But he was *so close*. He didn't want to overdraw, but he might have to. There was always the risk that this overdraw might be his last before the fraying gained a foothold. If it hadn't already.

He had good reason to overdraw. It might be his only way to not be stranded in the snow, something that could lead to his death. But nothing was more dangerous than temptation armed with a justification. He had to learn to get by without overdrawing, as difficult as that would be.

He knew the risks. Now, he had to see this through.

At last, most of the way to the western slope, both streams winked out. He crashed through the snow, finding solid ground about a meter beneath. Just a meter. As he had suspected, the snow was thinner up here, and passable.

He got up and brushed himself off. He was lucky. He'd escape with nothing more than a few bruises.

Lucian stood and waded the rest of the way out of the valley.

―――

When Lucian made it to the top, he let out a breath and hopped onto the boulder he'd originally bound. He gazed into the valley below, the ring of hovels basking in the dim, northern sunlight. He couldn't look long, though. There was only so much daylight left, and Lucian didn't want to push it.

He walked along the slope, sometimes using discs to bridge the rougher bits of terrain. He had a bit of ether, though it wasn't much. In this way, his progress was quicker than anticipated. Within the hour, the column of white smoke was closer. He still couldn't see the actual ground it was rising from. The landscape was too rough and twisted.

He'd only learn more by moving forward.

With the rate he was burning through his pool, he might not have enough ether for the return journey. It was something he hadn't considered. If this expedition turned out to be a bust, he'd have to find shelter for the night and wait for his pool to regenerate. Even with a fire, he didn't know if he could sleep out in the open, especially if it started snowing again.

The smoke was closer now, though the acrid stench of the lichen was absent. The wind might have carried the smell away. Another aroma, however, entered his nostrils – this one earthy. The temperature warmed quite a bit as he walked west. He could feel the warmth of the land through his boots. Thin rivulets of snowmelt ran down the shallow slope, coursing a path through deep drifts.

The moment he crested the next hill, a flat expanse spread before him. And he saw the source of the smoke.

It wasn't smoke at all, but steam, from hundreds of interconnected geothermal pools, spreading for at least a kilometer.

And lazing in one of the pools, about halfway across the field of hot springs, were two people. Both were male and shirtless, one with long gray hair and a beard, and the other bald and portly. Their clothes were cast off on the ground nearby.

It was too late to duck and hide. The gray-haired one was already waving at Lucian.

"Hullo!" The booming voice echoed off the ridges surrounding the pools.

Lucian could do nothing but awkwardly raise his hand in acknowledgement. He walked forward, mindful of the collapsed shockspear in his pocket. The men weren't making a move to dress or defend themselves, but that alone didn't mean anything.

It took about five minutes to weave his way through the pools. The hot steam was overheating him in his parka. He didn't want to take it off yet, though. Even if these two men were defenseless, it was likely they were mages, too. Who else would be on this forsaken island? Running was pointless since they knew where to find him. So, the only real option was to meet them head on and hope for the best.

By the time Lucian was close, they were still idling in the bubbling water, eyes closed, like two walruses in the sun. The bald one looked disappointed as Lucian approached, while the gray-hair laughed uproariously.

"*Told* you," the gray-haired one said. "It's a man."

The fat one shook his head. "Well, it's fresh meat, anyway."

"Where are your manners?" The gray-haired one smiled in apology. "We aren't monsters, believe me. The edges society once smoothed have now been quite roughened, I'm afraid."

Lucian wasn't sure how to take that. He tried to form a response, but he couldn't find anything to say. The portly man watched him with glinting eyes and a half-smile that somewhat creeped him out.

The gray-haired one barked a laugh. "Have a drink!" he said, nodding toward a leather-skin canteen. "There's plenty for all."

The bald one watched Lucian as he took a swig from his own canteen.

"If you're wondering about my idle comment," the gray-haired one said, "my friend and I made a small wager."

"Is that so?" Lucian asked.

He gave a yellow smile. "About whether you were a man or a woman. My friend here lost that bet. I have better eyes, but he was so sure."

"He looked pretty enough from a distance," the bald one said glumly.

"I'd watch yourself around Plato, if I were you," the gray-haired one warned.

At this, Plato tittered.

"Don't get any ideas," Lucian said.

"I would never dream of it, dear," Plato said. "I'm perfectly harmless. Right, Linus?"

"Hardly. You chased that other one off. Katya, was her name?"

"Wait," Lucian said. "Katya is here?"

Linus looked back at Lucian, brushing a strand of gray hair out of his eyes. "Not anymore. Shuttle came by a week ago. She decided to take her chances on the Mad Moon rather than with us."

"Quiet," Plato said. "You're *not* doing a good job of selling us."

"You're right, my friend. But honesty is the best foundation for friendship, no?" At Plato's lack of answer, Linus continued. "You must forgive us. It gets so lonely here, and we get so excited to meet anyone we flat out forget our manners. Welcome. Welcome, to the Isle of Madness!"

Linus gestured wildly, his blue eyes giving off a crazed gleam. These two weren't doing much for Lucian's confidence, especially as they both took mighty drinks from their canteens. Lucian knew from their rosy cheeks and general silliness that it wasn't water in there. He'd have to be careful.

Linus belched happily. "What's your name, friend?"

"Lucian."

Linus stood, doing nothing to hide his private parts. Modesty, it seemed, wasn't a value on the Isle of Madness. For his age, Lucian noted his form was lean and well-muscled. "I see you admiring my form, young mage. Believe me, Juan Ponce was looking for his Fountain of Youth on the wrong world. These springs are *delightful* for one's complexion!" He extended a hairy hand, connected to an even hairier forearm. "As mentioned, my name is Linus. Linus Wander. Isle of Madness inhabitant, and Mayor, for the past four decades."

Plato scoffed. "Mayor of my fat, hairy arse, maybe."

"Yes. And the mayor or arse that plants itself on a single

pebble of my island." Linus cleared his throat. "To our newest citizen, I apologize we didn't bring you your gift basket. The storm precluded us, though we were on our way there now. Only, the springs called out to us. I'm glad you came this way, because that valley is nothing but death and despair." He smiled widely. "Plunk here didn't want to come at all."

"That's *not* my name," Plato said.

"*Fine.* We just call him Plunk because..."

"*We?* We're the only two people on this island, idiot."

"*So far,*" Linus said. "If we play our cards right, our duo could become a trio." He turned back to Lucian. "This may look like pure paradise, but I assure you, life here is anything but. If you know where to look and how to finagle the environs for food and shelter, it's not a bad life." He frowned. "It could only use some women."

Lucian was still averting his gaze. "Are you going to, err... cover up?"

Linus looked down, abashed. "Oh. My apologies. You're not used to island customs. Nakedness, you see, is not considered a taboo here. But for the sake of you, our guest, I'll cover myself."

When he sat back down in the pool, Lucian found it much easier to focus.

"You seem at a loss for words, my friend," Linus said. "We saw your smoke a few nights back, as I said before." He nodded toward a leather satchel next to the springs. "That was to be your warming gift, but good Plato here could not resist a-plunking in these Pools of the Gods, as we are wont to call them."

"It was *your* idea, actually," Plato grumbled.

"Well, I agreed it would serve us greatly before heading into that bone-filled, snow-filled, ghost-filled valley."

"What's wrong with the valley?" Lucian asked.

Linus gave a guttural laugh. "What's *wrong*? Well, I'll tell you what's wrong. It's the worst spot to shelter on this island, especially in winter. How did you even *get* here?"

"A gravitational disc connected to a binding tether."

Linus's mouth made a rictus. "Oh. I see. Well, good for you, then. We get by without magic. That's how we've lived to a ripe old age. Ether is a poison we've learned to do without."

"I thought it was the springs?"

"Ah, that too. But mostly the lack of magic. A dangerous thing, that. Magic."

Plato held up a beefy hand, as if to say Lucian wasn't ready for that part. "Enough serious talk. Hop on in. I promise the heat's not coming from Linus's piss."

Linus scoffed. "Yeah, because it's coming from *your* flatulence, sir." Linus's expression twisted. "Whatever the source of this heat, it feels nicer than the cold air. Have yourself some refreshment, young Lucian. We have Sea Drink. That should loosen tongues as we all share our stories. You've been through much, friend. I would hear you laugh before daylight fails."

"I'm not doing that," Lucian said. "I don't know who the two of you are, anyway." And they couldn't be too noble if they'd scared Katya out of her wits.

"Why, we introduced ourselves," Linus said, abashed. "If you're worried about us robbing you, don't worry, we have everything we need on this island." He raised a questioning eyebrow. "Unless you have ... coffee?"

"I'm afraid not."

"Alas. One of the past exiles had some."

"That was ten years ago, Linus," Plato said.

"Be that as it may, drink with us, friend! It's impossible to know someone until you've gotten bloody drunk with them first." His nose wrinkled. "And you smell like you walked out of an hippopotamus's ass. Rose lichen makes for good fuel, but you must soak it for twenty-four hours beforehand. It'll get rid of most of the spores that cause that dreadful stench."

Lucian saw he had no choice but to join them. If they wanted to kill him, they would have done so by now.

He dropped his pack and stripped off his parka and pants. Now, he stood in his dirty Novice robes. The two old ones watched him for an uncomfortably long time. And Plato's eyes were hungry.

"Do you mind?" Lucian asked.

"Look away, Plato," Linus said. "We must protect the modesty of this youth, even if it's from your own eyes."

Lucian wondered whether he might get into the pool with his robe on, but that would make for a wet trip back. He decided to take it off but to leave his underwear on. Good as their word, the two old men averted their gazes, Plato even shutting his eyes tightly.

Lucian slipped into the warm water. He couldn't lie to himself, it felt amazing. Whatever misgivings he had were erased as soon as the warm mineral water soaked into his bones. That said, he kept alert, half-holding his Focus so he would be ready for anything.

"Good, then," Linus said, turning back. His manner grew more serious. "Wash out that hair, too. Looks like it was dragged through a trash compactor."

Lucian dunked his head underwater, but only for a couple of seconds. He felt relieved to see the two old men had remained on their side of the pool.

"So," Plato said. "Why are you here, Lucian?"

The fat old man tossed him a skin of what had to be the Sea Drink, which Lucian caught. He took a small sip, only to be polite. It was cloyingly sweet, with an alcoholic content that set fire to his throat. He only barely managed not to cough.

He wanted to ask them that very same question. This island was supposed to be empty, and if Linus had been here four decades, as he had said, then *how* was he still here? Why hadn't the shuttle taken him to Psyche? And Plato looked to be the same age as him and had obviously lived here a long time as well.

There was more to this island than met the eye. And Lucian meant to find out.

So, he told the story of how he got to be here. There was nothing to lose by telling the truth. When he got to the part about the Transcends stabbing him in the back, both of their faces darkened. Plato spat to the side while Linus punched the water.

"That's the Transcends for you," Linus said. "A bunch of dirty old frauds!"

"I take it you had bad experiences with them, too?"

"Bad experiences?" Plato gave a grim laugh. "Isn't that why we're all here?"

"That Transcend Violet is the worst," Linus said. "Huge, pointy, twisty stick up her wrinkled ass."

"He means Transcend White," Plato said. "She was Transcend Violet when we were Novices."

"Yeah," Linus said. "What's changed? The last one to come here didn't share all that much. She couldn't take to our island lifestyle. Figured the going would be easier on Psyche. More fool, her. Suffice it to say, we're here for the same reason you are. Well, your whole bit about being exiled for being *too good* seemed a little untruthful. But we'll let it slide. We're all friends here."

"I didn't lie," Lucian said. "I should be back there right now. If I had chosen one of them to train with, I wouldn't be here."

"Of course, you think that," Plato said, "but you don't know for sure. You wanted to be honest, and the honest path usually has a cost. Unfortunately, that cost is being forced to spend time with two hairy and irreverent sexagenarians."

Linus gave a bark of a laugh. "Well, I doubt he'll elect to remain with us, my old friend. Usually, it works like this. One, two, maybe even *three* exiles come here at a time. Then the shuttle comes, and they race for it as if it's a lifeline out of a stormy sea. You see, here there *is* no escape. Try to waterwalk across the ocean, and you'll never make it the four thousand kilometers to Krygos. Even if the entire sea were to freeze, the distance is much too far. Between this Isle of Madness and the mystery box that is Psyche, most people opt for the mystery box. And we expect you will as well when the time comes."

"They *always* choose the mystery box," Plato said, darkly. "They choose a literal hell over us! Confound it!"

"Well, sometimes they *try* to make it work," Linus said. "We had one man stay with us a couple of years. Then, it got to be too much for him. He jumped off a cliff."

"Oh, I forget his name. It was something weird, like Laurel."

"No weirder than Plunk."

"*Plato*," he said.

"Well, it must be hard to survive here," Lucian said. He took another swig of the Sea Drink, only this time, the taste hit him stronger. It started to gag.

Linus gave that barking laugh again. "You look as green as sweetkelp, friend." He took a swig from his own canteen. "The drink will grow on you, but it suffers not the weak-stomached. You need it to stay sane, here. It'll also keep the scurvy at bay."

"Doesn't appear to have worked for you on the sanity front, my dear Mayor," Plato said. "Quite the opposite."

Linus rolled his eyes. "So, what do you think, young Lucian?"

"Of what?"

Linus's gesture seemed to take in everything. *"This!"*

"I'm not sure what to think. The Psions told me no one was on this island."

"Ha! If the Transcends are clueless, the Psions are even more so."

"Why are both of you here, then?"

Plato shrugged. "Couldn't cut the mustard, as we used to

say. After five years at the Academey, I couldn't keep up. The Transcends noticed, and they sent me off. There was a good community of outcasts back then. Life was much rougher, though. Those who didn't die opted to go to Psyche, thinking at least on a prison world they might find a steady supply of food." He shrugged. "Who knows? Perhaps it *is* a better life, but in the years since, we've made things much better. I've learned to be content in the middle of nowhere at the edge of this blasted world. There's even beauty if you have eyes to see it."

There was a silence after this, and for once, Linus didn't seem to have a flippant remark.

"As for me," the mayor said, "where to even begin? I was a Talent to Transcend Gray. In those days, Transcend Gray was a fat old man. He's been dead for three decades now, I imagine. Well, one day I got into an argument with another Talent. First, it came to blows. Then it came to magic." Linus's face became stony as he remembered. "How I *hated* him. He was my rival, you might say, and both of us were competing for the position of being the fat man's Psion. Well, push comes to shove, and we went too far. We streamed magic that would get us expelled."

"So, both of you were caught?" Lucian asked.

Linus nodded, his gray beard dipping into the warm spring. "Aye, both of us were caught. But Rendar was raised to Psion. He's Transcend Gray now."

At Lucian's shocked reaction, Linus chuckled bitterly.

"Who knows, young man," Linus said. "That might have been me if I'd kissed as much ass as him." He stood, with a distant expression on his face. "I've had my fill of these springs. It's time we headed back, before the daylight gives."

"Transcend Gray is fraying, you know," Lucian said. "Might be you'll see him here before too long."

"Is that so?" His expression was grave. "Well, if that's true, I doubt we'll be seeing him. They either off themselves voluntarily or go delving the Manifold hoping to be the next Arian."

Linus seemed to think a moment, his face solemn. "It's time we headed back. Daylight's burning."

Plato nodded, dunking his bald head one last time before standing up. To Lucian's relief, his prodigious gut covered his manhood. The living here couldn't be so bad if he could maintain that weight.

Lucian stepped out of the pool. For the first time since getting here, he felt warm to the bone, and clean. He dressed, wrinkling his nose at his smelly clothing that reeked of sulfur.

"You got anything back at those cabins?" Linus asked.

"This is everything."

Linus nodded. "Good. Well, I thought we'd head back to the hideout. Show you the ropes, as it were. It's much more comfortable where we stay." He shrugged his bony shoulders. "I mean, if we haven't scared you off, yet."

Yes, there was what. Something about their story about driving away Katya didn't add up. If they did do that, why would they tell him? If they wanted him to follow them, they would have put their best foot forward. There was more to it, and Lucian would have to figure it out.

"Lead the way and I'll follow," Lucian said.

Linus nodded, and set off. Plato shrugged, and waddled after Linus, his stout legs doing a good job of keeping up with the taller man.

Lucian hesitated only a moment before following. It looked like these two old ones would be his guides here, and for now, it seemed best to follow their advice. There was no way he was surviving on his own.

Still, his most pressing question was left unanswered. How *had* they survived here for so long? And how had they eluded the prison shuttles?

Both were mysteries that Lucian resolved to find out.

27

GOING overland was easy after the hot springs. The gray, rolling tundra was mostly smooth. Streams of water trickled through carved gullies, forming cold pools next to the springs. There wasn't much in the way of life aside from the pinkish lichen. A dark, green moss coated the wetter bits of boulders, but there wasn't much else. The sky had become overcast, its heaviness promising even more snowfall.

The speed and limberness of both men surprised Lucian. Even Plato seemed to be in good health, and had no problem skirting up and down the hills with the nimbleness of a goat. He had two canteens, one of which had to be Sea Drink, and the other water. He drank from both just as often. Plato happily whistled a catchy song that Lucian didn't recognize. The melody sounded old-timey, like music from a Mage War propaganda holo.

"How much farther is it?" Lucian called.

"Almost there," Linus said. "Patience, young grasshopper."

As good as his word, the trio crested a rise, and Lucian was treated to the sight of the wide, gray Ocean of Storms. The expanse was chocked full of icebergs. Far to the north, he could see an endless wall of white on the horizon.

"Is that the ice cap?"

"It is," Plato confirmed. "About twenty kilometers north, give or take."

That explained the sheer number of icebergs, and the awfully cold wind blustering. Neither Linus nor Plato paused at the magnificent view. There were mere hours of daylight left, judging by the sinking sun at their backs.

They followed a trail down the cliff, and the wind was all but cut off.

"This is the best place on the island," Linus called back. "The cliff blocks most of the wind and storms. The trail goes all the way down to the shoreline. There's all the sweetkelp, mussels, clams, and crab you can eat. Fish too, if you don't mind getting your feet wet. The water soaks through the raft."

"*Actually*, they're not *exactly* crab," Plato corrected. "They're a native species of this world, called shellocks."

"Here we go again," Linus said, with a heavy sigh. "Must you *always* be Mr. Actually?"

"Well, *crab* comes from Earth. Shellocks are a completely different species, of a different evolutionary line..."

"If it walks like a crab and pinches like a crab, then it's crab."

"They're *not* the same."

They were like an old married couple. Lucian could only wonder if listening to them bicker for the rest of his days was his future. That was a depressing thought.

Linus chuckled. "What must Lucian think of us, clucking like old hens?"

"It's a nice view, at least," Lucian said.

"I'm glad you think so," Plato said. "Took us damn near two years to carve the trail into the cliff. And another year before we made the caves habitable."

"Quiet, Plato," Linus said. "Let's not spoil the surprise."

They rounded a bend, and Lucian saw it. The trail entered a great maw opening into the vertical rock face. As they drew closer, Lucian could see how vast it was – far more space than two people would ever need. Soon, they stood at the entrance, which must have been a good ten meters tall. The interior was spacious, with a central brazier that was down to coals by now. Lucian couldn't see much beyond it.

Linus strode forward and threw a few greenish looking logs on the fire. It didn't look like the lichen he'd used. Whatever it was, it didn't stink, and instead gave off an earthy, salty fragrance. Linus crinkled some herbs over the fire, and a fresh fragrance like jasmine filled the air. He turned toward Lucian, smiling widely. "Home sweet home!"

Deeper in the cavern, Lucian could see more tunnels. Torches, currently unlit, hung on the rocky walls. Lucian stepped up to the fire to warm himself. "This is incredible."

Linus gave a jovial laugh. "Well, there's little else to do here, I'm afraid. We still have to walk a decent distance for a bath to the springs, but here we can at least have a cold one." He nodded deeper into the cavern. "Come on, I'll show you!"

Lucian followed Linus deeper within, until Lucian heard the gurgle of a stream. Linus took a torch and lit it from the brazier, then walked toward the sound of water. They came to a fast-moving stream coming straight from the wall at about head level. It ran through a carved aqueduct of sorts hewn from the rock.

"Watch this," Linus said, proudly. He pushed a heavy stone, which blocked the channel perfectly. The water backed up a bit, and then changed course into a new channel. It tumbled over the aqueduct and into an empty pool below. That pool was about a meter deep. Lucian couldn't help but marvel at the ingenuity.

"We still take a trip out to the springs every few days, but Plato is trying to build a furnace so we can heat it up."

Lucian couldn't help but be impressed. "I can see why you haven't boarded the shuttle to Psyche yet."

His stomach rumbled. "What do you guys do for food?"

Linus nodded toward Lucian's bag. "Why don't we start with that? If I eat any more shellfish or kelp today, I'm going to puke."

Plato nosed his way forward. "Do you have peaches? I *love* peaches."

"No," Lucian said. "I'll share, though."

The two older men rifled through his bag while Lucian looked on. Not for the first time, he was having doubts about these two as they set aside two cans of beans and some rice.

"Man, they must *hate* you," Plato said. "Katya had peaches."

Lucian doubted that since he hadn't seen so much as a can of fruit in the Academy's larders. But perhaps the Talents had given it to her or had access to food the Novices didn't.

Within the minute, the men were throwing a mishmash of ingredients into a pot. Instead of water, they gave it a base of Sea Drink combined with the contents of Lucian's cans. They threw in some peeled crustaceans that looked like trilobites. Lucian's stomach went queasy looking at those. But once the pot was cooking over the fire, he had to admit the smell was appetizing, sweet and savory all at once.

Plato handed him a large stone bowl, along with a spoon. They sat around the fire, keeping warm and talking.

"Where're you from, friend?" Linus asked.

"Earth."

"No shit," he said. "You seem a bit uppity. Just like an Earther!"

Lucian shrugged. "Well, Earth *is* number one, and always will be."

"I see they're still indoctrinating the youth," Linus said. "I'm from Chiron myself. Never been to Earth. Wouldn't visit that piss pot for a thousand world creds."

"You *won't* have the chance, creds or not," Plato pointed out.

"Quiet," Linus said. "Well, Chiron is everything Earth is, except *better*. Blue skies? Yes, we have that, and without all the pollution. Breathable atmosphere? Got that, too. Yes, the sky-locust swarms are a problem still. But once they're gone, we'll have something more pristine and beautiful than Earth ever was."

"Sounds like Chiron is the piss pot to me," Plato said. He looked at Lucian. "I'm from Earth myself. Greater Macedonia."

"Ha! And you're one to talk about piss pots."

"Do you guys *always* fight like this?" Lucian asked.

"Not always," Plato said. "I grew up in Thessaloniki. Before the annexation."

"That war is over," Lucian said. "Has been for years."

"I know that," Plato said. "I got out in time. I have family in Nova Akershus, now. Or at least, I did twenty years ago. Who knows if they're still alive?"

There was a silence after that as they watched the stew cook. So far, these two didn't seem harmful. So, what had driven Katya away? They had made some crude jokes, but for some reason, Lucian felt as if it were a cover for something, though he could not have explained *why* he felt that.

"Stew should be done," Linus said. "Bowl over here, friend."

Lucian handed him his bowl. Linus poured a generous helping of the green concoction. He had to say it didn't look too appetizing. He couldn't tell whether his stomach rumblings were from his misgivings or his hunger. He poked around in the green broth a bit, seeing a mixture of rice, beans, and small sea life.

Lucian tasted the soup, and found it wasn't half-bad. It was better than the canned food he'd been eating, anyway, and the consistency of the broth was almost like a gravy. It lacked basic seasonings, but was at least salted.

"Not so bad, is it?" Linus said, beaming a wide smile. For the first time, Lucian noticed that he was missing a couple of teeth.

"Not bad. I have to ask, though. Why are you two the only ones here? The Academy must exile a few Novices each year. Do they *all* decide to go on to Psyche? Life would be hard here, but isn't this setup preferable to a literal prison world?"

There was an awkward silence for a moment before Plato began to explain. "We talked about it a bit before. That's a difficult question. Half of the ones we get are frayed already, so we can't take them here, obviously."

"They get themselves killed," Linus said, all traces of his former humor gone. "Frayed mages are dangerous indeed. They stream recklessly, and the madder they are, the more they stream. A lot of people lose it when they get here and let themselves go. We usually watch for a while to make sure a potential recruit isn't mad before we invite them in."

"What about me, then?"

"We didn't count on you trying to find *us*. We were testing you a bit when we first met."

"Testing me, how?"

"There are little tells that someone's starting to fray," Plato explained. "Mottled skin. Tremors in the hand. They say things that don't make sense. That's what happened with the one before Katya. We never even invited him back here, though we made sure he was well-fed. The stress of being on this island is enough for many mages to snap."

"But the both of you have been fine for years," Lucian said. "Forgive me for saying, but..."

"...shouldn't we have frayed by now?" Linus gave a somewhat maddened laugh, not doing much for Lucian's confidence. "I don't stream, young man. Not ever. Ether is poison."

That was impossible. If that was true, he should have died

of ethereal poisoning a long time ago. A mage *couldn't* stop themselves from collecting ether naturally from the ethereal background. Could they?

Linus went on. "Sometimes they last a few months, sometimes even years. But if you can't learn to stop streaming, the fraying will find you. The temptation is too much. We had one man, perfectly sane, who woke up one morning and decided it was a great idea to waterwalk all the way to Krygos." He shook his head. "There was nothing we could do. Those who are obviously frayed we leave for the shuttle. And when the shuttle comes, we hide in here. The stone walls are thick enough to hide our heat signatures. You can hear it thundering down long before you see it. And if we're out and don't have time to come back, we have hideouts all over the island. Someone who's frayed doesn't have the wits to hide themselves."

"How often *do* they come?" Lucian asked.

"It's supposed to be every few standard months," Linus said. "Last one was a couple weeks back. The one Katya took. The prison barges bounce around from world to world, but the end of their route is always the Mad Moon. It's not just mages sent there, anymore. The Border and Mid-Worlds dump a lot of their human trash there, the worst of the worst, even if they're not supposed to. I imagine the Mad Moon is getting quite crowded these days."

"Makes sense," Lucian said. "And it sounds like a place most would want to avoid."

And knowing all that, it especially didn't make sense that Katya would choose that over life here. Unless these two men were *especially* bad.

"You're one of us, as far as I can see," Linus said. "You're not mad, and that's all we ask. A few other things, too, but we'll get to that. Try not to use magic in the meantime. Some people think they can control it and limit themselves. But even a small amount causes the fraying, as far as we can tell. It's best to not use it. The withdrawals are the hardest part. Magic is poison. When you've gone a few days without it, you'll start to feel pretty miserable."

"What about ether?" Lucian asked. "It has to be released, or it can lead to death. My friend back at the Academy almost died that way."

"It can be done," Linus said. "In fact, it *must* be done. It's not easy, but it's possible. After all, we two are living proof of it."

"So, you're saying the Academy is wrong?"

"Yes," Linus said, without so much as blinking. "You never learned the purpose of the Academy, did you?" At Lucian's blank look, he chuckled. "Of course not. You never made it that far. Though I have."

Plato filled up his third bowl, and smiled, as if he were hearing a familiar story for the millionth time.

"What's the purpose, then?"

"You were a *weapon*, Lucian. Nothing more, nothing less. The academies are a way for the League to control the mages. To turn what would be a prisoner into an instrument of war. There hasn't been a major conflict since the Mage War fifty years ago. Even those scraps with these so-called Swarmers are nothing compared to that."

"They're back," Lucian said. "The Swarmers."

This was news to them both, judging by the surprised expression on their faces. "Katya said nothing about that."

"It's recent," Lucian said. "My mother died in the first battle." He looked at Linus. "It was in the Alpha Centauri system."

His eyes widened at that. *"What?"*

"They were turned back," Lucian said. "The Fleet won. I don't know anything else."

"So, Chiron is safe," Linus said. He looked up at Lucian, his long gray hair almost falling over his eyes. "Sorry about your mother."

It was quiet for a time, save for the crackle of flames and the howling wind outside.

"It may be the mages' time is coming," Linus said. "Magic is too useful a tool for the League to ignore. With one Atomicist, you can keep a ship going without the need to refuel, for example. Radiants can shield a ship from LADAR sensors, making it all but invisible. And in direct combat, magic is a terrible weapon. They want you to know how to use it, yes, but don't want you to fray *too* quickly using it. This path of Balance they speak of – it's all a sham. They just want to get the most magic out of you and the least amount of the poison that accompanies it. There is no safe dose. But if you can figure out a way to cut it off at the source, to not let ether trickle in, then you're set."

"So, the whole thing about your pool overflowing leading to ethereal poisoning – that's all a lie?" Lucian's thoughts returned to Emma then. "My friend back at the Academy had wreakings. They said it was because she couldn't stream her excess ether away. You're saying none of that is real? Or have you guys just discovered something that no one else has?"

"I don't think we've discovered anything new," Linus said. "Setting up a decent ethereal block, one that lasts for a lifetime, is highly dangerous. And if the League wants mages under its control, it also has no incentive to teach mages how to *not* stream."

All of this was so confusing. "This just goes against everything I've ever learned."

"Could be there's some that need to stream," Linus admitted. "The more powerful ones. But I know it's possible to stop, at least for some mages. Plato and I have both done it. I haven't streamed a drop of magic in years."

Lucian was skeptical of that, but he didn't want to deny it. There was a lot he didn't understand, and Linus seemed quite serious.

Linus took a pull from his canteen. "The Academy pushes

recruits far beyond what they should be doing. Those who fail get sent here. The only ones that remain are those who can stomach the poison of ether better than most. Humans aren't *meant* for it, Lucian. The mages have struck a diabolical balance between power and insanity. They're sifting through all the recruits to find those who are trainable and call them Talents. It's the same for the other academies, too, Mako and Irion. They're looking for those who are willing and able to become weapons. The day will come when the League uses the mages an official capacity. It's what they're being trained for. Someday soon, I warrant."

Khairu had even hinted at that what seemed a lifetime ago. If something like the Free Mages ever rose again, it would be the Volsung Academy that led the fight against them. But was it possible the League had another purpose in mind? The thought seemed unimaginable, but Lucian supposed it could be true.

"I knew we were being trained to fight," Lucian said. "But against rogue mages, or against groups of them banding together."

Linus nodded. "And the Swarmers, or any other threat in the Worlds the League has need to extinguish. There are rogue mages who escape the net and teach themselves to stream, right? Trust me, there are *much* more of those than mages at all the academies *combined*. Even with extensive testing, most mages slip through the cracks. Some get hunted down, but many more learn to stream on their own and elude capture. How?"

The question hung in the air for a moment. "I don't know."

"They learn to *control* it," Linus said.

"And that's how the two of you have lasted so long? By controlling it?"

Linus shrugged. "Forty years long, on this island. It's not easy. I think about streaming every day. The taste of power is sweet, isn't it? But it's only power. If you can learn to forgo the need for that, then magic will have no hold over you."

Lucian admitted that it *did* feel good to use magic. The idea of going without it was repulsive. So repulsive, that he wasn't willing to admit Linus might be right. But it also helped him to figure out the rest of the puzzle. Katya hadn't left because these two were bothering her. These two had forced her to leave because she hadn't been willing to give up using magic.

"That's how there's only two of you, then. The others can't resist the magic at their fingertips."

Plato nodded, coming out of his silence. "Precisely. That's something we usually break to people later, but it seems you've figured it out on your own. This lifestyle doesn't appeal to everyone. That's the main rule here: no magic. No matter how much you want to stream, no matter how bad your withdrawals get. No magic."

Lucian already felt himself protesting. "How can you tell the difference between withdrawals and poisoning? Wouldn't the mages of the Academy say that *withdrawals* are a symptom of your ether pool overflowing?"

Linus laughed. "That objection is the main reason most mages can't detox. They crave their magic so much that they aren't willing to suffer months of agony to live with freedom for the rest of their lives. So, they finally give in. As you said, that's why there's only two of us. This isn't easy."

"How'd you figure this out?" Lucian asked. "You have the answer for the fraying if I'm hearing things right. If mages could be taught to do this, then there *would* be no fraying."

"You can lead a horse to water," Plato said, softly, "but you can't make it drink."

Linus nodded sagely. "I discovered it quite by accident. I was trying to kill myself. I hid from the shuttle one day, forty years ago, and regretted not going. So, I held my magic in. It felt like holding my breath to the point of death itself. I was tortured with nightmares, seizures, and horrifying anxiety. But even in that darkness and despair . . . I could see a light I was completely blind to before. Like, magic had been blocking me from seeing it.

"I gave up after a few days and streamed. But I always thought of that light. About a year later, I tried again, determined to succeed. I gathered enough food and water to see me through a few months. So, I held my magic in again. Days passed, then weeks of hell. Many times, I almost flung myself from the cliff. Many times, I almost gave in to the temptation. Magic was always there, waiting. Easy to do, and it felt so damn good. At last, I reached a breaking point. All that ether was collapsing on itself like a neutron star. And neutron star, for lack of a better word, sort of transformed itself into my block. From that day forward, not a drop of ether has entered me.

"I woke up and wasn't dead." Linus paused, staring into the flames reflected in his blue-gray eyes. "My head was finally clear. And I knew peace."

Lucian was surprised to see tears forming. It was silent for a time, save for the crackle of the flames and the wind whipping past the cave mouth outside.

"Of course, I shared my findings," Linus said. "I told everyone here I could. But few could handle it. Most of the time, the ones who tried it, failed, and then they streamed more than they did before. It wasn't long for them to fray after that. I realized my teachings were making some worse. I would try to save them, but they ended up dying all the same. Only Plato here went through the Ordeal – that's what we call it – and lived to tell the tale. It took six months for his block to form." He shook his head. "What was that like, old friend?"

"Agony."

Fear twisted in Lucian's stomach. "What is it, then? What *is* magic? Why would it have this effect on us?"

"Nobody knows," Plato said. "Just as nobody knows why

some become mages in the first place. Magic is something that's pleasurable by design, but poisonous to use."

"Like hard drugs."

"It may be worse than that, Lucian," Plato said. "There is something insidious about it. Something that none of us can see that's been hidden. Hidden by what, or who? I can't say. I don't think anyone will ever know."

"I've often wondered what it *is*, exactly," Lucian said. "Why have we never had access to it before? It's only the last century and a half or so, or even less."

"Some might have been mages, but hiding," Plato said.

"No," Linus said. "Not likely. You and I have talked about this many times, and we don't always agree about everything. I keep telling you it corresponds to when we first started using the Gates. How do those work, if not by magic?"

"Are you saying the Builders *created* magic?" Lucian asked.

"I suppose it's possible. Almost certainly, they knew about it, and used it."

"And now they're gone," Lucian said.

"Makes you think, no?" Plato asked. "Magic is only magic. It's been here from the beginning, a byproduct of the creation of the universe, hidden until now, for whatever reason. Magic is the reality behind reality, the ethereal background, the Manifold manifested, and it exists outside of time and space and the universe as we know it. It may even be God. It certainly bestows the power of the gods. To say it was *created* stretches my credulity."

"Okay," Lucian said. "Suppose it's natural. Why *us*? Why now?"

Lucian wondered what Vera might have to say about all this. If anyone would have an opinion on the origin of the Manifold, it was her.

"All this talk has reminded me," Plato said, standing up. "It's long past time for bed."

Lucian was tired, too. To his surprise, the day had turned to night outside. The buzz from the Sea Drink had a way of making time pass. Lucian found himself wondering what they did with their days to keep from going insane. So far, it seemed like mostly drinking.

"I'm going to do it," Lucian said, deciding. "I'm going to do the Ordeal."

Linus looked at him. "Do you know what you're signing on for?"

"No," Lucian said. "If I can get through the Ordeal, then that means I can last as long as you or Plato. After that . . . we can think about escaping."

Assuming he really *could* form a block, as these two had, then in theory that meant he could get his old life back. At least, part of it. But it would mean he'd have to find a way off this island. Somehow.

Linus looked at him for a long time, and then laughed. "*Escaping*? And how do you plan to do that? It's impossible, even with magic."

Lucian didn't know, either. But there *had* to be something. But first, he had to prevent himself from fraying. And that meant getting through the Ordeal on the first try.

28

PLATO HELD a cup of Sea Drink to Lucian's lips. "Drink this."

"I don't feel bad yet."

"You'll need it," he said. "Trust the process."

There was nothing to do but drink. Only after three swallows did Plato nod, satisfied.

"You sure you're ready for this, son?" Linus asked.

The "mayor" was in one of his rarer serious moods. It had been about a week since Lucian moved into the cave. During that time, he'd had a taste of the Isle of Madness lifestyle. The long, dark nights seemed endless when there was little to do but drink. And Linus and Plato had plenty to drink.

Lucian soon discovered that whatever was in the beverage had a minor hallucinogenic effect at certain quantities. He could lie for hours, seeing past images of his life pass by in a kaleidoscope of vivid imagery, along with alternate realities of what might have been. He saw himself at the Academy, raised to Talent as a follower of Transcend Blue. He saw himself on the orbitally locked world of Halia, following Vera to explore Builder ruins under sheets of ice beneath a cold, star-studded sky. And he even saw a reality where he wasn't a mage at all, a reality where his mother was still alive. He had been about to leave home to crew a freighter based out of L5, having failed his civil exam.

But as always, the visions would end, and he'd return to the cave on the Isle of Madness. This reality, this truth, seemed to make the least sense of all.

Lucian warmed himself by the fire, ate some more stew, and lay on his hammock woven from ropes of lichen. Linus and Plato, to Lucian's surprise, hardly spoke to one another. Linus spent most of the daylight hours scrounging for clams and shellocks in the cold, icy surf. He had nothing but a fire built on the beach to warm him. He had taken Lucian with him several times, but it was cold, wet work. Lucian was shivering after a few minutes of wading in the shallow, icy lagoon at the base of the cliff. But Linus seemed inured to the cold. Lucian was huddling by the fire after a couple of minutes, having not found a single clam. Every time Linus emerged from the sea, frost clinging to his beard, he had a pot's worth.

Plato rarely left the cave. During daylight, he sometimes went to the flatland above to tend his "gardens." The gardens were edible fungal stalks, tubes, and lichen that grew in rocky crevices, damp with geothermal runoff. That only occupied a few hours of his time a week. His current project was building a furnace to heat the pool. Of course, any furnace would be primitive with the materials they had on hand. But once done, they wouldn't have to go to the hot springs when they wanted a warm bath. Lucian could hardly conceive how Plato could do such a thing.

"Time," Plato said, when Lucian asked. "Lots of time and experimentation. And it's not like I have anything better to do."

Plato showed him the work he'd done so far. It was nothing more than a chamber, really, hollowed out from the stone wall with a removable stone door. The fuel would be packed within, and a simple valve caused the hot air to enter a small chamber beneath the pool. The stone surface would heat, warming the water above. If all went according to plan.

"It won't be ready for a while," Plato said. "Depending on how efficient I can get it to run, I might bore out some airways around the cavern. That could give us some heating. That might not be doable, though." He smiled with pride. "Not even the Academy can boast central heating!"

"Not for lack of trying," Linus said, who was cleaning a pot of shellocks by the fire. "I don't understand the things you waste your time with."

Plato pursed his lips. "Why must you *always* denigrate my work, Linus? I'm only doing this that we all might live more comfortably."

"You do it because you're bored. Same reason I brew Sea Drink."

"The two things can't even be compared," Plato said, with a laugh. "One gets you drunk, the other betters our living conditions."

"I'd argue Sea Drink does both."

"I should have it done this winter," Plato said, turning back to Lucian. "You'll have to forgive him. We've been away from society too long. Manners have fallen by the wayside."

Lucian closed his eyes as another excruciating headache tore through him. This was his first day without magic, and already the temptation to stream was too much to bear. All the mages' warnings about ethereal poisoning ran through his mind. Why was he trusting Linus and Plato, anyway? Weren't they kicked out of the Academy for not being qualified, same as him?

Lucian knew he could never stop using magic if there were doubts. If the cost of staying here was not using magic, it was no wonder that most exiles chose Psyche. At least on Psyche, they could use magic, even if it would cause their minds and bodies to rot away. Here, magic was the only prohibition. And Lucian didn't know if he had it in him to last a few more days, much more the rest of his life.

Linus stood from his work. "Ah. Time for another drink. You can see he's sick, Plato, and your talk isn't helping."

Plato huffed, but in a way that said he must have agreed. He helped Lucian over to his hammock. The world was spinning already as Linus handed him a mug of Sea Drink. A wave of nausea passed through him.

"I know it's not easy," Plato said, kindly, "but you've got to get it down."

Lucian tried to open his eyes, but any time he did, the nausea was too much. He leaned over in his cot and heaved, though nothing came out. They had instructed him to fast, too. He couldn't decide if he was sicker, or hungrier.

Lucian took the cup and made himself drink. He tried not to taste the concoction. It left a sweet, grainy aftertaste on his tongue. "Water."

"Only a little," Plato said, handing him a cup. Lucian was only able to get a couple of swallows down before Plato took it away.

The worst part was Lucian knew streaming would make this horrible feeling go away. Holding his magic in went against everything he knew.

For all he knew, this was going to kill him. But he was determined to try. He needed the help of these men to not only survive the island, but to escape it.

"That's it, Lucian," Plato said. "Easy does it. Lie here for a while, and whatever you do . . ."

". . . Don't stream. I know." He held his breath, to keep himself from heaving again. "Why is it so bad?"

"Because the minute you learned to stream on your own, you never went a day without it," Plato explained. "The mages never gave you the opportunity to *not* stream. I've never seen the symptoms take on so fast, though. For me, it was four days, for Linus, he says he didn't get sick for a week. But you are already going through withdrawal. Either you were streaming a lot more than us back at the Academy, or your ether regenerates faster than anything we've seen before."

"So, you're saying this isn't normal?"

"Hard to say," Plato said. "The others who went through it developed symptoms later than you. Then again, some of them might have been cheating, streaming without us realizing." He smiled, and clapped Lucian on the shoulder. "Well, it's clear *you* haven't been streaming on the sly. This sickness can be thought of as the poison leaving your system."

And what if Plato was wrong? Lucian didn't have the heart to ask. The proof that it worked stood before him. Both Linus and Plato were old men, almost old enough to have participated in the Mage War themselves. They were alive during it, albeit as children. And here they were still, completely sane. Well, mostly. If there were signs of madness, it was only due to their isolation, which was understandable.

Another wave of nausea tore through him. How could he survive *this*? Was this what a magic-free life would be like? Would it be worth living in the first place? If there was even a part of him that wanted to answer "no," then there was no hope of making it through the Ordeal. But how could he make himself want it?

He almost told them then he wasn't ready for this. That he wanted to stream one last time. Both men were standing beside the fire, talking in low, indiscernible voices. When had *that* happened? Lucian had somehow faded out. It was already dark outside.

He needed to use the bathroom. Plato had carved a toilet in the rock about a meter above the lower part of the aqueduct closest to the ocean. Lucian sat up, barely managing to stand on his own. He didn't know whether it was his withdrawals, or the Sea Drink, but he could hardly keep his feet.

Linus rushed toward him. "Got to loosen your guts, I'll wager. We better get you there quick."

Lucian tried to wave him away, until he realized he wasn't going to make it on his own. Within a minute, Linus had guided him to the front of the cave, where it was much colder. Some of the harsh wind found its way in, all but sapping the heat from Lucian's fever.

The privy was in a small cleft of rock, covered by a curtain of hanging moss. Linus parted the moss for him, allowing Lucian to go inside.

There he sat on the cold stone seat, the water flowing about a meter under him. Once finished, he could hardly stand. He'd never felt so miserable in his life.

"You need help, boy?" Plato asked.

Had he been standing there the entire time? "I've got it."

He tried to stand, but he stumbled against the moss. In an instant, the older man caught him.

"Easy there." After keeping Lucian steady, Plato brought him a bowl of warm water, steeped in some sort of plant with small, white flowers.

"Put your hands in here for a good fifteen seconds," he said. "That's it, boy."

Lucian tried to thank him, but his tongue was swollen in his mouth. It was hard not to be humbled by this. He was twenty-one years old, and he couldn't even take care of himself. He had to let both guide him back to his hammock.

It went on like this for a while. Days, weeks, Lucian couldn't have said. After he counted the passing of daylight several times, his symptoms were at their worst and he could no longer keep track of the days. He couldn't move himself from his hammock. And in the darkness of his fever dreams, magic beckoned to him. He didn't know how many times he resisted its siren call, how many times he almost gave in just to feel normal again.

The men placed him on the floor at some point, on a bed of green moss which they freshened daily. Freshening was necessary because Lucian could no longer rise to use the bathroom.

This loss of dignity was almost enough to convince him to stream. But they always told him to keep going – to push through, no matter how bad it got. Or at least, that was what he thought they said.

But if it kept going like this, he was going to die. Hadn't they considered that?

The time came where it was hard to know what was real, and what was make believe. He floated through dreams. He saw Emma, hauntingly beautiful. There were his comrades from the Academy, frowning disapprovingly. Even Dirk was there, his face sneering with cruelty. There was his mother, too, her face younger than he remembered. There were periods of darkness. He relived his childhood, going back to that terrible day he learned his father had died.

His mother was crying in the living room. He didn't have to ask the reason. His heart pounded with helpless fear. His mother looked at him with reddened eyes, holding out her arms.

He ran.

"Go kiss your father, Lucian."

"No."

Why had Lucian been so angry? He could no longer remember. He was *leaving*. Why did he have to go again? He hid his face against his mother's leg.

He would not kiss him goodbye. He *wouldn't*.

He saw his father's face. The eyes were now open, yellow and rheumy. The mouth expanded into a silent scream ...

There were other dreams, too. Countless hours spent alone in his room, surfing VR interfaces. Looking for something to feel. School, where he had few friends and many enemies. Most of those confrontations had been his own fault, stemming from his own anger and shame.

And there was Luisa, too. With her, he had been afraid. Afraid of all she would see if he bared his soul, which was nothing at all.

Alone. He'd spent most of his life alone. And now he was here, on this island, never to escape.

One day, Plato and Linus would die. As good as they had made things here, they had perhaps a decade or two left.

Was it worth staying alive here, all alone? And to do so without magic, the only thing that made him feel anything at all, besides Emma?

It was hard to know. He could stick to the sad reality he knew, or pick the mystery box, as Linus had put it. Maybe the mystery box was as bad as what he knew. Or it might be even worse.

But after losing everything, what else did he have to lose?

Something told him the rest of his life did not lie on this island, as improbable as that seemed. He remembered Vera's words, under the waves of the ocean.

Greater things are meant for you, if only you have the courage to reach. Even from beyond, she had somehow spoken to him. Had that really been her? Lucian couldn't say. He no longer knew what to believe.

After the endless dreams, darkness finally came. At first, Lucian believed it to be death. It was a place without thought, without reason, without time. It was a place that might have been before the existence of the universe, and before the birth of magic itself.

He saw Seven Orbs burning like colored suns. Red. Orange. Yellow. Green. Blue. Violet. Gray. And in the middle the mind-bending shape, the maddening abomination he couldn't conceive that made him want to scream. What *was* that? To the core of his being, it felt wrong, against nature. It was like . . . an eye, but it looked nothing like any eye he'd seen. It stared into him, far harder than he could ever stare into it.

Reach, it whispered. *Take what is yours.*

I won't.

Would you deny my gift, Chosen?

Chosen? *It's not a gift. It's a curse.*

Only to fools who use it wrongly. In the right hands, magic can be your salvation.

His salvation? Did that mean it would help him leave this island?

I won't stream. I will make it through the Ordeal.

The Ordeal? Don't trouble yourself with that. You are meant for greater things.

The echoing of Vera's words seemed too coincidental. *Who are you? What are you?*

Long silence was Lucian's only answer. It stretched into eternity, until Lucian noticed a light, shining brighter than the rest. The Blue Orb. Another voice entered his mind, a voice that sounded female, but also a new voice he had never heard before.

It's close, the voice said. *Very close. Would you really leave it now, when all you must do is reach out and take it? Find it, Lucian. More is at stake than you know. You were meant to come. You are Chosen.*

What is at stake? What is Chosen?

There will be a new Time of Madness. Your race is in peril. Would you really let your kind be wiped from the face of Starsea?

Starsea? What are you talking about?

Come find me. I will tell you everything. But come alone.

All Seven Orbs shone with sudden brilliance that blinded Lucian. He screamed, the lights exploding like seven supernovae. Light and heat consumed him, as if the Manifold were a torrent of magma burning him to ash and bone.

And then it was done, followed by a moment of darkness.

When Lucian opened his eyes, the Ordeal was over.

29

THOUGH THE DAYLIGHT outside the cave was dim and gray, to Lucian's eyes it might as well have been high noon. It seemed to take forever for his eyes to adjust to the light. A steady scraping sound emanated from the direction of the fire, where Linus was cleaning shellocks. Each scrape sent a peal of pain ripping through Lucian's head. The sound stopped when Linus looked up at Lucian.

"You're alive." His voice said he found this fact surprising. He went to the aqueduct, filling a cup before coming to Lucian. "We thought you were going to die, to be honest about it." He held the cup to Lucian's lips. "Drink. The worst should be over."

Lucian guzzled the water until it was gone, downing the cup in seconds. He had never tasted anything so good.

When Lucian spoke, his voice was cracked from disuse. "Did I really almost die?"

"Seemed like it," Linus said. "How're you feeling?"

"I have a headache," Lucian said. "Correction. I have a *terrible* headache."

"That'll pass. Give it a few days, drink plenty of water. Till then, stay in bed." Linus broke into his wide, gap-toothed smile. "You made it! I'll be damned."

Lucian was wondering just how many Linus had watched die. Lucian knew he wasn't completely out of the woods, despite Linus's assurances.

Lucian slept more after that. When he woke again, it was evening. His fever was back, but not quite as bad as it had been before. The thought of using magic was tempting, but he knew doing so would undo everything he'd suffered. He knew he had some sort of block in place, but he wasn't sure whether it was permanent. The smallest trickle of ether might be enough to disintegrate it.

How many days had he been in this cave? He had lost consciousness somewhere around the fourth day, counting in Volsung increments. After the darkness, anything was a fair guess.

He faded in and out of sleep, until he felt well enough to eat. He had a light broth made from seafood and small bits of seaweed. He was no longer in his original clothes, but the same roughly woven tunics Linus and Plato wore harvested from some flax-like plant. His undergarments were clean, meaning the men had been changing him like a baby.

Why were these two going through so much effort just to keep him alive? Despite their eccentricities, they seemed to be good people. They helped without the expectation of a return favor.

It'd been a long time since Lucian had experienced that.

Plato returned, brewing a tea made with some herbs gathered from his gardens. It tasted vile, but after a few minutes, Lucian felt a sense of calm while his headache disappeared. It made him wonder where this stuff was when he needed it.

"Locals call this tundra tea," Plato explained. "The weeds grow wild here, in patches of lichen and damp places. Makes for an excellent pain reliever in the absence of morphine."

"Addictive, too," Linus said. "Almost as bad as magic."

"Yes," Plato said, agreeing with Linus for once. "It's best to limit it, and you were too sick before to make use of it. Believe me, this stuff does not help when the Ordeal pains are at their worst."

Lucian watched Plato. "How many people have you convinced to go through this?"

The two older men shared an uncomfortable look.

"Might as well be honest about it," Linus said. "About twenty actually gave it a try. They either give it up entirely, or more rarely..."

Lucian had only to look at their faces to realize the truth. "You weren't joking about dying, then. You could've told me."

"Then you would have never tried. It may seem harsh, but the only way out is through."

"And it beats the other option, dying on Psyche," Plato said. "Even if the chance of surviving the Ordeal is one in ten, it's better than fraying."

Lucian couldn't imagine anything *worse* than what he'd gone through. "Glad to see you're agreeing on something for once." The throbbing in his head had returned, but at least it was dulled by the tea. "I'm not completely through it, am I?"

"We can't say for sure," Plato said. "We haven't done it enough to have measurable results. This time, we made sure you fasted and had a bit of Sea Drink." He smiled. "Perhaps *that's* the key."

"See?" Linus said. "I *told* you so. And you said I was mad to give it to him!"

"What are you talking about?" Lucian asked. "You two don't know what you're doing, do you?"

Linus laughed. "You're only now figuring that out? The only thing I do know is that magic will kill you. Ergo, don't use it."

Plato nodded his agreement, but Lucian remembered his fevered dreams. There had been two voices; the first seemed to be the one that told him to find the Aspects. And the other one he wasn't sure. At the end of the darkness, he had seen the Septagon. And that not been his Focus. It had been something else...

And what did that second voice mean one of them being nearby? One of *what* was nearby? Surely, the voice couldn't have meant one of the *Aspects*, one of the Seven Keys prophesied by Arian.

Madness. Sheer madness.

He had to put this all behind him. He would live the life of a mage no longer, so far as it was in his power. As Linus and Plato had pointed out many times before, it was either this or Psyche.

And he most certainly didn't want to go to Psyche.

THE NEXT DAY, Lucian could get up from his hammock and take care of himself. He could use the bathroom, wash his face, and eat his own food. Plato made him a weaker brew of tundra tea, which helped him sleep and get through most of the long, dark hours. After a week, most of his Ordeal symptoms were completely gone. He didn't dare reach for his Focus. That might be too much temptation to stream, thereby undoing all his hard work.

When he was down on the shore fishing with Linus, he felt a sudden wave of nausea, which passed. As he was foraging for herbs with Plato, he was stopped in his tracks by a terrible migraine. As one brutally cold day passed into night, and back into day, the intermittent symptoms faded. Slowly, but surely.

Soon, it was cold enough for the snow to not melt on the ground, despite geothermal heating. Linus showed Lucian how to craft snowshoes. He made them from the sturdy reeds growing along the stagnant pools. After this was done, Lucian could walk on top of the deep snow.

And so, the days passed. The daylight hours waned until there was about four hours of weak twilight each day. The nights were almost as bright, with rainbow auroras painting themselves across the sky. Lucian had never known such cold, and they were never out for more than an hour or two. The older men had stocked the cave for the long Volsung winter, just in case the weather turned unbearably cold. A hoard of shellocks, crustaceans, and oysters lay iced in winter snow, while plenty of plants from Plato's gardens had been harvested.

Lucian did what he could to make himself useful. They had saved his life, and the only way to pay that back was by working. And he worked hard. He learned in weeks the skills of survival that had taken Linus and Plato years to develop. There was little hunting on the island, especially in winter. But Linus promised to take him hunting for rock crabs when the weather warmed. Plato tended his winter garden by the hot springs, using irrigation channels warmed by the ground farther inland, where the snow had yet to reach. The channels split into smaller arteries, feeding patches of tubular plants. They grew fat, purple fruits that Plato assured Lucian were safe to eat. After digging in the muddy soil, Plato showed Lucian a root vegetable. It looked like a strange cross between an eggplant and a toadstool.

"Were you an engineer or a farmer before you were a mage?" Lucian asked.

The plump man smiled. "Neither. Everything I've done here, I learned by trial and error. I've been here twenty years, Lucian. That's a long time to learn, and the best way to learn is to teach yourself." Plato went on to describe the various plants that grew seasonally. "Little but frost fruit grows in this weather. In summer, you can expect more variety. If the frost fruit is warm under the turf by the springs, they'll bear fruit. Not even harsh weather can freeze these things." For emphasis, he touched one of the tubes, about his height. Its outside seemed more akin to rubber than anything living. "The frost fruit saved the first colonies back in 2204. Resupply was impossible during the First Hegemon War."

Plato often punctuated his explanations with short history lessons. It was such a waste for an intelligent man like him to spend his life here in exile. What could this brilliant man have done if he had freedom? The alternative, though, was worse. He could be on Psyche instead, his skeleton lost in some chartless crevice.

"What's your story?" Lucian asked. "How did you come to be here? You've told me a bit, but not everything."

Plato paused his gardening, and smiled wistfully, and perhaps bitterly. "You don't want to hear my story, Lucian. I came here in my forties and I don't expect I'll live to see warm lands again. My family – what's left of it, anyway – could be dead as far as I know." He heaved a sad sigh. "What's the use of thinking about the past? I've trained myself to stay rooted in the present." He laughed, though there was no humor in it. "There are no shrinks here, unless you count Linus's Sea Drink."

Lucian didn't. "I don't understand. I don't mean to be harsh, but isn't life . . . *hopeless* here? It's so gray, dismal, and cold. I don't think I could go on for twenty years, like you."

Lucian almost regretted saying that, but he also had to know what gave Plato the strength to go on. To his relief, the older man nodded his understanding.

"Nothing is ever the end unless you decide it is." He pointed at a spot a few meters away, where a small rock crab was scuttling sideways. "Take that creature, for example. It's known nothing but this island its whole life. This island is its whole world. As far as it's concerned, nothing extends beyond the sea that bounds it. We're cursed with knowledge, Lucian. We know there is a world beyond. Even if we were to somehow forget, every few months a new exile arrives. Most can't manage to make it in this place."

"Then how have *you* made it here?"

Plato's expression darkened, as his brow furrowed in thought. "Many times, I have thought of leaving. Fear keeps me here, I think. Linus is more optimistic than me, though his harsh laughter is a shield for sorrow. Of course, Psyche could be less brutal than this island. Especially when you consider we must live without magic here. It's a matter of being content with less. To be grateful for the small things that make life livable." Plato shrugged. "And work. So much work, you can hardly think. People who can train themselves to not want the things of the world might learn to live without them."

Lucian listened. Could he learn that same lesson, or would he always be cursed with the knowledge of what could be?

Plato went on. "I do what I can most days to ensure this island is a better place to live. Not only for me, but for someone in the future, should they decide to stay. In that way, I might save a few from being tempted by Psyche. I believe I will outlive everyone who decides to take the shuttle. At least, until I'm on my deathbed. But I won't say I'm not tempted every time I hear that crackle in the sky. Several times, I've made the journey halfway to the shuttle, only to turn back for the cave. I came to this island at the ripe age of forty-four. I was a promising Talent of the Volsung Academy with my aim set on the Red Seat."

"The Red Seat?"

"Transcend Red's station," Plato explained. "It was between me and another woman, named Umbra."

"Is she the young one there now?"

"No," Plato said. "She's different. Umbra died hunting a rogue on Astravan. No, it was between Umbra and I for the Red Seat. I . . . made some mistakes, shall we say. Mistakes she was able to take advantage of, to the point where my very sanity was called into question. I'd rather not go into details. Things got desperate, so I did whatever I could to secure my place. I could not abide working for that damnable woman."

"You were a Red Talent, then."

Plato nodded. "In the end, I undid myself. I have no intention of going on to Psyche. I mean to live out the rest of my days here, in contemplation."

It sounded like a sad existence to Lucian. Then again, he was suffering the same fate. "And *have* you found meaning?"

Plato's face grew grim. "Some live their entire lives in ultimate freedom. They can hop on a ship and go anywhere in the Worlds they please. Yet they choose to remain where they are. Why is that? One could argue I'm freer than them, if I see this island as my world. A world in which it's possible to find happiness."

"And have you?"

From the scrunching of his brow, Plato seemed frustrated by Lucian's line of questioning. "I've been trying for twenty years. Some days, it seems like I have, like today. I need conversation – *stimulating* conversation – or I can't be happy. As useful as Linus is, he's not much one for deep thoughts. Great with the hunting and fishing. All people have their niches to fill. But two people do not make a happy community. And we can't allow anyone to live with us who can't pass the Ordeal." Plato clapped a hand on his shoulder. "But I have high hopes for you, Lucian. The time of your final test is coming soon."

"What do you mean, *final test*? Wasn't the Ordeal my test?"

"Linus and I were waiting for you to recover before talking about it. Few enough make it through the first phase, so we haven't done the second test in years. But despite the winter nights, it must happen soon, before the next shuttle comes. That could be days away." Plato looked at him seriously. "Are you feeling well enough?"

"I suppose," Lucian said. "What is this second test, though? If it's anything like the Ordeal, I don't know if I can handle it."

"No, it's nothing like that. It will be difficult in its own way. As far as Linus or I can tell, you've given up using magic. You haven't streamed since before the Ordeal. All that's left is to test your resolve. Only then can we accept your place here."

"And the other option is the shuttle."

"Yes."

They finished up the gardening and went back to the cave before dark overcame the island. Multicolored auroras danced above in the sky. Streams of pink, green, and violet colored the constellations. As beautiful as the lights were, it was far too cold to stay outside long. It was a relief for Lucian to be back in the cave and before the central fire, warming himself.

Over that fire, Linus was boiling a pot of shellock and herb soup. Lucian was getting tired of eating the same thing, but it was better than the fare served at the Academy. Here, there were no restrictions to flavor or texture.

Once dinner was over, the three of them sat around the fire, drinking and getting a decent buzz going. Sometimes, life here wasn't so bad. Only sometimes, though. He wondered what it might be like to have Emma here, too. He hated thinking about her. It was the easiest way to feel sad and lonely. What was she doing now? Nightly meditations, most likely.

"Something got you down?" Plato asked. "Drink will do that to you, if you're not careful."

"He's thinking about a girl," Linus said. "I see it on his face. Why don't you tell us about her?"

"It's not a girl."

"Ha! Look at him blush."

"It's the fire," Lucian said.

"Yeah, the fire right here," Linus said, pointing to his crotch. "A young man like you. It's cruel to be put up here with us two." He chuckled. "Those mages act all high and mighty, but there are liaisons on the sly. Always will be if you mix the sexes."

The idea that he and Emma might have been more was too painful to stomach. He had given up everything with her, and in the end, it didn't make a bit of difference.

"Are you done yet?" he asked.

"Struck a chord, have I?" Linus asked. "Let it all out, son. You won't feel better keeping secrets."

"What about *your* secrets?" Lucian asked. "Whatever this next test is, I'm ready for it."

Linus shot a frustrated look at Plato. "You told him?"

"It's about time for it, anyway."

Linus looked from one to the other, then stroked his long, gray beard. "Fine, then. The sooner the better, anyway. It's been a while since we've had a shuttle."

"Have you been checking the village?" Lucian asked. "Someone else might have arrived."

"There's no smoke," Linus said. "I've been walking far enough to see every day. As far as I can tell, we're ready for our trip to the Caverns."

The Caverns? That sounded foreboding. "When do we go?"

"We'll spend the rest of the night packing," Linus decided. "Leave a few hours before dawn. With luck, we can make it there before we freeze our asses off."

"And what's the test?"

"You'll know when you get there," Linus said. "I'll say this much. If the mages knew what *we* know they would have built their damned academy here."

30

THEY AWOKE in the middle of the night, packing enough supplies for five Volsung days. They didn't expect to be gone more than two or three but having a cushion in such weather was necessary. They filled their packs with smoked meat, potatoes, beets, frost fruit, various edible fungi, and seaweed bars. Besides this, they put on many layers of clothing – far more than Lucian would have thought they needed. Each of them had a parka, inheritances from past exiles. They had wear, but were still in good condition.

Even so, it was damned cold outside. But the older men had caches of food and supplies stashed around the island. If a sudden blizzard fell upon them, they would have the resources for a fire. Supposing they could get to a cache in time.

"The test is on the northern side of the island, in a system of caves," Linus explained.

"How far away?"

"Depends how fast we can walk. One standard day, if we are quick about it."

"Are we ready?" Plato asked.

Lucian gave one last review of the cave that had become his

home. He was going out into the cold, merciless world. Truthfully, he wasn't fully recovered from the Ordeal, and all he could think about was what Talent Hamil had said all those months ago about Volsung winter. It was coldness to freeze one's blood.

Even as they set out under an aurora-infused sky, Lucian couldn't imagine staying out here for an entire day. Whatever little sunlight there was would do little to warm them. Once they made it to the flatland above the cave, they trekked northeast, deeper inland, their snowshoes plodding on the fresh drifts. Their tracks coursed through unspoiled snow across a world of silence. A few flakes drifted down lazily, though Lucian couldn't see how. There was not a cloud in the sky.

The going was easy over the flat snows, though the shoes grew heavy. Dawn broke in the west, tinging the sky a sickly gray. A few hours later saw them still walking, single file, following the tracks Linus set. Linus never broke stride, as a man half his age might. The first obstacle came from a line of high, icy hills bisecting the island east to west. The orange sun peeked only enough to show half its face, casting the white-clad hills in hues of bronze and copper.

The wind was low today, a bit of luck. But even the soft breeze sent chills down Lucian's spine. Even if his body was warm, his gloves weren't enough to keep out the cold. He longed for a fire to warm his feet and hands, but that wouldn't come until tonight, long after the sun had set.

They were halfway up the mountains when they broke for their first meal of kelp bars and smoked fish. Both had to melt in their mouths before it was even possible to chew. It made for unpleasant eating, but at least Linus allowed a small fire in a cleft of rock, around which they huddled.

Lucian saw a single column of smoke on the southern horizon. It looked to be rising from the direction of the village.

"What do we do?" Plato asked, watching.

"Can't they last a week longer?" Linus asked. It was clear from his expression that he didn't want to switch course.

But Lucian had a vision of an exile there, cold, alone, and hungry. They might already be running low on supplies. And the snow would be even deeper in the valley.

All Lucian could wonder was whether it was someone he knew. Someone like Emma.

That thought alone was enough to make the decision.

"We should go down there," Lucian said. "See who it is and spend the night in the cabins."

"That would delay your test," Plato said.

Lucian thought about the problem. "With this weather, they might be *dead* in a week. We can at least check in with them and direct them to one of the caches."

Linus gave a chuckle. "You think your girl is over there?"

"It could be *anybody*," Lucian said. "We can delay the test."

The two older men thought about the problem for a few minutes. Long enough for Lucian to feel the cold seeping into his bones. He was ready to get moving.

"We'll let you decide, Lucian," Linus finally said.

The idea that it might be Emma, against all odds, made the decision for him.

"I want to go down there," he said. "We can vet them for fraying. If they are, we can leave them behind. If they aren't, we can take them to the cave to await our return."

"And if they try to follow us?" Linus asked.

"Hard to do, without snowshoes."

"He makes a good point," Plato admitted.

Linus thought for a moment, stroking his beard. "Well, if we are going down there, we better do it now. About an hour of daylight left, and these icy hills are treacherous."

LUCIAN TRIED NOT to think too much about who was down in the valley as he trekked across the snow in the direction of the smoke, though that was impossible. As small as the chance was, it could be Emma. That added urgency to his steps. By the time they crested the final rise that overlooked the village, the sun had sunk beneath the horizon, leaving a star-filled sky.

They watched for about a minute. Only one of the cabins, the very one Lucian had used, had smoke rising from its chimney. Lucian went downslope, the other two following tentatively. As he suspected, the snow drifts were higher, almost reaching the roofs of most of the cabins. Even with the snowshoes, he found himself sinking uncomfortably low in the snow. Lucian could see a path through the snow on the opposite end of the valley. That was where the exile had likely burned his way down. Someone skilled with Thermalism, then.

Once about twenty meters from the cabin, Lucian stopped. He looked back at his companions, who stood waiting for the next move.

"What now?" Lucian asked.

"This was your idea," Linus said. "First contact is on you."

Why did they think this was going to go so badly? Lucian supposed it was possible that the exile was frayed, or that he or she was starting to fray. But no Novice at the Academy had been like that, showing symptoms of rot in both mind and body. But maybe he was wrong. Maybe all this was a mistake. And after going through the Ordeal, Lucian couldn't stream anymore – not unless he wanted to undo all his hard work.

That meant he had nothing but his shockspear to defend himself with, and he couldn't even use magic to break through an energy shield streamed by an enemy mage. He took the spear from his pocket and extended it. Thinking for a moment, he collapsed it. Having it out would only panic whoever was on the other side of that door.

Linus and Plato were right to be cautious. Whoever was inside could be dangerous.

Then again, it could be a friend. Even Emma. They had already come all this way.

It was time to finish the job.

He turned to the older men. "Stay here. Or not. I'm knocking."

Without waiting for an answer, Lucian walked to the door. After a moment, Linus and Plato followed him.

31

LUCIAN WATCHED the door of the cabin, his heart beating faster. There were no windows, so there was no chance of anyone inside seeing him.

There was nothing to do but knock.

Lucian rapped three times, then took several steps back. He waited a good thirty seconds, his heart thundering. Part of him wanted to turn and go. Perhaps even *most* of him.

But curiosity got the better of him.

"Hello?" Lucian called. "Anyone home?"

There was still no answer. Lucian looked at Linus and Plato. Linus shrugged, while Plato nodded toward the door.

Lucian had started this. Now, he had to finish it.

Lucian turned the knob and pushed in, revealing a dark interior lit only by the embers of the hearth. It stunk in a way that had nothing to do with the uncured lichen. Lucian coughed, but couldn't see into the dark corner, where the bed was. Was there someone lying under the blanket?

"Hello?"

The form didn't move. Either it was asleep, or . . .

Linus touched Lucian's shoulder, making him jump.

"Geez. You're like a ninja."

"Sorry. I can check if you want."

Lucian let him pass. Linus walked to the bed and turned a body face-up. It was hard to tell who it was in the darkness, but the form was male, and the face young.

"Suicide," Linus said. "Ground here is too frozen to bury him..."

Suicide? Lucian made himself go closer, even if it was the last thing he wanted to do. He looked down at the face and recognized the exile.

"Marcus," he said. The realization was like a punch to the gut.

"You knew him?" Linus asked.

"He was in my Trial group." He shook his head. "We must have been just a few hours late. The fire is down to coals." Had they come straight here, Marcus might have found something to live for. What a terrible waste. "Could it have been an accident?"

Plato knelt on the floor, picking up a shockspear lying by the bedside. "This was no accident. Applied to the base of the skull, most likely, with a simple Dynamistic stream. It gives a death as painless as it is quick."

Lucian shuddered. "I didn't know him well. He was newer than me, but he handled himself well regardless. Why in the Worlds would he have been sent here?"

Of course, the Transcends could have exiled him for any number of reasons. It didn't necessarily have to be about his Trial performance. Whatever the case, Marcus was no longer alive to tell the story.

"There's not much we can do," Linus said. "We can go through his supplies, take what we need, and stash the rest nearby in case they send someone else soon. The body we'll have to burn."

"He wasn't a fray," Lucian said. "At least, he wasn't a month ago."

Had it really been so long since he'd arrived on the Isle of Madness? The thought seemed unreal.

Lucian remembered how he had considered the same choice Marcus made. The only thing that saved Lucian was seeing the steam of the springs in the distance. Surely, Marcus saw that same steam. He might have tried to get out of the valley, but couldn't. Perhaps the sheer effort of burning his way across the snow-filled landscape had pushed him past the point of no return.

Lucian felt a chill knowing that it could have been him.

"I doubt we have the fuel that'll make a fire that burns hot enough," Plato said.

"I say we leave it for later," Linus said. "It's cold enough to keep. We can bury it in the grove south of the springs. With the others."

It? The others? How many had these two buried over the years? Lucian didn't understand how they could talk about Marcus that way. Presumably, he had a family and others who loved him. Somewhere. What would the Transcends tell them about their son? The cold, hard truth most likely. Or even more probable, nothing at all. That would be just like them.

Lucian shook his head. "I don't see what else we can do."

Linus took Marcus's shockspear, collapsing and pocketing it. "We can never have enough of these. Great for fishing."

"More canned food, too," Plato said, rifling through Marcus's pack. "You think you can carry this, Lucian?"

"He was one of us," Lucian said. "An exile. And you would dishonor him like this?" Linus and Plato stopped what they were doing. "Maybe you didn't know him, but he was one of us."

At least each had the grace to look a little guilty.

Plato was the first to respond. "When you've seen so much death, you become desensitized to it."

"I don't care what you call it," Lucian said. "Just . . . have more respect."

Lucian walked out of the cabin. He couldn't stand being in there another moment.

About five minutes later, the two older men emerged. Plato didn't ask Lucian to carry Marcus's stuff.

Lucian looked at Linus. He had to focus on the current situation, and not the dead body in that room. "Do we have time to head north?"

Linus shook his head. "We won't find shelter north of the mountains, as I'd planned. We'll have to use one of the other cabins."

They took the cabin opposite of Marcus's and hunkered down for the night. Soon enough, they had a fire going, with some of Marcus's canned food in the pot over the hearth. They spoke not a word. Lucian couldn't emerge from his gloom. He kept thinking of Marcus's dead body, still lying in the dark cabin. He could only have been dead a few hours. It was almost too cruel to believe.

After eating, they each settled down in their own corner. Plato won the toss to get the cot. The other cabins were in such a poor state that they couldn't be used, and they hadn't the fuel for multiple fires, anyway. Linus and Lucian took up positions near the hearth; despite the stink, it was better than being cold.

And it was in that manner, with the cold wind howling outside and cold thoughts running through his mind, that Lucian fell into a fitful sleep.

When Linus woke Lucian, Plato was making a quick breakfast over the fire. They ate quickly, and within minutes were heading out the door without a single word being spoken.

They set off north, the auroras and starlight their only illumination. The long night would last for tens of hours. It was so cold that every intake of breath shocked Lucian's lungs. He covered his mouth with a scarf to protect his face from the dry, frigid air.

They left the valley, heading for the northern hills they had left behind the day before. They spent the greater part of the night scaling the ridge. Linus and Plato moved so quickly that Lucian had trouble keeping up.

The wind picked up as they neared the top. When they crested the ridge, the cold gusts were painful in their intensity. In the distance, Lucian could make out the vast ice sheet, several kilometers tall and stretching from horizon to horizon. The sheer scale of that ice wall took his breath away. It was a cold, desolate wonder, infused with the rainbow reflection of the dancing lights above.

All that was left before the ice cap was several kilometers of flat, gray tundra.

"We call the area north of the mountains the Wastes," Plato said. "As inhospitable as inhospitable can be."

What could be in these caverns, this far north? Lucian could only wonder as they followed the slope downward. Thankfully, it was not as sheer as the southern face, so it only took an hour of walking and sliding to make it to the bottom. There was no life Lucian could see. Not lichen, nor rock crabs, nor any of the tough life that eked out a living south of the mountains. He might as well have been walking across the bare surface of an asteroid or comet, from the clarity of the clear sky and the frozen barrenness of the landscape. A dusting of dry snow swirled upon the flat, frozen ground. At times, the wind would pick up sleet from patches of snow.

For as many layers as Lucian was wearing, it wasn't enough. They could not survive out here for long. They needed a fire, and Lucian couldn't stop his teeth from chattering.

"Almost there," Linus said. "Don't get frostbite yet!"

"I'm glad for the extra padding!" Plato said, patting his belly.

His words were almost eaten by the wind. Lucian didn't have the heart to respond. To think there was such a place as Miami, with sultry air and hot beaches, seemed the height of fantasy. He tried to imagine himself there right now. If he'd had magic, it would have been a simple thing to stream a heat shield, just long enough to warm up. That possibility no longer existed.

Lucian spied a deviation in the land ahead, a slight depression that wasn't visible until they were almost upon it. The ground sloped downward, then dropped off steeply.

Below them was the opening of a cave, what Lucian supposed would be their destination.

They hurried down the slope and entered the yawning mouth. Ice crystals clung to every surface. It was almost too dark to see, but at least there was no wind. Linus and Plato went straight to the back of the cave, seeming to know their way despite the darkness. At the back stood a pile of corded lichen, leaning against the ice-encased wall.

"Grab four good-sized ones, Lucian," Linus said. "Don't want to burn more than we have to."

Lucian did as he was asked, setting the lichen down in a small nook that would trap the heat. Within moments, Plato had a blaze going with his flint, and they were warming their hands and feet before it.

To Lucian, it was heavenly. It was life.

But for all its warmth, the fire was not enough. Linus allowed another two lichen logs, and the fire burned brighter and hotter. They cooked their dinner, some of Marcus's canned food. Linus announced they would head deeper into the caves once they'd had some rest. Though they were deep in the caverns here, Lucian could still hear the wind blustering outside.

Lucian had trouble sleeping, even if the nook had warmed enough to be somewhat comfortable. The wind sounded like the wail of a banshee. What was the point of even being here? He supposed he would find out soon enough.

THEY AWOKE AT DAYBREAK, if the paltry gray light entering the cave could be called that. The fire had burned low, and it was well below freezing. Lucian threw on more lichen and slept half an hour more. By the time he woke again, Linus and Plato were cooking a pot of stew over the fire.

They scraped the pot clean before packing everything up. Little of the insufficient daylight outside found its way inside. Linus assembled a torch from his pack and lit it with the remains of the fire. It burned brightly, revealing the rocky chamber with ice collecting in its corners. For the first time, Lucian saw a dark tunnel descending at the far end. His stomach dropped at the sight.

"We're going in *there*?"

"It'll be warmer, at least," Plato said.

"Let's go," Linus said.

The three of them left the fire behind to burn out and headed into the dark tunnel.

They walked for what seemed hours, generally downward. As good as Plato's word, the air warmed the further they descended. Lucian wondered why they couldn't have just slept here, even if the space was somewhat cramped. Lucian had to uncinch his parka. Sweat collected on his back until he had to remove it completely and carry it under his arm.

In the end, they found a small nook in which to place their extra clothing. According to Linus, it was only going to get warmer the further down they went. Lucian had a feeling there was a reason why they didn't opt to sleep in this tunnel.

It wasn't long before Linus's torch wasn't the only source of light. A dim, bluish-gray luminescence glowed at the end of the tunnel. At first, Lucian thought it was daylight. It couldn't be, though, or it would be far colder. Once they reached the end of the tunnel, Linus staked his torch in the sandy ground, in the beginning of a widening cavern.

The first thing Lucian saw was that this space was massive. Glittering blue crystals encrusted its sides and ceiling, lending ample light by which to see. The entire space could have fit the Academy in its entirety. They stood on a high ledge, looking upon an underworld of blue stalagmites and stalactites, formed over eons, all of which were coated with those same, blue-glowing crystals. But for all that ethereal beauty, it was not the main thing that grabbed Lucian's attention.

At the bottom of a winding trail leading from the ledge, stood a circular, domed edifice, supported by a ring of pillars rising above steps encircling its entirety. The structure glowed with blue radiance, the crystals of the cavern seeming to feed off its light. Its interior shone with light blue brilliance, almost blinding to behold.

Lucian had no doubt that this structure was left behind by the Builders. But what confused him most was that despite its age, surely hundreds of thousands of years, it looked completely unspoiled. His mouth hung agape as he stared at it.

"Now, you see," Linus said, with a knowing smile. "Not so bad, eh?"

"It's incredible," Lucian said. "But what does this have to do with a test?"

The two men looked back at the structure. They seemed to be taking in the sight just as much as Lucian.

"Everything," Linus said. "Inside those ruins, you will find your final test."

Ruins was the last word Lucian would have used to describe that structure. Majestic would be one. Magical, even. From what else could that light be coming from? He felt something pulling at him within its confines. Something familiar.

Whatever it was, he had to go down and see it. Linus and Plato's faces shone from the light emanating off the structure's surface. Unlike Lucian, it didn't seem to hurt them to look at. That was strange.

"Is there anything else you can tell me before I go in?"

"One thing," Plato said. "Remain steadfast."

"That's all?"

"That's all."

"We'll walk down together," Linus said. "But you must go in alone."

Lucian followed the older men down, until only a few minutes later, they stood before the massive structure. It was even larger up close than it had been from afar. Lucian felt small against it. The gaps between the columns shone radiantly, and it felt as if the structure would swallow him. Now that he was here, he was afraid to go in. But he also knew he *must* go in. Something compelled him.

He walked forward. As he neared the structure, he pondered Plato's words. Remain steadfast against *what*? Obviously, this place was more than a building left behind by the Builders. In fact, building seemed too common a word for it. A wonder, maybe? Or could it be a mausoleum of some forgotten alien lord? The light shining within was evidence that it was far from ordinary. Or perhaps it was a palace, and perhaps the Builders were not dead. Not all of them, anyway.

Xenoarcheologists had supposed the Builders vanished long ago. As much as a million years ago, by some estimates. If so, how could this building still be intact? Then again, Lucian thought, the Gates were still here, and they were surely as old. But the Gates had not been subjected to the same erosive forces as this planetary structure. How long had this place stood here forgotten in this dismal cave? How had it come to be here in the first place?

These questions ran through Lucian's mind as he approached the steep steps. Those steps wrapped around the domed edifice, seeming too tall for human legs. Perhaps the Builders had walked on two legs, like humans, but had longer limbs. Here on the cavern floor, the dome was taller than it had seemed from above. It loomed over Lucian, and he felt small in its glowing light. At a guess, it was fifty meters tall, and stood about that wide.

Lucian tried to take in the details as best he could before making his way upward. The pillars towered over him. He counted seventeen steps from the cavern floor to the entrance. There didn't seem to be any sort of design, artwork, or script written on the surfaces. Many archaeologists believed the Builders lacked a written language. No one had found anything of the kind. It was hard to tell whether there were any words, or even artwork, beneath the subtle glow that emanated from every surface.

Lucian peered beyond the columns. Bluish light radiated from within, making it impossible to see far. He walked toward that light, having to shield his face and squint his eyes. There was no sound or smell. Lucian got the feeling he was entering another dimension. A place where normal rules didn't apply.

Could that light somehow be magic? What was the test, exactly?

After ten or so steps, he could make out the lines of a pedestal, placed right in the center of the structure. Something seemed to be on top of it, the source of the mighty radiance.

That light felt as if it were *pulling* him. Lucian walked on, compelled to see what the object was. Despite the pain in his eyes, he couldn't keep them closed. It was only when he was standing right in front of the pedestal that he could see the object.

There sat a brilliant blue orb, shining like a miniature star.

He had to have it. He reached for it with his right hand, but some unseen force repelled him just centimeters away. He struggled against it, but his hand could not proceed any closer. He gritted his teeth. It was so beautiful, so luminous, with whorls of cloud eddying across its immaculately curved surface. He pushed as hard as he could, his hand meeting a resistance as steadfast as a diamond wall.

"Come on..."

He closed his eyes, to give them a rest from the terribly bright light. He worked his fingers around the orb, trying to find some space in which to pry it off the pedestal. But there was nothing. Lucian took a step back to examine the rest of the room for clues. Was *this* the test, then? To remove this orb and bring it back to Linus and Plato? That thought seemed reprehensible. This orb should be his. And obviously it was still here, meaning Linus and Plato had never managed to pry it loose.

With that in mind, Lucian considered the orb longer. Something tickled at his memory about it, but he was so overcome by its beauty that he couldn't think straight. The blue light no longer pained him as he circled it like a vulture, seeking some way he might wrest it free. He wandered the interior of the building, to make sure he hadn't missed anything. Perhaps there was a button or a switch that would allow him to access it. But there was no other ornamentation besides the pedestal and the treasure it held.

No, not treasure. Could it be that this was one of the Seven Keys that Arian had described? The possibility seemed beyond belief. And yet, he had seen it in his dreams. And the voice had said it was close...

How might he remove it, then? If it were one of the Seven Keys described as orbs, then it was undoubtedly an artifact of great power left behind by the Builders. If it *was* one of the orbs, and it was blue, might not Binding Magic convince it to come into his possession?

If that was so, then he couldn't remove it without streaming, without breaking the commitment he had made to himself.

This must be the test, then. He could have this treasure if he so desired. But it meant breaking his commitment.

The mere thought made his blood boil. It was so *unfair*. If he could only have this, then many possibilities would open to him. He might even use it to escape the island, though he knew not how. He sensed that it was his ticket to freedom. Or was that only wishful thinking?

Yet, the temptation to take it was powerful. More powerful than anything he'd ever felt in his life. How could he resist it? Would there be any harm to assuming his Focus and only *reaching* to feel the binding field surrounding the orb? That wasn't streaming. He wouldn't be breaking any rules.

If this site were ever discovered, thousands would descend upon it. His only chance of possessing the orb would evaporate into dust.

Even now, it was pulling at him. It *wanted* to be free of its prison. How was it possible that he knew that? The very idea of it wouldn't leave his head, that he might be the orb's rescuer. It was wrong to let such a beautiful thing shine in this place of darkness. He could become the orb's caretaker, its steward. Perhaps even bring it to a museum to get it appraised. One thing he did know: if he left it behind, he would regret it for the rest of his life.

And yet, there was his promise. His commitment. Was all that for nothing?

Still, he found himself reaching out, as if he were a puppet of a master beyond his control. He closed his eyes, reached for his Focus...

No. He couldn't.

He forced himself to look away from the orb. Forced himself to take a few steps backward. With each step, the pull and the temptation grew even more powerful. There was something special about this artifact. Something mesmerizing. The idea of holding it in his hand and unlocking its power was too great to resist. If not that, he could stare at it, discovering its essence even as its light blinded him.

He had to get away from here.

Despite the logic of this thought, he couldn't help but remain transfixed. He became aware of the fact that the longer he stood here, the harder it would be to leave. How long had he already watched it? Five minutes, or five hours?

Right here, right now, was his chance to commit, for good, to the life ahead of him. And a life without magic, without power, seemed a pale thing indeed compared to *this*. Would he be content staying on the Isle of Madness and making a new life for himself? Or would he die here, drawn to this orb like a moth to a flame? He tried to think of something – *anything* – that might get him away from this place.

Living on this island would not be enough. He needed something more. Nor did he want to choose the path Marcus had taken. That meant there was only one option left.

To take the orb.

He closed his eyes and saw Emma's face. She was smiling, and it felt as if she were in front of him. What would she make of all this, and what would she tell him?

He knew that answer without having to ask. She would tell him this wasn't right. She would tell him to back off.

Trust yourself.

The words came from seemingly nowhere, but they seemed

to come from her. Lucian *didn't* trust himself. Somehow, he knew if he streamed at this orb, it would be the death of him.

And what scared him was he would be smiling as it happened.

This orb wasn't his. It never was.

He turned his back on it and walked quickly for the entrance, between the columns and out of the light. The dim light of the cavern seemed like a world of darkness in comparison to the light and joy he left behind.

Linus and Plato were waiting at the bottom of the steps, but Lucian could hardly focus on either. His vision swam before him, still half-blind from the brilliance of the orb. He stumbled at the bottom of the steps, but Plato reached him quickly, breaking his fall. Lucian closed his eyes, trying to collect his thoughts.

"Well?" Plato asked.

Lucian blinked, and marshaled all his mental energy to respond. The orb was still boring into his mind. He wanted to go back and attempt to extricate it again.

The thought was madness.

"I'm done with this test," Lucian said. "I'm done with *being* tested."

Plato and Linus exchanged a glance, but neither said a word. In the end, Linus broke the silence. "What did you see, Lucian? What did you do?"

"I passed the test," he said. "The orb has no hold on me."

Linus and Plato shared another look – one of confusion, before they both looked back at Lucian.

"Orb?" Plato asked. "What do you mean?"

Did they not know? "The orb. That wasn't the test, then?"

"Neither of us know what you're talking about," Linus said. "Nothing in there spoke to you?"

"Who would have spoken to me?"

They couldn't mean Emma's voice. How could they have known about that?

"He must go back in," Linus said. "Or else, he can't have passed the test."

"What of this orb, then?" Plato asked. "Should we not investigate?"

"You *really* don't know what I'm talking about? There was this blue orb at the very center of the structure. You'll see it, clear as day."

"I'm going in," Linus said. "You two can wait here. I won't be long."

Linus marched up the steps and between the pillars.

"What was in there, Lucian?" Plato asked. "What happened?"

"There was this pedestal in the very center. And from it, an orb shining so brightly that I could hardly look at it."

Plato's brow scrunched in confusion. "Yeah, that's definitely not supposed to be there. Are you sure?"

"I'm not lying."

"No, of course not. It's just . . . strange. If it was there, why not pick it up and show us?"

"There's a barrier," Lucian said. "A Binding barrier, I think."

"Those are difficult to make, and *break*," Plato mused. "Binding shields are much sturdier than Dynamistic shields. Hmm." He thought about the problem. "But if that's true, then there must be a source for the magic."

At that moment, Linus appeared at the top of the steps. He shook his head before starting down. When he reached Lucian and Plato, he said, "Whatever you saw in there, it's gone."

"What?" Lucian said. "That's impossible!"

He started for the steps, but Linus grabbed him by the shoulder. "No. Your test is done, and I won't risk anything. It would seem your test is different from all the others, for some reason. I see your look. I don't doubt your story, boy. It's just mighty strange."

"*Why* was it different? What was I supposed to have seen?"

"A vision," Linus said. "A foretelling of your future." He gestured toward the building. "That's why we call this place the Oracle, and why we didn't call it that until just now. Didn't want you to think we were crazy. Are you *sure* you didn't hear a thing, and only saw this orb?"

Lucian nodded. "I . . . thought I might have heard my friend's voice in there. But it could have been my imagination."

That seemed to give both men pause. In the end, Linus said, "That could very well be. But the Oracle isn't anyone you know. Of that, you can be sure. Maybe what you saw was a vision, rather than a message."

"It didn't seem like a vision," Lucian said. "It seemed very real."

"This was not meant to be a vision, but a revelation," Plato said. "You should have learned your future. Whether this island was your fate. As the both of us did."

Lucian looked up at them with surprise. *That* was what all this had been about? If that orb *had* been a revelation of the future, then it couldn't have been on this island. Could it? He was only more confused.

"I should go back and see," he said. "If it's only a vision, it can't hurt me, right?"

"I wouldn't be so sure of that," Plato said. "Nothing like this has happened before. We should be careful."

"When you took others down here for *their* tests, what happened to them?"

"You're the only one to get this far in years," Linus said. "Some told us it was their fate to stay here. Others not. With you, though, we don't have a clear answer. I'm not sure what to do with that."

"Should I go back in or not?" Lucian asked.

"It would be irregular," Linus said.

"It's up to you," Plato said.

Lucian looked back at the entrance of the Oracle. That same, blue light emanated outward, giving the columns a sapphire luster.

Lucian knew what he had to do, but what if he *couldn't* leave this time? He almost second-guessed himself, deciding against what he knew he had to do.

But if there was a chance that this place would tell his future, he had to go in.

He went up the steps once again.

32

WHEN LUCIAN WENT inside the Oracle, it was completely vacant. The pedestal was gone, along with the orb it held. He blinked in surprise. Whatever had happened, it must have been a vision. Unless the pedestal had somehow retracted into the floor below. Lucian went to where the pedestal once stood, but there was nothing he could see. The smooth surface was as unbroken as any other part of the structure.

He couldn't help but be disappointed. He'd had his chance to take the orb, and he had ruined it. Now, it would never be his.

He hurried outside the columns, finding Plato and Linus waiting for him at the bottom. He was glad to be out of that place.

"Nothing?" Linus asked.

Lucian shook his head. "Empty."

Plato nodded. "That's what we expected. It was a vision."

"I don't see how this is possible," Lucian said.

"It's magic, boy," Linus said. "Sometimes, it can't be explained. We should go. We'll figure out what to do with your vision when we get back to the cave entrance. I need some time to stew on it."

"And by stew, you mean eat, right?" Plato asked. "I'm hungry."

The three set off back in the direction of the cavern's entrance. Before the tunnel hid the oracle from view, Lucian turned back to look. It was no longer glowing, and its state seemed far more dilapidated than before. Most of the columns still stood, but they had lost their luster. Pockmarks riddled the entire structure. Many of the steps were broken, and piles of rubble were strewn about. The roof held several large holes. Had it always looked like that, the glow obscuring the imperfections beneath?

Lucian no longer knew what to think.

"Has it always looked that way?" Lucian asked.

His two companions stopped and looked back.

"What do you mean?" Plato asked. "It's been that way for as long as we've seen it. And it's likely been like that for tens of thousands of years."

They both looked at him, but Lucian could only stare incredulously. Had his very *perception* of the Oracle, with all its untarnished glory, been a vision as well?

Lucian wanted nothing more than to be away from this infernal place. Something wasn't right about it.

"Let's move on," he said.

They left the Oracle behind, and with every step, Lucian felt lighter.

A SNOWSTORM WAS BLOWING by the time they reached the cave entrance. Plato built up a fire and the three crowded around it.

With luck, they might make it to the home cave in time for dinner tomorrow.

They heated stew by combining ingredients from their packs and melted snow. It was cold out here, but the last thing Lucian wanted was to seek shelter deeper in the cave. That would only bring him closer to the Oracle, and his vision of the orb.

Linus threw on more fuel, to better warm them as they settled down for sleep.

But Lucian found sleep impossible. It wasn't only the cold. He couldn't get the Oracle out of his mind. Nor could he stop thinking about the orb.

He could still go back. He could still try to figure it out. Now that the idea had taken root, he couldn't get it out of his mind. The passage down would take three hours. Two, if he ran most of it. If he waited too long, the opportunity would pass forever. Two hours there, two back, and an hour to investigate.

This was madness. Was he fraying already to consider such a thing?

But he was already standing. He watched the two older men, both fast asleep by the light of the fire. Odds were they would notice he was gone. But he couldn't stop now. He *had* to see if the Oracle had reverted to its former glory, or if it had only been his imagination.

Before he could doubt himself, Lucian lit a spare torch, and began his long descent into the darkness.

About fifteen minutes in, he paused and was thinking of going back. What if his torch went out in the tunnel and he became lost down here? What would happen if Linus and Plato discovered him gone? Despite these questions, he found himself running. He had to know, or he would be wondering "what if" for the rest of his life.

There was something about that Oracle. It was connected to *everything*. He didn't know, but he had to get down there to find out. If that orb had anything to do with Arian's vision, he had to find it again.

So, he continued to run. At least an hour passed, and then two. He was grateful for all the physical training he'd gotten over the last few months. Without that, he would have collapsed an hour ago. He was getting close.

At last, he came to the final bend. He could see the blue light emanating from the crystal cavern ahead. His heart thundered in his chest. In moments, he would be confirming the truth. He sprinted until he was out of the tunnel. Upon entering the cavern, he smiled.

It was as it had been. The radiant Oracle shone in its full splendor, its marble columns and steps glowing while its cerulean-domed roof shone with sapphire beauty.

Lucian didn't understand *how* it was doing this, or why. There was only one way to solve the puzzle.

The orb was in there. It was waiting.

Lucian hurried down the trail, and within minutes, was standing before the steps. This time, though, he didn't feel alone. Someone, or something, was watching him. Despite his fear, he climbed the steps. He tried to ignore the feeling that he might be a bug crawling into a flytrap.

Once again, he stood within the hallowed space. The radiance again was blinding, emanating from the central pedestal.

The orb was there.

He had a vision of Plato and Linus heading down the tunnel, having discovered his absence. He didn't know whether it was real, but it was enough impetus for him to step forward into the light. He was only a meter from the beautiful blue orb. If he could reach out and grab it, it was just small enough to fit in one hand. But when he did reach, the orb repulsed him once again.

This time, however, he meant to have it. Compulsion drove him. It was *necessary*.

For the first time since entering the cave, Lucian reached for his Focus. He felt his pool waiting beyond. There was a block.

But there were weaknesses, cracks in the dam he could exploit if he truly wished.

The orb would show him the way. He knew it.

Why was he doing this? Assuming he attained it, what would he do with it? For all he knew, the orb burned hotter than a neutron star and would obliterate him as soon as the field dissipated. Maybe the Builders had placed it here because it was too dangerous. Perhaps it was a religious relic, and the building a shrine. Whatever the case, it seemed to Lucian they *meant* to hide it. Why else would it be so deep underground on such a remote island? Then again, at the time they built the shrine, it might have been above ground, visible for all to see.

"Beautiful, isn't it?" came a musical, female voice.

Lucian almost jumped out of his skin as he pivoted. And there stood the most beautiful woman he had ever seen. She shone with blue brilliance, her appearance like a goddess from myth, so perfectly formed as to be eerie. Her wavy, raven-black hair fell past her shoulders, while her creamy skin was free of wrinkles and disfigurement. Her face was the glory of youth, but at the same time, had a strange, ageless quality. When her steely blue eyes gazed at Lucian, they seemed to see far more than the surface. Those eyes saw into his very soul and knew that he wanted her treasure. He stood paralyzed, unable to speak.

She looked familiar, but Lucian did not understand why.

"Who are you?" Lucian asked, his voice coming out cracked. It was a struggle to even meet her eyes. He was unworthy of them.

"Who am I?" she asked, smiling. "I'm the one who called you here. I'm the Oracle of this shrine. You can think of me as a spirit. A manifestation of the Manifold."

"A goddess?"

"If you please."

Lucian found another question on his lips, but at that point, she moved past him. Her hair brushed his arm, and in her wake, she left a sweet fragrance of apple blossoms and cinnamon. He lost his train of thought then and took a couple of steps back to gain some distance, and hopefully, his mental clarity. Her eyes met his again, inquisitive, before her attention returned to the orb. Its bright blue light reflected in her eyes, like sapphires in sunlight.

"What is it, then?" Lucian asked, doing his best to keep his eyes off her and on the orb. "What is this place?"

She placed her hand upon the orb. For her, there was no barrier. As she touched it, her entire body emitted radiance. When she removed her hand from the orb, the radiance receded. She smiled in a way that made Lucian ache.

"Do not be alarmed, but I can see into your mind," she said. "I know your thoughts, your desires, your fears, your memories. And I will use that information to tell you a story that makes sense to you, in a language you can understand."

Lucian found he didn't have a response. What *could* he say to such a thing?

The Oracle continued. "Long, long ago, the ones you call the Builders had an empire encompassing a thousand suns. They called it Starsea. Like your kind, they discovered the Manifold and learned to use it. They used the Gates to settle the worlds. They used magic for various arts – star sailing, construction, and the craft of war." Her face twisted. Even that expression was beautiful. "But after a time, the Madness visited them. As more awakened to the Manifold, more were taken by the Madness – and they destroyed each other. Their temples, their mansions, and their towers became dust. Their thralls rebelled." She smiled grimly and looked at Lucian. "Some like you were among the thralls. But that was long ago, and your kind looks different now. Starsea fell, a shadow consuming itself. The broken empire could not be reforged. The Time of Legends passed into the Time of Madness. And the Time of

Madness, into the Time of Darkness. Each generation, smaller than the last, grew ever sicker, ever more devolved, ever more depraved, ever more ignorant. Until one day, centuries after the Desolation, none of us remained."

Us? So she was one of them.

The Oracle paused to allow Lucian to absorb this information. What did any of this mean? Despite the thousand questions Lucian had, he couldn't bring himself to speak. To interrupt her was a travesty too great for words.

"Their fall was as great as their power," she went on. "It would be unimaginable to you. They did things with magic that humanity could never imagine. But like humanity, the Builders could not free themselves from baser instincts. And magic only served to magnify everything that was ugly about them. The galaxy became a dark place, even at the height of the Time of Legends. Power begets power, conquest begets conquest. The Lords of Starsea were locked into bitter war with one another, only subservient to the Infinite Emperor. But at last, they had reached their limit."

She paused, seemingly to give Lucian a chance to ask questions. He finally found his tongue, his former paralysis melting away. "What do you mean, they reached their limit?"

Her eyes became distant, even sad. "The *Alkasen* came. Despite the Builders' power, no amount of magic could compete with that dread menace. The Manifold . . . turned against the Builders. The Pristine Worlds were sieged and ran with our blood. And the Temples of Nai Shairen, which had never felt the touch of war, crumbled. And with them, Starsea disintegrated before the *Alkasen* hordes."

Lucian didn't understand a word of what she was talking about, though he sensed the sadness of her words, and almost mourned with her for those bygone days.

"You were one of them," he said. "Right?"

She gave a slow nod. "And I am now bound to this place."

"Why?"

She nodded at the orb. "I'm to guard *that*. Until I find one who is worthy to bear it."

Lucian realized that *she* was the key to gaining the orb. He had so many questions, but all he could think to ask was one.

"What is it?" Lucian asked. "Is it one of the Seven Keys?"

She smiled, as if that were funny. "I feared a time might come where knowledge of them would pass out of all memory."

"There was a man," Lucian said. "Arian. He delved the Manifold, and had a prophecy about orbs and Aspects..."

"The Manifold has revealed what once was lost. When knowledge is lacking, the Manifold can supply it. If it sees fit to."

Lucian wasn't sure what to say to that.

"Do you not feel the desire to hold it, Lucian?"

She knew his name, but he did not find that fact surprising. After all, she said she could see into his thoughts and memories. He looked at the orb again. "I do. But I've made a commitment to not use magic. And I will have to stream if I take that orb."

The Oracle watched him. It was hard to read those beautiful eyes. "This is an artifact of great power. One of seven in Starsea of its kind." She looked at it, with a strange mixture of pain and longing. "It was the dream of many to hold all seven. For a time, the Immortal Emperor did – he who ruled Starsea. But even in his great power, he was brought low by the peoples he subdued, despite the power of the orbs. Upon his death, the mages fought over his remains, and the Seven Vigilants took the orbs, rending Starsea asunder. But unknown in those days, when the orbs are separate, the Madness takes hold. If all are held by one, the Madness is kept at bay. There were none strong enough to regather what was lost, nor were any Vigilants willing to give up their orb for the greater good. When one died, another usurper took his or her orb, becoming a new

Vigilant. Thus several of your centuries passed. This was the Time of Madness, where Starsea slowly, but surely, disintegrated. When the *Alkasen* at last came, there were none left who could resist them. Starsea was laid waste, and the Builders no more."

"The *Alkasen*. Who are they?"

"The ones you call the Swarmers."

Lucian felt a chill at those words. The Swarmers *he* knew? Then they had outlived this Starsea Empire for hundreds of thousands of years, long enough to begin hunting humanity. If an empire of a thousand suns with inconceivable magic could not survive them, what hope did humanity have?

Lucian decided to ask about something else. "You said if one person holds these Seven Orbs, the Madness will be kept at bay. You mean the fraying, right?"

"Yes," she said, completing his thought. "This is known. Gathering the Seven would end the maddening effect of magic. Each orb grants a further boon, too. Whoever holds even one can stream the magic of its Aspect without fear of the Madness taking. It filters the Madness out of all the ether drawn from the Manifold." She nodded toward the blue orb before her, which Lucian watched with renewed awe. "This is the Orb of Binding. It is . . . mine. But my dream of holding all Seven is as dead as I am. Only the power of this orb allows my spirit to abide. To await one worthy of bearing it."

"And the other orbs do the same?" Lucian said. "If I were to have this, I could stream Binding without fear of fraying?"

The Oracle nodded. "This is so. It is not easy to do. It requires competence. But if the Orb respects your power, and your heart, then its power is yours."

Lucian had no idea of the implications, but his heart raced. This was power *beyond* power. "Yes. I can see how that might be useful."

The Oracle gave a sonorous laugh. "An understatement.

The Vigilants fought wars, with billions of dead on either side, for the mere dream of holding a single orb. Empires rose and fell in the bleeding carcass of what was once the Empire of Starsea. The Vigilants were nigh unassailable in their Aspect. Furthermore, each orb extends the life of the one holding it, but true immortality is not granted until all Seven are held. It is from this that the Immortal Emperor of old derived his name."

"I guess he wasn't so immortal if he was overthrown."

She stared at Lucian as if he were supremely stupid. "A being of his power does not simply die, Lucian. The Immortal lives on in the Manifold itself. His spirit endures, for I can hear his whispers in the darkness of my mind." Her eyes focused intently on his. "And I see that you have heard those whispers, too."

"Why am I hearing him?" Lucian asked. "How can that be possible?"

"Because, Lucian, you are a mage of unusual strength. And I believe you are the Chosen of the Manifold."

There it was again. That word. Lucian felt his hairs stand on end. He didn't know what that meant, but he didn't like it.

"Once every Cycle, one is born. And the Chosen has the power to end the Cycles once and for all. Or not."

"I don't know what you're talking about. Why would it be me?"

But Lucian thought back to yet another conversation he'd had with Vera on the *Burung*. She had said the Manifold had "marked" him in some strange way. Could that be the same thing?

"I'm not saying you *are* the Chosen of the Manifold," the Oracle said. "Only that I believe you may be. And it may be someone else. But I can sense you are unusually gifted with magic, though you are still limited by lack of training. Surely, your masters noticed unusual progress in all or most of the Aspects of the Manifold?"

"Only toward the end of my training, but . . ." He trailed off. "This can't be real!"

"It's very real," the Oracle said. "Just as real as you talking to an Oracle of Starsea who was the Last Vigilant of Binding."

Lucian felt as if he might faint. He needed a whole canteen of Sea Drink right about now.

"So if this is me, then I'm the only one that can end this Cycle . . ." He shook his head. "What the hell is a Cycle?"

It felt wrong to curse in her presence, but Lucian was done mincing words. If she was going to tell him he was one in billions chance to be some sort of "chosen one," then she had better give him evidence.

"As I said before, each Vigilant dreamed one day to hold all Seven. But holding a single orb, or even six, cannot keep decay or the Madness completely at bay. For at times, it was necessary for the Vigilants to stream other Aspects. The Vigilants could be sure of no one's loyalty, as every mage of Starsea coveted the orbs. Friends and family, overcome with greed, turned against the Vigilants. Some even succeeded in gaining the object of their desire, becoming the new Vigilant."

Tears streamed from her eyes. Lucian knew then she was speaking from experience. Had she been the one who was betrayed, or the betrayer? There might be ugliness beneath that beauty.

"You were a Vigilant, then. And then you became this Oracle. How? And why?"

She hesitated, but in the end, elucidated further. "When a Vigilant dies, their orb bleeds out from their heart. And by heart, I mean the point where soul meets magic, the gateway through which the Manifold streams. Whether that death comes from the cut of a blade, from magic, the Madness, or simple old age . . . the Vigilant loses the orb. And the orb goes to whoever finds it next. Even if that being possesses not a shred of the Gift, they possess the Gift as soon as they accept the orb as theirs."

"The Gift being magic itself," Lucian said. "So rather than die with the orb, you created this place. So none may have it."

"All of us agreed to such. I was the last Vigilant of Binding, just as the others were the last of their kind. The *Alkasen* were coming, laying waste to all. Even combining forces, we were too weak to defend the tattered remains of Starsea." She fell silent. "So, we made a pact, and we bound our word with magic, that our very orbs would destroy us should we not go through with it. For such was the distrust sown between us. We forced ourselves to work for a far distant future, where a future Chosen might find all Seven Orbs and end the Starsea Cycle."

Lucian could only think to ask one thing. "How long have you been here, then?"

It was a long time before she spoke again, her face a mask of sorrow. "Countless epochs. *Terrible* epochs, passing in silence. I . . . can't say how long it has been. I've been waiting for someone worthy to come. Someone strong and wise enough to fulfill my purpose."

"What about the other Vigilants? How do they factor into all of this?"

"Those Vigilants are now the Oracles, all the remains of the memories of Starsea. They each have their own secret places, to take their orb and hide it. They wouldn't make themselves easy to find. After all, it is necessary to prove one's worth to the Oracle in question to gain their orb. As you must prove your worth to me."

"You said if a Vigilant dies with the orb, it bleeds out from their heart. What would happen if a Vigilant died with an orb, alone, with no one around to find it?"

"I don't know," she said. "I've often wondered that myself. It has never happened, for a Vigilant was always surrounded by sycophants. I suppose it *could* have happened, as each Vigilant departed the summit to create their own place to guard their orb. However, the Manifold sleeps with the sleeping of the orbs. The Starsea Cycle came to a pause, and mages were no longer born."

"What do you mean, *came to a pause*?"

"Magic itself ended, except within the confines of each Oracle, and with the Gates – though one day, given time, their magic will end, too. They are far too powerful to be affected so easily by the sleeping of the orbs. And since magic slept, it's safe to say each Vigilant accomplished their mission, staying true to their word given at the Summit."

Lucian was confused. "But magic *hasn't* ended. And humanity can use magic. A few of us, at least."

"The return of magic coincides with the beginning of a new Cycle," the Oracle said. "As well as a new Chosen of the Manifold. And magic only returns when at least one of the orbs is active. Which has been the case for greater than one of your centuries."

If that was true, then it could only mean one thing. And Lucian reeled at the implications. "That means..."

"Yes," she said. "Somehow, somewhere, a human has found an orb. The Starsea Cycle has begun anew. Magic has returned, the Manifold imparting the Gift on select members of humanity. The Madness has also returned, and with the Madness, the *Alkasen*."

The thought seemed unbelievable. *Someone* had another orb. Who could it possibly be?

"Someone found an orb over a century ago," Lucian said. "And that caused magic to be released again?"

The Oracle gave a regal nod.

Some mage out there had unlimited power with one of the Aspects. Someone out there exploring the Gates probably happened upon one of the Oracles all those years ago. And by taking that orb, they had unwittingly released magic upon humanity, along with the Madness. The Starsea Cycle had resumed, the Desolation foretold by Arian.

"It seems unreal," he finally said. "Who could it have been?"

"I don't know," the Oracle said. "Nor do I know which orb was found."

"Where did the orbs come from, then?" Lucian asked. "Where did the *Manifold* come from? How did this Immortal Emperor find them all?"

"The Manifold is the unmoved Mover, that which remains still when all else is in motion. That is why, only with Focus, it can be sensed. As for the orbs, we don't know from where they came. They were from even before the Builders, perhaps the fundamental laws of nature manifested as single, physical objects – the meeting of the ethereal field and reality itself. Certainly, they seem to be the keys to the Manifold– whether its power is open to manipulation, or not. Somehow, the Immortal Emperor, who lived far before my time, discovered them, thereby preventing the Madness from destroying my species while he held them. He was our Chosen – he gathered them all before the Madness could take hold. But he could not save himself from the Insurrection, nor the *Alkasen*."

She was quiet then, for a long while. Lucian almost thought she wasn't going to say anything else.

"The real question, of course, is whether I should grant you *my* orb. If I do, you would be able to use Binding Magic without fear of being destroyed by it. But first, I must deem you worthy."

"And how would I do that?"

She smiled. "It's been a long time since someone strong enough has come to wield it. One who might be Chosen. I sense a purpose in you. A potential for greatness I haven't seen since I imprisoned myself in this place." Her expression hardened, and her glance made Lucian want to quail. "Even so, if you are *not* worthy, I will await another. Even if it takes a million of your human years."

"Why *would* you give it to me, anyway? What would you have me do with it?"

"That is what you are to tell me. Of course, you have every right to refuse it as well."

"I'm not following."

"The Starsea Cycle has resumed since an orb was discovered after all Seven lay dormant. The Cycle pauses when all seven lie dormant again. Who's to say how many times we've gone through these Cycles of creation and destruction? If there is one who holds all Seven orbs, the Madness is stayed. And the one who holds the orbs becomes the Immortal. Nothing will kill them, save a grievous wound." She watched Lucian carefully, as if to see whether he was following. "Magic has been dormant for over a million of your years, Lucian. But now, it has awoken. The cycle has resumed, and the Madness will take your race, one by one, until someone holds all Seven Orbs. The Manifold will *destroy* your race." She lowered her head. "Just as it destroyed us."

Despite all this overwhelming information, Lucian understood the reason she had called him here. She thought *he* had the strength to find the orbs. To gather them.

To become the new Chosen.

But why him? Why might he be worthy? What did all this even mean?

"This is what I wish of you, Lucian. I want you to find all the orbs. But not to become a new Immortal, a cruel master of a new Empire." If there was beauty in that intense gaze, then it was terrible beauty. "I want you to find the orbs and end magic. To destroy this reality's access to magic, once and for all."

33

LUCIAN WATCHED her in stunned silence. The sheer weight of that sentence almost made him laugh. End *magic*?

"You must be joking."

"I'm not," the Oracle said, turning her back to him. "I've waited here untold years for one strong enough to bear the orb. One who might be the Chosen. I may never get another chance."

"What about Linus and Plato?" Lucian asked. "You know about them, right?"

"Yes. But I sensed also that they would not be able to bear it. Linus is closed to using magic, whatever the reason. Plato has done the same. I sensed all that, and more. Of course, you are not without your weaknesses. And what I ask may be impossible, regardless. But if no one tries, then we are doomed to repeat the past. The Starsea Cycle will continue until the stars burn out and the universe is nothing but a cold, dark void. For more than a million years, I've waited for one worthy to come. But I will not grant you the orb unless you agree to find them all. Where the Orb of Binding goes, my essence goes, too. You must commit to complete the work none of us could accomplish."

Lucian shuddered at the mere *thought* that he might have to do this. He didn't know enough. He wasn't strong enough. It was too much of a burden.

"I don't know where the other orbs *are*. And who's to say the other Oracles will be willing to give their orbs to me? You've had a change of heart, but what if the others *don't* want magic to end?"

"Relinquishing the orb is the only way they can pass," she said. "If they cannot give it to you, there is likely no one they can give it to."

"Pass. You mean die."

She sighed. "It's been so long. But I refused to give my orb until one who might be the Chosen stood before me. The others, too, will sense your power. You must make them understand if they refuse to give you their orbs."

"But how would I even begin finding them? I can't expect to stumble upon them all accidentally, like I did here."

"The Oracles built their shines across Starsea. In places far, and in places wide. In places cold, and in places hot. Some do not wish for the orbs to be destroyed like me, Lucian. Some wish for the rise of a new Immortal Emperor, a new Time of Legends, in the hope that, by the new Immortal's power and magic, the new Immortal might revive them."

"Is such a thing possible?"

"Who's to say?" the Oracle asked. "But that was never meant to be. Perhaps the Immortal has magic enough to reverse death, to reverse a soul that's faded into the Manifold itself. But such a thing would not stop the Starsea Cycle. It would only stop it for as long as the Immortal drew breath. Even the Immortal Emperor of Starsea fell, at the height of his empire's glory."

"I see," Lucian said, though he wasn't sure he did.

"From the time an orb is found, it is only a matter of time

before magic lays waste to the species that has uncovered the orbs. As such, I don't know how much time there is left. But there is someone out there who has obtained at least one of the orbs."

"Another Chosen, then."

The Oracle nodded. "Most likely."

"Then why not wait for that other Chosen to find you?"

"I don't *know* if that Chosen would find me," the Oracle said. "And I don't know what they plan to do with the orb they have already found. Remember, a single orb does not grant eternal life, only longevity and unlimited, pure ether of that Aspect. Only possession of all grants immortality."

This had gone too far. "Well, *I* can't do this. I am an exile of the Volsung Academy. I'm the least qualified of all to do this."

Lucian looked at that orb, and again felt the desire to own it. Would it be possible to accept the Oracle's mission, but still follow his own path? The idea of the mission was laughably impossible. All of this was so outlandish. How could it be true? How could he even be sure of this Oracle's motivations?

"I can't."

"If not you, then who?"

Who indeed? Transcend White? Too old, despite her power. The Oracle had already rejected Plato and Linus. He thought of Vera, but she too was old, like her sister. Even with the power of one of the orbs, how long might it stretch her life? Lucian didn't know the answer to that. What he did know was another Chosen was out there somewhere. But as the Oracle said, it was impossible to know their motives. And he would not be able to find them stuck on this island, anyway. He doubted something even as powerful as the Orb of Binding could help him escape the Isle of Madness. What would unlimited ether in the Aspect of Binding allow him to do? A great many things, but he still needed the knowledge, and he was still restricted by certain rules of magic, such as having to see an object in the first place to be able to Bind it. That made crossing the ocean an impossibility, even with unlimited magic. Unlimited ether in Binding was an awesome boon to be sure, but not something that gave him limitless power.

He could refuse the Oracle and stay on this island for the rest of his life. But he didn't want that outcome. The only other option was to take the Orb of Binding and escape in the only way he knew how: allowing the shuttle to take him to Psyche. There might be new opportunities there, opportunities that could not be imagined from his position here.

He was out of options. The only option that gave him any sort of freedom was accepting the orb, along with the Oracle's mandate to destroy it, as impossible as that seemed.

"You never explained how I end magic," Lucian said. "I assume it's not as simple as breaking these orbs?"

She shook her head. "That's impossible. All Seven must be found . . . and they must be taken to the Heart of the Universe." She cradled the orb in both hands, almost protectively. "Where creation began, magic must end."

Lucian almost turned around and left right there. The Heart of the *Universe*? What did that even mean?

"The Manifold and the reality before us, the Corporeal, came into being at the same moment. You must return to that point, to the Heart of Creation. It is from there the orbs originated, and it is to there they must be taken."

Lucian gave a nervous laugh. "You realize how big the universe is, right? That's impossible."

"I understand that more than you could. But all the same, it must be done."

"*How*? So, I get the orbs by some miracle, and by some

other miracle I make it to this Heart of the Universe. Then what?"

"There is a Gate. *The First Gate.* And through that Gate is the Heart. The First Gate lies deep in Dark Space."

"Dark Space?"

"The abode of the *Alkasen.*"

"The *Alkasen.* Who are they?"

"They are the death knell. When magic awakens, so do they. And when magic sleeps, they sleep likewise. They are connected to the Cycles. They grow stronger and stronger until the Cycle ends. Only when magic sleeps again do they withdraw from whence they came. Their worlds – if indeed they even *live* on worlds such as we conceive – lie beyond the Last Gates of Starsea. It may even be impossible to pass *through* Dark Space. But it is the only way to stop the Cycles, for it is in that direction that the First Gate was raised."

It was impossibility on top of impossibility. "And through this First Gate is the Heart of the Universe."

"Yes. The Heart is the origin of the orbs. And what was made there, can be destroyed there."

"And how do you know that this place actually exists?"

"Because I've dreamed of it. And I believe that dream to be true." Seeing his reaction, she shook her head. "Yes, Lucian. It is a slender reed, but it is all we have to ride out the storm."

Impossible. It would be far easier to gather the orbs and become the Immortal, as impossible as *that* was.

"It's hopeless, isn't it?" Lucian asked. "Why not throw the orbs into some black hole, or a star?"

"Because they would not be destroyed. In the case of a black hole, due to time dilation in its gravity well, you would only ensure the orbs' preservation until the end of the universe. The gravity would not undo them. And in the case of a star, they would simply become buried in plasma and impossible to extricate. They are *magic*, and only magic can destroy them. That means they must be taken to the Manifold, into one reality that might undo them. And that can only be found at the Heart of the Universe."

"I would surely die in the attempt."

"We Oracles laid aside everything. Our pride. Our vanity. All for a shot to end the Cycles since none of us was strong enough to do it alone. We each went our separate ways. With the last of our resources, we built these hidden places. And here, we sacrificed ourselves to protect the orbs. Until one day, a Chosen strong enough might come to do that which we never could."

"You mean, never *would*."

The Oracle nodded, conceding this point.

"I'm not as strong as you," Lucian said. "And you want me to bear the burden? That's rich."

"We have no other choice. For an orb has already been found, meaning that you, or that person, are the only hope to stop the Starsea Cycle." When Lucian had been silent for a while, she approached the orb once again. "As soon as you touch it, it will cease to be a physical object. It becomes a part of you, only parting from your soul upon death or voluntary relinquishment."

"If I say I want it," Lucian said, "how will you know my motives are pure, and that I'll use it for what you intend?"

She gave a sad smile. "I won't know. I can only make my best guess at your motives. I am wiser than most, but even I can be wrong. Should you take it, you should seek the other Oracles. They might have their own conditions for relinquishing their orbs. Even if we agreed the Orbs needed to be protected for the future, we disagreed on how the future Chosen should use them. I only ask for your word, because one's word, when given in good faith and adhered to, is the greatest treasure of all. In the end, I suppose, we will discover which of us was short-changed. Nothing of worth can be accomplished until one person chooses to trust another, and they return that trust in kind."

Trust was a dangerous thing. It was the most powerful bond in the universe. Until it was betrayed.

And from the Oracle's tale, she had most certainly betrayed trust many times.

It wasn't that he was the Chosen. It wasn't even the fact he was marked by the Manifold, whatever that meant. Time had only run out. He was her last choice, one forced upon her because the Cycle had begun anew.

The thought chilled him to the core.

"I don't want this," he said. "You would give it to me, despite that?"

"Nothing in this is a sure thing, Lucian. Even *I* don't believe there is much possibility of success. And yet, I know it's important to try, despite all that. Sometimes, when we try, we end up surprising ourselves. Something that seems impossible becomes possible through the force of will. Never easy. But possible, as long as the odds are."

What he should have done was walk away. He should have done that a long time ago. Because the longer he stayed here, the more convinced he became of her vision. The more he saw himself wielding the Orb of Binding and seeking the others. If not to destroy them, then to use them for his own ends. Whatever those were.

"End the Starsea Cycle," he said. "End magic. Wouldn't that destroy everything? Destroy the Manifold?"

"No," she said. "Magic would die. Magic is how mages can manipulate the Manifold, so the Manifold would still exist. It would just be inaccessible. And of course, the Cycles would end."

"And that's according to your dream."

"Yes," she said. "My dreams are just a greater part in the

Prophecy of the Seven. That is, what the Seven Oracles have dreamed since we began guarding our orbs."

Lucian looked at the Orb of Binding again, held in her hand. And he knew his answer, as insane as it was. He didn't even know what possessed him to arrive at that answer. Maybe it was the fact that, like her, he had no other choice. He didn't want to live on this island for the rest of his life, eating seaweed and seafood with Linus and Plato. Even if he died, it was something to try. Something bigger than himself.

This was his path, at least for now. It was what the Manifold had set before him. He didn't understand why, or for what reason, but it was his path.

He let out a sigh. "All right, fine. If you're okay with me having no idea what the hell I'm doing, I'll take the orb."

The Oracle did not say anything – not for a long time. She stared into the distance, her face a mask of sadness. Finally, she faced Lucian. "Even after everything I've said, you still don't know what you ask, Lucian. And that is what saddens me. And yet, I will not refuse you. You are not our best hope. Not by a long shot. But you may be the best I ever get to see before the Madness destroys everything, along with the *Alkasen*. How this plays out remains to be seen."

Lucian felt anything but encouraged by that. But better the truth that cuts than the lie that inflates. It was an impossible task he had no idea how to complete. Who knew? Maybe in the future, he could find someone worthier to bear the burden.

A wind was now blowing, swirling around the interior of the shrine. It rose to a roar, and Lucian shouted, but the Oracle did not hear him. She cradled the Orb of Binding in both hands as the wind deadened. She touched it with tenderness, her face bathed with its light. Lucian could see tears falling like melting ice. Was it because she was giving up a priceless artifact that had been hers for eons? Because she believed there to be no hope? Or because she knew things beyond Lucian's conception, of the pain this object would cause him?

Then there was the simplest answer. She herself would end upon his acceptance of it. That was a sad thought, enough for a few tears to come to Lucian's eyes. But she would finally be able to rest after hundreds of millennia.

At least, that was what he told himself.

He had no time to ponder these questions. She stood before him and held the Orb of Binding out. He reached, seeming to be pulled by its gravity. At long last, he placed both hands upon it. It was warm as it vibrated beneath him. The light shone brighter and brighter, wrapping itself around him like a storm. It brightened until everything was blue whiteness projecting in all directions. He screamed, the orb seeming to obliterate him from existence...

Until the whiteness began to fade, and the world once again materialized in his vision. Broken pillars. Shattered stones. Cracked tiles. A half-collapsed roof. The interior of the shrine stood before him once more in its true, ruinous state. Drab, gray, lifeless. He looked around, bemused. Of the shining cerulean tiles, the resplendent pillars, the alabaster surfaces, there was no trace.

And the Oracle herself was gone, as if she had never been. He still held the Orb of Binding, which was now bleeding blue lines of light that ran along his arms. Those lines converged at his heart, uniting for a moment as a single point of light. And then, that too, faded.

The orb was his, soul-bound, and would only be unbound upon his death. He felt no different. It was as if he had imagined the whole thing. There was a part of him that still believed this was a dream, that he would wake up at any moment.

The only thing that dashed that notion was the unreal weight that pushed down on his shoulders.

He wasn't sure about this Chosen business, but the Oracle

had certainly believed it pertained to him. He could only find out more about that going forward. But of course, he hoped he wouldn't find out anything at all, and all of this was just some mad dream.

Reaching for his Focus, he meant to try his Binding Magic. But fear stopped him.

He was not ready to face it. Not yet.

Before he could think about it any further, he left the ruins of the shrine behind. He climbed the trail that left the cavern. His torch, left behind, had long burned out, so he chipped a glowing crystal off the side of the cave and used it to light his way. He turned around, one last time. He wanted a final glimpse.

But as he suspected, the shrine was still in ruins. It had served its purpose, and no one for the rest of time would ever see it as he had. He felt a sadness that its beauty had passed, along with the Oracle who kept it.

Lucian didn't understand the implications. He imagined he never would.

A voice entered his mind. It could only be her, her final words, that came to him as if in benediction:

Go now, with my blessing. Seek the other Oracles, who will tell you more. You are the only hope.

Don't fail us.

Lucian wanted to will that sad voice away, but soon, all it did was echo in his mind, a haunting refrain.

He ran down the dark tunnel, crystal in hand. He was back at the opening cavern in seemingly no time at all.

When he took up his place next to the fire, he found both Linus and Plato undisturbed. It was as if no time had passed at all. For all he knew, what was hours for him with the Oracle was only minutes for them.

He closed his eyes and slept.

34

LUCIAN FELT a light kick to the shoulder, rousing him from sleep.

"Up you get," Linus said. "We've got a long way to go today."

Lucian forced himself to get up, packing up camp while Plato got the morning stew ready. The events of the previous night ran through his mind. He would not have been surprised had it all been some insane dream. And yet even now, as he packed, the Orb of Binding was bound to his soul. Invisible, but present, like a second heart.

He couldn't deny what had happened. If it were a dream, it was like no dream he'd ever had.

They ate quickly. Linus and Plato were probably thinking of the long walk ahead. All Lucian could think about was the Oracle, her words, and the Orb of Binding.

The only way he could be sure it had happened was by testing the orb. But that would mean breaking his block, and he wasn't ready to do that yet.

They had a long way to travel. Testing would have to come later.

They bundled up and warmed themselves as much as they

could by the fire. Then, they doused it with snow. After Plato rearranged the lichen logs along the wall, the three men set off.

The weather was warmer than before, but that wasn't saying much. Or perhaps Lucian was only getting used to it. They set a fast pace, Lucian fighting his exhaustion with every step. If he needed any evidence that last night had been real, it was his sheer exhaustion.

He made his mind blank as he followed the path the two older men set for him. They walked across the gray, snow-ridden flats, each kilometer much the same as the last. Nor did they stop when night fell only a few hours after the sun first rose. But Linus did not pause – not for a minute. A fire would be hard to maintain in this blasted landscape, and there wasn't even the fuel to start one. They would be walking long into the Volsung night, not resting until they reached home.

The promise of good stew, a crackling fire, and his hammock were enough to keep Lucian moving.

Hours passed. They ate frozen fish and seaweed on the trail. When they reached the high hills, they took shelter in a cleft. Linus did a little digging and scrounged up one of their caches. Inside was lichen, which they used to start a fire to warm themselves. By now, Lucian's teeth were chattering, and his extremities were numb. Warmth was necessary if they wanted to make it back home with all their fingers and toes.

They also heated up some stew. Food was necessary to have the energy for the rest of the march. An hour later, they were off again. Trying to get up the slope was a battle of will, Lucian fighting exhaustion and cold with every step.

But Linus had steered them well. They passed through the hills, emerging in the relatively flatter terrain beyond. The two men knew the way so well that they had no need of torchlight. When Linus announced they were about an hour from home, their pace increased.

It was only a quarter of an hour later that a massive boom

reverberated across the landscape. Linus and Plato shared a worried look and hurried to climb a nearby hill. Once at the top, they scanned the southern horizon. An orange trail streaked across the aurora-infused sky, heading for the island.

Lucian didn't have to ask what it was.

"Run!" Linus called.

Lucian ran. He found it hard to keep pace with the hardened old men. Even Plato, with his extra heft, had no trouble matching Linus's brutal pace. The prison shuttle would have thermal scanners on board. A quick survey of the island would find all three of them out here in the open, ripe for the pickings. Only the shelter of the cave would keep them safe.

Under the dancing auroras, they ran across the snowy hills. Lucian's lungs burned with cold. When they reached the top of the next hill, he spied the ocean beyond the cliffs. They had about a kilometer to go. He ran hard, his legs rebelling, wanting to quit. But he couldn't quit, even if the cold felt like icy knives stabbing at his lungs.

He had already lost the two older men in the distance. Yet, he pressed on. He had no choice, even if he collapsed from exhaustion. The orange streak had dissipated by now, but a contrail was still visible in the southern sky. Even now, the ship was surely roving the island, seeking prey. It would likely be over the central village by now. If Lucian were lucky, they would investigate it despite the lack of heat readings. If he were unlucky, they would continue their scan of the island's southern half.

Lucian soon reached the entrance of the trail leading down to the cave. There was no sign of Linus or Plato, so they had to be down there already. He started down the path, but something stopped him.

He couldn't run. If anything about last night was real, he couldn't stay here. Even Binding Magic wouldn't allow him to escape this island. Civilization was simply too far away.

So, what was the answer then? To allow himself to be captured and be sent to a moon where there was *absolutely* no possibility of escape?

He remembered then what Linus and Plato had called Psyche. The Mystery Box. He didn't know what he would get if he went there, but there might be *some* chance of escaping, of figuring out the next step.

In all of Linus and Plato's years here, neither had figured out a way to escape this place. What made him think that *he* would? Then again, the same argument could be made for Psyche.

It now all hinged on this moment. Was any of it real? Was he the Chosen, like the Oracle had said? Was the best way to find the other orbs to leave this place behind?

Psyche was at least movement, changing his circumstances. He knew it was madness. But at the same time, he couldn't stop himself.

He turned away from the trail and walked inland.

He was only walking half a minute when lights rose above the hill ahead of him, blinding him with their brilliance, accompanied by the roar of a spacecraft engine.

He could only hope Linus and Plato were safe, their heat signatures hidden by the ground between them and the ship.

Lucian did the only thing he *could* do. He lifted his hands, placing them behind his head.

And he kept walking.

When the ship's engine ebbed, Lucian knew they had spotted him. He walked toward the light, taking in the sight of the vessel shadowed against the aurora-filled sky.

When the ship landed, a boarding ramp extended from amidships with a metallic whir. The boarding door slid open, and a stream of men with gauss rifles and energy shields clomped down the ramp. There were about a dozen of them. Would they shoot him on sight, or take him to Psyche? Lucian's heart thundered as he realized he might only have seconds left to live.

"I surrender," Lucian called out. The roar of the ship drowned his voice.

"Don't move!"

That was when something sharp pricked against Lucian's skin, right in his abdomen. He only had time enough to look down to see a hole in his clothing, and the very end of the dart which had punctured through multiple layers of clothing.

His head swam, and darkness took him.

HE AWOKE in a white-walled cell lying on his back. Head pounding, he forced himself into a sitting position, pushing his back against the wall. He kept his eyes closed, fading in and out a couple of times before coming to full wakefulness. The cell was small, though not quite as small as the one on the *Burung*. He had a small cot, a toilet, and a sink. There was no window except for the small one at head level in the door. And in the background, there was a strange whirring sound. An energy shield, maybe? He wouldn't only have to bust through the door to escape, but the shield lying beyond it.

Lucian was not inclined to test his abilities against that.

How long would he have to stay in this place, alone, without so much as a conversation to break the monotony?

He could only hope that they hadn't found Linus and Plato. He could never forgive himself if they'd been captured.

Panic clutched his chest, and almost by reaction, he sought his Focus and fed it all his fears. It didn't make them go away, but it allowed him to step outside himself and see the problem from a grander perspective. And beyond the Focus, he could sense the power of the Manifold. It was a sleeping giant, an entity he had not touched in weeks. How easy it would be to reach for it now, to let it consume him until there was nothing left of his block.

But there was more than himself to consider. There was the orb. He was its steward. A Vigilant, even, if he was interpreting the Oracle's definition correctly. And he had to find the others, as difficult as that would be. As *impossible* as that would be.

It was with that thought in his head that the door slid open. There stood a soldier, clad head to toe in crimson plasma armor. His personal energy shield was engaged, forming a protective bubble of light around him. In both hands, he clung to a gauss rifle. Over his head was a conical helmet with a tinted visor.

Lucian remained still, willing his heart to slow down. He needed to be calm, here. Nothing good would come from panic. He held his Focus, deciding it was best to be ready for anything. He didn't want to use magic, but he would do so without hesitation if this soldier so much as twitched that gun in his direction.

"You don't seem mad yet." The soldier's young, male voice came out garbled and robotic.

Lucian elected not to speak. He would do so only if the soldier asked him a direct question.

"You're on board the *LPB Worthless*. That's League Prison Barge. You're being transported to Psyche, per the treaty the government of Volsung has with the Academy of Mages of Transcend Mount." From the soldier's tone of voice, it was clear he was reciting a script. "Per the Treaty of the Magi signed on Chiron in 2314, you have no right to a Trial, but you must be informed of the League's decision to imprison you and the reasons thereof. Those reasons are that you are a registered exile of the Volsung Academy, and per the Treaty, a registered exile mage must be excised to the prison moon of Psyche, kept alive and hale in proper conditions aboard a reasonably protected prison ship, and safely put down on the moon's surface. Do you have any questions?"

"Yeah," Lucian said. "How long until Psyche?"

"A long time. For you and me both." The guard sounded bored, as if he would rather be anywhere but here. "The energy field surrounding your cell, in case you're wondering, will make your magic pretty much worthless. Prison barges have the biggest power plant of any League vessel, and those power plants make these shields impossible to break. And if you *do* manage to break out – which has *never* happened before – there's a Century of the League's finest to greet you with their own shields and gauss rifles. They're equipped with the best armor and energy shields creds can buy. If you somehow take *them* out, the ship itself can't be overridden. Any course deviation must be verified by every First World. So, unless you have people in place on Earth, Chiron, Volsung, Oceanus, and Nessus, then this ship's course can't be changed."

"Don't worry. I don't plan on trying."

"That's a good boy."

"You have a lot of confidence in this shield," Lucian said.

"Why shouldn't I?" The soldier's voice sounded a bit nervous. It hadn't been Lucian's intention to make the man second-guess his beliefs. But questions often had a way of doing that.

"No reason," Lucian said. "Can you be any more specific about how long it'll take?"

"Months?" He looked back over his shoulder. "Any hint of trouble, well, things won't go too well for you. Good behavior gets rewards. We're not maniacs here, though some of the guards are, to be honest."

The man was rambling, and Lucian was wondering what the point of all this was.

"Anyway. It gets damn boring on here, even for us. Oh yeah. I was supposed to ask. Was there anyone else on that island, or just you?"

"Just me," Lucian said. "There was another exile who committed suicide in the village."

"Yeah, we found him," the guard said. "Well, that's all I wanted to know. Like I said, if you don't raise a fuss, we might see about a slate to help pass the time. You need to stay quiet for a week, though. Think you can manage that?"

"Sure."

"Smart mage. All right. Take it easy."

The cell door slid shut, and once again, Lucian was left to his own devices.

Lucian found the guard's friendly nature strange. Maybe they found treating the mages well produced better results. It might even be more useful than the shields and cells surrounding the ship's perilous cargo.

Well, Lucian knew there was little hope in escaping. He didn't think the guard was lying to him about anything. And even if Lucian had the Orb of Binding, he still didn't know how to use it, or even if it would give him miraculous powers as the Oracle had said. What those possibilities were remained to be seen.

Lucian realized that there was only one way off this ship, and that was the Mad Moon. The main question was how to occupy his mind and not go crazy during the journey.

The only thing he could think about was his conversation with the Oracle. Whether he liked it or not, this was the path he had chosen on the spur of the moment. For now at least, it was the way forward. But just as he had an orb, someone else out there had an orb, too. Or even *multiple* orbs. And they'd had it for well over a century. That person could still be alive today. The Oracle said the orbs granted longer life, but also that it wouldn't grant true immortality until all seven were held by the same person.

Even if was hard to believe, he had to believe it was true. He had boarded this ship staking his future on it.

For the first time in a long time, he would have the chance to think. And so, he thought, even long after the first meal of a hot porridge was delivered through the wall. There were six more orbs out there, somewhere. And then he had to take those orbs to the Heart of the Universe. He could find that through the First Gate, in Dark Space. Where the *Alkasen* lurked.

He repeated the details over and over in his mind, until they had infused in his memory. Seven Orbs. Seven Oracles. And one other Vigilant who had at least found one orb. Was that person a Chosen, too? Could there be more than one? Alternately, there might be multiple Chosens by now who had found multiple orbs. He supposed it wasn't impossible. After all, he himself had literally stumbled upon his own orb. Of all the places in all the Worlds, Linus and Plato had led him into that cave. Or had something *drawn* him there?

Lucian had plenty to think about, but conjecturing didn't lead to solid answers. He knew some mages believed in the orbs and had even gone off to seek them. Was it so hard to believe that one of those dozens of mages had found one? For all he knew, there were seven Vigilants now, each holding one orb, with Lucian being one of them. Linus and Plato had known about the shrine, of course, but they had not guessed its significance.

Thinking of them filled Lucian with sadness. In their minds, they must have thought they left him behind. If they were wise, they hadn't come after him. Lucian could only hope so.

Whatever the case, Lucian realized that something new was coming with Psyche. Something he was not prepared for. No doubt hundreds of mages, mad and sane, had Psyche as their unwilling home. It wouldn't be possible to know how to prepare for the Mad Moon until he touched down.

There was no telling how long that would be. Space was vast. The Cupid system was two Gate jumps away, meaning it would be at least a few months to just get there. But if this ship was beginning its round by traveling *away* from Psyche, it might be well over a year before he saw the surface of the Mad Moon.

Lucian was not sure which he preferred. The cell was small, yes, but it was also safe. For all he knew, he might die the minute he set foot on the Mad Moon. That would be convenient for the League. As soon as a mage stepped outside the airlock, it was only to breathe a poisonous atmosphere. Lucian realized they *couldn't* do that, though, at least according to that treaty the soldier had just recited to him. If they didn't seriously intend to follow the Treaty, the League wouldn't waste massive resources to bring them here in the first place. Then again, that safety was only guaranteed to get him safely to the surface of the Mad Moon. It didn't guarantee his safety beyond that.

Lucian played many such scenarios in his mind in a nonstop stream. He even imagined that Psyche might be a relative paradise, where mages had made the best of things. Why not? Linus and Plato had done that with the Isle of Madness.

Lucian thought, he slept, he ate. There was nothing else to his life. Despite the guard's promise, there was no slate. Compared to the drab walls of his cell, the gray skies and rocks of the Isle of Madness were a rainbow tapestry. At night, he would dream of the auroras, the sharp cold wind with its clean salt-laden scent. He could hear the scuttling of rock crabs in the tundra. He could see Plato at his gardening, and Linus at his fishing. He hoped they were both doing well with whatever they had left of their lives.

And of course, he dreamed of Emma, longing for her warm embrace in the coldness of his cell. He dreamed of the Oracle, too, and her words to him. It seemed like something that had never happened, as the days and weeks ticked by. It became a dream, but a dream he chose to believe in.

He had nothing else.

He didn't dare stream. He had no doubt many mages had tried to escape and trying to do so would only speed up fraying. He had learned to live without magic, thanks to Linus and Plato's lessons. But he knew he would never know the truth of what the Oracle said unless he streamed Binding Magic.

That meant waiting for Psyche. He would try then. Something told him, in that brutal place, streaming would be a fact of life. One couldn't survive without it.

But if the orb was real, then he would have an advantage over every other mage there. Perhaps his *only* advantage.

If he died, though, none of it would matter.

Lucian only knew a day had passed every time the lights dimmed. This happened ten times. Then twenty. Then thirty.

By this point, Lucian had thought about everything there was to think about. He talked aloud, if only to hear a voice. He was moved to tears at various points. Soon, there was no emotion left but numbness. He felt divorced from mind and body, as much an object as his cot, sink, or toilet. Unmoving, uncaring, adrift in a sea of imagination and dreams.

He spent most of his time with his eyes closed. And in the darkness of his mind, there was stillness and calm. He found a new purpose – to prepare his mind as much for Psyche as possible. To do what no mage had done before.

Escape.

He reached for his Focus, willing himself to hold it as long as possible. He sensed his pool and the Manifold beyond it. He felt for each of the Seven Aspects, one by one. His block was still there, but he knew he could dissolve it at any moment. At some point, he knew, he would have to stream again. And he would stick to Binding Magic, as far as it was possible. He needed to be alive and healthy to complete his mission.

He always told himself to hold out another day. To wait. And to hold onto his Focus, from the moment he woke to the moment he slept. He would hold it until the day of his arrival.

He no longer paid attention to the light or his meals. He would eat and not be mindful of taste, almost as if he weren't eating at all. He no longer wanted to bathe himself, no longer smelled his own stink. His only goal was to keep insanity at bay.

Weeks bled into months. His beard had grown thick, falling to his chest. His hair was long and shaggy, nearly reaching his shoulders. What month was it now on Volsung? Winter was surely over, and the Novices would again be training under a northern sun. He had a vision of Emma training, learning, on the path to become a Talent of the Academy. He hoped she never thought of him. He hoped that she might forget him forever, and walk the path denied to him.

And then, one day, the door slid open, revealing an empty corridor outside. The buzzing of the energy shield, which had been a constant background drone for months, was gone.

Lucian's heart raced, his mind not accepting this new reality. It had to be just another dream. This cell was his home now. His life.

He had almost forgotten there was a wider universe out there. The only world he knew was the one inside his mind.

"Stand," came a forceful male voice, from some hidden speaker. "Walk outside your cell and do nothing more on pain of death."

It was only with that command that Lucian realized the truth.

They had arrived. Soon, he would be walking the surface of a new world.

35

LUCIAN STOOD, his legs shaking. He ventured out into the corridor, looking both ways to only see lines of metallic cell doors. There was no sign of any soldier. Only the empty corridor, extending for at least a hundred meters.

"Turn left," the voice said, coming from the speaker directly above Lucian. "Continue to the end of the corridor until you reach the open pod door. Step inside and strap yourself in. Do nothing more on pain of death."

This was how they were going to do it, then. Risk free, not putting any lives on the line. If Lucian resisted, they would kill him. No doubt, some had tried. But the fact that the ship was still here, and those mages weren't, told Lucian everything he needed to know.

There was only one real option.

He followed the corridor, past twenty or so cell doors. The corridor ended in an alcove lined with viewscreens. Every one of those viewscreens looked out onto a misty, violet-clouded surface. This must be it, then. Psyche. After the sensory deprivation of his cell, so much color was the most beautiful sight of his life. Tears filled his eyes.

He didn't pause to look long; he didn't know if staring down at that hazy surface counted as "doing something more" that might get him killed. He stooped his shaggy head below the frame and entered the small, confined pod.

From the small porthole in the pod, Lucian could discern only a small part of the surface. It was lost in a violet-tinged haze. If there were oceans or mountains down there, he'd have no way of knowing it.

He sat in the pod's single chair and strapped himself in. Despite these safety measures, he knew that this very well could be his last few minutes alive.

As soon as he had settled in, the pod door hissed shut. There was a moment's pause, followed by a foreboding creak. Finally, there was a hiss and a snap as the pod disengaged from the *LBS Worthless*. Trails of fire issued from the back of his pod, pushing Lucian against his seat. The purple surface crawled toward him, even as he floated against his restraints. It was only a matter of time until he entered the world's atmosphere.

The pod shook as a corona of fiery light surrounded it. There was only the surrounding purple air, impossible to see any distance into. Lucian clenched his hands and had to force himself to keep his eyes open. The clouds might clear, giving him a chance to see the surface below. Any amount of information could help him survive.

Assuming he survived the landing.

Something was already materializing from the haze, what looked like a pointed mountain peak. As he dove deeper into the thick atmosphere, more peaks revealed themselves. They were *impossibly* elongated and sheer, a nightmarish vision. There were entire ridges of them. They looked like needle teeth on the upside-down jaw of a primordial beast. The whole *surface* was like that. Though he was closer to the ground now, he could easily discern the curvature of the world itself. Psyche was a moon, and like most moons, it was a good deal smaller than Earth. He was falling more slowly than he had expected. The gravity wouldn't be much compared to Earth or Volsung. It was impossible to say at this moment, but it felt close to Martian standard.

He realized this might be less of a crash and more of a hard thud, judging by the air resistance rushing past the pod.

Lucian had sunk below the tallest of the mountains. As their shadows fell across the pod, he realized Psyche would be a dark world. As he sunk lower and lower into the narrow valley between, the mountains loomed ever taller. *Impossibly* tall, their dark slopes sheer. Is this why they were placing him here? There was no chance he'd be able to escape from this valley – assuming he survived the landing.

He sunk into deeper twilight. He could no longer see the tops of the wicked peaks outside the porthole. The atmosphere looked poisonous out there.

He had to be getting close. He felt like a caged animal in here. Even if the surface was dangerous, he wanted out of this death trap of a pod.

The pod's thrusters burned, pushing Lucian into his seat. He felt himself lifted for a moment before the craft landed lightly on the dark surface. The porthole revealed a dark, gloomy landscape. The only plants he saw were a few low things that might have been trees. They stooped over, as if bearing an invisible, oppressive weight. Lucian couldn't see how anything could grow in this darkness.

He unstrapped himself and weighed his options. He'd have to go outside at some point, and he had nothing but the clothes on his back and his wits to keep him alive. And of course, the orb. He could never forget the orb.

If the air were poisonous, death would come for him either way. When he stood, he felt light on his feet. He had been right about the gravity, that it was close to Martian standard. Now, the only question was whether the atmosphere was breathable.

There was only one way to find out.

Before he could think about it, Lucian pressed the button next to the door, which he assumed would open it. With a hiss, the door rolled back and a rush of cool, dry air flooded in. Lucian held his breath for a moment, but the air did nothing to harm his skin. Given the way it rushed inside, he supposed the air pressure was quite high. But it didn't seem to be harmful in any way, at least not obviously so.

He released his breath and inhaled. It was air. Normal, breathable air. It smelled of earth and rock, but the smell of vegetation was all but absent. He wasn't sure of the exact composition, of course, but it couldn't be too far off from Earth or Volsung. If there were any nasty surprises – like an undetectable but lethal amount of carbon dioxide – he'd have to wait for the results.

For now, there was one thing left to do. To walk out and survive a new world.

EPILOGUE

LUCIAN DIDN'T KNOW where to begin. He was in the same situation as the Isle of Madness when the Psions first left him. Only now, the Isle of Madness was an entire moon.

And unless he somehow found a way to get off Psyche, the Starsea Cycle would only continue, leaving desolation in its wake.

He had a mission and a purpose. It was most likely impossible, but what else did he have? He'd lost everything – his mother, his friends, his home. His mission to find the Seven Orbs, and then find the Heart of the Universe to stop magic and the Starsea Cycle, was all he had left.

He was aware of the brutal fact that it was impossible. And he worried that his determination to see it through was already evidence of a growing madness.

He couldn't think about any of that now. He had a more immediate concern: survival.

Lucian walked away from the pod. He headed into the dark rifts of Psyche, toward horrors unknown.

ABOUT THE AUTHOR

Kyle West is the author of a number of sci-fi and fantasy series: *The Starsea Cycle, The Wasteland Chronicles,* and *The Xenoworld Saga.*

His goal is to write as many entertaining books as possible, with interesting worlds and characters that hopefully give his readers a break from the mundane.

He lives in South Florida with his wife, son, and two insanely spoiled cats. He enjoys hearing from his readers, and invites them to connect with him through his Facebook page, website, or newsletter.

kylewestwriter.com
kylewestwriter@gmail.com

For information on new releases, please sign up for his newsletter.

facebook.com/kylewestwriter

ALSO BY KYLE WEST

THE STARSEA CYCLE

The Mages of Starsea

The Orb of Binding

The Rifts of Psyche

THE WASTELAND CHRONICLES (COMPLETE)

Apocalypse

Origins

Evolution

Revelation

Darkness

Extinction

Xenofall

Lost Angel (Prequel)

THE XENOWORLD SAGA (COMPLETE)

Prophecy

Bastion

Beacon

Sanctum

Kingdom

Dissolution

Aberration

Made in United States
Troutdale, OR
02/06/2025